THE HOUSE OF STARLIGHT AND SHADOW

THE MIRROR KINGDOM CHRONICLES

BOOK ONE

COREENE CALLAHAN

OLIVERHEBERBOOKS

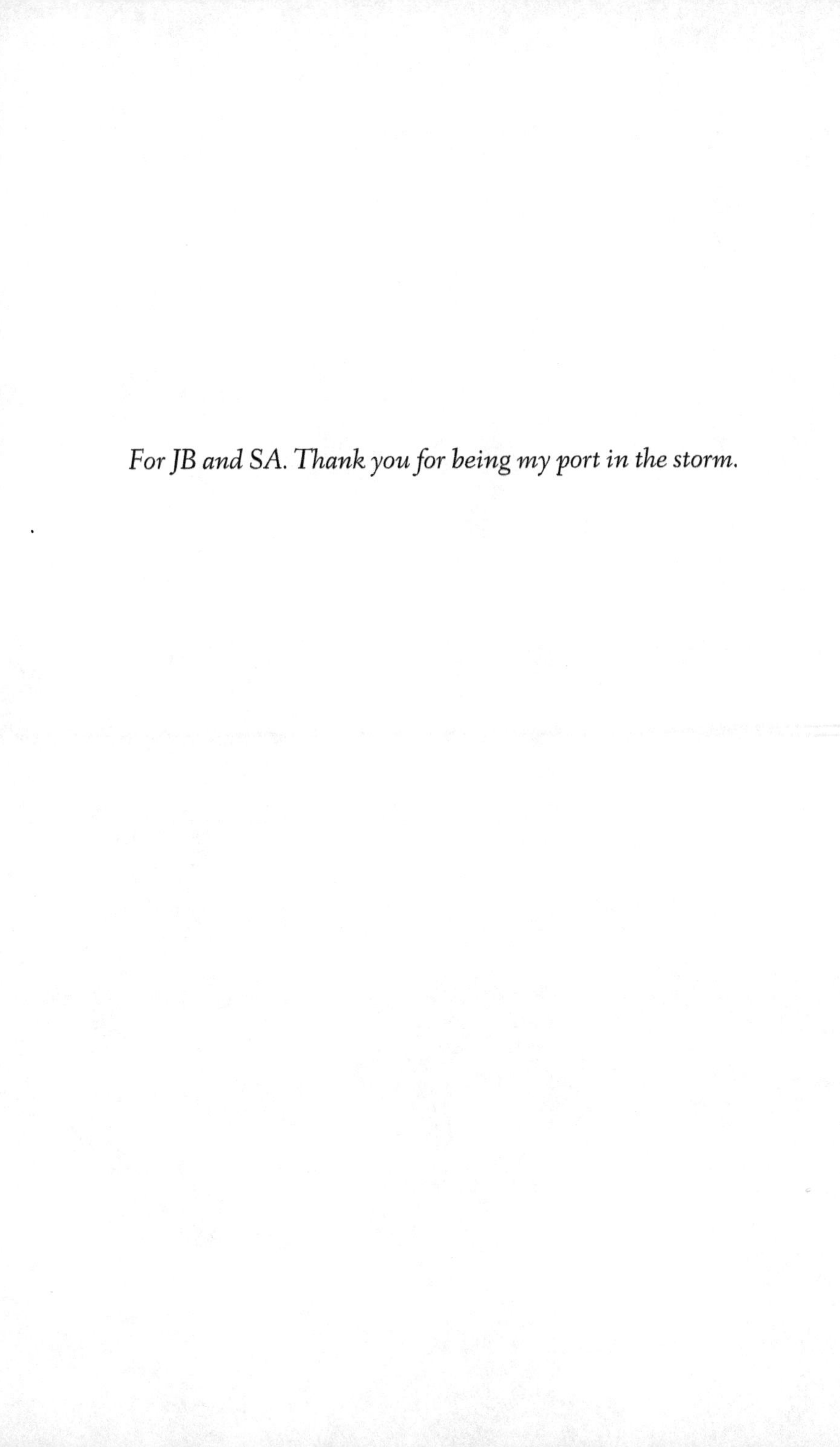

For JB and SA. Thank you for being my port in the storm.

SOMEWHERE IN PHILADELPHIA

Taking pictures of a couple through the window of a trashy motel wasn't Truly Langford-Bardot's idea of fun. Problem was, given recent income opportunities, it appeared to be her new job. How she'd gone from celebrated photographer to Mrs. Reeser's only chance of landing a seven-figure divorce settlement wasn't a mystery. She'd put herself here, slouched in the bucket seat of her '71 Barracuda, telephoto lens pointed at the lily-white ass of a man who should know better.

Or at least possessed enough gray matter to close the blinds.

Stupid. Also... gross.

Lifting the travel mug perched between her knees, she washed the bad taste out of her mouth, then framed another shot. Her camera shutter fired. The rapid clicking erupted through her open window to drift undisturbed down the sidewalk. Cracked concrete. Chilly autumn air. Just another late night in an about-to-slide-over-the-edge-into-poverty neighborhood. Shifting forward, she tilted her Canon for a better angle. She checked the images on the digital screen and...

There it was — the money shot.

Double, extra disgusting.

She hated the cheater assignments. Freelancing for workers' comp on insurance fraud cases was so much better. Taking those pictures didn't involve sex with prostitutes. It consisted of snapping photos of a guy claiming to have suffered a debilitating back injury at work, but didn't have any problem climbing a ladder to clean out rain gutters at home.

Again, stupid. Also, thankfully, a lot less gross.

Slouched in her seat, she thumbed the toggle on her camera, flipping rapid-fire through the images on screen. No need to stay any longer. The shots she'd gotten worked. Mrs. Reeser now possessed all the ammunition she needed to close the book on a bad marriage and open a new chapter. Truly didn't know what that looked like, but if Reeser could piece her life back together after twenty-five years with a jerk, who knew? Maybe there was hope for her yet.

Cranking her window closed, she put the cap back on and twisted off the long-range lens. She pocketed it along with her Canon into the padded interior of the large camera bag sitting on the passenger seat. A quick pull zipped her baby away as her cellphone rang in the holder on her dashboard.

Montrose calling.

Lovely. Just what she didn't need. Another go-around with a guy she didn't like, never mind want to admit employed her.

Taking a fortifying breath, Truly touched the flat screen.

A voice full of oil and smoke spilled out of the speaker. "Triple."

"Yeah," she said, gritting her teeth at the nickname. She'd asked him *repeatedly* to stop calling her that, but surprise, surprise, he never listened.

"You done?"

Of its own volition, her gaze flicked toward the window across the street. She grimaced. No sense looking at that again. "Money shots in the bank."

"You coming in now?"

She glanced at the time on her phone. 12:47 AM. No way in hell was she going in now. Later was soon enough to deal with Montrose. "Tomorrow."

"No good. Need you back at shop now."

Suspicion uncoiled in the back of her brain. "Why?"

"Got a visitor."

"Tell him to come back."

"Triple, there's a fucking troll sitting in my office."

Truly blinked. A *troll*? What the hell did that mean?

"Says he won't leave until he speaks with you."

"Come on, Rosy," she said, paying him back with a nickname of his own. Fiddling with her travel mug, she snapped the tab on the top open and closed. "It's going one."

"Don't care," Montrose said, sounding more than his usual amount of pissed off. "Get your ass back to shop."

Truly sighed.

Wonderful. She officially despised her new life. Who could blame her? The circumstances of her employment sucked, and her new boss wasn't pleasant. An affront to every sister in the sisterhood, Montrose said whatever popped into his head. Most of which was rude, insulting or downright disturbing. Staring at her keychain swinging from the ignition, she debated. Give in to the bonehead who signed her paychecks. Or hold the line and be out of a job.

The desire to eat in the next two weeks won out. "Be there in twenty."

Montrose grunted and disconnected.

She fired up the second love of her life. The engine caught and her car rumbled, sending a thrill through her. Never failed. Hearing her baby snarl always lifted her mood. The 'Cuda was one of the only things she'd managed to keep after being fired from her dream job.

The condo in the swanky downtown corridor — sold.

All her old friends — gone.

Her reputation — decimated.

And yet, the 'Cuda remained a steadfast companion, faithful in the face of adversity.

With a quick glance, she checked her blind spot, then cranked the wheel and pulled out onto the street. All quiet. No traffic on the boulevard. No one milling around or hanging out on street corners. A surprise. The seedier parts of Philly normally came alive at night.

Not here by the looks of it.

The small row houses across from the motel sat snug on their small lots, gates in crooked fences closed, interiors dark, no movement inside. She caught the occasional blue flicker of a television as she drove past low-slung wartime bungalows, turned deeper into the belly of the beast, toward the wasteland of *Montrose & Brim Investigations* and the 'troll' responsible for making an already less than stellar night even worse.

SOMETHING TRULY TERRIBLE

Montrose hadn't lied. The guy did look like a troll. Fitting, given the office he sat in resembled the inside of a hoarder's cave, minus the loot.

From her position on the sidewalk Truly eyed the man through a slit in Montrose & Brim's crooked window blinds. Seated in the chair in front of her desk with a beat-up briefcase in his lap, the man waited — eyes closed, peaceful expression blunted by the angular planes of his face.

Every so often, his leg would twitch, sending one of his too-big-for-his-body feet swinging like a pendulum. Her eyes narrowed as she studied him. Wide shoulders on a stocky frame. Short legs that didn't reach the floor. Deep-set eyes over a thick brow, bulbous nose accompanied by ears that veered into a slight point.

Truly pursed her lips. Definitely troll-like.

Also... dangerous.

One glance was all it took for her to know he was trouble. The kind that would shift the trajectory of her life.

Her stomach dipped as her chest tightened. She swallowed past the knot in her throat, wondering at her reaction. She trusted her gut. Always had. Intuition was a friend of hers. She followed it without question most of the time, and yet she hesitated to turn and go, even though the situation rubbed her the wrong way. It felt more like a set-up than a meeting with a new client. Farfetched? A tad alarmist? Unwarranted given she stood outside — safe, in control, able to walk away if she wanted to, but —

"Are you gonna stand there all night?"

The raspy voice slithered out of the shadows.

Sucking in a breath, Truly spun to her left. "Jeez, Earl!"

"Scared yah, did I?"

"Where'd you come from?"

"The alley," he said, the dirty blanket he wore like a poncho flapping as he lumbered to his favorite spot in front of the squat brick building Montrose called his shop.

He was limping, the side-to-side hitching motion not a good sign. His hip must be bothering him again.

She tipped her chin. "Need some Advil?"

Earl shook his shaggy-haired head and held up a dented pizza box. "Got all I need right here."

Dumpster diving. Another layer of gross to add to her night. "I would have brought you something."

"Breakfast tomorrow."

"You're on."

Flipping the box top open, he slid down the brick wall and took a seat under the eave next to the front stoop. "Best get inside before Montrose loses his mind."

"He been yelling?"

"Oh yeah," he muttered, around a mouthful of cold pizza. "Guy wouldn't budge though. Said he needs to speak with you. Sounded urgent."

"How urgent?" A detail she needed to know. Montrose was prone to overreaction. The guy labeled everything urgent.

"*Urgent,* urgent."

Dread slithered through her. "Bad omen."

"Could be," Earl said, eyeing her from beneath his bushy brows. "Won't know 'til you talk to 'im. Get moving, girl."

Adjusting the camera bag strap across her body, she squared her shoulders, preparing to meet the situation head-on. "Apple Strudel or bagel with cream cheese tomorrow?"

"Both, girl. Both. And don't forget the coffee."

"Do I ever?"

Earl grinned his gap-toothed grin and, with the flick of his fingers, motioned her toward the front door. A master at giving orders, the homeless man never hesitated to boss her around. For some reason, she didn't mind. Might have started out strange — with him asking her to buy cheese for Quint, the field mouse who lived in his pocket — but over the last few months, he'd become a friend.

He'd been hanging around since she started working for Montrose. At first, she'd thought him a permanent fixture on the block, someone who'd been around for years. Montrose disabused her of the notion. He didn't like Earl or the fact his arrival in the neighborhood coincided with her employment with M&B. Not a surprise, considering her boss hated everybody, homeless people topping the endless list of things he didn't like.

Not that she cared what Montrose thought.

Pissing him off was one of the only things she enjoyed most days.

At the front door, she reached for the bent handle. A clean grab and jerk opened grimy glass framed by steel. A fast pace walked her across faded linoleum, past the open interior door, into the office proper.

The visitor looked her way.

Her gaze tracked to Montrose.

Dark hair slicked back, phone pressed to his ear, long ash trail hanging off the cigarette perched between his fingertips, he glared at her through the window that provided a view of the main office from behind his desk.

She flipped him the bird in greeting.

He pointed to their unwelcome guest with stained fingertips.

With a nod, she skirted the counter separating the waiting area with three chairs (one of them broken) from four desks set nose-to-nose. The man hopped from his chair. Truly moved down the aisle between the desks, gaze leveled on him.

He shuffled from foot to foot, color rising in his cheeks as he bowed his head. Her focus sharpened. His reaction to her was weird. Was he shy, striving to be polite, or trying to be respectful? Good question. One Truly didn't know how to answer given what she saw in his expression. The look on his face read more like awe, the kind of reverence reserved for star athletes and A-list celebrities.

"Truly Isabeth Turnbolt?"

"Not my name," she said, stopping at her desk.

His brow furrowed. A moment later, his expression cleared. "Ah, yes. That's right. You were given a new one."

Swinging her camera bag off her shoulder, she dropped it onto her beat-up chair. "A new one?"

"When your mother left you at St. Redeemer's, she gave you a new name."

The knot in the pit of her stomach turned to stone. Her hands went from warm to cold. No one knew about her childhood. *No one.* She never shared the circumstance of her birth. Not with school friends. Never with a colleague. Not even with the boyfriend she'd dated in fine arts school. She'd hidden it, made up stories, told lies, her shame so great the words to explain wouldn't come.

"You know my mother?" she asked, the question abrading the back of her throat.

"No."

"I don't understand."

"To be expected," he said, his expression so somber old wounds reopened. The grief Truly struggled so hard to hide uncoiled inside her. "What happened is, for all intents and purposes, incomprehensible."

"You're not making any sense."

"I know." Clenching the battered handle of his briefcase so hard the leather creaked, he drew a deep breath. "But I don't have time to explain. We need to —"

"Make time."

"It's not my place, Truly. All will be revealed in time."

In time.

She hated that expression. In the beginning, during her years in foster care, she'd asked question after question, wanting to know everything, all the why's and how's surrounding her birth. Later, she'd learned to ignore the mystery. It had taken years, but practice had yielded the necessary results. Now, she didn't want to talk about it. Didn't want to dissect the past or dive into what it meant for her future. What she wanted was to forget her parents had left her in a cardboard box on the steps of a Catholic church and never looked back.

No love lost for her parents. Just complete abandonment framed by religious fervor.

Truly swallowed the bitter taste in her mouth.

She wanted to say she didn't care. Years had passed. She'd made a life for herself. Her origins no longer mattered, but even as she repeated the familiar refrain inside her head, the truth came calling, unearthing emotional landmines. All the questions she worked so hard to suppress resurfaced, rising like vipers, threatening to strike, making her want to know. Whom did she look like? Where did she get her creative drive? Why had she never felt like she fit in anywhere with anyone?

That last question always got to her. And as she studied the squat man standing five feet away, she finally accepted that ignoring the truth never made it go away. Denying she'd been left on the steps of St. Redeemer's as a baby, the only clue to who she was (first name and date of birth) written on a scrap of paper pinned to front of her tiny coat, wouldn't change anything. She was an orphan, a foster kid turned adult with a deep yearning to understand. Maybe then the hurt she hid from everyone would fade.

The unwelcome realization sharpened her edges.

Her focus riveted to the troll, she leveled her chin. "Who are you?"

"Minador," he said, watching her with rapt interest. "Your great-aunt's solicitor."

Right. Of course. Her *great-aunt*. "You have the wrong person. I don't have any family."

"Untrue. You simply were never told the truth about whence you came."

His words rang through her. She picked up the idiosyncrasies in his speech like candy dropped on the ground. *About whence she came* — strange turn of phrase. Who talked that way anymore?

Truly stared at him.

He stared back at her.

She opened her mouth, then closed it again.

"I apologize for the shock. I know it is a lot to accept, but you are Truly Isabeth Turnbolt," he said, tone soft, trying to be gentle.

"If that's true, then why now? Where have you and my great-aunt been?"

"Watching. Waiting. You've never been alone. Not for a

moment, Truly. You may believe you were abandoned, but we've kept tabs on you over the years and —"

"And that's not creepy at all," she said, sarcasm shoving her tone into deadpan.

He snorted, making a whistling sound. "Had you been raised in the bosom of your family, there would be no need to explain the name you carry now is not the one given to you at birth. It was changed to protect you. But now that you have reached your twenty-seventh year, we can delay no longer."

"What has my birthday got to do with it?"

"I was forbidden to come any earlier."

"Forbidden?"

He nodded, but said nothing, allowing her to absorb the news.

"But..." She frowned, skepticism warring with the desire to believe.

Stupid in many ways, naive in others. Believing often led a person into being deceived. Her eyes narrowed. Was Minador a con-artist? Over the last few months, she'd met a number of people who preferred grifting to getting a real job. Now she knew what to look for, how to spot a conman, and escape the net one cast. But as she looked at Minador, she couldn't discount him. He seemed more than just sincere. He seemed like a guy standing in certainty. Everything about him rang true, which was as upsetting as it was intriguing.

Setting her hand on the desktop, she leaned forward, arm supporting her weight, palm flat against cold metal. Truly welcomed the solidness. She needed it to ground her, to help keep her head in the game. "My birthday was a month ago."

"I am aware. Preparations needed to be made."

"What kind?"

"In this, I'm afraid, I can be of no help. You must find out for yourself. In the meantime, we must see to the paperwork."

Truly jerked upright. "The what?"

"Documents must be signed if you are to receive your inheritance — the house and funds your great-aunt left you," he said, setting his briefcase on her desk.

Leather scraped against steel, making her tense as he unbuckled the double clasps and flipped the bag open. With great authority, he withdrew a set of skeleton keys along with a thick file folder and set official-looking papers down between them.

"Please take a seat, my dear. No time to lose. The sooner this is done, the safer for all."

The safer for all.

Truly chewed on that for a moment before curiosity grabbed hold.

She sat down.

He began to explain, flipping through the documents, unearthing proof of her identity, convincing her of his veracity one page at time. After what seemed like minutes, but was no doubt hours, he pointed to the bottom of the last page and asked her to sign. Her gaze glued to the solid line, she put pen to paper. Ink crawled across the white expanse. A quiver of unease slithered up her spine. Call her crazy. Call it a promotion, but with the last loop of her signature, she knew everything had changed... and something terrible was about to happen.

3

THE HOUSE ON ISADORE STREET

Holding a ring of skeleton keys, Truly stood on the sidewalk opposite a house that had seen better days. In the early morning light, she studied the architecture, then turned her attention to the broad-sweeping crescent that harbored six other homes. Surrounded by silence, she picked over the details, letting her gaze roam before returning it to the Gothic monstrosity.

Old, sitting among ancient. Neglected, sitting among well-loved. Untapped potential, overshadowed by sagging eaves, peeling paint, and a mess of overgrown vines and unruly shrubs, standing under the watchful eye of two towering, old-growth oaks.

The ugly duckling in a house-proud neighborhood full of historical mansions.

Uncared for, like her.

A bit forlorn, like her.

In need of repair — just like her.

Disbelief warred with elation. A second chance gifted to her by a woman she'd never met and, until a few hours ago, hadn't known existed. Unbelievable. The turn her life had taken in a few hours was startling. Too fairy tale-ish to be true, if not for the paperwork tucked inside the camera bag hanging from her shoulder.

She breathed deep, held it a moment, then let it go, relishing the chill in the air, and scanned the Victorian again. It wasn't fancy. Didn't boast a ton of ornate moldings. Didn't have an elegant gate surrounded by scrolling fence work, like its neighbors. Then again, it didn't need the cage. Its solemn austerity (the chipped brick façade, faded moldings, and black shutters) said everything the architect intended it to — *no need to fence us in... or you out.*

Her focus jumped to the entrance.

A generous porch slashed across the front of the house. A stone path, uneven and worn, led to wide steps, pointing the way to double doors. Stained-glass windows looked out at the street like eyes that saw everything and didn't like any of it. Spooky, with a healthy dose of eerie. A house with attitude, a bit of snarl, some teeth to go along with its long-time neglect.

Her lips curved.

Nothing wrong with a bit of attitude.

She'd loved the place on sight. Felt an instant connection the second she got out of her car.

The keys she held jangled in her hand.

Truly curled her fingers around the cold metal bundle, drawn in some inexplicable way, as though the house wanted her closer. She resisted a moment, unable to take her eyes from the magnificence of her new home. It might be in disrepair, but money would fix what time had damaged. Soon, in a matter of months, she'd turn back the clock. Put the fortune, now sitting in a trust for her, to return the old girl to glory. The beginning of a new love affair. A worthy project, something to sink her creative canines into and make beautiful again.

A new sense of purpose struck her.

She started up the crooked walk. Each step echoed, ghosting out into the quiet street, the sound somehow profound in the silence, marking a moment in time. Her imagination flexed, making her think the closer she drew, the more the house came alive, drawing breath, exhaling in relief, welcoming her home. A tingle swept over her nape. The electrical charge in the air didn't slow her. It quickened her pace instead, blood rush filling her ears as she jogged up the front stairs.

Rotten treads groaned.

The soles of her boots slipped on the wet steps. She firmed her footing and crested the last riser. A whisper of something, a featherlight touch, brushed over cheekbones. A shiver rolled down her spine as she stopped in front of a pair of massive doors. Ten feet tall, at least. Solid wood. Simple design. Build tough, and so wide she'd be able to drive her car through when both doors stood opened.

The stained-glass windows, though, were spectacular. Up close, she could see the individual panes set in an intricate web. A woman walking through a colorful expanse, long robe flowing behind her, pinpricks of blue light sparking from her fingertips. A sorceress, maybe? A mythical god, perhaps? Someone of immense power determined to protect others — and the world — from harm.

A fanciful thought.

One that came out of nowhere, and for some reason, reached deep to stir her imagination. Images flooded her, flashing through her mind. The woman in flowing robes sitting at a long table, pen in hand, surrounded by books. One of her speaking to the masses inside a packed amphitheater. Another of her leading the charge into battle, weapons raised, blue light blazing around her.

Truly huffed, then shook her head. The lack of sleep must be getting to her. Montrose never cared if she got the recommended hours of zzzs. Work was work, no matter the time, day or night. Though... she pursed her lips... that had changed in a big way. With her money problems solved, she didn't need to go back to M&B.

The idea should've warmed her. It didn't. She might not enjoy every assignment Montrose gave her, but she'd learned a lot over the last few months. Enough to know her former career, master-minding photoshoots for glossy magazines, no longer held any appeal. She'd seen too much, had embraced the upheaval and become part of a world much more interesting than the corporate one.

Head bent to her task, she shuffled through the keys.

Quite an about-face on the job front. She frowned at the iron ring. What did that mean? Had she really changed so much? Had her old life really been that stifling — that empty and unfulfilling? The answer came to her at once.

Yes. A thousand times over, *yes*.

Despite the loss of what she'd considered her dream job, somehow over the last few months, she'd outgrown it. Become wiser and more savvy, better able to spot those who wore toxicity like a second skin. She'd always thought she knew what she wanted — the jet-setting, the glossy pictures of gorgeous people in beautiful places, the renown of having her name captioned in magazines and newspapers.

Having had it and lost it, now standing in a place filled with the unknown, Truly couldn't believe she'd fought so hard to keep the prestige. Or at least, the illusion of it. Nothing compared to standing in the fractured shadows of a broken porch light, about to step over the threshold her family had crossed for well over a hundred years.

Finding the key labeled 'front,' she fit it into the lock. With a firm hold, she twisted hard and...

The lock turned easily. No force needed. Surprising, given

the condition of the house. She figured getting in would be a fight. Might even include a call to a locksmith.

She nibbled on her bottom lip. Maybe Minador had visited, done a bit of maintenance before her arrival. Glancing up, she examined the front entrance, studying the wide, sloping trim, then dismissed the thought.

He hadn't been by.

The lawyer made it clear he feared the house. Refused to go anywhere near the old girl — wasn't his place to approach, or some such nonsense. The reason? No idea. Like so many things, he'd refused to clarify, stating she must discover her heritage without his interference. Some things simply weren't *permissible*. His word, not hers, but... whatever. What interested her now was the prospect of *discovering*.

She reached for the handle.

The tumbler clicked.

The door swung open without making a sound.

No squeak. No halting hesitation one would expect from an old house with little-used hinges. Boots planted on the wide-planked porch, outstretched arm hovered in mid-air, she hesitated on the threshold. A warm current curled over her wrist. Another round of prickles raised the fine hairs on the back of her neck and...

Invisible tendrils ghosted over the sleeve of her jacket. A gripping sensation took hold, pulling her forward, insisting she cross the threshold.

Rocking back on her heels, she stood firm for a beat. The pulling sensation increased from gentle tug to insistent yank. She stutter-stepped, and off-balance, peered into the darkness beyond the entrance.

Shadows played in the black, morphing into indistinct shapes — the fringed edges of an area rug, a table pushed tight against the wall in the corridor, the skeletal rise of a staircase further down. Squinting into the gloom, Truly looked harder, searching for trouble.

Elegant lines flowing over graceful bones. Nothing to get worked up about, and yet...

Unease kicked up. Uncertainty took hold. She let both roll a moment before obstinance hit the brakes on her overactive imagination. It was just a house — *her house,* soon to be her home, a haven in the midst of an unreliable world. No sense being afraid of it. Spookiness aside, embracing the place, instead of being afraid of it, was by far the better plan.

Forcing her feet to move, she stepped inside. The instant that she did, a strange sound rippled through the grand foyer. The breathy rush ghosted over the floor, along the walls, tunneling down the wide central hallway stretched out in front of her.

Warm air engulfed her, words forming in the drift, *"Turnbolt. At last, a Turnbolt."*

She blinked and stood still, wondering — had she really heard that? Or was it nothing but the shifting of fresh air in a place closed up for too long? She listened harder. Not a rustle. No murmuring. Nothing but silence in the close clutch of darkness. Truly drew a deep breath. Just her imagination playing tricks.

It had been known to happen.

She didn't like unfamiliar places.

In recent years, she'd gotten better at controlling her reaction. At belying her fears. At forcing the nightmares that had plagued her as a child to the back of her mind. All those monsters, ever present, always around the next corner. Even here, in a house with which she felt an immediate connection.

Now that she stood inside, the feeling became stronger. She belonged here. No rhyme or reason for the thought. Rational and logic held no place in the moment. Just truth, the kind that sank deep into her bones as she listened to the settling silence, trying to understand how she could feel so at home while her nerves jangled and pulled. She swallowed past the lump in her throat and —

The door slammed shut behind her.

With a jerk, Truly spun around and jumped back. The camera bag banged against her hip. Palm pressed to her chest, she stared at the closed door. "The wind. Just the wind. Settle down."

A sensible conclusion. Even better advice.

Speaking it out loud, however, didn't do what she wanted. She wasn't settled. Standing in the shadow of the door, the unreal quality of the house increased instead. A buzzing sensation sawed along her spine, deepening her unease, trying to tell her something. Seemed like an important message for her to grasp, and yet, she couldn't catch hold of it or decipher what instinct urged her to understand.

Tension gripping her spine, she walked deeper into the house and stopped beside the table set against the wall. Air stirred around her. Ignoring the strange rush, Truly reached toward the lamp. Her fingers found the toggle. She pulled. The chain zipped and rattled. Golden light spilled into the space, illuminating the central corridor, bouncing over wood floors to glitter off the enormous chandelier hanging from the high ceiling. Light refracted off hundreds of crystals, sending patterns over gleaming wainscoting and the sweeping flute of the staircase.

Her brows furrowed. Wainscoting and railings polished to a high shine. A clean, colorful oriental rug underfoot. She swept her fingertips over the surface of the hall table. Not a speck of dust... anywhere.

A wreck on the outside. Beautifully kept on the inside.

Not what she'd been expecting. Not what she should be

seeing, given Mirador's insistence no one had entered the house for years. *For years.*

Rubbing her lips together, she looked around again. Definitely odd. The spooky factor wasn't just her imagination playing tricks. The state inside the house rounded out her suspicions. Minador had set her down in the middle of a mess. What kind, she wasn't yet sure, but whatever it was couldn't be good. Or avoided, given the fact she now owned the Victorian currently freaking her out.

Signed. Sealed. Delivered.

The money transferred and in her name.

No way to back out of the deal.

The thought set a shiver through her.

Shoving aside her twang of distress, she set her bag on the table and began to explore, flipping on lights, walking through rooms, studying family portraits set in ornate frames. Relatives, she guessed, but she didn't recognize any of the people. No one seemed familiar. She couldn't say she looked like any of them. All she could say was that the house held a rich history of a family she'd never met, but must now claim as her own.

In the master bedroom, Truly ran her fingers over the quilt folded across the end of the bed, then moved to the bedside table. She touched the fringed bottom of the lamp shade. Spotless. Everything in its place. The room fresh-smelling as though windows had been recently opened. Even the bathrooms were clean, fluffy towels folded over warming racks, linen closets in order and organized — like a hotel, neat, tidy, clean — as though the house had been waiting for someone to arrive.

On her way back downstairs, she paused on the wide landing.

A wind gust rushed along the treads.

The eerie whisper came again. *"Turnbolt."*

She flattened her hand against the wall to steady herself.

Her stomach dipped as heat spilled from her palm. Blue light sparked against the paneling. Her internal temperature shifted to an intense chill, sending icy shards up her arm and across her chest. Her lungs seized. She choked, struggling to breathe as the house rippled around her. Clicking noises exploded inside her head, unlocking something inside her, sending waves of awareness cresting into unexplored mental places.

Light sparked behind her eyes. Thin blue lines, one after another, appeared in the darkened recess of her mind. She followed the ravening curves until she recognized the form — doorways, dozens of them, so many she lost count. Her heart kicked, galloping against the inside of her breastbone as she tried to pull her hand from the wall. No give. No way for her retreat, or stop the tide. Instead, she watched fingers of blue flames curl around a door edge, inferno-driven claws gripping the frame, trying to wrench the portal open.

Incredulity spread, arrowing into fear as Truly tried to put out the fire. She had to keep whatever stood on the other side of the door from breaking through. She didn't know why. Couldn't begin to understand, but instinct screamed, telling her chaos would ensue if she gave up... if she gave way... if the dam inside her head burst and monsters broke free.

Feet planted inside her house, mind somewhere else, Truly moved with precision, barricading mental doors, battling to turn the locks and beat back the flames.

A crack rippled through the quiet. Something shattered. As the splintering sound echoed, a latch on one of the doors gave away. A vicious roar pulsed against her temples. Tearing her hand away from the wall, she stumbled down the remaining steps. As she hit her knees at the bottom, the house hummed. *"Finally, a Turnbolt."*

A thump.

A twist.

A snarl rolled into a hair-raising howl.

The door she fought to keep closed flew open. A second one followed, then a third, heavy panels swinging wide, falling like dominoes in the dark. Gossamer threads pushed through the frames. Like sheets blowing in the wind, the frayed mist billowed toward her, glowing so bright white wisps obliterated the black. Her vision sheeted. Something unnatural stepped through the undulating flow.

Her mind took a snapshot and recoiled.

A monster. One that had stalked her at night, in her dreams, as a child.

Gripped by the nightmare, Truly drew a choked breath. She tried to scream. Nothing but a wheeze came out instead, as yellow eyes with vertical pupils locked onto her through the mist. Sharp fangs flashed in the gloom. A hulking silhouette reared, then charged through the doorway, sending her spinning as the beast escaped its world and came crashing into hers.

4

REALM OF AZLANDIA – BEYOND THE ECOTONE

The shockwave sent Queen Lyonesse stumbling backward. From her perch high on the cliffs, she looked out across the flatlands to the swath of blue beyond. Her gaze narrowed. The pulse had come from somewhere on the shelf, along the coastline rimming the southeast corner of her realm.

The ocean seethed in the distance.

The current turned, grew, whipping across her senses.

Another rumble shook the ground beneath her feet.

She felt the tear in the *Ecotone* widen, opening a doorway between worlds.

With a curse, she unfolded her wings and took flight. Five of her personal guard followed, the ruffling of feathers a symphony behind her as she rocketed into the warm, dark night. Her focus on the horizon, she flew fast, heading for the breach, already smelling the filth — the toxic swill of pollution — spilling in from Earth Realm.

Twenty-seven years.

Twenty-seven long, peaceful years without incident. Without the threat of Earthlings and their poisonous slop —

breathing fresh air, enjoying clean water, surrounded by abundance and the diversity nature offered.

She'd ensured it. Had spent decades hunting to eliminate the last Door Master.

Executing the Turnbolt ancestral line had been her duty, but also a privilege. She'd done it to protect her home. To help her people. To ensure humanity's slow poisoning of their world stopped affecting hers.

Exiting the flatlands, she reached the water's edge, then blew past the island tower. The light at its apex still glowed green, washing over the chop of whitecaps, but if she didn't act fast, that would change. Without her intervention, the doorway into Earth Realm would widen, allowing more toxic air to spill into Azlandia. The lamp would shift from green to yellow, and finally to red, sending panic through those she ruled.

Lyonesse clenched her teeth. It shouldn't be happening — or even possible. All the doorways between worlds had been sealed tight. In truth, the magical portals should never have been created in the first place.

Her predecessor hadn't agreed. He'd been foolish. A truly terrible king. Always benevolent, forever intrigued by humanity, Leonidas had taken pity, opening the *Ecotone*, mating their world with Earth Realm, using the magic in Azlandia to filter the toxicity Earthlings excelled at creating. Once clean, the magical weave sent fresh air back through a system of cosmic vents, ensuring humans breathed easy and their planet survived.

Leonidas had been an idiot. Trusting in ways she would never understand. In doing what he'd done, her father had jeopardized their welfare, enabling the slow poisoning of his own people.

Earthlings were vultures, taking more than their fair share.

No matter how many lessons the human race was given, their leaders refused to learn, squabbling like children, nation pitted against nation, raping their own world of natural resources in an attempt to gain more riches. Never a thought to the consequences. Stupid. Selfish. Lacking in vision. Earth Realm ought to be self-sufficient, an instrument for good, a balancing force in the universe, instead of a plague upon it.

Soon, however, it would be too late.

Over.

Done.

Nothing but a dead world floating in the shadow of hers.

Azlandia wasn't meant to be Earth Realm's filter. Her home wasn't meant to take the pollution humans flung into the air — day after day, month after month, year after year — clean it, and return it to ensure humanity flourished.

Flying over the ocean, out in front of her guard, Lyonesse spotted the structure atop Eckizbad Island. Remote, surrounded by water, the prison rose like jagged teeth in the snarling mouth of an angry sea. Worry uncoiled inside her. Not good. Worse, in fact, than she'd first thought.

The prison sat apart — far from land — for good reason.

Reinforced with magic, it housed the worst of the worst: mages and monsters so vicious even in Azlandia (where magic was encouraged and the most horrendous creatures embraced), it wasn't safe to allow any to roam free.

Her attention on the structure, she scanned open ground. Awash with light from eternal torches, the main courtyard was a flurry of activity.

The warden yelled out instructions.

Guards gathered into formation.

She dropped from the sky.

Her feet slammed into the ground. A ring of pink flame detonated around her. Dust blasted across the courtyard. Lyonesse controlled the magic, gathering the flames, drawing the tendrils to her before they incinerated the prison guards. With a flick, she folded her wings and turned to the Warden.

Her aura washed him in reddish-pink glow.

Out of breath, he hit one knee and bowed his head. "Your Majesty."

She ignored his greeting. "What escaped?"

"The Wendigo, Majesty."

Lyonesse snarled. "The doorway?"

"Still open," he said, fear in his voice.

"Anckar." Glancing over her shoulder, she found the commander of her personal guard. "Bring me the Slayer."

Anckar's blue wings fluttered, betraying his alarm. "Is that wise, my queen? He will not —"

"Bring. Him. To me," she said, tone soft, expression hard.

He bowed his head. "As you wish."

Yes. It would be... exactly how *she wished.*

She knew the dangers.

The Slayer couldn't be controlled.

A hybrid — half-Assenta (the hunter race on her world), half-Electi (a magic-wielder like her) — he was an abomination. An illegal aberration born of parents never meant to mate. Hierarchy was important to the continued success of society. The lines between different social classes must never be blurred. The intermingling of species and castes was strictly forbidden and brutally enforced. Why she'd allowed him to live, Lyonesse still didn't know. Maybe for a time like this. Maybe so she could put all those animal instincts, the grotesque monstrosity of him, to good use.

Cold and dark, blood lust ran in his veins. Maybe that was the reason.

Like any well-trained circus animal, she enjoyed forcing him to do tricks. To dance to her tune, putting him in his place while he justified his continued existence.

Moving toward the heavy gates, she swept by the Warden.

He quivered.

She hid her disgust, mounted the wide, stone steps, and crossed beneath the portico. The doorway between worlds must be closed. But not yet. She had a little leeway. Very little, but still enough to correct the situation, and as she walked deeper into the prison toward the Wendigo's cell, a plan formed. She would send the Slayer through the *Ecotone* into Earth Realm: to recapture the Wendigo of course, but for another reason as well.

The last Door Master wasn't dead. The threat hadn't yet been extinguished.

Surprising, but the evidence suggested the Turnbolts were more intelligent than she'd allowed. Somehow, they'd managed to hide one of their kind from her, preserving their ancestral line.

Clever.

Devious, even.

Traits she admired, but that didn't mean she'd admire it for long. The health of her realm hung in the balance, her people once again at risk.

No mercy would be shown.

Her lips curved. Ironic, really, how things turned out. Today's events made one thing clear — the Slayer would prove more valuable than first thought. He'd balk. She'd insist, using a carrot along with the stick she carried. If he did as she asked, he'd benefit, and she'd get what she needed — the Wendigo recaptured and returned to where it belonged... and the death of the Door Master missed during the last hunt.

Boot heels striking stone, Lyonesse hummed in satisfaction. Two birds, one stone. An absolutely perfect plan.

5

SOMETHING NEW. SOMETHING DIFFERENT

Given a choice between living in a cage and execution, Westvane had chosen the cage. Any sane person would, though the passivity didn't sit right with him. He wondered, in quieter moments, what his mother would've made of it. She'd raised him to be strong and fast, lethal to those who opposed him. She taught him to use cunning and brutality as weapons, and given her views, his imprisonment inside the Parkland felt too much like surrender.

Standing at his outdoor butcher block, Westvane stared at the blood-soaked surface.

No real reason for debate.

His mother would never have approved.

The mere suggestion made him flinch. He flexed his fingers around the hilt of his skinning knife. The feel of well-worn grooves settled him as he stared at the curved tip. One of his favorites, crafted by the most skilled blacksmith in Azlandia. A gift given to his mother in secret from a male who should never have been his father.

With a flick, Westvane tossed the dagger high, watched it revolve, blunt end over wicked tip, against the darkening horizon. Not quite night yet, but soon. Time to finish his task and call it a day.

Though it hadn't been much of one.

Westvane frowned at the dead animal on his table. *Bored.* He was so unbelievably bored. With autumn descending and his winter stores full, little hunting needed to be done. One hour ticked into the next with nothing much to keep him busy, and as he plucked the knife out of the air, his gaze strayed toward the sky.

Colorful leaves rustled and treetops swayed, thick branches creaking as evening wind pushed clouds across the muted sky. The setting sun burnished everything in gold — him, the clearing, the cabin he called home beneath the old oaks. Waning sunrays warmed his back, banishing the chill, soothing the memory of his mother away.

Soothing.

His top lip curled away from his teeth. Westvane despised the idea. He was an Assenta, the most lethal of his kind. He shouldn't need comforting. He shouldn't *need* anything at all.

Temper moving from bad to worse, he sliced through the marmot's carcass, gutting the animal, carving fur from flesh, fighting the emptiness, hating the frustration. He needed something to happen. Something new. Something different. Something that didn't involve thinking about —

A low chuff sounded from a nearby tree.

With a flick, Westvane cut a fatty piece of meat from bone and flung it across the clearing. Eastbrook didn't hesitate. The raven snapped the morsel out of the air, hooked it with his talons, and settled in to eat.

He watched the bird a moment, admiring his jet-black feathers before returning his attention to the marmot. "Too lazy to hunt today, my friend? You grow fat here with me."

Eastbrook tilted his head. Dark eyes scathing, the bird treated him to silent, yet snappish attitude.

Westvane grinned.

Eastbrook chastened him, cawing around a beak-full of fresh meat.

"I call it like I see it."

The raven puffed up in affront.

Westvane chuckled, enjoying the one-way conversation that was not one-way at all.

"Not to worry. You are always welcome," he murmured, gesturing with his blade to the half-carved carcass. "I have plenty to share."

His feathered friend wing-flapped in approval.

He threw him another morsel.

As his strong beak snapped closed, a pulse rippled through the air.

Westvane glanced toward the dome overhead. The fine webbing shimmered blue as light crawled across the magic-fueled surface. His eyes narrowed. He listened as the forest spoke, delivering information on a brisk breeze. And there it was...

Something new and altogether different.

Soldiers had just entered his prison, a place politely referred to as The Parkland.

Deeming him too dangerous to move freely among her people, the Queen kept him imprisoned under the dome, inside ten thousand hectares of pristine forest, boasting raging rivers and glacier-fed lakes. Lots of room for him to roam. An abundant amount of game to hunt and fish to spear. One of the most remote places in Azlandia. All the better to hide him from his own kind... and from hers.

Another ripple rolled into his clearing.

His nostrils flared, filtering scents, narrowing the scope of inquiry.

Odd. More than just the usual amount when it came to Lyonesse. No one but the Queen dared to enter his Parkland. She never arrived alone, always with her personal guard, to ensure his cooperation.

Not that she ever got it.

He fought her every time, forcing her to bind him in one of her magic spells. It wasn't that he thought he could win. His power in no way matched hers. At least, not yet. Still, he had to give her credit. The witch wasn't stupid. She didn't take chances, knowing his strength, understanding his cunning, aware of his predatory nature.

He couldn't be trusted, and she knew it.

Today's visit, however, appeared to be different. The magical wave that always preceded her wasn't present. The scent in the air told him the guards entered his prison without her, planning to approach him alone. Which signaled one thing — catastrophe.

Something terrible must have happened.

She wouldn't send a contingent into his cage, put a bull's-eye on her personal guard, unless Azlandia was at risk. Tipping his head back, Westvane drew a long breath. His nostrils flared. Magic curled in his veins as he sifted through scents wafting over the forest floor. Their stench reached him. Nine... nine very foolish males had just stepped into his domain.

Every step brought them deeper into his territory, closer to where he stood.

Westvane growled in satisfaction.

Eastbrook called in inquiry, reacting to his aggression.

"To me," he said, holding out his hand palm up to expose his inner forearm.

Eastbrook took flight, wings spread wide, seeking safety upon his skin.

He and the raven played at this often, testing his skill, connecting through the magic no one knew Westvane possessed. He wanted to keep it that way. No one needed to know what gifts his late father had given him. Least of all the guards tromping through his forest. But as Eastbrook landed on his arm and needled into his skin, flattening into a beautiful tattoo, he yearned to show them.

Westvane locked the urge down.

Showing his hand now would hurt his cause. He wasn't yet ready to admit he shared more Electi attributes than first thought. The magic he possessed was one. The second were his wings. The first time the pair punched through his shoulder blades had been a revelation. An accident that shocked him. Even more curious, however, was the fact he could tuck them away at will, keeping the pair caged beneath the surface of his skin.

A useful skill that ensured Lyonesse and the Electi High Table remained oblivious to the new threat he presented. Time would tell how fast and far his power grew. For now, he needed more practice. Allowing his secret out into the open before he understood his limits would end in disaster.

He wouldn't get a second chance. Which meant no matter how much it chaffed his nature, he must proceed with caution. The instant Lyonesse understood just how much he'd inherited from his Electi sire, he'd be executed with extreme prejudice. His plans to kill the queen and free Azlandians from a tyrannical regime would cease to exist.

Westvane refused to contemplate that outcome. His mother had wanted better for him. Had given her life to keep him safe and teach him what he needed to know.

Those lesson were burned into his brain:

Trust no one.

Be merciless in the face of his enemies.

Hide his magical abilities until ready to strike.

Twenty years later, and her rules still governed his life. Her wisdom continued to keep him alive. His survival depended on him hiding his gifts, who he was, and what he was capable of becoming. Not a challenge on a normal day. Others rarely visited him. He might hate his cage, but it had one thing going for it — seclusion and privacy. He required both in order to hone his craft without anyone being the wiser.

Softened by thick moss, approaching footfalls echoed.

Focus trained on the edge of the clearing, Westvane drove the tip of his blade into the surface of his butcher block. The knife bit wood. A thud echoed. Eastbrook shifted on his skin. The raven tattoo moved up his arm, over his shoulder to settle in on the side of his neck.

"Good idea," he murmured absorbing the burn of the bird's inky slither over his skin. "Keep an eye out, Eastbrook. Four eyes are better than two."

The raven repositioned his head, sliding closer to the front of his throat.

"Slayer," a man called, using the woods as cover. Not that Westvane needed to see him. Keen senses already seething, he knew where the guard stood. "We come in peace."

Westvane tried not to laugh. A huff escaped him. Not a bad plan on their part, all things considered. Warn him first. Make their intensions known. Live to see another day.

"Stop hiding," he said, eyes trained on the edge of the clearing. "Come out. I already know where you are."

Only fair he warned them in return.

He might not believe in fair play, but he wasn't opposed to playing by the rules when it suited him. Besides, toying with his prey before he killed it was one of his favorite pastimes. Add curiosity to mix, and he couldn't help himself. He wanted to know why Lyonesse sent them into his den, risking the strongest in her army.

Wary-eyed, the lead guard stepped out of the forest into the clearing. "Westvane."

"Anckar." His mouth curved, the smile not one of welcome, but of promised pain. "Nice of you to visit."

Raising his hands, Anckar held one out toward him, the gesture an appeal for mercy. The other he used to signal to the others following him. The soldiers behind him halted.

Westvane waited, unmoving.

Anckar swallowed. "We want no trouble."

"Then you should not have entered my cage." Flexing his fists, Westvane unleashed the predator he kept locked deep inside him.

"We come in the name of the Queen." Blue feathers aflutter, Anckar flexed his wings, settling each closer to his spine.

An unnecessary adjustment. A nervous, very telling tick. One Anckar would do well to subdue before Westvane decided to rip his wings off and shove both up his —

Anckar cleared his throat. "She has requested your presence."

"You lie. She doesn't request. She summons."

"All the same, we cannot return to her empty-handed." He unclipped the collar packed with magic and explosives from his belt. "Best if you come without a fight."

"By all means, come along, Electi," he murmured, soft tone full of menace. "Put the collar around my neck. I dare you."

Already pale-faced, the guards standing at Anckar's back palmed the barbed whips coiled to their belts. Westvane smiled even as he set his stance, preparing for battle. Excellent. Better than expected. A knuckle-bruising fight. Something new, though not altogether different. Exactly what he wanted, and everything he needed.

6

LIKE NOTHING SHE'D EVER SEEN

Ribs hurting, muscles burning, lying prone on the hardwood floor, Truly opened her eyes. Nothing but blur. She blinked to clear her vision, then realized she couldn't breathe. Heavy pressure sat on her chest. Pain moved through her as she sucked in a choked breath.

Too thin. The air was too thin. She couldn't get enough. Had her lungs collapsed? Had she fallen somehow? Was it —

Her brain rebooted, dragging awareness to the forefront of her mind.

Something had hit her and kept going, running right over the top of her.

Wheezing, she forced her lungs to expand and stared up at... something. She squinted through black spots. Slices of light refracted through the shards. The framework came into focus. A chandelier, light bouncing off hundreds of crystals, and it finally struck her.

The house on Isadore Street.

She was inside the old Victorian she now owned. Strange enough to be given property, but even more surprising was the fact she wasn't in it alone.

Drawing quick, short breaths, she forced her ribcage to expand. Blistering pain spiked behind her breastbone, then streaked around to her back. Her entire torso felt bruised. A broken bone or two wasn't out of the realm of possibility, given the size of the thing that collided with her. She didn't know exactly, couldn't check until she caught her breath, but...

She swore fur smacked her in the face as the thing thundered by.

A snarl seethed up the corridor.

Truly coughed as more air seeped into her lungs.

Another growl. Definitely an animal. Not of the cute, cuddly variety either. By the sounds of it, more like the ravenous, probably-going-to-gut her kind.

Tasting bile in her mouth, she turned onto her side and looked up the corridor. Cloaked in shadows, a figure stood by the front door. Not a someone, a *something*, and as she watched, horror pushed through the pain, tying a knot behind her breastbone, putting on pressure as the beast rose like a grizzly bear in the dim light. Hulking and predatory, it pushed from four feet onto two paws.

The stuff of nightmares, the monster was like nothing she'd ever seen. Smooth, blue skin streaked with red and white. A thick mane grew from its head, cascading over its shoulders. Six eyes, three on either side of a flat face, instead of the regular two. Seven long, lethal-looking claws tipped each paw. And a mouth full of sharp teeth.

Definitely not human. Also, not from planet Earth. Nothing normal about it. The thing smelled strange too. Its scent contradictory — a combination of freshly squeezed orange juice and ash.

Risking movement, she pressed her palm to the floor. Carpet fringe played between her fingers as she pushed to her feet. The air grew thick, almost stagnant as the beast stared at her. It bared razor-sharp canines. Muscles tense, anticipating attack, she prepared to flee, knowing —

"Door Master," it hissed.

Another round of surprise hit her. "You can talk."

The beast grinned at her and started to change shape.

Slack-jawed, she watched it shrink, beginning to transform into a man. Six eyes turned into two. Its long mane shortened into hair on a perfectly shaped human head. Two hooves became normal looking feet. Seven claws morphed into five fingers. All in the middle of her freaking foyer.

Stomping on a pair of boots, the thing turned to go.

A shiver swept through her, fear right on its heels.

Allowing it to leave wasn't a good idea. How she understood that, Truly didn't know. Nothing seemed real, or made sense right now. Not strange happenings in her house. Not the weird doors in her mind. And certainly not the creature about to walk out her front door. But with an instinct born of unproved certainty, she knew she couldn't let it go. She must stop it. The instant the beast escaped her house, disaster would follow, the wave of destruction so devastating, the city she loved would never be the same.

7

EIGHT WARRIORS DOWN

Fists raised, body loose, Westvane pivoted to avoid another punch. Short grass churned beneath his boot soles. The smell of damp dirt rose as he dodged, then ducked. The heavy fist whiffed over his head. With a low snarl, he spun in the opposite direction and unleashed his own fists.

His knuckles slammed into his attacker's side.

Bone cracked.

Westvane hit him again, each movement precise, striking without mercy. He felt flesh cave beneath his fist. Heard ribs splinter. Felt the corresponding scream in his gut as jagged shards punched through guard's skin, sawing into open air.

Wings bent, brown wings askew, the warrior fell to his knees.

A second, third, and fourth guard attacked.

Joy spilled through Westvane as he dodged another uppercut. The circle around him tightened. Anckar stood back while the others moved forward. Meeting his gaze over the other guards' heads, Westvane smiled at the bastard as he tussled with the others. Toying with them. Delivering pain with each strike.

Keeping his Assenta claws sheathed, each blow just short of lethal.

No sense gutting the males before he knew why Lyonesse sent them.

He kept the fight light instead. Decimating without killing. Leaving marks and broken bones in his wake. Downing one Electi after another with methodical precision.

Thuds echoed through the clearing. Groans raged against the treetops. The last guard fell. Eight warriors down. One more to go.

Stepping over one of the fallen, he engaged Anckar. The simpering coward. Talk about a terrible leader. The fool had allowed his comrades to attack first, hovering on the periphery, shielding himself from the brutality, watching the warriors under his command fall. Anckar ought to know better. He should've been first into the fray, not the last one standing.

Westvane wanted to be disgusted.

He found himself resigned instead. Expecting more always ended in a zero-sum game. The Queen's guard had never been "all for one and one for all." They looked out for number one, fighting over the scraps from Lyonesse's table. No thought to the good of others. No care for the Azlandians living under the High Table's rule. Just greed, driven by self-interest and self-ishness.

"Westvane," Anckar said, backpedaling, wings quivering, hands up, but not fisted. "Listen to me for a second."

Baring over-long canines, Westvane attacked.

A short series of jabs.

An uppercut to the chin.

A quick kick behind one of Anckar's knee, and he stood victorious, nothing but moans of pain interrupting the once peaceful state of his clearing. Westvane snarled and shook his head. A complete disappointment. No challenge at all. The fight had barely taxed him. He wasn't even breathing hard.

Taking in the chaos, he scowled at the Electi scattered on the ground at his feet. He waited for a sense of accomplishment to hit him. For the satisfaction of defeating warriors well-trained in weaponry and versed in magic to sink deep and feed his soul. It never arrived. Sad to say, but as he stood over his bleeding opponents, he didn't feel much of anything. Just mild revulsion that it took him less than five minutes to down all nine.

The queen should've known better and sent more.

Not that he lamented her lack of foresight. He wasn't inclined to explore his disgust at her tactics. Not right now. He had a job to do... and Anckar to take on a fieldtrip.

Scanning the ground, he searched for the crystals the guards kept clipped to their belts. Ignoring Anckar's pitiful moans, his gaze bounced between the Electi. Some lay unconscious, flat on their backs with legs and arms askew. Others curled into tight balls, wings ripped, bloody bones exposed, trying to absorb the agony of dislocated joints and cracked skulls.

His focus narrowed on their belt loops. Not a crystal to be found.

Concerned by the lack, Westvane turned toward Anckar. With a quick hand, he grabbed him by the throat. Muscles tight, grip sure, he lifted the captain of the queen's guard from the ground. He held him that way, broken ribs exposed, blood streaming down his side, feet dangling off the turf.

"Look at me." The second he saw the white of the Anckar's eyes, Westvane murmured, "Take me to your queen."

Larynx convulsing against the palm of his hand, Anckar coughed, and grasping Westvane's wrist with one hand, unearthed the crystal hanging from a leather cord beneath his shirt. Choking on the words, the guard spoke in a language long forgotten.

The rasped incantation slithered through the clearing.

The rough, oddly shaped crystal began to glow.

The dome overhead flexed. Cascading light rushed over his skin, dragging him into a kaleidoscope of color. The teleportation prism pulled. Cool evening air warped, and the clearing whirled. Massive trees, along his small cabin in the wood, disappeared.

The sensation of flying took hold.

Seconds later, his feet thumped down, finding solid ground in a different place.

Westvane smelled the putrefaction of the prison before he saw it. Suffering, after all, was easy to recognize. He should know. He dished enough of it out as often as he could, laying waste to whatever Lyonesse sent his way.

Feeling his body solidify — muscles and bone returning to normal — Westvane scanned his surroundings. The main courtyard, the steep stairway into the hell of Eckizbad Prison, topped by a wide landing where public executions took place, rising hard in front of him. Stark recollection transported him to another time and place. Images of his mother — standing so proud and strong on the landing as she awaited her execution.

Rage swelled, rising like a serpent up the back of his throat.

Controlling the pain, Westvane killed the urge to strike. He buried the agony of childhood memories deep instead. Showing weakness here would be the kiss of death. The second Lyonesse saw his agony, she would exploit it. Rub it in. Revel in the fact, she'd taken away the only person who'd ever mattered to him with a single stroke of her blade.

As ever, the witch stood on the top step, looking down her nose at him, lording over the rabble that stood in the courtyard. She thought her guard would protect her. Westvane swallowed a growl. So foolish to have left him alone so long. In the span of things, two decades didn't seem like a long time.

To him, though, it felt like the good kind of forever. He was stronger now. More experienced. Older. Wiser. Better equipped to deal with her idiocy. Better able to exploit the fact Lyonesse wasn't yet aware of what Eastbrook already knew — that the potency of Westvane's magic would someday rival hers.

Digging his fingers into the scruff of Anckar's neck, Westvane tossed him toward Lyonesse. The warrior landed and rolled, coming to rest at the base of the stairs.

"Slayer," she murmured, amusement in her tone. "Still up to your old tricks, I see."

Westvane didn't answer. He waited instead for her real reaction, for the consequences of leaving the captain of her guard broken at her feet.

At his silence, she shook her head, like a mother might when faced with a recalcitrant child. Stepping closer to the edge of the landing, she gazed down at her injured soldier. The movement caused her scent to drift. His predatory nature took over, hearing and smelling everything, noticing even more — the whisper of her wing-tips against stone, the perfume she wore made from morning dew and lilac petals... the distance between his hands and her throat.

With an ease that spoke of decades of practice, he stilled his killing instinct.

The queen rolled her eyes, then changed tact, focusing on the warrior lying broken at the base of her stairs. Lyonesse waved her hand. Magic pinwheeled down the treads, sparking over stone. The red-pink glow swirled around Anckar, mending muscle, reknitting bone, breathing oxygen into lungs gone without for too many minutes. The male twitched, gasping in pain before managing to take a full breath.

Without taking her gaze from him, she spoke to her captain, "Be gone, Anckar... and take the rest of the guard with you."

"As you wish, Majesty," Anckar said, gaining his feet, hugging his ribcage.

The whisper of footfalls against hard-packed earth rose behind Westvane. Iron hinges creaked. A heavy wooden door opened, then closed as the Queen's Guard left him alone in the courtyard with the merciless witch who ruled their realm.

Keeping his stance relaxed, he raised a brow. "You called?"

Painted blood red, her lips curved. "And like an ever-faithful hound, you came."

The muscles along his spine tightened as instinct urged him to attack. He quieted the impulse and locked down his body. He refused to give her the upper hand. The second he responded to her verbal jabs was the instant he lost control of the situation. He would have time and more to put her in her place.

Now, however, wasn't the hill he planned to die on.

Crossing his arms over his chest, Westvane tipped his chin. "What do you want, Lyonesse?"

The use of her given name got her attention. Her dark eyes flashed in warning. No one called her by name. No one, but his father... and now, him.

"I'm having trouble remembering why I let you live, Slayer," she said, tone sharp enough to cut most males. But then, he wasn't *most*. "Your insolence knows no bounds."

"You know why," he said, doing some goading of his own. "Now again, what you do want?"

Gaze aglow with fury, she unfolded her wings and took flight. Her feet touched down at the bottom of the staircase, less than six feet away. Her nostril flared. She recoiled as she came close to him, walking a wider path around him. "You wear the stink of your mother upon your skin."

Again. Like always. It always came back to this — a slur against his ancestral line.

Accustomed to it, Westvane didn't react. What Lyonesse

thought of him didn't matter. He knew who his mother had been, what she'd stood for — on the right side of all things good. Nothing the queen said would change that... or take away the blood-bond, a gift from his mother for doing nothing other than being born of her womb.

His mother had loved him. Even more than she'd loved his father.

An incredible claim, given his parent's affinity for one another.

Class hadn't mattered to his parents. His sire and mother had fallen in love anyway, ignoring the laws written and enforced to keep them apart. He knew the story. Had listened to it over and over in his mother's retelling. By the time the queen discovered his parents' deception, it had been too late. He'd been nestled inside his mother's womb. Already illegal, considered an abomination in the eyes of his countrymen before ever being born.

His parents had fought long.

They'd fought hard.

The rebellion lead by his father dividing an already divided world.

In the end, his parents died for their beliefs, fighting to abolish the law separating *Cropper* from *Assenta*, and *Assenta* from *Electi*, legislation that expressly forbade a union between classes. Magic wielders (Electi) stayed with Electi, Assenta with Assenta, and the low-class Croppers with those born as serfs. No exceptions. No mercy. Examples made of all who defied the royal edict. Which meant...

Despite the year-long battle, the law remained the same. And he continued to be reviled and ostracized for something he couldn't change — the mixed blood in his veins.

Lyonesse completed her circuit around him.

Westvane smoothed his expression, giving none of his

thoughts away. The history that made him must remain in the past. Nothing mattered now but the present, his ability to not only avenge his parents, but do what they had been unable to — right the wrong and change the law through any means necessary.

"Forever a beast, never any manners." Distain in her expression, her attention left his physique as she moved away from him to mount the first step.

"And yet, you keep calling on me."

She turned from her ascent, whipping around to face him.

He quirked a brow. "Why call if you do not like the look of me?"

"Slayer, do not tempt —"

"You can't help yourself," he murmured, going in for the kill. Usually, he had no need for words. His fists spoke for him, but in this, he knew her weakness. "Did you love my father so much you need a glimpse of his son to get your fix?"

"Insolent cur. You are nothing like your sire."

A lie. A bold one, given the painting that hung in her Great Hall. He was the spitting image of the male who'd sired him.

"Your Grace," a guard called from the landing, braving his queen's wrath. "Time is —"

"I am aware, Garrod." Soothing her ruffled feathers, Lyonesse folded her wings neatly as she climbed the steps. Halfway up, she glanced at him over her shoulder. "Come, Slayer, like the good dog you are. Stay seven paces behind me. You come any closer, and I will strike you down."

Westvane nearly scoffed. He doubted it. Lyonesse wouldn't kill him. She wanted something from him first. Intriguing. A mystery. A puzzle only he could solve — just the 'something different' he'd been searching for, and so...

He followed, keeping his distance, curiosity piqued.

Garrod's expression — along with the urgency Lyonesse

tried to hide — warranted attention. Very close scrutiny. Something was more than just wrong. Whatever problem she needed him to solve must be dire. So huge, she courted the consequence of releasing him from his cage.

As he reached the landing and passed beneath the soaring stone archway into the prison, an unwanted shiver shook him. The first years of his life had been spent sharing a cell inside Eckizbad with his mother. He knew this place. Every brick. Every flagstone and well-travelled tread. All the cracks and crevices marring the interior corridors' thick stone walls. The darkness, musty smell, and moans of agony. He remembered it all too well.

The place was a giant torture chamber. One designed to bring a person's worst fears to life.

Trying to ignore the ripple of unease, Westvane followed Lyonesse down one corridor into a connecting one. Around another bend. Through an intersection, down more steps, only to turn a corner and encounter more. The faster she walked, the more memory assaulted him. She was headed to the maximum-security wing, a place so deep underground an ordinary male would never find his way out.

A set of iron bars clanged behind him.

Keys rattled as the guard at the next gate prepared to unlock it.

Lyonesse came to a stop at the end of a narrow corridor. She faced him and, with a flick of her hand, indicated the lone cell door in the long hallway... in a section of the prison set apart from the rest.

He breathed deep, picking apart scents, searching for clues, detecting in the way of a hunting Assenta. His brows collided. He glanced at Lyonesse in surprise. "The Wendigo."

She blinked a second before eyebrows popped up "How can you know?"

"The scent... orange peel and ash. Unique. Powerful. One that should not be present here," he said, stopping alongside her. "Why is it still alive?"

The accusation made her flinch. "You of all people know the answer to that."

Clenching his teeth, Westvane glared at her. Of course, he knew. She liked to keep powerful things as toys — force them to dance to her tune any time she grew bored.

"Orange peel and ash," she whispered. "You smell it that clearly?"

"Yes." Sidestepping her, he walked into the cell. Every instinct he owned recoiled, screaming for him to get out. To get free. To never be caged again. Rolling his shoulders, he reached for calm, and with a deep breath, forced himself to hunt for information.

Big creature. Very small space. The scent of powerful magic in the air.

He frowned at Lyonesse. "What happened here?"

"It escaped." Looking uncomfortable, she shrugged her shoulders, sending the tops of her wings arching. "Can you track it?"

Busy examining the walls, he shook his head, not in the negative, but in bafflement. "How did it get out? These walls are thick, the stone sound and magic strong. The Wendigo should never have been able to — "

"Westvane."

Surprised by her use of his name, his focus sharpened on her.

Expression intent, she asked again, "Can you track it?"

"Of course," he said, wanting to say *no*, but unable to deny the seriousness of the situation. The Wendigo was a powerful creature if loosed upon an unsuspecting population. Every conflict in the history of Azlandia and Earth Realm, including two World Wars, had been started by the Wendigo before it had been captured and imprisoned. "Question is — why can't you?"

The question was a valid one.

Her magic fueled unprecedented power. She should be able to run it down herself. No need to call on him at all.

"It's no longer here," she said, looking as though admitting it gave her stomach pains.

"Impossible."

"And..." she continued, ignoring his incredulity, "where it's gone, I cannot follow."

"Earth Realm."

"Exactly," she said. "I cannot cross the *Ecotone* without damaging my magic. And you're the only one with enough skill to track it."

A compliment instead of the usual insult.

Incredible. Mark the occasion.

"How did it get out?"

An excellent question.

He needed the clarification. All the portals between Azlandia and Earth Realm lay closed. Bricked up by the very queen he stared at with growing impatience. Her assertion made no sense. Only a magic-wielder of equal power could open rifts between worlds. Lyonesse didn't own that skill, only a Door Master born on the human side of the *Ecotone* possessed the ability.

"The Wendigo escaped through a doorway."

"How is that possible?"

"That is the question," she said, standing on the threshold between the door jambs. "One I will have answered by you. Recapture the Wendigo, Slayer. Bring me the one responsible for opening the doorway between our world and Earth Realm."

Westvane indulged in a few quick calculations. "What's in it for me?"

She scowled. "You will be a hero to your people, you —"

"What do I care? I've never wanted titles and don't need fanfare."

"I cannot allow the Wendigo to run free."

"Then allow me to run it to ground, but..." he said, gaze boring into hers. "If I do this for you, you grant me my freedom. No double-crosses or tricks. I want a normal life with my own kind."

"There are no others like you."

True enough. As a hybrid, he existed outside the norm. "You want the Wendigo recaptured and the Door Master dead?"

"Yes," she said through clenched teeth.

"Then freedom is my price."

Her hatred for his ultimatum hung between them. Dark pink feathers rustling, she stalled, refusing to answer in haste, searching for a way out. He refused to give her one. If she wanted him to hunt, she needed to make it worth his while.

Kicking at a pile of straw, she turned to face him. Rage ignited in her eyes as she stared at him. "Agreed."

He growled in triumph.

Looking sick to her stomach, Lyonesse raised her hand. Magic rippled from her palm. The iridescent wave hit the stone wall, tearing in half the illusion she held together. The scales fell away, revealing a vortex of clear white light, allowing him to perceive the doorway beyond the prison cell.

A portal into another world.

Awe made his heart beat faster.

The *Ecotone*, unaltered beauty untouched by time. Stories had been passed from one generation to the next, telling of a time when people moved freely between worlds, but he'd never seen it. Never scented anything so fresh, so pure, so light. The portal smelled of nothing and everything, all at once.

"Go, then." Raising a black-tipped fingernail, Lyonesse pointed him toward the breach. "I will await your successful return."

"And I, my prize," he said, moving toward the doorway.

"Do not fail me, Slayer."

He didn't plan on it. Freedom lay at the end of his mission. A chance to put his plan into action while living free. To right past wrongs and build a better future for Azlandia, one filled with hope and new purpose. He could finally see the light at the end of a very long tunnel, and nothing and no one would stand in his way.

8

THE SUCKAGE OF HER LIFE

alf frozen in fear, half hopped up on adrenaline, Truly struggled to decide. Did she want to start a fight with the beast? Seemed an incredibly stupid thing to do given the size of the thing transforming from monster to human being in her foyer. Thinking fast was better than fighting. She needed to figure out how to talk it down — or at least, waylay it — given tackling the creature wasn't a plan she wanted to employ.

She didn't want to tangle with the thing.

Letting it escape her house, however, felt like a worse option.

Looking around, she kept one eye on the beast and searched for a weapon with the other. Maybe if she lassoed it, she could trip it, tie it up, then —

Bright yellow eyes trained on her, the beast hissed while backing toward the front door.

"Stop right there." Both hands raised, she took a step toward it. "Don't move a muscle."

"Or what, Door Master?" Half transformed, looking more human by the second, the creature positioned its new head on top of a thinning neck.

"You won't enjoy my reaction," she said, injecting authority into her voice. Not that she held out much hope of it working. She might sound convincing, but the thing had a mind of its own. "You're not going anywhere."

It laughed, the cackle almost human. "How're you going to stop me?"

Good question. One in need of an immediate answer.

Truly knew her own strength. Understood her weaknesses too, which helped her come to an inescapable conclusion. No matter what she said, she wasn't going to be able to stop it. A major problem in the ever-growing pile of trouble inside her new house.

She might not understand what was going on, but having a giant, saber-toothed monster with six eyes standing in her entryway was a real eye-opener. The fact the thing continued to morph into a man added that extra special something to already thickened sauce. Which didn't inspire confidence. Or the requisite amount of sanity to carry on a conversation.

It tilted its head. "I didn't think so, though..."

"What?"

"If you were stronger, able to control your magic..." Trailing off, it crouched to tie its bootlaces. "You might've given me a run for my money."

"Magic," she whispered, not understanding. "What magic?"

"You have no idea who you are, do you, little Truly?"

"You know my name."

"I picked it out of the air. The house keeps few secrets."

Terrific. A haunted house. An irreverent monster. The suckage of her life had just rocketed into the stratosphere. "You wanna maybe stay a while, have a chat... clue me in?"

"Nice try, but no need for me to educate you. The queen will see to that soon enough."

"What in the hell is going on?"

"Wise up, Door Master. Do it fast," it said. "If you don't, Lyonesse will eat you alive."

Dread spooled down her spine. The tips of her fingers tingled as she raised her hands, trying to delay the beast's departure. Bad things were on the horizon. The creature's presence might as well be the harbinger of death.

"Listen," she said, then paused, having no idea what to say next.

"No time." Finished morphing into a man, it glanced at the open hallway behind her. A warm current of air hit her in the back. As she swayed forward, a sting nipped the nape of her neck. The man-beast tipped its head back to scent the air. "The queen has mobilized. The Slayer will not be far behind."

"Who — what are you talking about?"

Her question rushed down the corridor and...

The monster-now-man turned. She saw the yellow of his eyes, then... nothing. Like vapor, it ghosted through her solid wood door.

Shocked, Truly stood paralyzed in the hallway. What had just happened? What in the hell was going on? Frustration streamed through her. Urgency prompted her, reminding her of a self-appointed mission — *don't let it leave.*

Forcing her muscles to unlock, she lunged toward the front door. Her feet hammered the floorboards as she sprinted down the corridor. The work of seconds, she made it to the entrance. Without thinking, with no plan in mind, she grabbed the door handle and yanked.

The door swung open, then wide.

She clamored over the threshold, skidded across the porch and jumped over the front steps. Her feet hit the front walkway. The thud echoed, blasting out onto the street and —

Thank God.

She wasn't too late. The thing still stood in her yard, bathed in the glow of streetlamps, standing at the end of the cracked pathway.

The importance of that fact registered.

Attention riveted to the beast, she plotted a moment, grasping for what to do next. Stalling sounded like an excellent idea, but... why, exactly? What good would stalling do? It was already outside her house, free to go where it wanted and... God. She needed someone to explain a few things. Her night had gone from weird straight into bizarre. Given more time, who knew what else might walk though her front door tonight — pixies, elves, a whole battle contingent of Orcs.

The thought made her stomach ache.

She powered through the reaction, and racking her brain, tried to figure out the best way to keep it from escaping into the streets of Philadelphia.

"Hey!" Not exactly pithy, but given the strain, it would have to do. "Hold on a second."

It glanced over its shoulder. "You grow tiresome, Door Master."

"Nothing good will come of this."

"For you, perhaps," it said, a hideous grin on its face. "I'll be just fine."

"No, you won't," she said, leading with intuition. "Someone will come after you, hunt you down and —"

It growled at her, baring sharp teeth in a now-human mouth.

"I'm right, aren't I? You might have escaped, but..." She paused, realizing she could read its intention. The skill startled her, but didn't knock her off course. *Stall. Stall. Stall.* The longer she kept it talking, the better off she would be. "You won't stay free for long."

"You are more powerful than you know, Door Master." Breathing a lungful of fresh air, it stepped off her walkway onto the sidewalk. "But you can't stop me. I've been imprisoned for decades. Since the last great war. Nothing, not even you, will stand in my way."

Decades. The last great war.

Truly frowned. World War Two, maybe? Or was it talking about a different war — one that occurred in the place it came from? All good questions. Facts to ponder... some other time, when she didn't have a monster to stop. "What are you?"

"I am Wendigo, destroyer of worlds."

The declaration hit her like a punch to the solar plexus.

She sucked in a shaky breath as words stalled in the back of her throat. How was she supposed to respond to that? A witty comeback. A smart-ass retort. Neither of those conversational avenues seemed the way to go. Especially given his title. Nothing about *destroyer of worlds* sounded the least bit promising.

"You have no one to blame but yourself, Door Master. Without your help, I would never have escaped."

Worse and worse. How could keep getting worse? "I didn't do anything."

"You opened the door and set me free."

"No." It wasn't true. *Couldn't* be true, but then, the strange shift she'd experienced after entering the house couldn't be denied. She'd felt the heat in her veins. Heard the clicking inside her head and the sound of doors being unlocked. Only one had opened, but that didn't mean she hadn't unlocked more.

The enormity of it hit her.

Somehow, she was responsible for what had happened tonight. From start to finish. The cause of the Wendigo's escape included.

Stupid troll.

No wonder Minador acted as though she was on a covert operation. The lawyer knew exactly what would happen the instant she stepped inside the mansion. Instead of the ally she believed, the troll had turned out to be the enemy, the catalyst that propelled her straight into the middle of the mess.

Laughter echoed down the street. "I see you're getting it, Door Master. Good luck with that and also... brace."

"For what?"

"The Slayer," it said. "He will show you no mercy."

No longer able to see it, she shouted, "You really think I'm going to take advice from you? You're going off to eat people!"

Or something.

Praying it wasn't so didn't make it untrue. The Wendigo probably *did* make meals out of people. Covering her mouth with her hand, she tried to hold in her distress. She didn't want people to die — or to be eaten by the Wendigo. It wouldn't be a pretty death or fast clean-up... for anyone.

A chuckle drifted down the street, rolling out of the darkness. "Don't be foolish, Door Master. Heed me well. *Beware the Slayer.* He will hurt you, do you allow it."

Lovely. Another thing to worry about. The list got longer by the second.

"Just what I don't need," she said, the icy air making each breathe puff white in the dim light. "Seriously — what the hell is going on?"

She asked that question into the stillness.

The Wendigo was already gone. Vanished into the night. No trace of him but the lingering scent of oranges and ash. Leaving her alone in front of a house-made-in-hell, with no idea what to do next.

The realization wasn't a welcome one. She'd always been the girl who got things done. But as she stood in her yard on a silent street in a strange neighborhood, the lingering whisper of an alien heat in her veins, she admitted to being at a loss.

One thing for sure, though — she needed to prioritize. Start making lists. Formulate different plans, one for every scenario.

Zero in on the best methods of attack. Yes. Exactly. A perfectly reasonable way forward considering what lay in her future. A Slayer who planned to hurt her — according to the Wendigo. A killer queen bent on ruining her world — potentially. More weird and unexplainable events — perhaps. But first things first...

She needed to find Minador and strangled some answers out of him.

With Step 1 of her plan in hand, Truly turned back toward the house. She sighed. Too bad, really. It was such a pretty place, with its columns and sweeping front porch. Lord knew she needed a refuge, a safe place to land after months of being out in the wild, but... she should have known better. The minute she signed the papers and Minador put the keys in her hand, she should've expected the worst. Things like that didn't happen to normal people.

Normal people struggled.

Normal people scraped by.

Normal people fell down and got back up every day.

Normal people were not given houses worth three million dollars in nice parts of town.

Pursing her lips, she kept walking, boot soles ringing against flagstone, gaze on the open front door. Something moved inside the house. Cloaked in shadows, a figure stood just beyond the reach of her porch lights.

Truly jerked to a stop.

She fumbled in her coat pocket, searching for her cellphone "Stop right there, or I'll call the police!"

The shadow stepped forward.

A boot crossed her threshold, thumping down on her porch. Wooden planks creaked. The air shifted, banishing the chill, swirling into an odd pattern. The man connected to the foot moved forward, striding into the light. Black eyes riveted to her, he halted on the lip of the stairs. Shock whispered through her. She'd never seen a man that size. He was more than big. The guy was enormous. A tall, broad-shouldered, mean-looking heavyweight.

"Shit," she whispered, yanking her hand out of her jacket pocket. She searched the other one, then patted the back of her jeans.

The guy raised his hand. Perched between his thumb and forefinger, her cellphone winked in the low light. "Looking for this?"

"Double, extra shit." Truly swallowed past the lump in her throat. The guy had snooped through her camera bag. She'd left it sitting on the hall table. A bad move. The wrong one, given she'd been walking into a strange house in an unknown neighborhood. "The Slayer, I presume?"

Expression set to unhappy, his hard gaze raked her. "Good guess."

"Yeah, well," she said, beginning to get angry. Enough was, well, *enough*. There was, after all, only so much a girl could take. "I'm batting a thousand tonight."

Her snotty response drifted between them.

He shifted on the top step, threatening to come closer.

Truly stood her ground, assessing, wondering... debating. Should she run or power through the fear?

She took a second to think about it, then decided. Option two, definitely. He was a Slayer. His title stated the obvious. He enjoyed killing things. Making her evisceration fun for him by running was, quite simply, one affront too many on an already bad night. So yeah, might as well stay put. If she died in the front yard of her new house, so be it. At least the neighbors would notice her dead body and call the police in the morning.

9

YOU'VE GOT THE WRONG GIRL

Standing on the top step, Westvane stared at the human, trying to read her. The Door Master gave nothing away. Expression neutral. Body language closed, yet alert. No fear in her scent. Strange and unexpected. Most beings feared him on sight, making immediate moves to avoid him.

Gaze fixed on her, he descended the porch steps to join her on the crooked stone path. He expected her to retreat. She didn't twitch. Not a muscle. Not a fingertip. No shuffling of feet or the slightest quiver of anxiety.

Westvane frowned at her.

She raised a brow, her expression one of challenge.

He wanted to pick up the gauntlet, grab her, and go, but curiosity got the better of him. Tilting his head, he examined her a little more closely.

Hmm. Interesting. Definitely not what he expected.

He'd anticipated fear. Lots of running. Maybe even some begging. He hadn't counted on the Door Master standing her ground.

Locked in a staring contest, he crossed his arms, intending to wait her out. But as seconds ticked into minutes, he butted up against her fortitude. She wasn't going to break. Everything about the standoff suggested long-term resistance. No surrender. Non-negotiable terms. Devil-may-care strategy front and center, her defiance shoved right in his face.

A spark of admiration ignited inside him.

She might be female, but she wasn't weak. Everything about her said bold, brash, big attitude packed inside a small package.

Mirroring his stance, she crossed her arms, allowed the silence to thicken, bright blue irises boring into his dark ones.

His mouth curved.

Her eyes narrowed.

Taking another step toward her, he held her gaze. His regard firmer, much blacker, the menace he exuded easy for her to see and feel. He intended the added proximity to intimidate her. Even with him looming, the Door Master refused to back down. She widened her stance instead, claiming the space around her, and like any self-respecting magic wielder, flexed her fingers, chilly demeanor gathering more frost.

His admiration grew even more as he tried to decide what bothered him most about her. Her size, maybe. She was slight of frame, short of stature, too fragile-looking to be one of the most powerful mages in two different worlds.

The air surrounding her shifted.

Interest rapt, Westvane watched the magical current swirl in her aura. Driven by preternatural power, molecules buzzed like fireflies, bouncing off her shoulders, breaking apart only to rearrange into a new pattern. An elaborate deception. Misdirection designed to do one thing — disguise the threat she presented and throw him off.

Like one of the lake lizards in his Parkland, she changed her colors, camouflaging her gifts, masking her power, allowing none of her true nature to shine through. If he was full-blooded Assenta, instead of a hybrid, the strategy might have worked.

But despite her effort at evasion, he saw through to the heart of her.

His magic allowed him to perceive hers.

"Nice try, Door Master," he murmured, tired of the stalemate. "But you cannot hide what you are. Not from me."

"Hiding?" She tilted her head. Blonde hair tied into a tail at the back of her head swung, brushing her shoulder, stirring the air, shifting the charm-spell into another gear. Her power butted up against him, pulling at his senses. Westvane clenched his teeth as magic disrupted cold temperatures, dusting her aura in blue shimmer. "I'm not hiding. I'm standing right here."

"Don't lie to me. You've made a choice."

"You think?"

"I know it. Not a smart one either."

Annoyance puckered her brows. A muscle flexed in her jaw as she held her hand out. Her fingers curled into a flicking motion... and pure challenge. "My phone."

Westvane glanced down. He'd forgotten he'd taken the toy away. "Come and get it."

She scoffed. "What — and get close enough for you to take a whack at me? I don't think so."

"You can't stand out here all night."

"Wanna bet?"

He snorted before he caught it and smothered the sound of amusement. Such a pain in the ass. She might be small, but despite himself, he liked her spirit. "I'm not going to kill you."

"Right," she said, sarcasm in her tone striking like a whip. "'Cause you're named *Slayer* for nothing."

"No. The title's well-earned," he said, returning her temper with honesty. "I'm simply stating the facts. I have no intention of harming you."

"Seriously?"

"How will I navigate Earth Realm if my guide is dead?"

"Something tells me you'd manage."

"True," he said, beginning to enjoy the verbal battle. "But as a rule, I never make things harder than they need to be."

"How very practical of you."

"Practicality is a virtue."

"When it comes to killing people."

"In everything." Might as well give her fair warning. He always took the path of least resistance. Unless, of course, he needed to make a point — like he so often did with Lyonesse. "Have I reassured you?"

"No." A look of consternation on her face, she studied him like a strange object.

His shoulder blades began to itch.

Westvane clenched his teeth. The little witch. She was tapping into his glamor, making his magic react to hers — and making it harder for him to keep his wings tucked safely beneath his skin. Even as he fought it, the clawing sensation grew. He felt his muscles split beneath his marmot-skin jacket. Flexing his mind, he turned his attention inward, sealing the seam, forcing his wings to stay under wraps. He refused to lose control. Not now. Not in front of her. Not when he was so close to getting what he needed to begin his hunt of the Wendigo and secure his freedom.

"Why are you here?" she asked. "To hunt that thing?"

"Good guess."

"As I said — I'm batting a thousand tonight."

The disgruntled comment made him want to laugh. Again. Not optimal considering his plans. Enjoying her wit would make it more difficult to execute her when the time came. An interesting tangle, the push-pull one he might've enjoyed another time, in another place, but he refused to allow her likability to stop him from achieving his goal.

He was on a mission.

She was nothing but a stepping stone on the way to victory.

But even as the thought occurred to him, Westvane wondered what would happen if he chose to leave her alive. He couldn't deny she intrigued him. All indications pointed to the fact she didn't fear him. She seemed set in her ways, more obstinate than angry. And yet, anger was definitely a part of her. He read it in her posture. He saw it in the stubborn way she faced him. He recognized it in humorless depths of her eyes.

She was different, unique — an anomaly, here and in Azlandia.

Just like him.

Nothing like Lyonesse and the Electi the queen commanded.

Taking a step back, he sat down on steps. "Your name?"

"Truly," she said, focus still razor-sharp even though he'd backed off. She didn't trust him. He didn't blame her. "Yours?"

"Westvane," he murmured, wondering how else to put her at ease. "Relax. Nothing to worry about, Door Master. We're just talking."

"Talking. Finally," she grumbled, sounding set upon. "The Wendigo wouldn't tell me anything. Also —"

"It talked to you?"

She sailed on without acknowledging his interruption. "I have no idea what's going on. You keep calling me Door Master. The Wendigo did too, but you've got to know I'm no one special. I'm not that — it isn't who I am."

He stared at her, bewildered. "Not that?"

"No."

"I can see the magic. It's in your aura. In your eyes. All around you."

"But that's..." Taking a deep breath, she uncrossed her arms. As her hands dropped to her sides, she shook her head. "Impossible. You have the wrong girl."

"You felt it, Truly. Deny it all you want, but the door opened at your command, freeing the Wendigo, ensuring my arrival."

"I don't understand any of this."

"Come inside," he said, looking over his shoulder at the front door. "And I'll explain."

"I'm safer out here."

"No, you aren't." With a flick, he tossed her the rectangle she called a cellphone. He watched her catch it, then stood, and with long strides, approached. She jerked back. He moved with her, shadowing her, putting his strength and speed on display. "If I wanted to harm you, it wouldn't matter where you stood. I am faster than you. I am stronger than you. Your magic is immature, not yet sufficient to protect you from me."

"Terrific," she said. "My night keeps getting better and better."

Westvane bit down on a smile. Even in a fit of temper, she was funny. "I've given you my word. I won't hurt you. You're safe with me."

"For the time being."

He nodded. "For the time being."

She sighed. "Shouldn't you be out..."

"What?"

"Hunting that thing down?"

He gazed up at the brightening sky, gauging the time. "The Wendigo will wait."

"Are you sure that's wise? It seemed dangerous to me."

"It is, but the sun is rising. The Wendigo will go to ground until nightfall."

"The trail won't go cold?" she asked, shoving her phone into her coat pocket.

"Not for me. I am an Assenta... a hunter. There isn't a creature alive that can hide or escape me."

"Annoying and arrogant," she muttered, re-crossing her arms. "Both'll get you killed, you know?"

"Unlikely, but thanks for the warning," he said, as sunlight peeked over the treetops, casting long shadows on the lawn. "Now, come inside and —"

"You'll explain."

"Yes."

"Everything — to my satisfaction," she said, index finger pointed at her chest.

"As much as I know," he said, lying through his teeth. He had no intention of telling her *everything*. He might not want to hurt her, but that didn't mean he planned to take her off the board. He needed every pawn to win against Lyonesse. He played a dangerous game with a powerful queen, a match he couldn't afford to lose. "If it is within my power to give, the information is yours."

Wary, unwilling to trust him too far, she studied him. Molecules buzzed, shooting out from her to surround him. Pleasant prickles grazed his skin. Eastbrook shifted on his throat, causing the ink to burn deeper. Westvane stayed still through the sting, blocking the barrage as her magic attempted to pry the information she needed out of his mind. He should've felt bad about holding firm. He didn't. Guilt was a waste of time, so instead of spilling secrets, he withstood the cosmic assault, giving nothing away. Truly would learn the truth soon enough. It wasn't his place to tell her what Lyonesse planned.

Chewing on the inside of her lip, Truly broke eye contact and, deciding to take him at his word, moved toward the house. Her boot soles tapped against the flagstones, echoing across the yard. He held his ground, shifting at the last moment, allowing her to skirt past him.

Reaching the porch, she jogged up the stairs.

Pivoting in her wake, he followed.

Halfway up the steps, she glanced over her shoulder. "Don't get any ideas, Westvane. After our talk, you're leaving. You can't stay here."

He snorted. "Well, I'm not staying anywhere else."

"It's my house."

"You're my guide."

Truly threw him an extreme look of irritation.

He swallowed his laughter. Stubborn little witch. Endlessly amusing with her opinions and bad attitude. Not that it mattered. She might be an excellent source of entertainment, but that wouldn't change the facts. Like it or not, the Door Master had just gained a new roommate.

No way in hell would he let her out of his sight.

Not until he completed his mission. Not until he figured out how best she fit into his plans. Even if that meant handing her over to the queen in the end.

HYPER-AWARE WESTVANE STALKED BEHIND HER, Truly trudged up the front stairs. Each step cost her, making her bow beneath the weight of fatigue. The stress of the past few hours had gotten to her. Add her unrelenting work schedule — all the sleepless nights — and she felt as though she'd been hit by an eighteen-wheeler. Then run over again. And perhaps, one more time.

She should be dead.

Instead, she was simply dead on her feet.

Bad timing, given Westvane didn't seem the type to give her a break.

He was too brutal for that — not a soft spot on his body or in his mind. His determination pressed against her back, pushing her forward, pressing nervousness toward anxiety. Which caused her mind to skip from one worrisome detail to the next. Now she couldn't settle on anything. Nothing made sense. Not one thing since Minador threw her to the wolves and hightailed it in the opposite direction, lined up with what she knew of the world.

The muscles along her spine began to ache.

She forced herself to keep moving, wishing she could sleep for a few hours before slogging into a conversation. The mass of muscle-bound testosterone hulking in her wake said "fat chance." His manner, the lethal aura he wore like a bad attitude, told her the talk he wanted to have wouldn't be delayed. Truly frowned. Come to think of it, she didn't want to delay it either.

She needed information.

Westvane possessed answers.

Match made in heaven. Or on the dark side of hell.

Truly didn't know. All she knew for certain was he promised not to hurt her, and for some reason, she believed him. Stupidity fueled by sleep deprivation, maybe. Wishful thinking, perhaps, but whatever the logic, she couldn't back out now. Self-preservation forged ahead, setting her on a prescribed path. She needed to know how much trouble she was in before something else jumped out and surprised her.

"Truly — calm down."

"Westvane — shut up."

He huffed, the sound coming from right behind her.

"You don't get to do that," she said, voice soft in warning.

"Do what?"

"Boss me around." Standing on the top step, she whirled to face him. He stepped down two treads. She pointed her finger right in his face. "Don't think for a second that's the way this is going to work. You might be bigger than me. You might be stronger than me. But I won't stand for it. I won't."

Dark eyes steady, he met her gaze head-on. "I'm not bossing you around."

"Sounded like it to me."

"You misheard."

She slammed her hands onto her hips.

"It was a suggestion."

"Yeah, well, don't do that either."

He blinked in surprise. "Make suggestions?"

"Exactly. You do what you do, I'll react the way I want. Got it?"

"Thought you wanted answers."

"I do. What's that got to do with anything?"

"If you don't want me to talk, how —"

She growled at him. "I never said you couldn't talk."

His eyes danced, laughing at her. "I'm starting to feel under-appreciated."

"I'm starting to feel the need to maim you."

"I'm game, princess," he said. "I'm always up for a good fight."

Truly sighed. She could already tell. He was going to be a *huge* pain in the ass.

Forcing herself not to take the bait, she spun toward the house, marched across the porch, through the open door and into the foyer. Childish, maybe, but she didn't care. She'd earned the right to riot months ago, when she lost her job.

A pang tightened her chest.

Truly clenched her teeth. Lodging a formal complaint had been a mistake. A miscalculation on her part, but then...

The inability to stay quiet in the face of unfairness — which she'd just proven by arguing with Westvane — wasn't her strong suit. She was a doer. A put-idiotic-people-in-their-place kind of person, but filing a sexual harassment complaint against her boss qualitied as short-sighted.

Resigning would've been better.

At least then, her reputation would still be intact.

She could've found another job. She could've called on friends and landed a freelance photography jig. Instead, she'd been blackballed for doing the right thing. For standing up for herself. For protecting others. For hoping to save her coworkers the same kind of aggravation and heartache.

Stupid move. Far too idealistic in a world gone to hell.

Men who occupied corner offices excelled at covering up wrong-doing. In a time when shareholders ruled and bottom lines prevailed, she hadn't stood a chance. Big bonuses always won in the end.

Heavy-hearted, Truly walked down the corridor and pushed through a swinging door into the kitchen. Navy blue cabinets. Carrera marble countertops. White, gray, and cream mosaic backsplash. Six-burner gas stove, and vintage appliances with curved corners and charming steel handles, the white enamel as glossy as the day it rolled off the assembly line. A large table held court in the center of the room, eight ladder-back chairs stationed around it.

The instant warmth, the ready welcome, helped dissolve some of her disillusionment.

The past didn't matter anymore.

She was *here*. HR and the man who wronged her were *there*. No sense wallowing in what she couldn't change. Especially with a new crisis on the horizon and Westvane casting a dark shadow across her light-filled kitchen.

Skirting the table, she headed for a long bank of cabinetry. As she moved through the kitchen, information filtered in, telling where to find things. Odd, but all of an instant, she knew the location of the pantry, which cabinet held the booze, along with the contents of the old-school refrigerator. The house offered up the intel without her having to do any exploring.

The layout and contents simply appeared in her head as if by magic.

A nifty trick.

One she appreciated at the moment. It put her that much closer to the drink she needed.

Stopping in front of the liquor cabinet, she caught a glimpse of Westvane from the corner of her eye. He lurked in the doorway, as though unsure he wanted to enter. She read the hesitation on his face. His body language echoed his uncertainty and...

All of a sudden, she felt better. The exhaustion lifted, raising her spirits a bit. Even Slayers, it seemed, suffered from a lack of confidence sometimes.

The realization made him seem human, even though she knew he wasn't. He'd come from somewhere else — another world. It would behoove her to remember that tidbit. Trusting him didn't qualify as a good idea.

With a flick, she opened the door and reached inside. She grabbed what she wanted — what the house told her would be there: a bottle of fifty-year-old Glenfiddich and two heavy crystal glasses. Turning, she set the tumblers down on the table. Heavy crystal clanked against wood as she glanced at Westvane. Cracking the seal on the whiskey, she tipped her chin in his direction. "Want a drink? I know I could use one."

His attention slid from her to the bottle, then back again. "You're inviting me to your table?"

"Yeah. Game?"

An odd look crossed his face before he nodded. "Pour, Door Master. Make mine a double."

Tossing the cap, Truly smiled. Well, all right then. Let the games begin.

Pouring equal amounts into both glasses, she pulled a chair

away from the table. As she planted her butt in it, she pointed to the other across from her. "Sit, Westvane. I won't bite."

"Shame," he murmured, teasing her.

She rolled her eyes and picked up her glass. "Start talking."

"You're not tired?"

"Honestly?"

He took a seat. "The truth always works best."

"I'm exhausted," she said, hating to admit it, knowing she couldn't hide it. No sense trying. Exhaustion lived in her, was etched in her bones... and probably written all over her face. "But I need to know. Ignorance is not bliss, Westvane. And anyway, I won't sleep if I'm stressed out."

"Wise," he said, palming his glass.

"Or stupid. Jury's still out."

Something flickered in his dark eyes. He shot his double in one go.

She refilled his glass and set the bottle down. "Stop stalling, Slayer. Sun's coming up."

"Don't call me that."

"What?" Taking her first sip, Truly savored the burn as the Glenfiddich went down. "Slayer? Thought that was your title."

"I'm an Assenta. A hunter," he said, voice edged with something she couldn't identify. Fury? Or was it sorrow? "Only those who wish to provoke my wrath call me that."

Truly blinked. A moment passed before understanding struck. "She calls you that. It's an insult."

A muscle jumped along his jaw. He tipped his chin in the affirmative. "What do you know of Queen Lyonesse?"

"Nothing. I'm working blind here." Tipping her glass, she frowned at the amber liquid. "Until a few hours ago, I'd never heard the name Door Master. Five hours ago, I was working a job, struggling to pay my rent. Now, I'm the owner of a house in an upscale neighborhood dealing with scary-ass monsters. You do the math."

"Well then," he murmured, shooting his second Scotch. "Guess I need to start at the beginning."

Sipping her drink, Truly nodded. The beginning would be good. The beginning would be great. The beginning and end, along with everything in the middle, would be perfect. Exactly what she needed from him.

10

YOU'RE NOT ALONE ANYMORE

Examining the alcohol in his glass, Westvane resisted the urge to pinch himself. Sitting in the Door's Master kitchen. Sharing a drink like friends sometimes did. The situation struck him as surreal. He didn't know what to make of it. Nothing had prepared him for the invite. His encounter with Truly thus far qualified as strange. And yet, oddly enough, it was as though he'd been waiting for it to happen his entire life.

Raising the tumbler, he took another sip.

Truly raised her glass. As amber liquid crested the rim, he watched her take another drink. He paused, the lip of the tumbler against his mouth and sipped again. She did the same, mirroring his movements, making him wonder — was she aware she was doing it? Seemed a safe bet to say no, but... she'd done the same thing outside, mimicking each gesture, becoming his reflection.

The idea left him at a loss.

Other than Eastbrook, he'd never had a companion. Never engaged in friendly conversation or let anyone close. But sitting across the from Truly felt different. She didn't act like an adversary. She treated him like he belonged. Her easy acceptance overwhelmed him. He'd never experienced anything like it. He didn't know what to do with it. Block out the experience and ignore what she made him feel? Or take what she offered and enjoy the drink. No one had ever invited him to sit at their table. No one had ever thought enough of him to offer.

Truly hadn't blinked an eye.

The gesture, her interest in him and what he knew, was genuine. No malice. No manipulation. She wasn't shying away. Setting her elbows on the table, she leaned toward him, bridging the distance, getting closer, unconcerned by his violent nature.

Westvane frowned.

How was that possible?

What kind of game was she playing?

Everyone he encountered gave him a wide berth. *Everyone*, warranted or not, but not her. She wasn't scared. Didn't seem bothered. Settling back in his chair, he studied her some more, trying to unpack her like a puzzle. Fit the pieces together, and he'd understand.

Without looking away, he held her gaze and downed the third glass of what she called whiskey. Good stuff. Better than what he'd been allowed in Azlandia. Setting the tumbler down, he sent cut crystal spinning across the table. Light refracted. Color tumbled across the oak surface. Stopping the slide with a fingertip, Truly picked up the bottle, refilled his glass, then pushed the drink back in his direction.

He caught it before it slid off the edge. "You're not afraid of me at all, are you?"

She paused mid-sip, then tipped her head back and shot the rest of her drink. As her hand dropped, she raised a brow. "That bother you?"

A question answered with another question. She'd been

doing that from the beginning too. Not a bad strategy. Deflection was a useful skill to possess. An annoying one, when aimed in his direction. "Answer the question, princess."

"Princess?"

With a sigh, he set his glass down with a thump. "You're determined to be difficult, aren't you?"

She smiled, the sparkle in her eyes arresting him as her magic spiked. Blue stardust spilled into the air, coating her with ethereal light. She didn't notice. As unbelievable as it sounded, she had no idea who she was... or what she was capable of unleashing.

He scowled. "Are we really going to have an entire conversation with nothing but questions?"

"Not very productive, is it?" she asked, pouring a finger of whiskey into her glass.

"You are," he said. "You're determined to be difficult."

She shrugged. "It's me."

"That's what worries me."

"Why?" Dragging her fingertip around the rim, she made her glass sing.

A soft sound. An enchanting melody. Pretty in its simplicity. Soothing in its softness. The music made him relax against his will.

She nodded her approval. "Better. I'm not the only one who needs to chill."

Charmed by her, not wanting to be, Westvane glared at her. She was making it exceeding difficult not to like her. Irritating to no end. "Fair point, princess."

"Despite what you think," she said, leaning in again. Her forearms landed on the tabletop. "I'm far from stupid, Westvane."

He tipped his chin, conceding the point.

"I know how serious this is — believe me. In the span of a few hours, I've met a troll, been run over by a monster, now I'm sitting here with you. None of that says everything's going to be okay. It shouldn't even be possible..." She waved her hand. The flurry pushed stardust across the table at him. "Yet here you sit, in all your scary-killer glory. I'd have to be an idiot not to understand the strange turn my life has taken. Given the craziness, I don't have time to be afraid of you. You'll either kill me or you won't. Nothing I can do about it, so I'm choosing to let that worry go... for now. I've got enough on my plate."

"Very grown up of you."

Picking at the label, she peeled the paper off the bottle. "I'm a big believer in controlling what I can, and leaving the rest to the universe. When I trust in that, things have a way of working out."

Westvane opened his mouth to reply. He closed it again. Who was this woman? She kept surprising him. After readying himself for a brutal fight, he couldn't believe she sat so peaceably with him.

He'd expected resistance.

He'd expected disdain.

He'd expected her to act like Lyonesse.

Truly refused to give him anything of the kind. She accepted his presence instead. Wasn't making assumptions or painting him with a black brush. She wasn't hampered by a closed mind, a hard heart, or entrenched ideology.

She might not trust him, but she was willing to try.

He could see it in her eyes. Felt it in the open way she regarded him. Read it in the way she spoke to him. No condescension. Zero ridicule. She didn't believe he was less than. She welcomed him as an equal.

The realization floored him.

"You've grown quiet, Westvane."

"I'm thinking."

"Trying to decide how much to tell me?"

Definitely not stupid.

Her keen mind was going to be a problem. She continued to surprise him, picking his thoughts out of the air. Somehow, he needed to guard himself against her magic. It might be wrong, but she was right — he didn't plan to tell her everything.

He must maintain the upper hand at all times. Otherwise, he'd lose his ability to maneuver and his plan wouldn't succeed. No matter how cruel, he would do as promised. Catch the Wendigo. Hand the Door Master over to Lyonesse and the Azlandian court. It all came down to one thing — *his* freedom mattered more to him than hers.

"The queen has given me a task."

"Capture the Wendigo."

He nodded. "I must return it to its cage. It will wreak havoc here — start wars, kill Earthlings, manipulate the future, and change the past."

"What's it got to do with me?"

"You are a Door Master. Without you, the *Ecotone* remains closed, and I cannot cross back into Azlandia."

"You need me to reopen the door?"

He shook his head. "Doesn't matter which is opened, just as long as it's close to where I reacquire the Wendigo."

"No way." Her hand tightened around the glass, making her knuckles go white. "You're on your own with that thing. I'm not going with you."

"No choice. No one can open doors but you."

"If Queen What's-her-face —"

"Lyonesse."

"Whatever," she muttered, making a who-cares gesture with her hand.

"Details matter, princess."

She glared at him. "If she's so powerful, why can't she —"

"Only a Door Master has the ability to command the *Ecotone*. It will not welcome, or answer to, anyone else."

"I don't know how to do what you're asking," she said, unease making her talk faster. "It was an accident the first time. I have no idea what I did to open that door... or how to do it again."

"I'll teach you."

Her mouth fell open. "You?"

"Don't discount me, Truly. I may be an Assenta, but I understand how magic works," he said, tempting her with knowledge she didn't yet hold. "I can help you while I'm here... if you allow it."

Uncertainty rose in her scent. She chewed on the inside of her lip. "You'll have my back?"

"Yes," he murmured, regretting the lie, unable to do anything about it. He'd made a promise to keep her safe... until the time came to let her go. A little bit of something, after all, was better than nothing.

"All right," she said softly. "But you need to remember something."

"What's that?"

"You have my back, I'll have yours. You're not alone anymore, Westvane."

Her statement made his chest tighten. Wicked, wicked woman. For a clueless Door Master, she wielded her intellect incredibly well.

"You hear me?"

"Loud and clear."

"Good," she said. "Don't ever forget it."

Not knowing what else to do, he downed his drink, powering through what her words made him feel. Westvane didn't want the emotion or need the turmoil. He wanted to keep her at arm's length and hold onto his secrets. He needed to remember who he was — and how he'd always survived. Otherwise, he'd forget Truly wasn't his friend and tell her everything he didn't want her to know.

11

HOW DRUNK ARE YOU?

Westvane was hiding something. Something important. Details he didn't want her to know. He wasn't lying... exactly. But the longer Truly talked to him, the more she picked up. He twisted her inquiries and turned them inside out, dodging her questions by delivering interesting tidbits that answered nothing while refusing to tell her the full story.

The terms of her "partnership" with him weren't negotiable. He wanted her help. She needed the truth. And whether he liked it or not, she would get it before he got a scrap of information out of her.

A dangerous game. One she might not win, but as she stared into her empty glass, hoping it morphed into a crystal ball and gave her clarity, she wondered how best to proceed. Forcing answers out of him wouldn't work. Westvane wouldn't tell her until he decided to, which left her drifting on a strange current without the equipment required to steer back on course.

She must learn to read between the lines. Find an avenue of understanding, then she'd be able to... to...

Truly blinked, a slow up and down, as she lost her train of thought. She tried to recapture the thread, but her mind kept drifting. Now, she had nothing but blank. Which was odd. She'd been full of clever ideas earlier.

Tipping the glass up, she rotated it in her hand. Light refracted through the bottom. Her vision blurred, then came back into focus. Something was wrong with her eyes. She wasn't seeing straight. Might be the strange, prickling rush in her veins. Could be the odd heat circling the center of her palms. Or —

She squinted harder at the bottom of her glass.

Could be the Glenfiddich.

A good guess given the tip of her nose had gone numb five minutes ago. A sure sign the effects of the Scotch were about to hit hard. Not surprising (though incredibly foolish), given Westvane hadn't slowed down while she tried to keep up.

Westvane poured more into her glass, then refilled his own. Struggling to sit straight in her chair, she watched Scotch sloshed against cut crystal. He set the bottle down and continued talking, his deep voice weaving a spell around her and...

She had no idea what he was explaining.

Truly heard the cadence of his words, was tracking the rise and fall of syllables. Knew he spoke in full sentences that flowed into cohesive paragraphs, and she was missing all of it.

She ought to be filing the information away.

Instead, she struggled to grasp the basics.

Raking her hair out of her face, she shoved long bangs behind one of her ears. All right. Okay. She could do this — follow along, identify the holes in his story and piece together the rest. All she needed to do was concentrate.

"And that's how it works," he said, leaning back in his chair.

"Hang on a second." Holding her hands up in self-defense, she shook her head. He was going too fast, not giving her a chance to ask questions. No doubt his plan, but that didn't work for her. "Back up."

"To where?"

"The beginning."

Shifting in his seat, he stretched out his legs. "What for?"

"I need to process."

He gave her a look she couldn't read. After a moment, she realized it was extreme irritation.

She set her glass down with a thump.

"How drunk are you?"

"I can't feel my nose, so... sliding towards blotto."

"Seriously?"

"It's your fault!"

"How?"

"You kept drinking. I felt I had to keep up."

"I have a hundred and fifty pounds on you."

"At least."

"Truly," he growled, irritation tipping into exasperation.

"Probably your plan all along. Clever Westvane, getting me drunk, hoping I wouldn't be able to follow along."

"You got the bottle out, princess," he said, pointing out an unhelpful fact.

"I had a bad day."

"I'm aware," he said, borrowing from her bottomless well of sarcasm.

She hiccupped.

His mouth curved.

Truly took a cleansing breath. She really needed to pull it together. If she didn't, Westvane would continue to slip important information by her. Something intuition warned her she didn't want to happen. Whatever he planned wouldn't end well for her unless she screwed her head on straight.

"Playtime's over," she said, forcing her brain to work. "Go back to the part about the Mirror Kingdoms."

He sighed, sounding aggrieved.

Somehow, though, she knew he wasn't.

He was too relaxed, too comfortable sitting in her kitchen to be truly annoyed. She might not know him well, but she was learning. The big, bad Slayer had a few things going for him. One — he possessed a sense of humor. Two — he wasn't impulsive. Three — he liked her. He didn't want to, but (despite trying his best) was failing to hide that he did. He viewed her as difficult, an obstacle to be hurdled, but all her poking and prodding made it clear he wasn't a thoughtless thug.

Violent when needed? Yes.

Lethal when warranted? Absolutely.

But behind his predatory nature lay an active mind. He might be a hulking beast of a man, but he thought things through, ensuring an end that best served his purposes. Not his queen's. Not his world's. *His.* And that gave her an advantage. One he kept trying to take away by blowing past the facts. She understood his game now. The less she knew, the safer he would be. But then, two could play that game. She planned on dancing the dance, and not making anything easy for him.

Twirling her glass on the tabletop, she met his gaze. "Have you tasted Scotch before?"

"Never been invited to anyone's table to enjoy it before."

"Never?"

He shook his head.

"No friends?"

"I've been caged for years, Truly. Kept apart from the population. I've had no one but Eastbrook for company."

"She should be shot," she said, reacting to the pain in his undertone.

"I'd prefer to strangle her with my own hands," he murmured, knowing she referred to Lyonesse.

"Fair enough," she whispered, her compassion for him becoming a bosom buddy. Caged for years. Left to languish alone when it was clear Westvane enjoyed company. His willingness to spar with her proved his social bent. Everyone, after all, needed somebody. "Who's Eastbrook?"

He ran his fingertips down the side of his neck.

She watched him trace the tattoo. A bird, of some kind. Black ink. Precise lines. Each feather drawn in exquisite detail. It wasn't as though she hadn't seen it. She had, the instant she laid eyes on Westvane. But his artwork hadn't registered. She'd seen it, without *seeing it*, more concerned for her safety than about the bird inked into his skin.

Wanting a closer look at the tattoo, she leaned onto her forearms. Inky eyes looked out from Westvane's throat, staring back at her. Odd, but she got the impression intelligence lived in its gaze... that the raven wanted to caw in greeting. Perception narrowed, making her skin itch with unease. The raven felt alive to her, as though its place on his skin wasn't permanent.

"You'll meet him soon enough," Westvane said, dropping his hand. "Now... the Mirror Kingdoms."

Another of his distractions. One that worked.

She needed to know all about the other realm — the one she'd opened a doorway into — in order to keep herself alive.

Picking up the bottle, Westvane tipped it toward her glass. She waved him off. More alcohol wasn't a good idea. He might not agree, preferring to keep her addled, but surprise, surprise, he accepted her denial, topping up his tumbler, leaving hers alone. As he set the Glenfiddich down, he settled back, got comfortable and took a sip.

Dark eyes met hers over the rim. "Earth Realm and Azlandia are twin worlds. Two planets interconnected, each dependent on the other."

"For what?"

"A variety of things."

"You can do better than that, Westvane. More..." She flicked her fingers, making a 'gimme' motion with her hand. "How are we dependent?"

"Think of Earth and Azlandia as conjoined twins."

"Two bodies sharing one heart type of thing?"

Westvane nodded. "Exactly."

"So the *Ecotone*..." Fiddling with the label she peeled from the bottle, she folded it in half. "It sits between worlds, like a passageway, allowing people to cross the divide."

"If it stays open."

"The queen closed it?"

"Twenty-seven years ago. After she killed the last Door Master."

"She missed one."

He raised his glass, saluting her. "Lyonesse has been hunting and killing your family for years."

"And the last Door Master was —"

"Your mother."

"My *what*?"

The news flashed through her.

Her chest started to burn.

Something cracked inside her, slicing her open. Pain streamed through the fissure. Prickles of heat rolled across the tops of her shoulders, then down her arms. Her vision sheeted white as iridescent glow circled the center of her palms, spilling onto the tabletop.

Her *mother*.

A woman she couldn't remember. A woman meant to love her. A woman who hadn't been given the chance. She'd never hugged Truly. Never put her to bed or tucked her in. Never read her stories from thick, leather-bound picture books. Never kissed her child or wiped away tears, ensuring all the bad things became better. Truly had spent years yearning, wondering, longing to understand why she'd been left on the steps of a church.

Why she'd been abandoned.

Why no one loved her enough to stay.

Why she'd always felt so empty and alone.

Westvane set his glass down... slowly. "Calm, Truly."

"Calm?" Pinpoints of blue light sparkling around her, she started to hyperventilate. Too hot. No air. Nothing but suffocating weight sitting on her chest. "You want me to... to —"

"Breathe through it."

"I c-can't."

Shifting forward in his chair, he prepared to move. "You have to, Truly. If you lose control, you could kill me. You will be left alone, without the answers you seek."

"I'm going to —"

"*Breathe.*"

About to come out of her skin, Truly trembled with the effort. Cool air in. Hot air out. Each inhale a challenge, every exhale painful.

Gritting her teeth, she pressed her hands against the table. The itch in the center of her palms grew hotter. The glow intensified. Ribbons of blue light spilled between the wide spread of her fingers. The internal inferno fueled her. The heat raging in her veins pushed her. Shock and sorrow collided, giving birth to fury, as tiny tornados of fire twisted up from beneath her hands, licking over her skin without harming her.

Her touch scorched the tabletop.

The flickering blaze should've worried her. What she was seeing and feeling qualified as insane. It wasn't normal. *She wasn't normal.* The glow and heat didn't leave room for denial, but as she watched ribbons of flames dance — over her fingers, under her hands — and smoke curled up from the wooden surface, she embraced the pain. Felt the fury. And tasted the power, her heart and mind churning, her rage so bright she wanted to lay waste to it all. Burn the house, her grief, the whole world down until nothing but ash remained.

Her mother was dead.

Dead. Never to be seen or heard from again.

No second chances, or late-life reunions. Just... *gone.*

When had it happened? Right after she set Truly down on those church steps?

Agony sliced even deeper. The blaze under her palms burned brighter. Truly let it, wanting to use what she didn't understand to burn the hurt away. To cause death. To wreak destruction. For others to hurt as much as she did now that she knew her mother hadn't left her by choice. She'd been trying to protect her baby by giving her away. By placing her with those who could see to her care until she came of age. Until Truly was able to step into her power and...

"Truly!" Westvane barked, locking eyes with her. His black gaze bored into hers, reflecting the blue glow shimmering in her own eyes.

The sight made her flinch.

Braving the flames, he stood, leaned forward, and set his hands, palms flat, on either side of hers. "Calm."

The band squeezing her lungs loosened. She sucked in a shaky breath. "She's dead."

"I know."

"I didn't."

"I'm sorry."

Holding his gaze, she used it as a lifeline and pulled herself back from the edge. Her palms cooled. The fire-tornados spun low and vanished. The furious glow dimmed as, little by little, she gained control, breathing in, exhaling out, playing catch and release until her chest stopped heaving and her throat stopped burning. Now, all she felt was raw.

Her nose stung as she fought the tears she'd spent a lifetime denying. "Why? Why, Westvane?"

"She was a Door Master. Of equal power and authority. A threat to Lyonesse's rule," he said, tone soft with understanding. "Just as you are."

"I'm going to kill her."

"Not if I reach her first."

Her eyes narrowed on him.

He stared back. "I'll make you a deal."

"What kind?"

"Start the fight, weaken Lyonesse all you want, but..." His dark eyes flashed. Something dark. Something dangerous. Something so lethal, it made her skin prickle. "I deal the death blow."

Unwilling to concede, but knowing now was not the time to argue, Truly took another steadying breath. "We'll talk about it later."

"Princess —"

"She killed my mother, Westvane."

"I understand. Believe me, I am well acquainted with that kind of pain, but —"

A loud bang slammed into the kitchen.

Westvane pushed away from the table and shoved his chair back. The ladderback rocked, tittering on its back legs as he spun toward the swinging door.

More banging.

She pushed to her feet. "What the —"

"Who knows you live here?"

"No one."

Moving with intent, Westvane crossed the kitchen. He flicked his fingers. Without him touching it, the swinging door whipped open. Hinges squawked in protest. Truly wanted to do the same, but instead hustled around the end of the table.

Without slowing, Westvane dipped his head beneath the lintel and strode over the threshold into the central corridor. Unable to see beyond the set of his shoulders, she avoided the backlash of the door and ran after him.

The barrage of knocking continued. Someone shouted her name.

"Ah, hell."

Already in the foyer, Westvane glared at her over his shoulder. "What?"

"I know who it is." Shoving past him, she grabbed the handle and pulled the front door open.

"About time, girl. You think I got all day to stand around out here?"

"Earl," she said, eyeballing the homeless man on her front porch. "Eavesdrop much?"

He grinned, treating her to the gap between his front teeth. "Been keeping track a' you for months, girl. You think I'm not gonna pay attention when a troll comes calling?"

She really should've guessed. Earl had always been nosy. And bossy. And far too opinionated for her own good. "What are you doing here?"

"You promised me breakfast." He shifted the duffle he carried, transferring it from one arm, shoving it under the other. "Sun's coming up. Breakfast time."

Truly bit her bottom lip. How best to explain? She didn't want to hurt his feelings. Earl spent too much time on his own, and honestly? If she was alone, his sudden appearance on her doorstep wouldn't have been a big deal. "Listen... now's really not a good —"

Westvane muttered something.

Earl's attention snapped up. It landed on the hulk of man now planted behind her. His bushy brows collided. "Who the devil are you?"

Truly opened her month to warn him about Westvane.

She didn't get the chance. One moment she stood in the open doorway. The next, Earl tossed the duffle at her. The heavy bag hit her in the chest. Air puffed from her throat as momentum pushed her off balance. She stumbled away from the door, back into the house.

Johnny on the spot, Westvane steadied her before she took a header into the hallway.

His expression thunderous, Earl stepped over the threshold and —

Transformed into a creature she didn't recognize.

Clutching the bag, Truly jolted as surprise grabbed hold. Earl didn't appear to be *Earl* anymore. He shifted the moment he entered her house, morphing into something she didn't understand. His top half looked normal — like regular old Earl. His bottom half elongated into the body of centipede with more legs than she cared to count.

Shock slammed through her. "What the hell, Earl?"

"What?" he snapped, shoving her to one side, trying to get between her and Westvane. "Never seen a Mantipede before?"

"Is that what you are?"

"Well, I'm certainly not a Slayer!" he shouted, waving his fists at Westvane.

"Don't call him that," she said, sounding like an idiot. But really? Who could blame her? She had Earl — half man, half bug — standing in her foyer. "He doesn't like it."

"He doesn't?"

"No."

Earl threw her a wild look. His fists dipped, dropping his guard. Not that he had much to guard against. Westvane didn't appear to be contemplating retaliation.

"A Slayer?" Earl asked, looking horrified. "Have you lost your marbles, girl?"

"Probably." Earl's observation wasn't far from the truth. Her mental acuity began to slip the second she signed the damn papers. Nothing to do now but make the best of it... and the introductions. Dropping the duffle to the floor, she waved her hand between the two. "Earl meet Westvane. Westvane, this is Earl."

"Seriously, princess?"

"Don't start." Warning Westvane with a look, she slammed the door. "I really don't want to hear it."

Earl jumped out of the way, the wooden edge missing his creepy-crawly hind-end by less than an inch. She didn't care. After months of lying to her, it would serve him right if he left her house one leg shy of a full load.

12

———————

AS YOU WISH

Deep in the ancient lands, far from the capital, Lyonesse stood alone on the fortress balcony. *Alone* was a good word for her state of mind. *Forlorn* might be better. Old as the rock that cradled it, as inhospitable as the mountain it rested upon, Ramstein Palace had never been a friend to her.

Set apart from the world.

Unmoved by time.

As beautiful as it was unwelcoming.

Resting her hands on the wide stone railing, she tipped her face up to the darkening sky. Brutal winds whipped across glacial terrain. Summer. Winter. The temperature never changed. Always cold. Forever icy. Permanently frosted by hostile forces that refused to relent.

She breathed deep, drawing the chill into her lungs, feeling the harsh air bristle against her wings. Settling her feathers, she returned her eyes to the view. Stark gray mountain peaks rose high, only to fall, plummeting toward snow-covered valleys.

It had been years since she'd visited. Twenty-seven of them. Not since her father ruled Azlandia.

The thought jabbed at her.

She disliked the reminder. Didn't want to acknowledge her father's failure or enjoy standing in the place he'd once called home. Too many memories lived inside the palace, lying in wait against the walls, ghosting through empty rooms and the many archways she'd played beneath so often as a child.

Everywhere she looked memories persisted. Reminding her. Shaming her. Blaming her for what she'd done. It mattered little that she'd been right. Or that her actions had been necessary to ensure the health of her people. Being right didn't make the reality any less painful — or mourning the loss of her father any less difficult to bear. She carried the manner of his death with her every hour of the day. Heartache weighed more than one might believe. Certainty more than she anticipated, given the time spent with her sire never faded from her mind.

The truth stared her in the face.

Especially here, in the high nesting place of a beloved king.

Unlike her, her father had enjoyed solitude. Liked the chill in an all-but-forgotten corner of the realm. He'd told her spending time away from the capital and court made him a better ruler, a wiser leader to the people, but she knew the truth.

He'd come here to be with *her*, to feed the connection so it would burn bright and never fade.

She hadn't understood it then. She did now.

Leonidas had betrayed them all.

She'd set it straight, ending his rule, closing all avenues to the *Ecotone*... ridding the Mirror Kingdoms of the Door Master her sire had loved so much. And yet, here she stood — in a palace she swore would never house another living soul. She'd regressed, come back in time, returning to a place she despised to ensure all she'd accomplished wouldn't be undone.

Lyonesse drew another deep breath.

Stalling much longer wasn't wise.

A decision needed to be made.

Damn the Slayer. If only he could be trusted.

She had no doubt Westvane would neutralize the Wendigo. Not for her sake. No, never that. He'd recapture the beast for the fun of it. For the challenge of it. For the chance to pit his skills against another's in the real world.

The Parkland bored him. His loneliness grew by the year, leaving him restless and wanting, more dangerous than ever.

His willingness to hunt for her didn't mean he would do as she asked. He'd do damage in Earth Realm. Create something for himself. Become what she most feared — exactly like his sire. She'd dreamed of Nygard while he lived, hoping one day to make him hers. Like her sire, he'd betrayed her in the end, joining forces with an Assenta whore, breaking the law, siring a child never meant to be born.

Now, she dreamed of his son.

Dangerous yearnings lived in the dreamscape. Bad things stalked her in the darkness. Premonitions of the future plagued her now. Sending Westvane through the *Ecotone* had been a mistake. How big a mistake, she'd yet to determine. Her visions blurred before she caught hold of the details, leaving her with an unclear picture of things to come.

Unusual for her.

Normally, she saw the future with all-seeing eyes. Not so with Westvane. The moment he crossed over, her leash on him snapped. Now, the threads tying him to her unraveled, causing her casting pool to turn gray with uncertainty. The shift toward black days worried her. How was she to manipulate and control the outcome if she couldn't see the future clearly?

An excellent question.

One without a good answer.

The wind rose, howling across snow-capped peaks, whipping ice along the palace walls. Nature's fury whirled, tempting her to take flight and play in the updraft. Lyonesse ignored the impulse.

A decision needed to be made.

She hated to do it. Didn't want to kill Westvane, but long experience with him made the way forward undeniable. She closed her eyes. *Damn the Slayer.* If only he didn't remind her so much of his sire. Removing such beauty — such divine brutality and supreme skill — from the Mirror Kingdoms counted as a tragedy. Something to mourn, if she were so inclined.

Good thing she was immune to such things.

Grief was a waste of time. A human emotion, more ailment than constructive skill. No queen worthy of her crown had time for such idiocy. A Monarch must show nothing but strength. Her people expected it. Her position demanded it, which meant...

Time to do what she'd been avoiding.

A decision must be made.

Turning from the vast winter-scape, she walked across the balcony, toward the wall of frosted windows. Little more than shadows behind towering double glass doors, her personal guard waited. Waiting to be told why she'd made the trip. Waiting for her to decide. Waiting on her orders, forever ready to do her bidding. She felt the weight of their gazes, but ignored the yoke. Such was a powerful queen. Her life had never been, nor would it ever be, her own.

The doors swung open at her approach.

Two of her guards stepped over the threshold, blocking the wind as she walked into the warmth. Halting just inside, she turned toward her captain. "Anckar."

He bowed, awaiting her command.

Despising what she must do, Lyonesse stared at the top of his head. Her hands curled into fists. Magic exploded in her palms. Hot pink sparks rained down on the floor tiles beside her feet.

"Majesty?"

"Proceed," she said, her tone tight. "Open the chamber."

Keeping his gaze downcast, Anckar straightened and stepped back. "As you wish."

As she wished.

Here and now... so very far from the truth. Some things, however, couldn't be avoided. Some things must be met with sword and shield. In the heat of battle. No surrender. No weakness shown. Strong in the face of the ferocious.

Footfalls echoing against hand-painted tile, Anckar exited the room.

Lyonesse followed, refusing to look at the portraits lining the walls, ignoring the dust covers draped like ghosts over furniture as she left one corridor and entered another. The door she dreaded lay in the belly of the beast, deep in the heart of Ramstein Palace. In no time, she stood before the portal, watching her guard slice through the seal preventing entry into the room.

The wax fell away.

The iron lock stamped with the royal symbol clamored against the floor.

Using brute strength, Anckar set his shoulder to the door and forced it open. The hinges moaned. She stood stone still, fingertips itching to do damage. Lyonesse quelled the urge, refusing to use her magic to enter the room. Some things could not be borne. Breaking into her father's secret chamber on her own was one of them. She didn't want to enter. Her father was no doubt rolling in his grave, but time and necessity dictated the play.

She needed to use the machine.

It was the only way for her to get a message through to Earth Realm — to those who would understand the urgency. The idea made her itch with impatience. She wanted to hurry her guard, but waited for Anckar to push the door all the way open. The moment he did and stepped aside, she entered, and with a whispered word, lit the torches ringing the chamber edge.

Light splashed over barren walls and bare floors.

She scanned the chamber in a single visual sweep. Lyonesse frowned. She didn't know why, but she'd expected more. Something better. Something closer to what her father enjoyed in the capital: thick floor rugs, comfortable chairs, ornate tables and fancy wine goblets, beautiful artwork crafted by a master's hand.

What she found was the exact opposite.

A round, windowless room with a high ceiling, capped by plain wooden planks. Stark stone walls without any ornamentation. A stout table with a rough top made its home in the middle of the chamber, and on it sat a black metal box.

Her wingtips swished across tile as she strode toward the machine. On closer inspection, it wasn't just a box. The front of the frame boasted a host of buttons, round keys with a single letter stamped in the center of each one. A system of letter writing, one Earthlings used to communicate with one another.

She'd never seen the machine. Had never wanted to, but she'd seen the missives. Her father had taken great pains to hide the correspondence, but she'd watched him read them from her secret spot inside his chamber. Even now, she remembered the smile on his face as he read the words stamped on paper, his excitement when letters arrived from Earth Realm every week.

Reaching out, she stroked her fingers over the keys. The buttons moved. She pressed a little harder. A slim bar flew up, striking the sheet, leaving a letter stamped in black ink on white paper. She stared at the mark a moment, then with the flick of her fingers, beckoned a chair to where she stood. Wooden legs scraped across the floor. The chair settled. She sat down on the worn cushion.

Dust drifted from the upholstery.

The letter on the paper faded, then disappeared.

She smiled. Excellent. The machine still worked. The single letter she'd pressed into the paper was on its way, traveling through time and space, flying through the *Ecotone* to land on the page of the person who now owned the Door Master's machine.

Ignoring the musty smell of the chair, she set her fingers to the keys. The type bars struck. The name of the person she needed to reach appeared on the page as the machine clanked, sending an awful racket clamoring through the quiet.

She shoved the carriage to the right.

A tiny bell rang.

The machine waited, patient and unassuming, as she stared at the blank page, deciding what to write.

Not that her message needed to be perfect. The group she wanted to reach didn't care for formality. The human militia excelled at stealth and intelligence gathering, hunting and killing magic wielders in Earth Realm. One of the reasons she and the people of Azlandia weren't safe crossing the *Ecotone*. The Yeomanry didn't discriminate. Their hatred of magic was legendary, and had been for centuries.

An unlikely ally to call upon, but uncertain times called for unusual methods.

She only hoped the group was still operational.

Whether Isaac and his merry band of "witch killers" still hunted was anyone's guess. Twenty-seven years was a long time to go without news. But as she typed her message, relaying information about Westvane — along with what she'd gleaned about the Door Master — Lyonesse prayed the Yeomanry responded. She might not like Earthlings, but they'd proven useful in the past. A valuable resource to be exploited. A strategy she wasn't above using to ensure Westvane returned to his cage, and the Door Master ended up dead.

13

BLACK AND WHITE. NO SHADES OF GRAY

One hand pressed to the shower wall, Truly stared at a simple pattern set in shades of black and white. Handmade, the glazed tiles were wavy with rounded corners, as though each had been left out too long, the edges worn down by time. Imperfect beauty. Perfect precision, laid by the hand of a master.

Breathing in steam, she traced over an uneven spot with her fingertip. Hot water streamed over her hair. Blinking droplets out of her eyes, she slicked the wet strands out of her face and tried to reboot her brain. She should be taking advantage of the quiet, leaning into relaxation instead of rehashing the events of the last few hours, stewing about things that couldn't be undone.

Would never be undone.

The fact Westvane had slept in her house, under her roof in a bedroom down the hall, was all the proof she required to know nothing would ever be the same. She might not have the full picture yet, but the information he'd given her about the Mirror Kingdoms — along with the unfamiliar spark she felt sifting like hot sand through her veins — couldn't be denied. Neither could the blue smears left behind on white tiles every time she moved her fingertips.

She traced over one of the uneven edges again. Her finger bumped over the wavy surface. A trail of tiny blue shimmer drew a line across ceramic. Drawing symbols with sparkles, Truly leaned in to rest her temple against the shower wall. She watched her fingertip move. No sense pretending it wasn't happening. Sticking her head in the sand wouldn't change anything.

Something had happened to her. Something was still happening to her, and no matter how frightening the shift, she must face it without flinching. Past experience told her ignoring a problem never made it go away. It simply made whatever had gone wrong even worse.

Exhaling long and slow, she returned to studying the tiles. *Black and white.* No shades of gray. If only life was that simple.

Closing her eyes, she pushed away from the wall and lifted her face into the spray. Steam rolled across the enclosure, fogging up the glass. Another example of stellar craftsmanship. The house was so much more than she expected. Everything worked. The pipes didn't groan, just delivered what they promised — hot water and the promise of a few minutes alone.

The ultimate way for any girl to start her day.

She frowned. Actually, it was coming on night now. She'd slept long, hard, and comfortably — in a strange bed that felt like home. Another anomaly to add to the sum of odd things she kept tabulating. A good night's sleep had never been in her arsenal. Restlessness. Insomnia. Hours full of interrupted rest followed by exhaustion. Her cross to bear as she rolled out of bed in the morning. The fact she felt comfortable enough to sleep in a place she didn't know should've rung alarm bells.

A sense of peace, along with relief, came calling instead.

She'd been desperate for the rest.

She needed the break.

She'd gotten both, and yet, her mind continued to spin, digging up potential problems while trying to map out future pitfalls. *What ifs* kept cropping up, surfacing one at a time, telling her she needed to understand how to navigate a shifting landscape — along with the power she possessed and now must learn to control.

Even with Westvane lurking, her change of circumstance didn't feel real. It felt... well... like a farce. Like a farfetched scheme cooked up for a TV show.

Tightness pulled at her chest.

The unpleasant pinch invaded muscle and bone, squeezing her ribcage, stealing her air. Inhaling past the pain, she shook off her sense of foreboding. She couldn't hide in the bathroom much longer. Westvane wasn't patient. He wouldn't wait for her to get her act together. Even now, she sensed him, moving on the fringe of her perceptual field. Roaming around her house. Picking things up to examine them before putting them back down.

Rolling her shoulders to break the tension, Truly shook her head. She really wished he'd keep his hands to himself. But oh no... he wasn't that polite. He kept snooping through family heirlooms — objects, keepsakes, her ancestral home and history. Things she had yet to see, acknowledge, or pick up herself.

His curiosity felt like an affront. Like a personal attack, one akin to an invasion.

Westvane had no right to any of her things. He was a stranger. An outsider in her world. Someone to keep an eye on, not befriend. And yet, she had offered him friendship of a kind, inviting him into her house, treating him like a trusted confidant while she stepped into a new life. Seemed like a stupid decision to make. Intuition, though, disagreed, telling her no matter how rough (or annoying), Westvane would prove useful to her in ways she couldn't yet predict.

Raking the hair out from her face, Truly reached for the controls. She twisted both knobs, leaving sparkles of blue shimmer on brushed brass. The water slowed to a trickle and stopped. No more stalling. She needed to face her future and whatever Westvane planned tonight.

She hoped it didn't involve her death. Or any sort of maiming, though she should probably resign herself to the possibility. With a Slayer squatting in her house, running around the outskirts of death would no doubt become the norm, if not the rule.

Though, she had to admit — a *brush* with death sounded better than being the target.

Opening the glass door, Truly reached for the towel on the heated rack. As thick terry cloth settled in her hand, she stepped out and dried off. Wiping the fog from one of the mirrors, she wrapped her wet hair into a messy bun on the top of her head and started getting ready. Moisturizer went on her skin. Mascara got swiped onto her lashes. Lip balm made an appearance before she turned to her outfit.

Dressed in jeans and a long-sleeved tee, she swiped her socks off the bathroom counter and headed for the door. Westvane was getting restless. His aggressive energy electrified the air, occupying the house like a foreign invader — focused, impatient, snapping in the quiet. The swirl invaded her mind, raising awareness, keeping her informed, helping her pinpoint the source.

Magic — strong, unrelenting, dangerous.

She sensed the power. The rise and fall as strong as ocean tides. The push-pull undeniable, waiting somewhere deep inside her. The problem was...

She didn't know how to access it.

The surging waves came and went, rolling in one moment, ebbing the next, staying long enough for her to notice, but not long enough for her to capture. Understanding the magic she now wielded topped her list of priorities. Controlling it hit the list next. Westvane insisted he could help her learn how. He knew about magic, after all. Their conversation in the kitchen made that plain. Less clear, though, was whether or not he possessed magic of his own. He claimed he didn't, explaining he was an Assenta warrior, not a magic wielder. He hunted. He killed. He thrived on both activities, which didn't bode well for her.

His mission took precedence. Nothing else mattered to him. Not her well-being... or Queen Lyonesse's wishes. He stood in the breach, unplagued by conscience or concepts of mercy. He'd pivot when needed, change tact when warranted, sacrifice those he believed pawns, willing to throw both allies and enemies to the wolves in order to accomplish his goal.

She wasn't stupid. Reading his intentions, understanding his aim, wasn't difficult.

He had an agenda beyond recapturing the Wendigo. How would his tactics play out? What effect it would have on her own plans? Anyone's guess. One thing for sure, though — she needed to figure out what he planned, and do it quickly. Otherwise, Westvane would walk all over her, and she'd end up in the crosshairs. A place Truly knew she didn't want to be with a Slayer.

Walking through a cloud of aromatic steam, Truly moved toward the bathroom door. She breathed deep, preparing herself for a confrontation while also enjoying the scent of flowers. She loved lavender. Candles scented with lavender littered the window ledges in her apartment. How the house knew her preferred brand of shampoo surprised her, even as she accepted the quirk was something she'd never be able to explain. The magic that fueled the house embraced symbiosis, pulling her preferences out of thin air.

Everything around her matched her personality. Master bedroom done up in her favorite color scheme — check. The beauty products she preferred neatly set out on the vanity — yup. Good food in the fridge — all there. None of it her doing. If she thought about it too hard, she'd end up with a complex.

Pulling the door open, Truly exited the bathroom, stepped into her bedroom and —

"About time." Camped out on her bed, back resting against her headboard, big boots planted on her bedspread, Westvane glanced up from a book. "Thought you drowned in there."

Her eyes narrowed. "Do you mind?"

"No."

"Well, I do." Seriously. For real. Everything about the guy made her want to maim him. "A little privacy would be nice."

"I'm being nice."

"How do you figure?"

"Gave you lots of time in the bathroom, princess." Using his index finger as a placeholder, he closed the book. "That's about as much privacy as you're going to get from me."

"You're annoying."

"Probably best you get used it."

"One thing's for sure," she said, un-balling her socks with an angry yank. Grabbing her boots from the floor by the dresser, she marched to the armchair opposite him. She sat, dragged on her socks, then followed with her boots... while glaring at him. "Either you're going to annoy me to death, or I'm going to figure out a way to kill you before that happens."

"Excellent," he murmured, dark eyes glittering with amusement. "Threats before supper."

"I'm learning."

"Bodes well for me."

She sighed. "You're a bit warped, you know that?"

"Says you." Uncrossing his ankles, Westvane swung his feet to the floor, and with a quickness that defy logic, rounded the end of her bed.

She stood up, then sidestepped, giving him plenty of room. "Says everyone who's ever had the misfortune of meeting you, I would imagine."

"You've a quick wit," he murmured, approval in his tone. "I'll give you that."

"Thanks," she said, returning fire, using sarcasm instead of humor. "I'm relieved you approve."

Book in hand, he walked past her toward the exit. "Let's go."

"Where?"

He didn't answer.

Her question floated into the upstairs hallway, following him out the door. She hustled to catch up, crossing the threshold just as he reached the stairs. Running her fingertips across the polished banister rimming the u-shaped landing, she rounded one of the hand-carved posts of Griffin heads and started down the steps after him.

She caught up halfway down. "What are you reading?"

Without looking at her, he held the hardback up for inspection.

Surprise made her blink. "Philadelphia landmarks? History of the city?"

Pausing on the landing between floors, he looked up at her. "Need the lay of the land."

With a hop, she jumped over two steps and landed beside him. "I know everything there is to know. Born and raised in Philly, remember?"

"You know where the Wendigo might go?"

"Depends."

"On what?"

"What you tell me about it," she said, taking the lead, heading toward the central corridor. The crystal chandelier winked, sending tendrils of light bouncing off wood paneling down below. "What does the Wendigo enjoy most?"

"Chaos."

"Well, we've got plenty of that, but you'll need to be more specific."

A few steps behind her, Westvane jogged down the remaining stairs. "Busy places. The more crowded the better. A target rich environment where it can push people to anger and —"

"Cause fights to break out?"

"That's the idea," he said, his footfalls so light she couldn't hear him. Fleet of foot. Guess that made sense. He was a Slayer — a predatory hunter by breed and training. Stealth seemed like a necessary part of that package. "The Wendigo feeds on brutality. The more chaos it can cause, the more pain it can create through confusion and the manipulation of others, the stronger it becomes."

"It hasn't had that for a while." Nearly a century spent in lockdown, imprisoned somewhere the Wendigo couldn't get what it needed. "It'll be hungry."

"Exactly."

"And when it becomes stronger? What then?"

"It'll move onto larger prey. Government leaders. Those in powerful positions."

"Decision makers."

"Yes."

"It'll try and start another war." Reaching the last step, she entered the corridor. "We don't need any more of those, Westvane."

"No one does, Truly."

True enough.

Pausing by the hall table, she grabbed her cellphone from where she left it earlier, thinking about how best to locate the monster. No one wanted global tensions to explode. Western leaders were already at China's throat, and with Russia on a rampage, and the Middle East forever angry at Israel, leveler heads needed to prevail. But... she frowned at the dark phone screen... how best to find it?

She tapped her index finger against the glass. "I have an idea."

"What?"

"We need to go by the shop before we start looking."

Stopping next to her, Westvane frowned. "The shop?"

"Montrose & Brim Investigations."

"Why stop there?"

"To grab a police scanner." Pocketing her cellphone, she moved past him toward the kitchen. Something smelled good, and she was hungry. "It's Friday night... lots of people will be out. The Wendigo can take its pick — sporting events, bars, clubs. Alcohol will be flowing. Ample opportunity to shake up crowds and —"

"Wreak havoc."

"Exactly. The scanner monitors police channels. Any serious problems — fights, shootings, angry protestors — will go out over the wire. It'll give us direction. We won't be forced to search blind."

"Good idea."

"I have them occasionally."

Westvane snorted.

Pushing the swinging door open, Truly strode into the kitchen and spotted Earl. Creepy-crawly half hidden from view by the table, he stood in front of the stove. Bushy head of hair a wild mess, his back to her, he stirred something in a pot.

Banging a wooden spoon on the stainless-steel rim, Earl glanced over his shoulder. "Evening, girl."

"How's it going, Earl?"

"Spaghetti and meatballs," he said, frowning at Westvane. "That's how it's going."

"Awesome," she said, seeing drops of sauce splattered across white countertops. "I'm starved."

"And I'm a great cook."

"You're hired."

Earl smiled so wide the gaps between his teeth showed.

"You shouldn't encourage him, princess."

"Not your call."

Westvane sighed, the sound full of aggravation.

Throwing him an annoyed look, Truly grabbed a chair, pulled it from beneath the table, and sat down. Elaborate table setting complete with three-headed candelabrum Earl had been busy — cooking, organizing... unearthing the fancy stuff from the back of the China cabinet. Like jewelry, expensive cutlery sat next to antique plates, accompanied by fine-cut crystal tumblers.

Doing her part, she picked up the Waterford water pitcher, filled all three glasses, then glanced at Westvane. "Waiting for an invitation?"

His dark gaze roamed over the set-up.

She pointed to the chair on her right. "Sit. First, we eat, then —"

"We hunt," he said, his expression clearing. A new one took its place, the hard gleam in his eyes promising the kind of violence most people never saw.

The quick shift in his mood should've given her the shivers. Truly shoved the thought — along with her reaction to it — into a lockbox at the back of her brain. She and her unwanted house guest had a plan. Stupid or not, she was sticking to it. Only thing left for her to do now was pray Westvane remained loyal long enough for her to get some answers — while hoping like hell being on his side meant he'd stay on hers a little bit longer.

14

IT'S EVEN WORSE INSIDE

In his usual position — breathing down her neck — Westvane followed her onto the after-porch (Earl's word for it) attached to the back of the house. After years spent studying fine art, Truly didn't think "after-porches" were a thing, but given she'd never lived in a Victorian — and arguing with Earl about anything never ended well for her — she took the sane route, avoiding a head-on collision with the Mantipede by refusing to contradict him.

She didn't need the added aggravation... or another lecture.

Her new cook liked rules. During supper, Earl had lectured her about the mansion. The ins. The outs. The dos and don'ts. In less than an hour, she'd learned more than she ever wanted to about the house she called home. Which made her current escape from said place timely — even with Westvane hot on her heels.

Ignoring the jumbled mess of greenery in her backyard (along with the detached garage listing to one side like a drunken sailor), she hopped off the after-porch onto the drive-way. Gravel crunching beneath her boot soles, she rounded the front of her 'Cuda. Sleek body. Aggressive lines painted flat-black and accented by spit-shined chrome. Her baby was second to none, the epitome of muscle-car beauty.

A tug on the handle, and the door swung wide on silent hinges. Dipping her head, Truly slid inside. The smell of leather and a well-contoured interior greeted her. The sense of relief hit her first. Pure joy rolled in on its wake. No matter how many times she fired up her 'Cuda, it always felt like coming home.

With a murmured greeting to her car, Truly closed the door and settled in. The key went into the ignition, the jangle of metal reassuring as she reached for her seatbelt and...

Realized she was missing something.

Peering out the windshield, she searched for her wing-man. Motionless, Westvane stood in the driveway staring her car, a look of consternation on his face. Her lips twitched. No need to guess what he was thinking. He didn't believe he would fit. Truly didn't blame him. Her 'Cuda hadn't been built for a guy his size.

Trying not to laugh, she met his gaze through the glass and tapped her wrist. Her finger landed on the face of her watch. *Tap-tap-tap. Tick-tock, time's a-wasting.* The gesture came off as impatient. She was nothing of the kind. Might be a little mean-spirited, but his uncertainty struck her as funny. His hesitation bolstered her spirits. She wasn't the only one struggling to adapt to a new normal. Westvane was maneuvering through a field of firsts too, and besides...

He deserved the discomfort. God knew he didn't mind hers.

The big bad Slayer loved watching her squirm. She'd lived through an example of it an hour ago. She hadn't wanted him in her bedroom. Westvane knew it. He simply didn't care, entering uninvited, invading the only space in the house she claimed as her own. Worse, he planted himself on her bed. No sense of civility. All personal boundaries ignored. No apology on the horizon. Supreme arrogance on display, as though he'd gone out and retained exclusive rights to boss her around.

His attitude irritated her.

Everyone needed alone time along with a little privacy. The idea he didn't agree shouldn't bother her. He was who he was — a grown, well... *Slayer*... already set in his ways. No changing him. Somehow, though, the lack of respect he showed made her itch to put him in his place.

Where that place was exactly, Truly hadn't yet figured out. Time seemed to be moving at the warp speed. Westvane's ability to dodge important questions didn't help. She needed more information from him. She wanted to understand how she fit into the fractured puzzle that was her mother's life. The small pieces Westvane gave her provided the broad strokes. The larger picture, however, remained out of focus.

She needed him to tell her more. Everything. Down to the most insignificant detail. Quick on his intellectual feet, Westvane gave her just enough. Enough to paint a vague picture. Enough to keep her chasing her tail. Enough to keep her curious, wondering what would pop up next to blindside her, so... yeah. Absolutely. He'd earned the discomfort.

Palming the steering wheel, she pointed toward the passenger door, and mouthed, "Get in."

Scowling, he approached the car, slowly, acting as though the 'Cuda was a venomous snake about to strike. She swallowed a snort. With a single fingertip, he reached out and popped the latch. The door swung open. He bent in half, eyeing her from beneath the sweep of the curving roofline.

"Westvane — get in."

His gaze swept the interior. "How?"

"Never been in a car before?"

He shook his head. "Looks like a death trap."

"Only if you don't know to drive it. And since I do," she

said, letting the statement hang, "just for you, I'll keep it under one-twenty."

He threw her a horrified look. "Miles an hour?"

"I'm an excellent driver." She wasn't lying. *She. Could. Drive.* Better than most race-car professionals. One of her foster fathers taught her. A total gearhead, he hadn't minded when she helped him in the garage — handing him tools, carting supplies, helping to re-build carburetors and transmissions. Visits to scrapyards all over the city to look for engine parts, though, had been her favorite activity with him. Time spent with him had made up the better part of three years. Until he got a divorce, and she lost her foster family. "And I like my car too much to kill you by crashing it. Get in."

He frowned.

She reached over the center console and flipped the release handle. The locking mechanism clicked. The passenger seat slid back, giving him more leg room.

"If I die in this thing," he grumbled, folding his large frame into the bucket seat, "I'm killing you."

"Paranoid freak."

He growled at her.

"Close the door," she said, laughing at him. "We gotta go."

The door slammed.

Truly turned the ignition key. Her baby roared, coming to life with a snarl.

"Nice," Westvane said, hearing the engine he couldn't see. The hood shimmied, moving as the Hemi rumbled beneath steel. "Sounds fantastic."

"You ain't seen nothing yet." Throwing the 'Cuda into reverse, she hit the gas and streaked down the driveway backward. The second her tires hit asphalt, she cranked the wheel. The muscle car swung into a one-hundred-and-eighty turn on the street. The heavy frame rocked. The powerful engine growled. She shifted into first, then second and third in quick session, rocketing beneath tree branches arching over the avenue.

Westvane cursed.

She grinned. "Buckle up."

He reached for his seatbelt.

One hand on the wheel, the other on the shifter, Truly put her foot down, maneuvering around slowpokes on one-ways, avoiding parked cars, pausing at stop signs without stopping completely. Traffic was light. On a couple of side streets kids were out, one group playing basketball, the other with a ball hockey game on the go. She slowed to let them move the nets, then kept going. A few more turns took her out of the neighborhood and onto the Schuylkill Expressway.

The on-ramp turned into an elevated highway.

She took advantage, changing lanes, weaving between cars, catapulting her 'Cuda into stupid speeds.

A death grip on the door, Westvane tore his attention from the road. "Where are we going?"

"Devil's Pocket."

"Montrose & Brim is there?"

"Yeah," she said, downshifting before swinging around a mini-van. "It's a bad neighborhood, so keep your eyes open."

"This is where you work?"

She nodded, speeding around two motorcycles. "I'm not there a lot. I usually call in to get my assignments. M&B's isn't my favorite place."

Blowing past a Corvette on the left, she moved into the center lane, then across the next to reach her exit. She took the off-ramp fast. The front tires bucked, leaving the pavement for a second. As the rubber touched back down, Truly sped toward bottom of the exit.

The light turned yellow.

She hit the gas. The 'Cuda rumbled and jumped, racing toward the intersection.

Westvane sucked in a breath. "Truly —"

"Hang on."

Big hand pressed to the dash, he reared in his seat.

She sped through the intersection just as the light turned red.

He released the breath he was holding. "Next time, I'm driving."

"Over my dead body."

"That can be arranged."

His threat made her smile. Why? No clue. Insanity, maybe, but for some reason, she found his disgruntlement hilarious. Satisfying, even. She knew with instincts that rivaled a predator's not much bothered Westvane. The idea of her driving might freak him out tickled a long-forgotten part of her — a place that encouraged laughter and accepted joy. A place she hadn't visited in a while.

Feeling lighter, she turned into a bad part of town. Rundown buildings populated street after street. Questionable people hung out on corners with cracked sidewalks fronting seedy stores. The wide boulevards narrowed, leading deeper into the belly of the beast. Philly at its most stark. A city in waiting, a gray lady hoping for better days. A place Montrose had planted his business, sinking deep into an underbelly where nothing but bad things grew.

She hadn't lied to Westvane.

She came to Devil's Pocket as little as possible. Safety wasn't something she took for granted here. It wasn't lost on her that Montrose hadn't tried to find better. Not once. He stayed instead, terrifying people in a neighborhood that boasted the scariest criminals around. Even stranger, everyone gave her boss a wide berth. No one wanted his attention, and...

Everyone who owed him paid on time.

He must have serious connections. She'd never asked. Didn't really want to know. All she wanted was for gang members and drug dealers to leave her alone. To date, they had — no doubt thanks to Montrose — so, no complaining. She took what little she got when in Devil's Pocket. Only a fool, after all, got uppity in the face of bad elements.

Taking the last turn, Truly slowed as she drove down Spindle. She spotted the parking spot from a block away. Located on the side street next to the shop, the space along the curb always sat empty. No name tag above it to explain the vacancy, but it never failed — whenever she showed, the spot was available. A quirk of fate? A gift from the Gods? She didn't care. No sense risking the wrath of Montrose to find out.

She parallel parked, zipping into the gap with little effort. The second her car settled, she threw it in neutral, yanked the emergency brake, and shut the engine down.

"See?" Truly glanced out of the corner of her eye. Looking pale, Westvane sat still as a statue in the passenger seat. "Got you here in one piece."

"I don't know how," he said through clenched teeth. "You nearly hit three cars on the off-ramp."

"Did not. I had inches to spare."

"I didn't realize it before, but now I do."

"What?"

"You're out of your mind," he said as though he'd just discovered the secret to the universe. "Should've known. Door Masters — certifiable."

"Met many of us, have you?"

"No, but I read."

"Good for you." Palming the handle, she popped her door open.

Westvane looked out his window. He eyeballed the chipped

brick exterior with peeling paint before shifting focus to look at the faded sign hanging above cracked windows: *Montrose & Brim Investigations.* "Not much to look at, princess."

"It's even worse inside."

"Something to look forward to at least."

Swiveling in her seat, she got out of the car. "In and out, Westvane. I don't want to be here long."

"Agreed." Already standing on the sidewalk, he scanned both sides of the street.

She watched him, trying to gauge his mood. Serious. Intent. Hyper alert, more than the usual amount. The realization sent a shiver down her spine. Something was wrong. The smell, perhaps. The odd vibration in the air, maybe. Westvane's reaction, without a doubt. At the moment, however, putting her finger on what bothered her wasn't important. Getting out of the open, into the office and behind closed doors, seemed more the priority.

Westvane's eyes narrowed on a junkyard down the street. "Truly."

"I feel it." Rounding the hood, she joined him on the sidewalk. "Front door's around the corner."

"Go. I'll follow."

She didn't question him. Truly moved instead, her focus on making it to the office door. An engine revved on the street. The low rumble fractured the quiet, raising the hair on the back of her neck as Westvane pivoted, moving out in front of her to face the coming threat.

HIS ATTENTION SPLIT, Westvane kept his gaze on the vehicle at the end of the street, but listened for Truly. Her footfalls struck concrete. The rapid rap-rap-rap rippled down the sidewalk, joining the sound of an engine revving, drifting on the stench of exhaust fumes, into dark corners best left undisturbed. A few more strides, and she'd clear the corner of the building. The entrance lay beyond that, a straight shot from curb to front stoop.

He needed her through the door before he made his move. Otherwise, she wouldn't make it inside.

The set-up in front of the junkyard didn't look good. Two sedans. Dark paint. Engines running. Headlights off. Drivers crouched behind dashboards, focus locked on him, as multiple passengers sat hunched in the backseats. He resisted the urge to shake his head. How the idiots expected to hide from him was anyone's guess. Not the sharpest tools in the shed, but that didn't make the humans any less dangerous.

The street-side ambush was a bold move. Open air. An adequate amount of room to maneuver. Lots of time for him to react. Advantage — *him*. Certain death — *them*. As he'd first thought — not the sharpest-minded he'd ever seen.

Which left him two options.

Turn and follow Truly into the relative safety of Montrose & Brim. Or approach the idiots and start cracking skulls.

Option number two suited him best. He excelled at breaking bones, but as he stood on cracked concrete lining the street, Westvane questioned the brutal thrust of his plan. He was in a new world with a different set of rules, and the fools inside the vehicles hadn't offended him yet. He didn't like their eyes on him. He didn't like the swell of hostility emanating from the sedans on a silent street. He didn't like the idea they might be lying in wait for Truly... or him.

His lip curled, baring the tips of his pointed canines.

Lyonesse had been busy. He'd expected her to pull some strings, but not so soon. The fact she'd mobilized support on this side of the *Ecotone* in less than twenty-four hours impressed him. He should've seen it coming. Honoring her word had never counted as a moral imperative for the queen, so no real need for him to speculate. She was hedging her bets, sabotaging him before he began, and yet, Westvane paused to consider his next move in the game.

Confirming his suspicions about Lyonesse by taking his prey alive might benefit him more than killing them all. He needed to know who his enemies were in Earth Realm, and the interrogation methods he employed always provided results, along with all kinds of interesting intel.

No surprise there.

He was an Assenta, born and bred. A hunter without equal, and playing with his prey came with the territory. Even so, he never attacked without provocation... or proof of wrong-doing. He would defend himself if approached. He would maim and destroy to preserve his own life and complete a mission. Sad to say, but the humans sitting in cars that matched the dilapidated condition of the neighborhood hadn't crossed any lines. Or met what he considered the prerequisite burden of proof.

Not yet.

Maybe, they wouldn't cross the line. Maybe, the group wasn't interested in him — or Truly. A pity if it turned out that way. After dealing with the Door Master — and her attitude — since crossing the *Ecotone*, he needed a good fight. Smashing heads together never failed to improve his mood.

Headlights came on in the lead car.

Only then did he hear it — a series of clicks.

Quiet sounds.

Barely there.

Hardly noticeable.

His keen senses picked up each noise. He wasn't human. His abilities — physical and magical — gave him skills humans couldn't match. He saw in the dark. Heard things even his own kind couldn't. Was able to tear apart a magic-wielding Electi with his bare hands, so... humans weren't much of a threat to him.

The weapons they used, however, were another matter.

He recognized the quiet clicking sounds — guns being loaded. Westvane heard the tinny rattle of shell casings. He never seen or held a gun, but he knew all about human weapons. Killing machines. Death dealers. The method cowards used to end a life. No hand-to-hand combat. Nothing up close and personal. Killing happened from afar. Point and shoot, then speed away without having to look at the devastation left behind.

A weak approach. An affront of every Assenta sensibility he owned.

The engine of the first sedan revved.

The inside corners of his shoulder blades itched. A bad sign, one that spelled disaster if what he suspected happened and —

The driver put the vehicle in gear and wheeled into the street.

A second car roared in behind the first.

Windows on the passenger sides of both cars rolled down.

Spinning toward the building, Westvane turned away from the curb. His gaze landed on Truly. She glanced at him over her shoulder. Her eyes widened in horror. She shouted a warning as barrels of multiple weapons cleared open windows.

Westvane lunged toward her.

Slipping from its leash, magic darkened the edges of his vision. Westvane pushed against the powerful tide, trying to stem the flow as heat bubbled through him. He heard the shooters disengage the safety locks. The burn in his veins inten-sified. Magic boiled over. Pain rippled along his spine. The sharp claws crowning his wings punched through his skin, shredding his shirt, tearing through his leather jacket.

One instant, he was wingless.

The next, jet-black feathers beat against his back. On full display. Out in the open for all to see.

He snarled, and knees pumping like pistons, grabbed the Door Master. Her feet left the ground. His boots slid over the sidewalk as his wings bucked in the autumn air. Truly gasped as she collided with his chest. His arms and wings came around her as he heard guns ratchet and tires screech.

"Tuck," he growled, turning away from the street.

Truly reared in his grasp. "What are you doing?"

"Tuck!"

His hard tone produced results.

Giving him all her weight, she tucked her head and curled her legs up, turning herself into a compact ball, improving his ability to shield her. Smart girl. Bullets wouldn't kill him. Hurt like hell as each one hit? Yes. The barrage would be agonizing, but he healed fast. He was built to last, which made him very hard to assassinate. His flesh would knit, his body pushing the bullets out the second the metal entered his flesh. A few holes would only serve to piss him off.

Truly was a different story.

Her magic might be powerful, but it was still in its infancy. Until she matured and mastered her skills, she remained vulnerable, unable to throw up a shield in defense, without the accelerated ability to heal. At this stage, she was little more than flesh, blood, and bone. Susceptible to the weapons of her world. Which meant...

He must do what she couldn't yet do for herself. Ensure she stayed whole until his mission ended and he evened the score.

Lyonesse awaited his wrath. Nothing would stand in the way of avenging his mother's murder and years of unwarranted confinement. He needed Truly. She would ensure his success, keeping possibility alive until he finished what he promised his mother on the day of her execution.

A series of pops beat through her air.

Time slowed.

"Eastbrook," he said, calling on his friend.

The raven answered, peeling off his skin. Half inked on his throat, half his body in the open air, Eastbrook craned his neck, lending Westvane his eyes. An image bloomed on his mental screen, allowing him to see what the raven saw.

Three cars now. Windows down. Metal muzzles pointed at his back. Bullets leaving the barrels. He had just seconds before the first projectile hit.

Curled around Truly, Westvane ducked around the corner of Montrose & Brim. Raven feathers fluttered over his cheek. More gunshots, the spray coming from multiple weapons. Car engines roared. Men shouted, the words incomprehensible as staccato of weapons screamed.

Bullets struck the building inches above his head.

Brick exploded. Shrapnel rained down, coating him with dust, bouncing off his shoulders and wings, abrading his skin. Eastbrook squawked in protest, the vocal array sounding like cursing. Westvane leapt onto the front stoop and —

The door flew open, slamming into the exterior wall.

Light from the street bled into the entryway.

Armed with an automatic weapon, a beast stepped over the threshold. Still moving, but feeling suspended in time, Westvane jolted in recognition. A gargoyle. Big. Muscular. Gray fur covered by a battered green jacket.

Blue eyes aglow, aggressive features set in severe lines, the gargoyle set a gun butt against his shoulder. "Get her inside!"

Truly jerked against him. "Rosy?"

"Shut it, Triple." Stepping to one side, the gargoyle hit his haunches next to the door. With one knee pressed to the concrete, he leveled the machine gun at the attackers. Fangs bared, he pulled the trigger. The weapon jack-hammered in his grip. Bullets sprayed the lead vehicle. The sound of steel jackets annihilating metal echoed down the street, over building tops to reach the elevated highway.

Tires squealed.

The men inside the cars shouted.

Truly tucked tight, Eastbrook peering over his shoulder, Westvane entered the shop, one thought top of mind. He hoped Montrose didn't kill the humans before he stashed Truly somewhere safe and joined the fight.

15

SHOOT FIRST. ASK QUESTIONS LATER

Truly couldn't hear anything but the raging echo of automatic gunfire. Not her heart beating. Not the blood rush in her veins, or cloying rasp at the back of her throat. She knew it was happening. Evidence of panic was everywhere — throbbing at her temples, in her wrists and ears as her heart slammed against the inside of her breastbone. The constriction stole her breath, making the air in her lungs hitch and her stomach clench.

She was suffocating. Drowning beneath waves of machine gunfire as bullets slammed into the front of Montrose & Brim. Stone dust exploded into a cloud around the building. Chunks of brick flew like shrapnel. Terror tightened its grip, choking off her ability to think.

Truly knew she was moving... but not under her own power. A strange cage surrounded her. Black. Dense. Soft, somewhat lightweight. Which seemed odd, given she couldn't see through it. The barrier seemed impenetrable, everywhere all at once, keeping her from being hit as the staccato of shooting intensified and shards of window glass and brick flew.

"Oh, my God."

Westvane's hands flexed on her. A wall of what looked like feathers tightened around her. The movement jarred frozen thoughts loose. Perception realigned, dragging her back into awareness. She was in his arms, curled in a ball, tucked in close, and he was running. Legs fired like pistons. Heartbeat raging against her ear. His pace so fast, the lamplit sky blurred into streaks as she looked up through the slim cove made by the protective curl of his dark wings.

Wings.

How did Westvane have *wings* all of a sudden?

"Westvane," she rasped, shifting in his hold.

He growled in response, firmed his grip on her, and kept running. The sound and fury of gunfire roared, peppering M&B. More shrapnel. More dust. Tons more shouting. What in God's name was going on? Westvane hadn't mentioned anything about people wanting to kill her during their conversation. Not that she could berate him for the omission now. Staying alive took precedence. Which meant she needed to pull herself together and do her part. Montrose kept a gun safe in the storeroom at the back of the shop. And given the firepower currently pointed in their direction, arming herself and returning fire had just become priority number one.

Pain spiked through her ribcage.

Truly forced a half-breath and refocused. "Westvane... ease up. I can't breathe. You're crushing me."

Taking a sharp turn, he came to an abrupt halt. The vice around her ribs unlocked. Her feet hit the floor. Off balance, she listed sideways, bumping into a wall of feathers.

"Open." Chest heaving, she shoved against the plumes. "Let me out of here."

The wings surrounding her opened, allowing her to see more than black feathers and the column of his throat. Grabbing her arm, Westvane propelled her backward, past the half-wall of the reception area, deeper into the bullpen. Grabbing the nearest desk, he flipped it over. The metal edge slammed into the floor. Bullets blasted in from the street. Window glass shattered, exploding into the room, ripping the blinds from the wall.

With a curse, Westvane spun toward her, using his body to shield her.

Both arms curled over her head, Truly lunged for cover. Her knees slid on worn linoleum, carrying her behind the desk. She expected Westvane to follow. When he didn't, she glanced at him. Her lips parted a second before she jolted, incredulousness shoving fear out of the way. He was crazy. He must be *crazy*. Unlike her, Westvane wasn't shaken. He was furious. Murderous. His expression so black she suffered an involuntary shudder. Attention leveled on the front of the shop, he turned away from her toward the battle.

Crouched behind a desk, she reached out and grabbed his pant leg. "Westvane — get down!"

With a jerk, he broke her hold.

Shrapnel blasted overhead, slamming into the overturned desk. Metal dented. The steel frame bucked, banging into her. Bullets continued to fly as she watched Westvane walk — not run, not dodge, zigzag or army crawl, but *walk* — toward the wall of windows.

"What are you doing?" Truly flinched as bullets sprayed the back wall. Plaster puffed from the holes, clouding the air. "Get down!"

Dark eyes blazing, he glared at her. "Stay there."

"But —"

"Don't move." Black wings folded, he strode toward the front door, dismissing her without looking back. "You do, I'll kill you myself."

Under normal circumstances, she would've taken umbrage at his nasty tone. The threat of murder didn't thrill her either.

Toss in his dismissal and... yeah. None of those things ranked high on her list of favorite things. While under fire, however, didn't seem an appropriate time to be offended, or voice opposition to his demented, death-trap of a plan.

Hunkered down, she watched him go, then made plans of her own. Holding a stationary position wasn't smart. She might not want to walk into the fray, but that didn't mean she couldn't hold down a secondary position and ensure no one broke through the back door. Which meant she needed to open the gun safe and get her hands on a weapon. Or several of them.

Glancing over her shoulder, she calculated the distance to the back of the shop. Fifty feet of open space between her and the storeroom. She knew the code that opened the safe. Montrose had made her memorize it her second day on the job. "Just in case of an emergency," he'd said, which definitely qualified as now. So...

Only one hurdle left to jump — the fact she'd never fired a gun.

Not exactly encouraging. Her lack of education in this area didn't say much for her, given the assignments Montrose sent her on. Safety should, after all, come first. And self-defense fell under that umbrella. Knowing how to shoot, however, didn't matter right now. She didn't need to be a marksman. All she needed to do was aim and pull the trigger. After that, she'd worry about whether or not she hit the bad guys.

She was, after all, a Door Master. Or at least, was supposed to be. She might not understand her role yet — or know exactly what being a magic-wielder entailed — but necessity was the mother of being-brave-enough-to-learn-on-the-fly.

The thought made her pause.

Her mind stopped racing. A sense of calm descended. Automatic gunfire bombarded M&B as the realization she wasn't defenseless took hold. She was a Door Master. No... she was *the*

Door Master. The only one left of her kind. That had to count for something. Which meant Westvane was wrong. She could help instead of stand by and watch. Maybe, if she concentrated hard enough, she could access the magic. Put the power Westvane insisted she commanded to good use, but... her eyes narrowed on the storeroom door... how?

She hadn't lied. Opening the door, releasing the Wendigo, had been an accident. A one-off she didn't know how to replicate. More understanding — and practice — would no doubt change that, but for now, she needed to help any way she could.

Inching across the debris-littered floor, she peered around the corner of the overturned desk, then slide onto her belly. Army-crawling toward the storeroom, she stayed low and searched for the spark. The one she'd felt, then seen in her mind's eye, at the house. There must be a way for her to access the magic — a method or sequence to follow, a resource to tap that would result in her conjuring a door. If she managed to open one, she'd dragged Westvane and Montrose into the *Ecotone*, away from the danger, into a place they could regroup and figure out what the hell was going —

Bullets zipped over her head.

Flat against the floor, she slithered to her right, sliding behind the next desk in line.

"Truly!"

"What?"

Westvane snarled. "You want to die?"

"You're not going to kill me!"

"Try me."

"Shut up and, for the love of all that is holy, listen for once!" she yelled, trying to locate him in the chaos.

Long fluorescent lights hung from the ceiling, plastic casings smashed, some of the long bulbs blinking, others shattered and buzzing. Bright light strobed, throwing shadows across the walls, cutting through drifting drywall dust and —

"Holy hell," she whispered, gaze locked on Westvane.

The odd glow wasn't coming from broken ceiling lights.

The shimmer emanated from Westvane. Like an avenging angel, he stood near the broken window, a shield of smoke in one hand, a crackling black-flamed sword in the other. A spray of heavy ammunition slammed into the shield. Westvane's feet slid back a foot, absorbing the assault. A moment passed before the smoke-shield spun and hurled each bullet back, acting like a machine gun. Return fire peppered the street, ripping across asphalt.

Baring his teeth, Westvane swung his sword. A bolt of black lightning left the tip. Electricity slammed into a car. Steel shrieked. Metal twisted as the jagged stroke blew the vehicle sky high.

Men on the street screamed and scrambled. A single voice cut through the confusion, shouting directions. The gunfire stopped. Smoke from burning cars and buildings billowed into Montrose & Brim.

Curling the scarf from her neck, Truly wrapped it over her nose and mouth. "What's happening?"

"They're regrouping." Down on one knee, gun pointed at the street, Montrose slid out of the entryway. "Bringing in heavier artillery."

"Shit," she whispered.

Westvane moved right, covering Montrose's retreat, seeking a better vantage point. "Told you not to move, princess. Where were you going?"

"Storeroom," she said, trying not to freak out. Stark quiet after such calamity seemed wrong, heralding the arrival of something much worse. Clearing the dust out of her throat, Truly watched blood trickle from the tip of Montrose's pointy ear and roll across his fur. She stared at his bat-shaped face as he bared huge fangs, thinking, not for the first time, she understood how Dorothy felt when she landed in Oz. She was not in Kanas anymore. "There's a gun safe, and better cover. I need a place to work."

"What do you mean — work?" Montrose asked, stopping beside a control panel mounted to the wall inside his office.

"I'm going to try and open a door."

Treating her to a load of stink-eye, Montrose flipped the panel open to reveal a bunch of buttons. "You know how?"

"No, but now seems like a good time to learn."

"No need," Westvane said, eyes on the street, shifting toward the front door.

"Westvane — don't go out there."

"Ending this now, princess."

"Don't. There are too many of them, and anyway..." She paused, trying to think of something to say. A clever argument to keep him from attacking. She didn't know how, but intuition warned her if he went into the street alone, he wouldn't come back. "This isn't Azlandia. Someone's probably called the police. You can't be seen, you know..."

Black eyes aglow with citrine light, Westvane raised a brow as she trailed off.

She pointed to his wings. "Like that."

"Princess —"

"The police will shoot first and ask questions later. They're as likely to shoot you as the bad guys, and honestly? We don't need more guns pointed at us."

Flaming sword and smoke shield raised, Westvane unfolded his wings, glanced at the feathery appendages, and scowled.

She read him instantly. His expression said violent aggressor. His body language said he didn't care what happened to human police. He wanted blood. He wanted death. He wanted to deliver both to the men outside. She could see the intention in the rigid lines of his face. His sword and shield weren't for show. He knew how to wield the weapons and planned to use both.

On anyone who got in his way.

Policemen.

Pedestrians.

Innocent bystanders and Neighborhood Watch inductees.

Truly refused to let him.

Crouched across from Montrose, she shook her head. "Westvane — no. Tuck the wings. Shelve your weapons. You're not allowed to kill police."

Dark eyes filled with fury, Westvane bared his teeth.

"She's right. Never a good idea to kill lawmen, Slayer." Montrose said, surprising the hell out of her.

Montrose never agreed with her. Her boss seemed allergic to all forms of cooperation. As she blinked, battling the shock, he pushed a series of buttons on the control pad.

Something rattled near the front.

A sheet of steel sliced down from the battered ceiling. Heavy. Thick. Slab-like. The security shield covered the picture window and door, blocking out streetlights, anchoring into the floor, keeping the shooters out and Westvane in.

For now.

Fingers crossed, it would last.

But as she watched him struggle to control his temper — aggressive nature in overdrive, magical weapons clenched in his hands — she didn't hold out much hope. With his lethal instincts raging, calming him down, keeping him contained inside the shop while she figured out how to open a magical door seemed more work-of-fiction than here-and-now reality.

16

WHETHER SHE LIKED IT OR NOT

The frantic shuffle on the street outside M&B went still. Aggression swelled in the ensuing silence, mixing with the taint of adrenaline. Truly smelled it in the air. She felt it in the ether. Tension rippled through her, tightening muscles over bones, warning her peace didn't always mesh well with quiet.

Hanging by a thread, a chunk of drywall lost the battle with gravity and hit the floor. Dust swirled. The thud echoed as broken fluorescent bulbs swung, creaking against their metal casings.

Westvane's fingers flexed around his sword hilt.

Truly stayed still, afraid movement might light the fuse on the powder keg of attitude growing inside an office turned war zone. Westvane wasn't happy. Neither was Montrose. The difference? Westvane wanted to kill her boss for cutting off his path to the street — the most direct route to unleashing carnage.

Montrose, on the other hand, pretended not to notice. Not the best approach when dealing with a Slayer. Enraging Westvane didn't amount to a good idea. But then, Montrose didn't care what anyone thought — or for her opinion. He made that clear on a regular basis. The owner of M&B went his own way, wielding his ability to irritate like a superpower.

Some might call the skill endearing. Right now, Truly called it certifiable, given Westvane's reaction made it clear Montrose stood precariously close to a line he shouldn't cross. Not with Westvane. Not with her either, but... whatever. She didn't have time to deal with the chaotic churn of male idiocy circling the room. She had bigger problems, along with a few additional worries.

Moving slowly, she stepped in between Montrose and Westvane, using her body as a physical deterrent to discourage murder. "Tell me what's happening?"

"Quiet," Westvane growled, gaze fixed on Montrose. A clang rippled in from outside. Dragging his focus from Montrose, he looked toward the steel barrier. He tilted his head. His eyes narrowed as he listened to something she couldn't hear.

"What are they doing?" she asked.

"Cars reversing," Westvane said. "Heavy vehicles approaching."

Worry tightened her chest. "Tanks?"

"In the city?" Frowning at her, Montrose shoved aside a broken chair. "Where do you think you are, Triple — the Middle East?"

Well, it felt like a war zone. Looked like it too. Debris everywhere. Bullet holes in the walls. Smashed lights hanging from the ceiling. Given current conditions, armored vehicles didn't seem like much of a stretch. "What then?"

She needed to know.

Too busy listening, no one felt inclined to answer. Which made her even more twitchy. Silence, after all, didn't mean safe. The lack of gunfire didn't mean larger weapons weren't being moved into position... and pointed in their direction.

An ache started behind her breastbone.

Each inhale tightened the invisible band wrapped around her ribcage. Her breathing became shallow. A sharp pain radiated over her shoulder. Heart attack territory. She had all the symptoms, but... no. This wasn't that.

Not heart failure. Extreme anxiety — the beginnings of a panic attack.

"Westvane," she said, some snap, more wheeze. "What're they doing?"

"Relax, Triple. Don't freak out."

Don't freak out? Terrific advice, but... was he crazy? Freaked out was a distant memory. The ramp up into terror kept shoving it out of the way.

Fighting to hold it together, Truly glared at her boss.

"There she is," he muttered, a satisfied smile on his bat-like face. "Always so ornery."

"I know the code to the gun safe," she said low, struggling to pull in full breaths.

"So?"

"Keep it up, and I'll load one and shoot you. No one'll fault me for killing a..." She paused, staring at him. "What are you anyway?"

"Gargoyle."

She blinked. "You've been a gargoyle from the beginning?"

"Beginning of what?"

"My employment," she said, exasperation pushing panic to the side.

"Of course," he said, slamming a new chip into his machine gun. "Saw you. Knew who and what you were. Couldn't let you run all over town. Someone had to keep an eye on you until the magic kicked in."

Truly opened her mouth, then closed it again.

Her bafflement prompted Montrose to go on. "Your power

is good and set now, though, isn't it? Scales are off, so you see me as I truly am... in all my gorgeous gargoyle glory."

Gorgeous gargoyle glory.

Truly snorted, half laugh, mostly disbelief.

"Don't know what your problem is, Triple," Montrose said, taking exception to her reaction. "You're running around with a Slayer —"

"Assenta," Westvane growled.

Montrose rolled his eyes. "And a hybrid, at that. You're not worried about Westvane and his wings, so why're you so bothered by me?"

Good point. Irritating, per usual, but Montrose wasn't wrong.

Her attention snapped to Westvane. "Seriously? You couldn't have warned me about the wings?"

"None of your business, princess."

Ah, no. No way would she let that pitch sail by. "Double-edge sword, Westvane. You can't invade my privacy and expect to retain your own. Everything about you became my business when you entered my house uninvited. You told me you had no magic."

"I lied."

Her brows popped up. "You lied?"

"Of course," he said, his tone conveying 'no big deal.' "Never promised you honesty, Truly."

She scowled. "What else have you lied about?"

Tipping his chin down, he looked at her from beneath furrowed brows. What he didn't do was answer. Not a good sign. A stubborn Westvane might prove to be too much for her. She suspected when an Assenta warrior dug in, he became an immovable object, and there wasn't a living soul capable of shifting him. Not that she planned on giving up. Westvane possessed the answers she needed. No way would she let him off the hook.

Avoiding the flaming tip of his sword, she stepped in close. "You're a hybrid. What does that mean?"

He hesitated, predatory nature piqued as he studied her, no doubt trying to decide how much to share. He took his time. Truly allowed him to look, hoping he not only picked up on her curiosity, but also read the intent behind her inquiry. She wanted him to trust her. She needed him to know she accepted him, warts and all. No one was perfect. Everyone walked around with scars on their hearts and unaddressed issues inside their heads. Emotional turmoil didn't play favorites. Trauma might take different paths, but at some point, it came for them all.

A muscle ticked in his jaw.

She held his gaze, refusing to look away.

His brow furrowed. "Stubborn."

"Yes," she said. "Tell me what you don't want me to know, Westvane. Say it out loud, share the fear, and it loses power."

He looked away, breaking eye contact.

She moved a bit closer. "Westvane."

"I'm half-Assenta, half-Electi. My father belonged to the royal house, my mother born to one in the second-tier caste," he said, voice soft, expression set in hard lines. "Different castes are not permitted to mingle socially or form romantic attachments. It's against the law, which makes my birth an illegal act. In Azlandia, I'm considered an abomination, a *thing* that never should've been born."

How awful.

How unfair.

How absolutely wrong.

Through no fault of his own, Westvane would never be accepted. Never be anything other than a stain upon Azlandian society. Truly clenched her teeth, disliking the way he was viewed in his world, the way he'd been treated, but also what it implied.

Different castes, classes kept separate at all costs. Sounded like feudalism in the Middle Ages, and a lot like Azlandia needed its own civil rights movement.

"It's weighed, isn't it?" she asked, taking a guess. "Some castes are considered more important than others?"

"Electis are magic wielders, the dominant caste and ruling minority."

"Top of the food chain." Shifting the gun, Montrose flicked the safety off. "Bastards like to keep us in our place."

"Where do Gargoyles sit along the chain?"

"Separate class, specially grouped caste." Montrose spat on the floor. "Above Assentas and Croppers. Below Electis."

"Gargoyles are members of the House of Scholars. Record keepers, supreme judges, the deep thinkers of Azlandia," Westvane said. "Investigators of things both known and unknown."

"A prestigious link on the chain, Rosy, so..." she said, seeing her boss in a whole new light. "Why are you so grouchy all the time?"

Montrose's whiskers twitched, first one way, then the other. "You'd be pissed off too, if you'd been trapped in Earth Realm for twenty-seven years."

"Twenty-seven years?"

"For as long as you've been alive."

Truly blinked. Trapped in Philadelphia when the queen sealed the *Ecotone*. Unable to return home to the House of Scholars. Separated from family and friends. Had it happened to her, she'd be angry too.

"But now, you're going to fix it, Triple."

"Who's Brim?" she asked, listening to her instincts instead of the steel in his voice. She'd asked before — more than once —

wanting to know who owned the other half of the shop. Seemed like information she should have, given the criminal element in the neighborhood and the company Montrose kept. No matter how many times she asked, he refused to answer. Seeing his expression now, though, Truly knew she needed to press him. If she didn't, he'd never tell her the truth. "He's more than just your business partner, isn't he?"

"She," Montrose said, his tone so soft she almost didn't hear him.

Her throat tightened. "Your wife?"

"My mate." Blue eyes intent on her, he stepped closer. She titled her chin up, getting a crick in her neck to maintain eye contact. "I miss her, Truly, so I need you to fix it."

"What if I can't?"

"Bullshit."

"Rosy —"

"Knew it the moment I saw you. Imagine," he said, throwing a bewildered look at Westvane. "Been trying to get home for years, and one day, just like that, in walks a Door Master. No idea who she is, wandering around the city all by herself. No magic. No protection. Bull's-eye on her back. Totally clueless. I tell you, man... what was I supposed to do?"

Amusement sparked in Westvane's eyes. "Only thing you could."

"Exactly. I hired her. Got her clueless ass off the streets and a roof over her head," Montrose said, his eyes narrowed on her. "So now... pay back. Open a door, Triple. I want to go home."

She sucked in a breath. "I don't know how."

Montrose scowled at her. "'Course, you do. You're a Door Master."

Truly glanced at Westvane, hoping for help. Montrose wasn't wrong. She was clueless, and had been for a while. She didn't know how her magic worked, or what triggered it. Since entering her new house, she'd caught glimpses of it — the faint, shimmery smudges left behind when she touched something, the strange current in her veins, the vague hum inside her head — but the glimmer disappeared almost as fast it arrived. Her magic wasn't stable, her grip on it unsure, which left her grasping at straws. She didn't understand it. Couldn't access the power at will, never mind control it.

Discouraged, she pressed the heels of her hands into her eye sockets. What had she been thinking? Less than five minutes ago, she'd planned to crawl into the back room and open a door.

Open a door.

Something she had no idea how to do. So, yeah, in all seriousness... *what had she been thinking?*

With bullets flying, reaching for the power had seemed like the best option. Now, with the quiet stretching and her mind spinning, stress tightened its grip. No way would she be able to do it. She needed guidance. She needed practice. She needed to be in a place where bad guys weren't aiming heavy artillery at the front door. A minute to breathe. And think. And figure her way through without feeling as though she stood inside a pressure cooker.

She shook her head. "I want to help, Rosy. I really do, but —"

"Open a door, Triple."

"Listen —"

"Concentrate, Truly," Westvane said.

Anxiety tied a knot in the center of her chest. "I can't."

Westvane flicked his fingers. The sword and shield disappeared. "You can."

Holding her hands up, she pressed her palms toward him. "Forget about doors, Westvane. You have wings. If we get to the roof, you can fly us out of here."

Shrugging his shoulders, he flexed his wings. Black feathers fluttered, the inky sheen mesmerizing in the low light. "I don't know how to fly."

Her mouth fell open. "What?"

"A fine pair you two make," Montrose said, laughing.

"Shut up, Rosy." Not understanding, she pointed at Westvane's wings. "What do you mean — you don't know how to fly?"

His expression grew stark. "I have yet to learn."

"How can that be?"

"The wings are new to me, a recent addition to the magic I command. Like you, I've had no one to teach me," he said, his tone tight. "I couldn't test them or practice in the cage. I'm watched too closely by the queen's guard for that. Lyonesse —"

Montrose snarled. "She put you in a cage?"

"The Parkland."

"Alone?" her boss asked, brows drawn tight.

"But well-monitored."

"The faithless witch," Montrose said, sounding raw, as though he'd swallowed a glass full of acid. "Must have been torture."

Westvane's chin dipped in acknowledgement. "Close to it."

Interesting information. Curious exchange. Every bit of it making Truly want to know more. She wanted to know how someone as strong as Westvane ended up in a cage. His skill and strength were formidable. What would it take to subdue him? How had the queen managed it? What had Lyonesse done to keep him contained in a place he didn't want to be? Imprisoning him seemed unfathomable. Impossible, even.

Truly frowned.

Lyonesse must possess tremendous power. The kind a smart person would avoid.

Come to think of it, *she* was a smart person. Westvane might be right. Escaping into the *Ecotone* might be the best way to avoid the army of men outside, but it also came at a cost. The biggest one entailed her being brutally murdered.

"Truly," Westvane murmured, using his voice to soothe her.

She drew a shaky breath. "I'm not ready."

"I'll help you."

"No."

She didn't want to end up like her mother — buried six feet deep in an unmarked grave. A distinct possibility if she entered Azlandia. The second she set foot inside Westvane's world, the queen would know. Lyonesse wouldn't hesitate to end her life. She'd put the most ruthless killers on her trail. The name of the game would be *Seek and Destroy*. Or maybe, *Find and Torture*.

Neither scenario sounded fun.

She'd be a sitting duck. Like fresh chum thrown into the shark-infested waters. Out of her depth. Unable to navigate. Without a lifeline, no way to pull herself to safety. But as Westvane walked across the office toward her, and she back-pedaled, stepping around overturned desks and over wrecked ceiling tiles to avoid him, Truly knew it was too late. She was already in deep water. The way Westvane moved, the look in his eyes, the direct path he took to reach her screamed, *"Time's up"*.

He intended to force the issue. Pit his will against her own. Whether she liked it or not.

17

TRY, TRIPLE

Truly retreated as Westvane advanced. Avoidance was key, and escape the best course of action. Problem was, she didn't hold out much hope of accomplishing either.

Confined space. Limited options. An army outside the front door. Everything seemed stacked against her.

Not surprising. Her plan wasn't rooted in rocket science — more in the inane hope Westvane would change his mind. A long shot, given his nature. With Slayer-driven intensity, Westvane boxed her in, mirroring her movement, moving her backward, herding her toward a corner of the room.

Stumbling over debris strewn across the floor, she continued to retreat. A sharp pivot turned her toward the storeroom. Gaze steady on her, Westvane shook his head. She didn't need his non-verbal form of communication. Truly already knew her strategy sucked. Retreating instead of standing her ground was a bad idea. Westvane enjoyed chasing. He liked to hunt, and she was running out of places to run.

M&B had never been huge. Now, it seemed more than just small. The outer office felt tiny, full of dwindling space, too little air and few options.

Panic nibbled around the edges, hovering like a Spector on the horizon. One that threatened to engulf her as her chest compressed, making it difficult to breathe.

"I can't, Westvane," she said, as he moved closer. "Believe me... I can't."

"Triple," Montrose growled.

The intensity in his low tone ripped her attention from Westvane.

Her gaze snapped in her boss's direction.

The first thing she noticed was his scowl. Ever a fixture on his face. Nothing special about it now. More of the usual, but also, different. The contrast of bright blue eyes against gray fur held a quality, a softness, she'd never seen before from him. Knowing she must look terrified, unable to catch her breath, she threw him a wild look.

"*Try*, Triple." Gun still leveled at the door, he jerked it toward the metal barricade. "The men outside are well-armed, and we're outnumbered. The assholes will breach the building eventually. You've nothing to lose by trying, and everything to gain."

Sound reasoning. Perfectly logical.

Truly hated the suggestion the second it left Montrose's mouth. In light of the mob outside, he'd chosen to make sense. A startling about-face for him, but Truly couldn't deny *trying* was the right thing to do. Opening a door, attempting to connect and own her power, was the safest way out of a dangerous situation. The singular avenue by which she could ensure Westvane and Montrose didn't get hurt — or worse, killed — by the madmen outside. The solution made sense, but for one rather large problem. If she opened a door and escaped into the *Ecotone*, Westvane's original mission went unattended and ignored.

Walking backwards, she raised her hands to ward him off. "You're forgetting something."

He raised a brow. "And that would be?"

"The Wendigo."

"I haven't forgotten about the Wendigo, princess."

"It can't be left to run wild." Her shoulder blades bumped against the wall. "It'll —"

"I know what it'll do," Westvane said, stopping a foot away.

Not far enough.

Not nearly far enough.

He stood too close, within striking distance, making her aware of his size. Funny... at her house, in the car, standing alongside him on the sidewalk, the obvious signs of his strength hadn't bothered her. She'd barely noticed. Under threat, however, all she saw was the wide set of his shoulders, the enormous curve of his black wings, the hugeness of his hands. He could kill her without breaking a sweat.

It wouldn't take much.

Just a flick of his wrist, and she'd be dead at his feet. A broken neck. A snapped spine. A fractured skull. Anything was a possibility. Which made the idea of running look more attractive by the second.

She shifted sideways, sliding along the wall.

Westvane hemmed her in, leaving no room for escape. "I gave you my word, Truly."

"I remember." And she did. The problem was, could she trust it?

"I promised I wouldn't hurt you. My word stands."

"Right," she said, starting to sweat. "We leave now and the Wendigo goes unchecked. We can't —"

"Sure we can," Montrose said, his bias showing. "Who gives a shit about this place?"

"I do! Along with the people in it." The snap in her voice bounced around the shop. What sounded like a heavy truck rumbled up to and stop just outside the front door. Trying to ignore the likelihood of imminent attack, she scowled at her boss. "They don't deserve to die just because you're pissed off that you haven't been able to go home, Rosy."

"Shame," he murmured.

Westvane sighed. "We'll come back right after."

"What do you mean?" she asked, still scowling at Montrose.

Montrose shrugged. "You open a door. We walk through it into Azlandia. You open another, you and Westvane circle back into the city from a different location. Hunt the Wendigo from there."

"Oh, really?" She had to give him credit. Her snotty tone didn't faze him. "That easy?"

"You're a Door Master, Triple," Montrose said, attitude just as snarly as hers. "So yeah, that simple."

Truly swallowed. "But the queen and her guard are there."

Understanding dawned in Westvane's eyes. "There and gone, Truly. She'll know we landed. Your magic is powerful. The ripple effect of your presence won't go unnoticed, but Lyonesse won't be able to pinpoint our location that fast. Before she does, we'll already be moving back through the *Ecotone* into Earth Realm."

"And those guys?" She pointed toward the front door.

"The Yeomanry?"

"Is that what they're called?"

"Yes." His expression sharpened, taking on lethal edges. "Don't worry about them. I'll deal with the Yeomanry once we're back."

"Who are they?" she asked.

"The queen has allies on this side of the *Ecotone*," Montrose murmured. "The Yeomanry are one of them, a human militia. They have existed for centuries. Their hatred of magic folk is absolute. Their sole purpose is to hunt and kill us. You've heard of the Salem witch trials?"

"Of course."

A muscle twitched along Montrose's jaw. "Orchestrated by the Yeomanry."

"Zealots."

"Fanatics lead by a charismatic sociopath. That is who stands outside." The fur on his snout twitched, making him look like a feral, oversized bat. "You're one of us, Triple, the most powerful of our kind. I understand your fear, but stalling is no longer safe. Let Westvane help. Let him spark you. The sooner we're through a door and out the other side, the better."

Freaking Montrose. Despite all evidence to the contrary, he knew her well.

She *was* stalling. Putting off the evitable. Looking for a way out, instead of finding the way through. She kept telling herself she needed more time to prepare, but that was a lie. Nothing and no one could prepare her for what was to come. Maybe her mother might have done, but...

Bowing her head, Truly closed her eyes.

The former Door Master was dead. Murdered in cold blood by a queen the universe made certain Truly wouldn't be able to avoid. Here. Now. Tomorrow or next week. The time frame didn't matter. At some point, she and Lyonesse would come face-to-face. And from what Westvane said, something must be done.

Wrongs must be righted. The discrimination and inequality needed to stop.

The injustices suffered by those under Lyonesse's rule couldn't go unchecked. Everyone, no matter where they came from or what they believed, deserved to be treated with fairness and dignity. The dial needed to be turned, and as things came to a head inside her mind, Truly understood what it meant.

She must step into her calling and be the catalyst for change.

"Courage, Truly," Westvane murmured.

Courage. The word spilled through her. Yes, above all else... *courage.*

Swallowing the lump in her throat, Truly opened her eyes and met his gaze. "All right. Let's go."

"Good, now..."

As he trailed off, his large hands settled on her shoulders. The heat of his palms seeped through her jacket, invading muscles and bones, then turned tact to coast along her spine. A low-grade hum buzzed over her temples.

Truly released the breath she'd been holding.

"Deep breath," he whispered. "Hold it — one, two, three, four... let it go. Take another."

She obeyed, beginning to relax beneath his touch.

"Again."

Inhaling deep, she counted off the second, then exhaled long and slow.

"Perfect," he said, his deep voice dipping even lower. "Close your eyes."

She hesitated, her gaze drilling into his, assessing. No malice that she could see. Not a hint of anything unspoken. Just the steadying force of his dark eyes. After a second spent searching, she did as he asked. Her eyelids fell, lashes fluttering against her skin.

Westvane murmured in approval.

She followed his voice, allowing its cadence to draw her deeper.

"See anything?"

"Just darkness."

"Good. It'll make the spark easier to see."

"Spark?"

"The burst will be small at first. Infinitesimal. Barely there at all," he said, sounding like he stood far away instead of right in front of her. "I want you to go hunting, Truly."

"Seek and ye shall find," she whispered, mind beginning to blur.

"Yes," he whispered back. "Go way, way back... into the deepest recess of your mind."

Diving deep, she went swimming, stroking through the black, allowing the rise and fall of inky swells to carry her from honed intellect into something softer. Something elemental. Something ethereal. Something she knew lay waiting, dormant in the dark. Westvane's hands firmed on her shoulders. She welcomed the anchor and drifted, moving closer to the void she sensed, finding comfort in the silence, choosing faith over —

A glimmer winked through the blackness.

Truly turned toward the frayed outer edges of her mind. Faint at first, the light refracted, becoming a revolving beacon from distance shores. Her focus narrowed. Thought propulsion took hold, and she flew toward the small starburst. Its dimension expanded. Tendrils slithered from its center. Fireworks exploded into a colorful array, bursting onto the dark canvas of her mind.

Edges formed. Ridges grew. A light-filled shape grew out of the darkness.

She sucked in a breath. "I see it."

"Reach out. Push through. Open it up, Truly."

With an invisible hand, she prodded the edges. A strong wind blew through her mind, then gusted into the room. The icy chill clawed at her ponytail, whipping it across the back of her neck. Goosebumps rose on her skin. Westvane's heat retreated. She felt the weight of his hands, but the warmth... his heat no longer touched her.

Startled, Truly opened her eyes.

His fingers flexed on her shoulders. "Look."

She followed the tilt of his head. Her gaze tracked left and…
"Oh my God."

The door she'd seen in her mind now stood open on the other side of the room. Floating above the floor near the far wall. Tangible. Touchable. Unmistakable. As solid as Westvane. As plain as the nose on her face.

"It's real."

"Yes."

"I did that."

"Yes."

Wonder filled her. "I'm a Door Master."

"Was never in doubt." Lifting his hands, Westvane let her go. "Well done, princess."

His praise made her smile.

The corners of his eyes crinkled.

Amazed by the sight of the door, Truly pushed away from the wall. "Let's go."

"About time," Montrose said. "I told you th —"

"Move. Now," Westvane growled, cutting off the gargoyle.

Truly didn't argue. Pivoting toward the door, Truly hopped over an overturned chair, and dodging the lights dangling from the ceiling, ramped into a run. She heard the guys roll in behind her. Felt the thump of their footfalls on sagging floorboards, but something else, too. The building vibrated. A loud screech walked shivers up her spine. An engine roared. Steel groaned. The security wall ripped in half as it was yanked from the front window and door.

A thin, whistling noise tore across the shop.

Westvane cursed.

Montrose shouted, "Get down!"

Halfway to the magical door, Truly looked behind her. All she saw was Westvane. A fierce expression on his face, he closed the distance. Rough hands grabbed her. His wings came around her, protecting her as he lunged for the portal she'd opened.

A missile slammed into the shop.

The front of Montrose & Brim exploded.

A fireball raged into the room. Shrapnel blew inward as heat licked over her skin. One arm wrapped hard around her, Westvane stumbled sideways. The smell of burnt feathers and singed skin bubbled into the air.

With a snarl, Westvane spun into a quick rotation. Truly held on, trying to look past his wings, desperate to oriented herself. She didn't get the chance. One moment, he carried her. The next, he threw her, hurling her toward the portal ten feet away.

She yelled in protest.

Too little, too late.

She was already flying, heart in her throat, feet no longer on the ground, careening out of Earth Realm into the unknown.

THE DETONATION BLEW shards of brick and glass into the room. Fire followed, swelling into fury around him. Westvane felt the heat, endured the burn, smelled his singed feathers beneath the lashing flame. His back to the explosion, he stood firm, his eyes trained on Truly.

Her trajectory was true.

His throw pinpoint accurate.

In full flight, arms and legs wheeling, her back to the portal, she reached the threshold. She yelled his name, eyes wide with incredulousness and a healthy amount of rage. Like any warrior, she didn't want to leave the fight... or her comrades behind.

He understood the instinct. Welcomed the news she'd come

fully into the fold. No longer disbelieving, she'd accepted him and Montrose. No doubt in her scent. No shying away from the truth. No more resistance to the idea magic existed and that she played a key role in their kind's survival. That, however, didn't mean he'd permit her to be anywhere near the battle.

Her welfare was too important. Giving Truly time to grow into her power — into who and what she would become — was paramount. More important than his own survival.

She'd be angry when he caught up with her on the other side of the *Ecotone*. But at least she'd be alive. He could handle her temper. What he couldn't do was complete his mission with her dead.

With a murmur, Westvane conjured his weapons. Black flames engulfed his right hand as lightning sword formed. Smoke swirled around the other, the shield solidifying in front of him. Feet planted, fighting stance set, he watched Truly sail through the open doorway. Only then did he turn toward the battle. Weapons raised, he snarled at the armed men advancing on the building with guns raised. Aggression rolled through his veins. His eyes began to shimmer. The ravening luminosity washed into the street, striking at the contingent who were approaching with one mission in mind — the annihilation of Magickind.

As one, the men hesitated, stutter-stepping at the sight of him.

He bared pointed canines, raised his sword and —

"No!" Montrose roared behind him. A desk went flying, flashing through his periphery as the gargoyle rolled to his feet. "The door! Westvane, the —"

His focus flicked to where Truly had exited. The door expanded. The frame contracted. A loud *pop!* rippled a second before the glowing panel whiplashed, closing with a snap. The slam reverberated through the office. The light-filled seam sealed and went black, disappearing into thin air.

His heart contracted.

"No," he whispered as realization struck.

He'd miscalculated. His plan possessed a fatal flaw. One he hadn't considered.

Truly couldn't control her magic. As a Door Master, portals opened upon her command, but once she walked through, a door did what it had been designed to do — close in her wake, preventing others from slipping into the *Ecotone* behind her. She wasn't strong enough yet to hold a portal open. Hadn't learned the necessary tricks of her trade.

His hand flexed around his sword hilt. Goddess forgive him. He should have known. Should have anticipated and planned in accordance with the information available. If he had, she wouldn't now be in Azlandia — little more than a sitting duck without him to protect her.

The realization unleashed his rage.

Westvane turned back to the armed men crossing the sidewalk. He would kill them all. Eliminate the threat. Level entire buildings. Leave no trace of his enemy. Only then would he turn his attention to the new problem — getting across the *Ecotone* without Truly's help. He refused to leave her there: alone, vulnerable, easy pickings for a queen who would stop at nothing to see her dead.

18

ROTTEN LUCK

Pinwheeling across Montrose & Brim, Truly revolved into an uncontrollable flip in mid-air. A high-pitch whine whistled in her ears as she flew over the magical threshold. White fog swirled into a thick soup, blurring her view into Earth Realm. She lost sight of Westvane as high velocity blew her hair around. She clawed for a handhold, but found nothing but the air, her field of vison sheeting bright white.

She screamed for Westvane and Montrose.

They needed to reach the portal she'd opened. She couldn't leave either behind, stranded in Earth Realm, alone inside M&B with bombs exploding and a militia beating down the door.

Spinning through the air, Truly searched for a point of reference. Something to grab, the door frame, a ledge, something, anything to stop her flight into the murk. Soft as silk, wispy tendrils brushed over her skin, pulling at her limbs, drawing her backward, sending her tumbling toward darkness.

The haze thickened into milky shadows.

The outline of the door tunneled. Flames sparked around the frame. As fingers of fire licked over the seal, Truly grabbed for the handle. Her fingertips brushed against the warm surface.

The door slammed closed. Her mind screamed as she cursed between clenched teeth. Without meaning to, she'd closed the portal, walling off Westvane and Montrose's only avenue of escape while madmen attacked with rocket launchers, armored vehicles, and automatic weapons.

The realization ripped through her. Her friends were in serious trouble, and now, so was she.

Without Westvane by her side, she wouldn't stand a chance. She hadn't stood much of one when in Philadelphia — a city she knew, a place that knew her, too. If she struggled to survive in her hometown, how would she survive what awaited her beyond the *Ecotone*?

Westvane hadn't painted a pretty picture, and he lived in Azlandia. He'd been born and raised there. Grown up in the shadows of the Electi's cruel laws, rules, and regulations. As a hybrid, he was reviled for his mixed blood. As a Slayer, he was respected for his skills. He could hold his own in ways and in places she couldn't. At least, not yet. Landing in Azlandia — as an outsider, a magic wielder who didn't know how to use her power — without her guide was a bad idea.

If the people of Azlandia were anything like Earth Realm's human population, her sudden appearance would raise alarm bells. Fear would rise. Mobs would form. The queen's guards would be called. Lyonesse would come, and Truly would be executed on sight without the courtesy of being given a fair trial.

Over. Done. Zero paperwork to sign, nothing but a grave to dig.

Which meant she needed to go back. Right now. Before she landed on the other side of the *Ecotone* and the residents of Azlandia caught sight of her.

A great strategy. Slight problem in the execution of it, however.

No matter how much she fought the pull, the *Ecotone*

refused to reverse course. Moving like a fast conveyor belt, the strange mist carried her forward, racing toward something she couldn't see. She flailed. Twisting around her, it tightened its grip, spinning her upright, sitting her down in an invisible cradle that felt a lot like a first-class seat inside an airplane.

A death grip on the armrest she couldn't see, Truly slammed her feet down. The heels of her boots skipped over something. Water splashed up, splattering over her ankles to soak her pant legs. As damp air swirled, wind tugged at her ponytail. Sweat bloomed beneath her clothes as an unseen force lifted her feet, prompting her to sit cross-legged in her seat. The chair swayed, then dipped, cutting through milky-white film.

The veil tore open.

Heavy mist cleared, exposing an incredible vista.

Dark skies rimmed by blue shimmer. Mountains capped by snowy peaks on the distant horizon, a border beyond an expanse of inky sea. Patches of translucent fog hovered above the smooth, black surface, floating like boats, bobbing in a light breeze. An invisible web flexed across the sky, coming alive as it drew a breath. Truly sensed the inhale. Experienced the exhale, lived and breathed with the *Ecotone*, aligning with the spirit that called the sliver between worlds home.

Worry dropped away. Wonder sufficed her. Lost in time and space, she reached out. Her fingertips met slight resistance, trailing across the invisible weave. Tiny sparks cascaded, diving like falling stars toward the sea.

The still, glass-like surface rippled.

Huge cobra-shaped heads popped up like periscopes, slicing out of water into open air. Astonishment battered her. Terror made her tense. She froze in her seat as the sea serpents spotted her. As a group, the nest followed her flight across the top of the water. Brilliant green eyes glinted in the lowlight. Serpentine bodies covered in white scales uncoiled. Water rippled as bladed fins glimmering, three giant snakes swam out of the shallows, watching her approach from far too close.

Truly tucked her limbs in tighter.

A forked tongue flicked out as the lead serpent spoke, "Turnbolt."

"Door Massssster," the second one hissed.

The third chimed in. "Finally."

As a unit, the trio stilled as she sailed past. "Welcome. Welcome, welcome, welcome."

The chant echoed over the ocean.

Turning in her seat, Truly glanced over her shoulder at what any sane person would consider monsters, then did something odd. By rote, as though she did it every day, she lifted her hand and waved. Needle-sharp fangs flashed in the gloom as the trio grinned back.

Incredible. Also... really, *really* strange.

Then again, normal was a distance memory for her. She'd blown past it twenty-four hours ago. The past was so done, it was gone. The world she inhabited now operated under different principles. She needed to stop being surprised by the oddities. Part of that included tossing out obsolete definitions to make room for new ones. The sooner she acclimated and accepted the seeming inconsistencies, the quicker she'd get to play by her own rules.

Speeding away from the sea serpents, Truly bumped over an uneven patch. The chair underneath her swung one way, then the other. Her stomach pitched. Blue shimmer disappeared. The silken bonds wrapped around her vanished. Her seat bucked, tossing her overboard. Water rose up to meet her. Heart in her throat, she tucked into a ball, preparing to hit, knowing it would hurt, about to —

White-tipped claws speared out of the darkness.

Truly jerked as leathery fingers grabbed hold. The hand

jerked her sideways, dragging her through the air. Darkness faded. Light bloomed. Streaming from corner to corner, the blazing trail formed into a doorway. Heat rippled around her. Hanging like a ghoul in mid-air, covered in vines, half-eaten by decay, a door materialized over open water.

Hinges squawked as the portal creaked open.

Seeing nothing but blur, Truly flew over the threshold. One moment, she was weightless. The next, gravity took hold. She landed hard, slamming into the ground, then rolled. Gravel scraped over her jeans. A jumbled of sticks raked over her side. With a curse, she twisted mid-slide. Dust billowed up as she dug her heels into the ground, and using her jacket to protect her forearms, pressed down with her elbows to halt her skid.

She came to a rasping stop on a compact surface and noticed three things straight off. One, it was dark, obviously night in Azlandia. Two, she'd come to a sudden stop in the middle of a one-lane street. And three, squat brick buildings lined both sides of the narrow road.

Breathing hard, ignoring the scrapes and bruises, she rolled to the balls of her feet. Crouched in the moonlight, she shuffled backwards, sinking into the shadows along the side of the road. Her back butted up against the side of a one-story building. The dust cloud settled. Her line of sight improved. A town of some kind. A small one, given what she could see, which meant she'd landed in a place populated by Azlandians, instead of in the middle of nowhere.

Truly scowled at the brick building opposite her. Of all the rotten luck. Landing in a field, far from anyone or anything would've been safer. Better for her continued good health. An easier environment to navigate, a quieter place for her to figure out the next steps.

Scuttling along a stone wall, she stayed low and kept to the shadows. She needed to get out of the street — and find a place to lie low — before one of the inhabitants decided to come out and investigate. A distinct possibility. Her landing hadn't been quiet. She'd fallen straight out of the sky and hit the ground... hard. Sleepy village or not, someone, at some point, would pop their head out of their front door. She wanted to be far, far away before that happened. Maybe even back through a —

Realization scored through her. "A door."

She needed to conjure another door. If she managed to open a portal, she could walk out of Azlandia, back into Philadelphia, with no one being the wiser.

On her haunches next to a garden wall, Truly took a shaky breath and closed her eyes. Inky waves swelled behind her lids. Clinging to Westvane's advice, she sank into the darkness, searching for the spark. Side to side. Up and down. Nearer, then farther. She traveled miles inside her mind, but went nowhere at all... and found even less. Not a single pinpoint of light. No answering pulse of power in her veins. Just a great swath of blackness, and a stillness so absolute Truly knew the magic had deserted her.

"Goddamn it," she murmured, worry mixing with fear. "Move. Get to safety, find shelter, then try again later."

Sound advice. A wise approach, even if the whispered words didn't comfort her. Forging ahead into the unknown was scary. Truly told herself to go anyway. Move quietly. Do it strategically. One step at a time, instead of rushing ahead. Imagining all the terrible possibilities wouldn't serve her. The second she got too far ahead of herself, panic would set in, pushing her into making a mistake that would alert the Electi who lived in Azlandia.

Looking both ways, she scooted around the end of a garden wall. She kept her footfalls light and her eyes peeled, using thick shrubbery to shield her movements, searching for the quickest route out of town. After she left the Azlandian settlement behind, she'd look for a hidey-hole. A place to rest and recharge. Somewhere she wouldn't be spotted. Somewhere she could blend in, a place people wouldn't immediately identify her as an outsider. A city would be best, one with a large population, too busy to notice a stranger walked amongst them.

She might even be able to locate Brim.

Other than opening another door, finding Montrose's wife seemed like the next best option. Brim might not know her, but she'd know what to do. Westvane said gargoyles were scholars, teachers, the intellectuals of Azlandian society. Astute individuals who loved learning, and she hoped (at least for her sake) hated Lyonesse as much as Montrose.

Blood rushing in her ears, Truly crept across an alley, then sprinted across someone's lawn. Please God, let Westvane be right about gargoyles. If he spoke true, Montrose's biting personality broke the mold, running contrary to a normal gargoyle's nature. If she got lucky, Brim would be helpful instead of hostile, calm and calculating, able and willing to hide her until she found a way back through the *Ecotone*.

Wet grass underfoot, she moved from house to house, dodging rain barrels and stone pathways, slipping through hedges and raised garden beds with well-tended vegetable patches. Picking her way past some stables, she entered another backyard. She glanced over her shoulder. Her foot slipped on heavy dew. Stumbling sideways, she reached out to stop her fall and —

Her hand collided with the side of a stone cottage. A hoe and two shovels started to fall. She reached for the long handles. Her fingers brushed against wood, but slipped out of range, hitting the stone walkway with a *clang*!

Heart hammering, Truly froze.

A light came on, slashing across narrow porch steps, cutting across the yard. The thud of heavy footfalls sounded. Metal creaked. The door swung open. A man stopped on the threshold, his shadow cutting a swath across freshly cut grass. He waited. She remained unmoving next to a wide trellis.

Stay still. Stay calm. Be smart.

The instructions unspooled like ticker tape in her mind. Night blooming roses nodded overhead, smelling sweet, as a huge figure stepped onto the porch. Shadows concealed his front, throwing his silhouette into sharp contrast, making her realize it wasn't a man. Her first clue was the rap of hooves hitting wooden planks as he strode to the edge of the deck. Her second was the tall, twisted horns rising from his temples. She couldn't see his face. Didn't need to either, for her imagination to conjure up all the horrible possibilities.

The urge to run thumped through her.

Contracting into a smaller ball, she stayed still and silent, her gaze locked on the beast now walking down the steps. Treads groaned beneath his hooves. A thick dark mane fell around his horns, brushing his shoulders, as he scanned the backyard.

Hidden beneath a fall of leafy foliage, Truly pressed her hand over her mouth, quieting her breath, wanting to run, knowing she wouldn't make it. No way would she able to outdistance, well... whatever Azlandians called his species. The hooves suggested swiftness. The horns on his head promised violence. Not the best combination when planning a foot race against an opponent, never mind a full-frontal assault.

His nostrils flared as he scanned the yard again.

She held her breath.

His eyes narrowed on the back wall where she hid.

Adrenaline hit her like rocket fuel. Her muscles quivered. She quelled the urge to run, and focus locked on him, pictured the interior of M&B. Her senses contracted. Perception expanded. Information filtered in, allowing her to sense the

Ecotone and what lay on the other side of it. A picture formed in her mind's eye. Westvane appeared on her mental screen. Wings folded, weapons raised, a snarl on his face, dead bodies littered the ground at his feet.

Her breath caught as realization struck. Even here, on the other side of the *Ecotone*, she remained tethered to Philadelphia. She could feel and see Westvane through the vast expanse, knew exactly where he stood. All she needed to do was find the thread and pull him through.

Gaze glued to the porch, Truly allowed her mind to tunnel. Body present in the here and now, mind combing through the mental-scape, she searched for the spark. She failed again... and again. Over and over, unable to find the light as the Azlandian stepped onto the path, casting a long shadow over a rambling pumpkin patch.

With no assistance on the horizon, Truly started to pray. For a little luck. For more time. For her magic to come back and open a door, allowing her return to Philadelphia.

Luck was all she asked. Time all she needed. Magic all she desired. Before the man-beast spotted her, and she died a horrific death in the middle of small town Azlandia.

19

FAR TOO RISKY

The window seat wasn't comfortable. Then again, nothing inside the Winter Palace aspired to those levels. Comfort had never been a priority inside the great stone fortress. Form followed function. Necessity lorded over luxury. Utilitarian came before beauty. Her father hadn't aspired to anything else. Well, other than charity and the human witch who'd beguiled him.

Adjusting the lumpy pillow behind her back, Lyonesse curled her wings close, creating a cocoon for herself, and stared out into the abyss. No beauty to be found out there. Just howling wind, barren mountain peaks, and miles and miles of snow. Ice crystals formed on the windowpanes, mocking her while she waited for the machine to work.

She'd hear it from where she sat in the dusty antechamber, a short walk across the corridor from her father's favorite room. The place the machine called home.

Picking at her cuticles, she frowned at her nails. Filed into sharp points, the ink-black tips lightened to pale pink paint. Glossy. Perfect application. Stunning in its effect. The artistry made her feel pretty and powerful. Her father would've scoffed at the idea, calling her fascination with the beauty industry an exercise in vanity.

The thought set her teeth on edge.

Maybe Leonidas was right. Maybe she enjoyed primping too much. Maybe that made her vain, but what did she care? She was a queen with a vison for the future — strong-willed, powerful, chosen by divine right. And a king who abandoned his blood kin in favor of an outsider didn't deserve the privilege of opinion.

Shifting on the hard bench seat, Lyonesse glanced toward the entrance. The double doors stood open, providing a clear view across the hall into the machine's chamber. She glared at it. Ridiculous contraption. Such an antiquated way of communicating. What the devil had her father been thinking...

And what the devil was taking so long?

Time in Earth Realm mirrored Azlandia's, same flow, same twenty-four-hour clock and 365 days a year. Hours had passed without word. More than enough time for Isaac to hunt and capture the Door Master. *Honestly — what the devil was he doing?* The Yeomanry should've contacted her by now.

Impatience rolled into restlessness. She readjusted her wings. Snow pelted against the glass panes next to her, dragging icy fingers over the sill. Cold air drifted into the room. Eyes narrowed on the icicles hanging from the roofline, Lyonesse clenched her fists and spun in her seat. Her feet hit the floor with a thump. The wood of her well-heeled shoes struck stone. The rap echoed as she strode across the room. Probably a bad idea, but she couldn't sit still any longer.

Standing post in the hallway, Anckar looked around the jamb. "My queen?"

"I'm tired of waiting."

"We all are, majesty," he said, blue eyes fixed to her face.

"But we knew it would take time. Humans are unreliable creatures."

"Hang them all," she muttered, her temper slipping. If she could, she would rip the *Ecotone* from its moorings and leave Earth Realm to float away. Into the abyss. Into emptiness. Let them stew in the filth they created. Reaching the threshold, she stopped beneath the soaring archway. "Have you and the others eaten?"

"Yes, majesty," he said, gesturing to the long table that had been set up in the main corridor. "Only you have not."

She wasn't hungry. She'd lost her appetite the second she realized a Door Master breathed, living carefree in Earth Realm. "Make sure the table is kept well-stocked. I don't want any of you to suffer while trapped in this God-forsaken —"

A rumble shook the granite slab beneath her feet.

Air left her lungs in a rush.

"No," she rasped, the infinitesimal threads of her feathers standing on end.

"Another door." Stepping close, Anckar raised his fists, intent on protecting her from an invisible threat. "So soon. It's too soon. My Queen —"

"Quiet," she said between clenched teeth. Magic seething, her vision-eye opened inside her mind. Perception expanded as she set the magical eye sailing above her lands, seeking the location of the open door. Rage stirred behind her breastbone. "The faithless witch. She's crossed over. She's in Azlandia."

Anckar growled, low sound full of affront. "You're sure?"

"She's here," she snarled back at her guard.

"Where?"

Lyonesse tilted her head, fine-tuning the eye to pinpoint the signal. Pink shimmer washed in, dusting her cerebral landscape. The magical flight stopped. She hovered over the red cliffs, not far from the ocean shore. "Near Forrestarian."

"But that's close to —"

"Ipsalar." The Capital City... the seat of Azlandia, Lyonesse's home. A small town in the Southern Kingdom, Forrestarian lay nestled against the cliffs, not far from the endless sea, on the edge of the lands given to her at birth by her father. An Assenta stronghold, a place where Electi rarely ventured and were not welcome. "Assemble the guard."

"Majesty," Anckar said, deep voice rumbling. "We're too far north. It'll take a day of flying to reach it. And with this weather —"

"Even longer." Pacing into the corridor, Lyonesse pivoted toward her guard. "Who remains in the Capital?"

"That we trust?"

She nodded.

"Priestly. Although..." her guard paused. "He remains unmotivated."

A diplomatic way of putting it.

Priestly was a wild card — at best a lazy, self-indulgent prick; at worst, a cunning, insubordinate jackal. Add spoiled by his doting mother into the mix and...

Lyonesse sighed. Not the best guard to send after a Door Master. Then again, as inept as she considered Priestly, he did do one thing well — fight. He never missed an opportunity to embarrass her favored guards with his skills.

"Majesty," Anckar said, "If Priestly doesn't please you, we have another option."

"The crystals?" Flexing her hands, she shook her head. "Not optimal. We'll need to make multiple jumps. With no guarantee of landing close to Forrestarian."

"Too risky."

Far too risky. She didn't want to make a mistake. Too many had been made already, and with dematerialization crystals involved, she couldn't predict the outcome.

The precious stones taken from the core of Azlandia (mined in the deepest recesses of her realm) no longer generated the same power. For generations, her people had taken the natural resource for granted, using crystals for everything from ready light sources to teleportation. The stones had been taken from the ground by the trolley-full for centuries. Now, few remained, the quality of each less powerful. Which made rematerializing in the correct spot almost impossible while bending time and space.

If she opened her dwindling cache and used one, she might end up ten thousand miles from the location she needed to land.

"Get word to Priestly," she ordered, whirling toward the machine room. "And prepare my guard. We fly the moment the storm clears."

Anckar murmured his assent.

Lyonesse nodded in approval. Perfect obedience. Such a lovely trait. She only hoped Priestly behaved half as well.

20

SLOW AND STEADY

Broken by the call of crickets, eerie quiet stretched as Truly watched the horned behemoth from her place in the undergrowth. Right now, slow and steady won the race. Silence added a key element, but she needed to be ready for anything. Ready to inch forward. Ready to stay put. Ready to run without looking back, though intuition warned her running would be a mistake.

The man-beast staring into his backyard looked fast. Far too quick for her to outrun.

Truly swallowed as he turned his head. As he scanned, the twist of his horns cast horrifying shadows across the lawn. He continued searching. She remained frozen, waiting for him to decide all was well. Insects chirped, chipping away at the quiet, pushing a soothing song into the garden.

A lost opportunity, given she didn't feel soothed at all.

She was stretched thin, fragile skin wrapped over hollowed-out bones. Barely breathing, she watched and waited, the beat of her heart throbbing in her ears.

He turned on the stone path. Toward his home. Away from her.

Releasing a pent-up breath, she ghosted from beneath a branch of night-blooming roses. Her strategy was simple. Her plan straightforward — move soundlessly to, then around the end of the stone wall. Get out of his yard unseen, but more importantly, unscathed.

Focus fixed on the man-beast's back, she crept sideways. Open blooms the size of a closed fist bobbed above her head. Thick foliage brushed her shoulders. A thin whisper of sound escaped her hidey-hole.

His head snapped back in her direction. An instant later, he lunged across the yard. His hooves slammed down next to the flower bed. She heard him land. She felt his aggression. Terror raged into a wildfire, ripping good sense away as Truly whipped around. Feet churning in loose soil, she grabbed the wooden trellis anchored to the back wall.

He growled.

She cursed. Stupid, stupid... *stupid*. She should've remained unmoving until the front door closed behind him. But like an idiot, she'd given herself away. Too late now to change a bad decision to good. She was committed, and now must climb. *Climb* as though her life depended on it.

Catapulting herself over the brick wall remained the only option. It didn't matter what lay on the other side — a prickly thorn bush, another monster, Dante's Inferno and its nine circles of Hell. Nothing mattered but avoiding the man-beast and getting away. Before he grabbed hold of her and dragged her out of the darkness into the light.

Thin, sharp wooden edges scraped across her palms. Thorns from the rose bush nicked her skin. Blood welled on the backs of her hands.

Truly ignored the pain and listened to self-preservation. Her heart took up the cause, thumping hard, delivering adrenaline, propelling her upward. She climbed fast, fighting through foliage, searching for handholds, refusing to look back. Getting caught wouldn't end well for her. She was an outsider in a strange land, a human surrounded by a host of magical creatures. Who knew what Azlandians would do to her if —

A clatter rose behind her.

A large hand fisted in the back of her coat.

She yelled, and with a quick twist, shed her leather jacket. He snarled. She kept going, eyes trained on the top of the wall. Ripped from their mooring, rose petals flew into freefall around her, the sweet smell spoiled by the scent of her fear.

"Oh, no you don't," the behemoth said, latching onto one of her ankles. "Come here, you."

He yanked.

Truly lost her handhold.

She landed on the grass beside his hooved feet. Not wasting a second, she rolled to avoid him. She wasn't fast enough. One second, she lay on the ground. The next, he latched on, subduing her with ease. She struggled. He reacted by tightening the stranglehold. Grasping her by the throat, he heaved her off the ground.

Chin pressed to the top of his fist, feet dangling in the air, she got her first good look at him. Twisting black horns. Umber-hued skin and angled cheekbones. Big hands with hooked claws, strong limbs, pale hazel eyes with almond-shaped pupils.

"Let go," she rasped, kicking at his midriff with her feet. Her boots swung wide. The man-beast shook her, making her teeth rattle. "Put me down."

He bared sharp teeth. "Shut up."

Light footsteps echoed along the garden path. "What is it, Samarin? Another warbel?"

Samarin lifted her a bit higher. His brow crinkled, making her aware he had no eyebrows as he examined her. A look of disgust crossed his features. He glanced over his shoulder at whoever stood behind him. "A human."

A female version Samarin blinked in confusion. "A what?"

"A thing from Earth Realm."

"Good eating, do you think?" she asked, staring at Truly as though she hadn't eaten in a month. "Something for the stew pot?"

Samarin shook her again.

Leaves dislodged and fell from her hair.

He tilted his head as though considering. Truly held her breath. She needed this to go her way. No way would she allow anyone to eat her. Samarin's eyes narrowed. He studied her a second longer, then shrugged, glancing from her to his companion. "Let's find out."

Breath stalled in the back of her throat.

"Hang on a second!" Flailing in his grasp, Truly wrapped both hands around his wrist. She yanked, trying to loosen his hold.

Rolling his eyes, expression annoyed, Samarin dropped her. Her bootheels struck the garden path. Her backside followed with a thump. A gasp escaped her. Surprise made her slow, giving him time to re-establish a grip on one of her ankles. With a grunt, he began dragging her across the lawn toward the cottage.

Desperation took hold.

She didn't care how hungry the pair were, she couldn't allow it. Refused to let it happen. She had options. She had friends (sort of, if Westvane could be called a friend). All she needed to do was try to reach him.

Try.

Then, if all else failed, try again.

Squeezing her eyes closed, Truly ignored the draw of the cold, wet grass against her jeans and searched for the spark. The black expanse of her mind greeted her. She looked harder, clawing through mental fringes as Samarin dragged her closer to his back door... and his wife's stew pot.

Terror dredged up an echo of magic. Light eked out of the darkness. Not quite a spark. More of a sputter, but she refused to complain.

She zeroed in on the source instead.

Holding an image of Montrose & Brim's, the street, her car in its parking spot, inside her head, she aimed her magic. If she could open a door close to the shop, Westvane would be able to detect it. If he reached it, the Slayer would walk through it.

Truly wondered, a bit hysterically, if she'd lost her mind. Her unshakable belief in Westvane suggested she was spinning into uncharted territory. She didn't care. What other choice did she have? She was no match for Samarin, or the perils that lay inside Azlandia.

So she did the only thing she could.

She blew on the spark, fanned the flame, trying to build it into an inferno, praying her magic obeyed and her gamble paid off. Hoping she was right, and if she provided the way, Westvane would walk through the door she opened before Samarin reached the stew pot and made a meal out of her.

21

JUST STARTING TO HAVE FUN

Pivoting on the sidewalk outside Montrose & Brim, Westvane kept his eyes trained on the enemy. Protected by a line of vehicles angled in the street, the Yeomanry retreated as he snarled. He wanted to laugh. He settled for baring his teeth instead. The idiots. Did they really think they stood a chance? Against him? With his magic humming — and the sword and shield in his hands — the combat unit assembled fifty feet away was all but finished.

About to be done.

Cooked. Flambéed. Skinned alive.

Whatever.

Five minutes tops, and the fools would be dead. Nothing but disarticulated corpses. Lying in bloody piles in the middle of a city street.

A human in charge yelled out instructions, calling for further retreat.

Westvane smiled, flashing elongated canines. Eyes wide with fear, an enemy solider panicked and raised a rocket launcher. The fresh-faced youth fired the weapon. Time slowed. A high-pitched whine erupted as the missile shot from its casing.

Ducking his head, Westvane brought his shield up and shifted to his right.

The missile rocketed over him. The smoke inside his shield seethed. The bomb slammed into the building behind him. Concrete, brick, and glass exploded up and out, then rained down. Spinning out of a crouch, Westvane swung his sword, aiming for one of the armored vehicles.

Lightning flashed from the tip.

Electricity arched, burning a path through smoked-filled air, then struck. The military truck blew sky high, flipping end over end, sailing above the streetlamps. The group hiding behind it shouted and scrambled. The smell of gasoline suffused the air. Westvane slammed his shield into the pavement. Sparks snapped against the edge. The accelerant caught fire. Blue flames streaked toward the puddle of fuel as the truck finished going up and started to come down. The wind rush scraped over the fine threads of his singed feathers.

He folded his wings.

Pain burned through him. Rage rippled in its wake.

The human platoon didn't know whom they faced. The burns he'd suffered in the first explosion inside the shop only served to piss him off. Now he didn't want to just kill the Yeomanry. He wanted to give the task special attention. Tear each man apart. Make the dissection painful. Ensure the torture lasted... and lasted... and *lasted*.

Twisted metal that used to be a truck slammed into pavement.

Fire burst from the engine block, over the hood into the cab.

Smoke billowed into the street.

Stepping off the concrete curb, Westvane cut a swath through the fray. Tossing a car aside, he slammed his shield into the soldiers rushing him. Three went flying. Blood sprayed, painting the asphalt red, the crunch of bones echoing as he sighted the leader. Standing behind an array of armored vehicles, his men between him and danger, the commander shouted orders.

His eyes narrowed. New prey. The yeoman he wanted. The one who needed to be killed most. The one he'd —

"Westvane!"

"What?" he snarled, kicking the limp body off the end of his sword. Pivoting right, he skewered another human, then glanced toward Montrose.

Blood dripping from his claws, the gargoyle finished snapping a yeoman's neck, then pointed toward the side street. "Look!"

The black death trap Truly called a car sat unscathed next to the curb. And beyond it — the shimmering edge of a doorway. Not open completely, just cracked at the frame. Enough for him to see the glow beyond the threshold.

"Hell," he growled. Talk about bad timing. He was just beginning to have fun.

"We need to go," Montrose yelled, running toward him. "She can only hold it open so long. We need to —"

Something exploded.

Shrapnel flew in a wide arch.

Blown sideways, the gargoyle stumbled to his knees.

Knowing Montrose was right, Westvane didn't hesitate. With a muttered curse, he sheathed his sword, putting it away inside his mind as he reached for Montrose. Precious seconds passed before he grabbed hold of the gargoyle. Raising his shield, he protected their backs as he turned and lunged toward the portal.

More yelling. The rumble of chaos behind him.

He heard two more missiles launch.

Reaching the doorway between worlds, Westvane hammered the opening with his shoulder. The panel resisted, the seam half sealed, holding firm. He pushed harder. An explosion rocked the ground. Fire licked up his back, attacking his wings. The smell of burnt feathers and flesh rose, making him stumble. The door gave way. Opening. Widening. Hinges groaning as he shoved Montrose into the *Ecotone* and followed in his wake.

TRULY TWISTED, fighting the hand wrapped like a shackle around her ankle.

With a grunt, Samarin continued to drag her toward the house. Fresh-cut grass clung to her pant legs. She clung to hope, kicking her out with her free foot, clawing at the ground to keep from being dragged forward.

Her effort didn't make a difference.

Samarin kept walking. She kept struggling. What she needed was leverage, a weapon of some kind, something to make him stop, drop her and back the hell off.

Too bad all she had were her fists... and fingernails.

Bent in half, she clawed at the back of his hand.

Samarin growled at her.

The nasty sound settled low, vibrating through her ribcage, making her heart pound harder as he heaved her up the stairs. Her knees fired like pistons. The backs of her boots clattered against the wooden treads. She arched wildly, rearing like a stallion, gaze ping-ponging, thoughts jumbled and chaotic.

She needed something to grab onto. The edge of a board. One of the porch columns. A piece of outdoor furniture. Whatever. The object didn't matter as long it stopped Samarin from hauling her through the door and into the house.

Chest heaving, fighting for each breath, Truly grabbed the edge of the last step with both hands. Samarin yanked. She held firm, clinging to the board like a lifeline.

"Stubborn little thing." Fingers twisted in her pant leg, he adjusted his grip. "Probably terrible eating. Tough and sour, I bet."

The pause, his musings about how she'd taste coming out of the stew pot, allowed her to suck in a full breath. It also gave her a second to think. She scowled at the behemoth trying to pry her from her perch as she flipped through possible strategies, searching looking for a solution — *the* solution — that would stop him where he stood.

She held one advantage.

Well, more than one — if her magic worked as Westvane assured her it would. Some day. At some point. Probably at a date too far in the future. But that complaint needed to wait for another time. Right now, she didn't have Westvane's sword at her disposal. All she owned was smarts, guts, and a little bit of knowledge. Not a lot, but maybe enough to turn the situation in her favor.

The way forward came to her like a lightning flash. Maybe if Samarin understood who she was, he'd get on board with the idea she wasn't meant to be anyone's meal.

Leaning down, Samarin reached for her hand. His intention clear — he planned to pry her loose.

Curled on her side, Truly protected her grip on the tread. "Don't you dare!"

"Stop fighting."

"I am a Door Master. Release me at once —"

He snorted. "Sure you are."

His amusement ignited her temper. "I am! How do you

think I got here from Earth Realm? Humans don't live here. We live over there, you live over here. Simple enough to understand."

Thick fingers flexed around her wrist. Samarin paused in his attempt to pry her free.

"Look, I know it's weird," she said, determined to convince him.

"Weird? Don't know that word. What's it mean?"

She translated, tossing out synonyms. "Odd. Strange. Unusual."

His grip on her wrist lightened.

Porch planks creaked as he hit his haunches next to her.

Truly remained still, every muscle tense, refusing to lessen her grip on the board. Her statement might've stopped his forward progress, but that didn't mean the drag-and-tow wouldn't start up again. Distrust combined with a healthy dose of prudence seemed the way to go, given the level of his commitment. He could be trying to trick her. Could be hoping she'd let down her guard. Could be deciding what seasonings to use before trussing her up and tossing her into a human-sized stew pot.

His odd hazel eyes met hers. "Well then, Oh-Exalted-One — open a door."

Her stomach clenched. Bile touched the back of her throat.

She swallowed the burn, knowing she was in even bigger trouble now. Samarin wanted proof. And her magic was shot, winking out, barely sparking. The faint glow persisted, swimming around the edge of her mind, but she could hardly see it now. Blackness kept washing back in, rolling over the light, erasing the glow a little at a time.

Truly searched for it anyway. All she needed to do was —

A brilliant starburst broke across the backyard.

Like a welder's rod sparking, magic zigzagged into sharp

blue lines. A crack appeared in the open air. A doorframe took shape, hovering above the grass. Illumination streamed across the pathway, up the stairs, nearly blinding her.

Shrieking split the night, quieting cricket song.

The door slammed open.

Montrose sailed over the threshold. He landed with a thump. Arms and legs flailing, cursing like a drunken sailor, her former boss spun across the grass. Billowing like a sheet of gauze, wispy edges of *Ecotone* floated out of the portal. Fresh air blew across the yard. Stride even, pace steady, a winged shadow approached from inside the breach. Truly held her breath as Westvane dipped his head beneath the curved lintel and stepped into Samarin's backyard.

His boots touched down, flattening the grass.

Magic swirled inside her mind, heating her temples and...

The door swung shut. A gradual closing. Quiet and clean, absorbing all sound, a soft stirring sigh carried away on a warm wind.

Westvane caught sight of her. Her brows snapped together. An instant later, he snarled.

Samarin flinched. His hand spasmed around her wrist. Tearing her eyes off Westvane, she looked up at the man-beast. Startled by Westvane's appearance, he remained motionless as fear drew his features taut. Color leeched from his complexion, turning the beautiful umber hue ash-gray.

"Thank God," she whispered, sagging against the steps. "Thank God."

Ignoring her thankfulness, Westvane raised a brow. "Got yourself into some trouble, princess?"

She ignored the sarcasm. Right then, at that precise moment, she didn't care about his warped sense of humor. She was too grateful, so relieved to see him she wanted to hug him until his ribs cracked.

"A little," she said, bumping down the steps on her backside.

His brows popped up.

"Okay, maybe more than just a little."

"Figures." His lips twitched as she collapsed in a heap at the bottom of the stairs. Humor warmed the usual chill in his eyes.

An illusion, no doubt. A flight of fancy, the wild flickering of her imagination. How did she know? The warmth in his gaze didn't last.

Ice cold, the chill came back, leaving a cruel expression in its place as his attention shifted to Samarin. Dark eyes flat with the threat of violence, Westvane tilted his head, the viciousness he conveyed so profound Truly shivered in reaction. No need to translate. Things were about to get messy in a very unpleasant way.

Rolling his shoulders, Westvane resettled his wings.

Hooves clattering, Samarin scrambled to his feet. He raised his hands, palms up, and stepped back, distancing himself from her. "She belongs to you?"

Westvane's nostrils flared. "Close enough."

Samarin swallowed. "I didn't mean —"

"Are you hurt?" he asked, lethal tone cracking through the quiet.

Slow to understand, Truly blinked. "Who — me?"

"Not talking to Montrose, princess." Focus locked on Samarin, Westvane stepped onto the stone path.

"No." The response came out weak, unsure, completely unconvincing. Brushing a clump of hair out of her eyes, she pulled in a steadying breath. "Freaked out, but not hurt."

"Forgive me, Slayer." Hitting one knee, Samarin bowed his head. The horns on his head quivered as he exposed the back of his neck. Not a good sign. She'd seen her fair share of war movies. Medieval warriors acted much the same when faced with certain death, inviting a quick strike. One that would sever the spinal cord and result in a clean kill. "I didn't mean to trespass."

Silence stretched, then widened into something else. Something more. Something harsh and lethal and altogether intolerable. Violence rode on the wind, beating like a drum, raising the fine hairs on the back of her neck, making her skin crawl. What was Westvane doing? Trying to decide how to kill Samarin? End him quickly? Or draw the brutality out into something slow, agonizing, and bloody?

Truly's mouth went dry.

Her eyes bounced between the two.

The idea Westvane might kill Samarin rubbed her the wrong way. The man-beast might've intended to eat her, but executing him over a misunderstanding didn't seem fair. Granted, she wasn't from Azlandia. Didn't know the customs or traditions — or how one warrior atoned after insulting another. Death, though, seemed too steep a price to pay. She'd been the one trespassing on his property, which meant...

Truly sighed.

No way around it — she must intervene. And do it fast, before Westvane did whatever he planned, and she lost the opportunity to stop him.

Formulating her argument, Truly opened her mouth.

Westvane beat her to it. "Your name?"

"Samarin," he said, horns twisting into tighter spirals. Head still bowed, he gestured toward his companion. Kneeling by his side, the woman stared at the porch floor, tears in her eyes. "My mate, Meniva."

"You're an Assenta."

"Yes, my liege."

"Get up, Samarin," Westvane said as he reached for her. Truly didn't hesitate. Given the vicious vibe in the air, she accepted the invitation and slid her hand into his. With a tug, he pulled her to her feet. "An Assenta kneels for no one."

Samarin glanced up, surprise in his eyes.

"Up. Now. On your hooves," Westvane said, growling at him before his attention returned to Truly. Raising her hand, he held it out to one side. A furrow between his brows, he looked her over again. "You sure? Nothing broken?"

"All good." Standing a bit taller, Truly nodded to reassure him. Two sets of hooves scraped across wooden planks. She glanced at Samarin and his mate, seeing they'd gained their feet, then moved her focus back to Westvane. "A few scrapes and bruises. Nothing serious. I'm ready to roll."

"Good." He dropped her hand and, ignoring the pair on the porch, glanced over his shoulder. "Montrose?"

A horrible racket came from the hedge on the other side of the lawn. A clawed fist punched through the foliage. The plant reacted, thick wooden vines slithering, tightening, creating some kind of cage. Montrose cursed. His snout appeared through the greenery. A second hand punched through. Fangs flashed in the low light. A fight ensued. With a snarl, her friend emerged, yanking off sticky foliage, cutting through the horde of clinging vines.

He stepped free.

The plant reacted, green limbs reaching out to re-establish a grip.

Montrose hopped out of reach. Standing a safe distance away, he glared at the hedge and shook like a dog, dislodging the leaves stuck in his fur. "Stupid Verbanthamum. Didn't miss *that* fucking stuff while I was away."

Truly wanted to reply. She didn't bother. After witnessing a plant try to eat him, she had no idea what to say, so instead of trying, she turned to Westvane. "I'm tapped out. No way I can reopen a door right now."

"Recovery time?"

She shrugged. "Your guess is as good as mine."

"Shit," Montrose said. "We need to move. We stay here much longer, the queen's guard will find and track us."

Moving to stand between her and the steps, Westvane glanced at Samarin. "Where are we?"

"Forrestarian," Samarin said. "Seventy miles south of Ipsalar."

"I've never been." Westvane glanced at Montrose. "Are you familiar with Ipsalar?"

Montrose tipped his chin.

Truly threw him a sidelong glance. Something in his expression tweaked her. Warned her. Made her watchful as she asked, "How familiar?"

An odd light entered his eyes. "Very. I know the city like the back of my hand."

She became even more alert as understanding struck. "Brim's there."

"Bull's-eye, Triple." Montrose's mouth curved, exposing the tips of his fangs.

"As good a place to hide as any. At least, until I can access my magic again." She turned to Westvane, gauging his reaction. "Sound like a plan?"

"It'll be a trek, princess," he said. "You up for a road trip?"

"Do I have a choice?"

"No."

"Then why're you asking?"

"Attitude," he grumbled. "The trip through the *Ecotone* did nothing to improve your personality."

She huffed.

Shaking his head, Westvane turned from her and mounted the porch steps.

His wing-tips slid across the treads, rustling against wood.

Inky feathers fluttered then settled as he stopped in front of Samarin. While struggling with him, Truly thought Samarin was huge. Too broad. Too strong. An unbeatable foe, but... Westvane was taller, broader, much more menacing.

"You'll cover our tracks?" Westvane asked, studying his fellow Assenta.

"Should anyone come looking, my liege, no one will know you were here." Thumping his fist against his chest, Samarin bowed his head, showing respect like a solider would his commander. "On my honor. You have my word."

"Good enough," he said, clasping hands with Samarin. "You have my thanks."

The Assenta nodded. "My sword is yours should you need it."

"I'll keep that in mind." Retracing his steps, Westvane walked to where she stood on the path. "Time to move. Fast and light, princess. No trace left behind."

"Okay," she murmured, hoping she could do as he asked.

She'd never been pursued before. Never feared for her life in a world not her own. Never been forced to run across rough terrain to stay alive. But as she left Samarin's house, jogging at a fast clip behind Westvane, Montrose falling in at her back, Truly prayed for strength. Not only for the ability to run and run hard, but for the kind of luck that would keep the queen and her guard off their trail.

22

QUICK AND QUIET

The sun came up over fields of gold, burning across wide-open plains. Miles and miles of wild wheat undulating in the wind. Top shelfs laden with grain no one would ever harvest, waiting for someone to step into the long grass, danger disguised as beauty and abundance.

Running lead in the procession of three, Westvane scanned the fields on either side of the trail. Long strides. Light footfalls. Pace steady. No snakes yet. Although, he saw of plenty of holes for nests of vipers to hide in.

Too late in the day, perhaps. Too cold on the plain for the venomous creatures to be anywhere other than tucked deep in their dens.

Whatever the reason, he was grateful. Battling giant snakes while on the run (and protecting a Door Master) wouldn't be optimal — or an activity he considered fun.

Always the way things went on the Great Plain. Fun never factored in, the entire reason Azlandians didn't venture here. No one who valued their life risked the inhospitable expanse.

Assentas, though, prided themselves on being braver than

most. His kind liked to nibble around the edges, play the odds, and still they remained wary, venturing only so far into the hinterland.

For the most part, the area had been left to wildlings, to the underthings that roamed the open plains and dense forest. Westvane could smell the trees in the distance. The scent of rich loam, leaves, and deep root systems called to him. The aroma opened a yearning so deep, he struggled to keep his pace even. He wanted to lengthen his stride and speed up, but quelled the urge. He couldn't leave Truly in the dust. Not yet. Maybe, not ever. He was still on the fence, confused about what to do about her, so...

His affinity for woodlands would have to wait.

Especially since the one he approached owned an interesting reputation.

Not much was known about the forest beyond the Great Plains, but rumors abounded. Some said the woods teemed with caustic magic. Others insisted the trees had minds of their own. Westvane only knew what he'd been told — and now scented on the evening breeze.

Running at a steady clip, he scanned the trail ahead. Shadowy edges of woodland rose in the distance. Unnatural power simmered above the canopy, rolling like a slow boil as tall trees stood strong against an endless sky.

Beautiful, formidable, luring weary travelers in, only to kill them.

Westvane huffed. His thoughts had grown fanciful. Perhaps even idiotic. He knew better than to become distracted by a myth. Something Truly would no doubt categorize as an old wives' tale. A warning to the already wary. A story told to misbehaving children late at night. Viciousness given a name and a place to keep people in line. The promise of violence sufficient enough to keep the greedy away.

Not a bad plan. Clever, all things considered. The land benefited from the lack of outside interference. That didn't mean, however, all the stories were lies.

Dangerous creatures lived in the treetops, beneath the ground, and hidden in the underbrush. So far, he'd hadn't seen any, but that didn't mean they weren't there, crouched in the long grass, following his progress, waiting for the right moment to strike.

Westvane already knew a pack of Hyraxes trailed them. He smelled the musk of the rock badgers' thick fur coats. Scented the funk of acidic saliva in the air. Heard the whisper of venomous claws scraping over compact earth. Not too close to worry about... yet.

So far, the pack had kept a respectable distance. Maintaining the gap. Not rushing in to flank him. Not exploiting the weakness in his group. His strength, the scent he carried on his skin, warned of danger. The Hyraxes smelled him and, like every other creature in his world, reacted with uncertainty.

Not surprising.

Accomplished killers recognized the presence of another, more skilled member of their class. Westvane understood the pack Alpha's thinking. Proceed with caution. Gather more information. Investigate the potential of his quarry. Assess. Determine. Then attack.

Most predators aligned in the same way, waiting for the right opportunity to increase the odds of a successful kill. Which meant the faster he crossed the plains and navigated the Stepping Stones, the better for Truly. A hungry pack in need of a fresh meal wouldn't hesitate long. His strength wouldn't keep the Hyraxes at bay forever.

Tracking the proximity of the pack travelling in their wake via scent, Westvane upped the pace. Truly breathed heavily behind him, the rush raspy and harsh. Remorse simmered through him. He was pushing her too hard, permitting no breaks, making her drink from water pouches on the run. The pace didn't faze him. He could run for days at greater speed and not tire. He heard Montrose stumble on the uneven trail. Build for speed, not distance, the gargoyle cursed under his breath, quietly protesting the tempo. Truly, however, had yet to utter a single complaint.

Her stoicism surprised him.

Humans, as a group, weren't known for stamina. Or stalwart attitudes.

As a male born of an Assenta female, he'd taken his lessons seriously as a child. His mother had been thorough in their delivery. Aware his existence was a serious threat to Lyonesse, she armed him with knowledge. From an early age, the lectures began. She'd taught him of Azlandia and all those living in it — people, plants, animals, and creatures. She'd instructed him in the ways of Earthlings. As an Assenta from a lauded family, her education had been extensive. She'd passed on all she knew, making him memorize whole passages, weaponizing his intellect.

Knowledge was power, truth its handmaiden. And according to his mother, humans made terrible teammates.

Most didn't know how to work together in order to achieve a shared goal. Their thirst for power always got in the way. Obstinate. Quarrelsome. Vain and poisoned by self-interest. His mother had actually used those words to describe those who lived in Earth Realm. But after observing Truly, he suspected his mother might have missed some of the finer points.

Maybe even gotten a few things wrong.

Glancing over his shoulder, Westvane checked to make sure she was still behind him. He clenched his teeth to keep from laughing. He had to give her credit. Even coated with dust and exhausted from exertion, she stayed the course. Breathing hard.

Refusing to break stride. Bent, bruised, but nowhere near broken.

Meeting Montrose's eyes, Westvane tipped his chin. The gargoyle nodded, understanding what he wanted, and lengthened his stride. Montrose narrowed the gap between him and Truly, close enough to protect, far enough away to not impede her run. Westvane sprinted ahead. He needed to find the best spot to enter the Stepping Stones. Some of the rocks would need to be climbed. Others could be skirted, the narrow trails between acting more like labyrinth than path. He wished he could go around the rock field, but avoiding it would take too long.

A week, perhaps. But in all probability, much, much longer.

Wings tucked to his back, he upped his pace. His feathers reacted to the uptick in speed. Wind rustled through the singed plumes. A wave of pain clawed over his back. He clenched his teeth, then dismissed the discomfort, searching for the landmark on the horizon.

There.

In the distance.

Less than a mile away.

Closer than he'd thought — the main entrance. Two tall, flat-faced standing stones. One crevice-like entry point.

His focus narrowed on it. Not optimal. He would've preferred another way in, one with the potential to throw the Hyraxes off his scent. Needing a better view, Westvane murmured, sending out a magic-infused call. Eastbrook answered, peeling away from his throat, morphing from tattoo to physical bird. Feathers ruffled, brushing his cheek as the raven settled on his shoulder and adjusted his wings.

"Time to fly, my friend," he said, without breaking stride. "Need eyes in the sky."

With a chuff, Eastbrook leapt skyward. A black blot against

blue sky and golden fields, the raven reached altitude and began to soar. Angling his wings, he flew toward the giant Stepping Stones.

A light touch tapped along his temples. A sinking sensation took hold as mind-meld locked into place. Images flashed on Westvane's mental screen, showing him what Eastbrook saw — a bird's-eye view of the expansive rock field ahead.

Carved from reddish-orange stone, individual pillars rose from the valley floor. Some boasted jagged crowns, others had tops smoothed out by time, each one began and ended with high cliffs. Westvane refocused on the main entrance. The triangle-shaped fissure didn't seem safe to him. Too many entered there and never came back out.

Eastbrook's gaze snagged on a smaller opening half a mile to the North. A better bet. Less predictable. A safer place to stop and recalibrate.

Given a choice, he wouldn't stop at all, but Truly needed a break. Five minutes to catch her breath, drink some water... rest and recuperate.

He wished he could give her more.

She'd done well all day. Running hard. Keeping pace. Asking no questions. An accomplishment for anyone, but especially for her. She was dogged in her pursuit of information and answers. The topic didn't matter. The moment a subject snagged her attention, she peppered him with questions until he ended up telling her things he wasn't yet ready for her to know.

Ahead of his companions, Westvane slowed to a jog. His senses contracted as he checked Truly's progress behind him on the trail. He heard her before he saw her — the labored breathing, the light strike of footfalls, Montrose at her back.

Waiting until he saw her crest the hill, Westvane veered onto a rough, little-used path. She caught his movement and followed, moving at a steady clip. Impressive by any standards. Especially given her magic wasn't working at full capacity.

If that day ever came, she would become a force. Someone to be reckoned with, a human with the capacity to control his world. Framed that way, he supposed her boundless curiosity was normal. Were he in her position, he'd want to know everything all at once too. Still, her ability to ask one question after another never ceased to amaze and —

"Why are we stopping?"

— annoy the hell out of him.

Standing at the secondary entry point, at the base of an enormous boulder, Westvane turned to look at her. Red-faced and out of breath. Doubled over with hands planted on her knees, blonde hair matted with sweat, face streaked with dirt.

He stared at her, then pointed out the obvious. "You need a break."

"Not a good idea," Montrose said, sucking in a raspy breath. "There are —"

"I know what hunts us," he said, throwing the gargoyle a warning look.

"What do you mean — *hunts us?*" Pushing up from her half-crouch, Truly drew a hitched breath, then exhaled slow. "Are we being followed?"

Westvane sighed.

Reading his expression, she scowled. "By what?"

"You don't want to know."

"You're probably right," she grumbled. "Though, just gotta say — I shouldn't be surprised, given the huge pile of crap we're already buried under."

The sarcasm made his lips twitch. He couldn't help himself. Her reaction tweaked him. Most humans would be screaming by now. About sore muscles and dirt-streaked skin, the heat, and hostile terrain.

Resuming her half-bent position, Truly braced her hands on her knees. "Please tell me you're able to kill whatever it is."

He threw a water skin between her feet. "Probably."

"Probably?" she said, sounding alarmed.

Unable to contain it, Westvane huffed in amusement.

"Now is not the time…" Swiping the water skin off the ground, she popped the top and drank. After a couple of long swallows, she passed the kidney-shaped bag to Montrose. "To locate your sense of humor."

He ignored the jab in favor of scanning the field behind him. "We'll stay another minute, then move on. Quick and quiet. I would prefer to avoid the Hyraxes if possible."

"The what?"

Montrose took another drink. "Rock badgers."

"You don't want to kill them?" Truly asked.

Westvane shook his head. "Hyraxes are important here. As the dominant predators in the region, they keep wildlife populations in check. Kill the pack, unbalance the ecosystem."

Truly stared at him, eyes steady on his, then nodded. "Good enough reason. Although, push comes to shove, I would prefer not to be eaten by one."

"I'll keep that in mind."

"Thanks," she muttered, accepting the skin from Montrose, taking another drink before handing it to him. "Though, just want to point out…"

She trailed off.

He raised a brow.

Her focus cut to the wings rising above his shoulders. "At some point, we need to get you flying lessons."

Montrose guffawed.

Westvane scowled. "There it is."

"What?"

"First complaint of the day."

"Not a complaint," she said, eyes sparkling. "More of an observation or... you know... a *fact*."

One he didn't need pointed out. Particularly since she was right. Learning to use his wings landed near the top of the pro side of his tally sheet. Still...

"Fine form, princess," he said, acknowledging the direct hit. "But now that you've recovered —"

"I'll never recover," she said. "Secret magical abilities, killer Yeomanry, nearly getting eaten by a horned Assenta and his bride — I'm scarred for life."

Westvane clenched his teeth to keep from laughing. "Suck it up, princess. Time to move."

She sighed.

Ignoring the attitude, he turned toward the Stepping Stones. Best not to go through any fissures just yet. He wanted to get a better look first. With Eastbrook flying, he already knew the best way forward, what path he planned to take, but better safe than sorry.

Capping the water skin, Truly lifted the strap over her head.

He examined the surface of the stone in front of him. A hundred-and-fifty feet high, give or take. Good hand and footholds. Still, a long way up for Truly. A challenging climb. The first of many between him and the other side of the rock field. *Quick and quiet*. A good strategy. More of a surgical strike than a journey to the other side. He must cut though the many twists, turns, and cliffs ahead of them.

Be efficient.

Leave little trace behind.

Quick and quiet.

More than the Hyraxes trailed them now.

He wasn't yet sure who else had picked up their scent. The

read he held on what stalked them lacked direction and clarity. Too much distance stood between him and it to get an accurate lock. The creep and claw across the back of his neck, however, told the tale. Someone else had joined the hunt. A powerful someone. Someone other than Lyonesse, but just as dangerous.

23

THE STEPPING STONES

Truly had never been a kidder. The few who knew her well would never make the mistake of thinking so, but that didn't mean she wasn't right. Westvane needed flying lessons as soon as humanly (or rather, *Azlandianly*) possible.

The ability to fly would've been a game-changer. Made life so much easier. Hers — without a doubt — but, for all his physical prowess, Westvane's too. Free-climbing huge red rocks wasn't her idea of fun. The scrape and claw against her sore fingers sucked. Which naturally led to unkind thoughts. Murderous thoughts. Lob-a-grenade-at-the-big-bad-Slayer thoughts.

Truly clenched her teeth. If only she had one...

And knew how to throw it.

Digging her toes into a crevice, she searched for her next handhold. Small bits of debris tumbled down the cliff face, clouding the air with dust. Her nose twitched. Hanging on for dear life, battling the need to sneeze, Truly glared at Westvane. Not that it did her any good. Her grievance continued to be lost on him. He was well ahead, a black splotch above her, scaling each boulder with cat-like efficiency. Annoying. Frustrating. Admirable, if she forgot for a moment she wanted to kill him.

She scowled at the backs of his wings.

The plumage was a little worse for wear.

Even from a distance, she saw where the fire singed him. The feathers on his left wing looked sparser than on his right. Thinned out, balding in patches, some plumes bent at odd angles. He'd been shedding ravaged feathers all day. She'd watch each one fall. Studied the hole opening up in the middle of his wing. Jogged over the remains on the trail all day as she struggled to keep up.

He'd been burned badly inside Montrose & Brim while trying to shield her. The realization made guilt rise. She shouldn't be angry at him. The current circumstances weren't his fault. He was doing his best. His job. Leading where she couldn't.

Truly wanted to let the thought raise her spirits. In truth, she'd been trying to stay positive all day, using it to battle the worry and cage her anxiety, but honestly? After hours of climbing, so late in the day? She only had two options left — give in to despair or channel the fury.

Tears weren't her style.

Anger, however, was another story.

She excelled at shaping it. Living inside the Foster Care system had taught her a thing or two. She'd learned early, and often, turning anger into a friend. She knew how to mold her temper and the safest places to direct it. Right now, she needed rage to fuel her climb, and fair or not, Westvane made for an excellent target.

Still, she was glad he healed fast. Even in the gathering gloom, she watched the skin covering his wings shift from black char to pink healthy glow. New feathers pushed through the repaired flesh, growing over the bare spots. The plumage so glossy, the inky shimmer mesmerized her. The fascination lasted a second before he disappeared over the next rock, and she slid back into uncharitable thoughts. No one (inhuman or not) should be able to climb like him — rhythm steady, handholds swift and sure. It made her question everything. Like why in the hell she scrambled in his wake, struggling to keep up. Keeping pace with him was an impossibility.

With a grunt, she heaved herself upward anyway. Her foot slipped. She grappled, clinging to the rock face with two hands and one foot to keep from falling. It wasn't too far down. Maybe fifteen feet, twenty if she wanted to be generous. Not enough to injure her if she landed right, but...

"Suck it up," she gritted. "Keep moving."

No way would she give up now. She needed to go up not down. And if she fell, she'd be right back where she started. At the base of the boulder she needed to summit, instead of closing in on the top.

"Climb faster, Triple."

"Shut up, Rosy." Breathing hard, she glared at the gargoyle. Another place to direct her anger. He was irritating the hell out of her. Like Westvane, he scaled the tall boulders with relative ease. Using his claws, he scampered along the rock face. Although, unlike Westvane, he kept pace with her. Always a little in the lead. Always off to her right.

"Want a piggy-back ride?"

"Touch me, and I'll kill you."

"You get your magic back online, you could fry me from all the way over there."

"Something to look forward to," she huffed, reaching for the next handhold, trying to pretend she wasn't intrigued. Though, it was irritating. Imparting important information while she clung to the side of a cliff (and lacked the energy to ask questions) wasn't fair. "If I wasn't afraid of falling, I'd hurt you the old-fashioned way and plant my fist in your face."

His whiskers twitched.

Truly read the amusement in his eyes. Hers narrowed on him.

He shook his head. "Hurry up. We're falling behind."

"I know." Resuming the climb, she fought her way closer to the top. "Westvane's too fast. He's so far ahead, I'll never catch up."

"Part of the plan," Montrose said, his gaze in constant motion, scanning the towering stones on either side of them. "He's scouting. Charting a course through the rock field. Ensuring the Hyraxes don't flank us."

"Rock badgers." The name worried her, in no way inspiring confidence. Just a guess, but an animal with *rock* in the title was no doubt accomplished at — oh, say — *climbing rocks.*

Cresting the top, she crawled to the middle of the pillar. "Terrific. Super, uber fantastic."

Huffing, puffing, feeling as though she might die, Truly shifted into a crouch. She planted her forearms on her bent knees and looked at her hands. Caked with red dust. Cuts and scrapes underneath the layer of dirt. Shaking a little, she flexed her fingers, trying to stop them from trembling. She drew a calming breath and scanned the terrain. More brutal cliffs ahead of her, although...

Truly looked over the rock field again. Even with late day folding into dusk, she made out the edge. The shelf and drop-off. The place where the huge stones fell away.

The gloom deepened.

She squinted, forcing her eyes into focus.

Tall treetops swayed in the distance. Some coniferous with dense pine needles. Some leafy and full, the foliage so thick, the green so deep, the sight gave her hope. Good news. A forest meant shelter, relative safety and... water. Cool depths instead of the hot, dusty expanse of the rock field and more climbing.

She glanced at Montrose. "Is that where we're headed?"

"Not if we want to live."

"What do you mean?"

"Weeping Hollow is not a friendly place," Montrose said, unease and reverence an odd mix in his tone. She threw him a questioning look. He shook his head. "The woodland is full of magic, Triple. Strange creatures and malevolent spirits. Those who enter don't come back out."

"Sounds like an old wives' tale."

"Might be." Westvane landed with cat-like grace beside her. Quick, sure and... soundless.

A black blur, Eastbrook descended and, talons outstretched, landed on his shoulder. The raven cocked his head. The feathers at his throat rippled as he greeted her with a cooing call.

Truly huffed. "Well, I'm glad someone's enjoying themselves."

Eastbrook replied, the bird-sound more chuckle than chuff.

With a sigh, she pushed away from her knees and stood. As she brushed off her hands, her gaze bounced from Westvane to the direction he'd come, realizing he'd leapt the crevasse between two standing stones. The gap at least twenty feet across.

She scowled at him. "If you can jump like that, why the hell are we climbing?"

His dark eyes lit with humor. "I'm scouting."

"And I'm tired of climbing."

He smiled. "You really want to me carry you?"

Maybe. The thought pricked her pride. "No, but you could throw me. You know, like a human caber. Just chuck me from one boulder top to the next."

Montrose snorted.

"While tossing you sounds like fun," Westvane said, pausing for effect. "You'd end up sliding off the other side."

"Might be a good death," she said, pursing her lips. "Maybe even an advisable one."

His lips twitched. Westvane shook his head, then extended his hand. She did as bid and settled hers, palm up, in the cradle of his. He examined her scrapes along with the raw patches of skin on her fingertips. "You good to go on?"

"No choice. Gotta keep going." Removing her hand from his, she flexed her fingers again. Pain bit, making her knuckles ache. She ignored the discomfort, her attention drifting to Weeping Hollow. Even from a distance, she sensed the magic. Could see the vivid tumble in the air. Drank in the cool forest breeze like a tonic as silent spells surfed over red rock, smoothing caustic currents into gentle breaths of air.

She exhaled in relief. The breeze felt good. The forest felt like a true friend. Just what she needed, and at the moment, everything she wanted.

"Can you feel it?" she asked, gaze locked on the woods.

"Don't, Triple."

Montrose's sharp tone turned her attention. "Don't what?"

"Allow it to beguile you."

Her brow popped toward her forehead. "The forest?"

"Weeping Hollow calls to those who come close to it," Montrose said. "It tempts. It lures. It —"

"Destroys," Westvane rumbled, sending a shiver down her spine.

"Doesn't feel dangerous to me. Feels..." Inhaling through her nose, she exhaled through her mouth. The scent of pine and earth assuring her of sanctuary and safety. "Like home."

"It isn't, princess. The safest route is around it."

She opened her mouth to challenge Westvane's claim.

"We go around. Anything else is folly," he said, tone firm.

Stroking Eastbrook's feathered head, he held her gaze, waiting for her to argue. "Clear?"

Given his tone, it would have to be. Westvane knew this land, she didn't. Butting up against him wouldn't be wise. She must trust he knew what he was doing. Still...

"A topic to be revisited later?" she asked.

"No, I don't want to go in there either," Montrose said, looking to the sky. "Plum crazy, Triple."

"I think it's been established I've got some crazy in me." How else could she explain the last couple of days — the one-hundred-and-eighty degree turn her life had taken. Anyone faced with magic and twin worlds, brutal Assenta warriors and talking gargoyles, needed to be a touch nuts to believe a quarter of it.

"Maybe just the right amount."

Nice. Truly's mouth curved. A compliment of sorts. From Westvane. Unexpected, but she'd take what she could get. "Listen, can we rest awhile? Maybe —"

"Quiet." A furrow between his brows, Westvane looked over his shoulder. His eyes searched terrain already covered. His body tensed. He curled his hands into fists.

Boot soles churning through red dust, Truly pivoted, following his movement. "What is it?"

"They're closing," he said, unfolding then refolding his wings. "We need to move."

Dragging her attention from him, she focused on the spot his gaze rested. Something moved six or seven rocks behind them. As she watched, a huge paw, sharp claws extended, crested a stepping stone. The body of the animal followed, and she got her first look at a Hyrax.

Massive head with tufted, short ears. Thick reddish-brown fur covering a sleek, muscled physic. Dark patches on its forepaws, underbelly, spine, and tail that looked like scales:

armor in the most vulnerable places. White stripe down the center of its snout. Hooked fangs the size of a saber-toothed tigers.

Scary looking.

Vicious looking.

Leader of the pack. A hungry predator on the hunt.

Westvane was right. They needed to go... and they needed to do it now.

24

MAKE THE JUMP

Leaning into the run, Truly sprinted toward the edge of the cliff. Her boots felt heavy. Each breath came fast, hot air rasping in the back of her throat. Balls of her feet churning, she pushed herself harder, gauging the distance to target. A little off-angle. She made the infinitesimal shift, correcting the trajectory, praying she was strong enough to land the jump.

Her feet left the ground.

She went weightless.

A second later, she landed with a bone-jarring thump.

Her soles skimmed over the stepping stone. Dust swirled. Her muscles burned as she slid across orange rock worn smooth by desert winds. With a skipping hop, she ramped into another run. Pumping her arms and legs, she leapt from one boulder top to the next. *Don't look down.* Repeating the chant, Truly visualized the outcome she wanted instead — the initial jump, the landing, the physical coordination required to cycle into the next leap.

Her pace was good, her determination set. No faith required, just quick feet, working muscles, and the will to live. She heard Westvane running in her wake — footfalls silent, his breaths even and steady, the quiet rustle of feathers. Montrose made more noise, but she refused to look back. The pair stayed behind her for a reason. Probably to shield her from what dogged their trail.

Dwelling on the Hyraxes, however, wasn't productive. She needed to concentrate and keep moving. Easier to do now as the rock field leveled out. No more jagged cliff faces and hard climbing. On the smaller side of tall, the towers in front of her turned into true stepping stones. The gaps between rounded edges continued to narrow, allowing her to jump from one to the next. Exhaustion dragged at her, though, threatening to pull her under as she made another leap.

Pain clawed through as she touched down.

Breathing so hard her chest hurt, her body urged her to take a break. Truly pushed harder instead. Slowing down would lead to disaster, so instead of listening to her muscles, she lined up the next stone. Tired legs propelled her forward. She eyed her target zone. The rock top slanted at a bad angle, down and to the left. Landing in the middle would be best. She needed to clear the edge while lining up her approach. If she didn't, she might lose her footing and slide off the other side — right into Hyraxes' claws.

The thought sent a shiver down her spine.

Sweat dripped into her eye.

With a swipe, she rubbed the droplet away and refocused. Balls of her feet grinding over stone, she launched herself into the air. Her feet slammed down. Fatigue broke her stride. The toe of her boot caught a rough patch. Truly hissed as her body rocked forward. Her muscles flexed. Agony tightened its grip as she struggled to keep her feet under her.

Red-orange stone revolved beneath her.

Her shoulder slammed into the uneven surface. Air

exploded from her lungs. Rock scraped across her hip, and she spun into an uncontrollable tumble.

Westvane cursed behind her.

Montrose shouted in alarm.

Truly fought to recover by digging her heels in. Her hands scraped over rock. Pain pushed panic past the pressure point as she clawed for a handhold. Blue shimmer bled from her fingertips, smearing red stone, leaving an uneven trail in her wake. She felt the heat on her skin. Sensed something fierce spike inside her as starbursts flashed behind her eyes. She recognized the pulse a split second before she embraced the meteoric rise of her magic. Potent, burning like wildfire, power streamed from her palms, trying to slow her down.

Digging her nails in, Truly directed the flow, using the magical shards like claws. Friction carved grooves in the stone, rubbing her fingertips raw. The trail of blue shimmer burst to flames, roaring across the rockface. Smoke billowed around her. The scent of scorched earth rose as dust fogged the air orange.

One moment tipped into the next.

Unable to stop the slide, she ran out of runway.

Gasping, grappling, she looked across the flat surface of stone. Dark eyes aglow with citrine light, Westvane yelled something. Too little, too late. She was already gone, spinning over the cliff edge, disappearing into the canyon below.

TOO FAR AWAY TO STOP IT, Westvane watched Truly careen over the cliff.

The Door Master.

Over the edge.

Falling toward certain death.

Unless he reached her in time.

Powering through his alarm, he forced his muscles to unlock. To propel him toward the same edge she slid over. Footfalls hammering against stone, he focused on the spot she disappeared. An odd sensation slithered through him. He'd never felt anything like it — the urgent blood rush in his veins, the slamming thump against the inside of his chest, the roaring rush in his ears.

It took a moment for realization to strike. Understanding followed quick on its heels. *Fear.* Cloying. Awful. Clawing up his throat as he heard the pack of Hyraxes mobilized. Growls drifted up from down below, shifting fear into terror.

A new experience for him, foreign and unwelcome. Nothing raised his pulse point. He never allowed himself to care enough to get worked up about anything. Self-control had always been the goal. A necessary state of being in a place that viewed vulnerability as weakness. Strong. Silent. Suppress his feelings. He existed inside an emotionless void. The cocoon of ice-cold helped him survive every day. But the sound of Truly's scream caused everything inside him to tightened. The usual calm abandoned him, shoving him into unknown territory.

She was his last hope. The one who would restore balance to Azlandia. The one with the power to change it all. Make it right. The possibility of equality and justice, the shattering of a caste system that served few and brutalized many, lay within his grasp. He could do what his mother and father hadn't been able to — through her. Which meant Truly not only needed to live, she needed to thrive, so...

Like it or not, he must be the one to safeguard her.

Westvane snarled as the truth struck. No one would believe it. *Him,* (a hybrid, an abomination, loathed by his own kind) the self-professed protector of a Door Master. Somehow, though, that's what he'd become — Truly's shield. And now, when she needed him most, he was failing.

Baring his teeth, he ran harder. Air whistled though his feathers. An updraft grabbed hold of wings, lifting his bulk. His feet skated across stone. His muscles tightened as the seesawing motion threw him off balance.

A black blur in the sky, Eastbrook wheeled above him.

Montrose shouted something to his right.

Westvane ignored them both, fighting to stay level. The gust died down. Hot air whispered around him, becoming heavier, leveling him out. His feet slammed into the top of the stepping stone. He didn't bother correcting the pitch and tilt. Tucking his wings, he rolled into a somersault, regained his feet, and leapt across the crevasse between stones.

He scanned the ravine.

Large paw prints dimpled the sand below, but...

No sign of Truly. No blood splattering the ground. No Hyraxes in sight either.

He took a moment to absorb the details and frowned. Something was wrong. The anomaly wasn't huge, was barely detectable, but...

He scanned the rocks again. His gaze narrowed on the steep drop.

Scorch marks marred parallel cliff faces. Five smooth tracks: blunter, wider than claw marks, bright blue in color, the glow inside the impressions faint. More droplets littered the ground, leaving indentations across the red sand. His attention sliced up trail. Even from a hundred feet up, he smelled it.

Magic. Powerful and persistent. Traces of Truly everywhere.

Jumping to the next stone, he followed the spray of blue droplets. Seven stones ahead, Eastbrook circled above, a shadowy stain in a darkening sky. Gaze on the raven, Westvane opened a channel inside his mind.

The connection sparked.

He spoke to Eastbrook. *"Got her?"*

Eastbrook chuffed in answer.

"Show me."

An image moved through mind-meld. A glowing blue sphere, Truly at its center, surrounded by Hyraxes appeared on screen. In pursuit, holding the picture Eastbrook sent him in his mind's eye, Westvane watched rock badgers attack the sphere, clawing, biting, batting it like a ball. Truly went spinning. The sphere skidded between towers, slamming into stone walls, throwing her around like a ragdoll.

Running hard, Montrose came abreast of him. "Anything?"

"Just ahead," he said, veering left to flank the pack. "Follow me. Be ready for anything."

"With Triple, I learned that months ago."

Smart gargoyle.

Westvane clenched his teeth. He should've picked up on it immediately. Been quicker to understand. Learned faster, been smarter, realized sooner... the moment she'd gone toe-to-toe with him on the front porch. Truly might be human, but she wasn't normal, and nothing ever went to plan with an undisciplined Door Master gumming up the works.

25

HAMSTER ON A WHEEL

Shimmering liquid splattered across stone as Truly tumbled by inside the ball. A ball she wasn't controlling. A ball drawn from a mysterious place. She tried to tap into it, but the source of the conjuring remained hazy. Though she knew it emanated from her.

She felt the pulling claw of magic beneath her skin, sinking deep to infuse muscle and bone as the sphere warped, moulding into a protective shell the instant she started to fall. No warning. Zero explanation. Evidence of her abilities once more on display, even as she struggled to pinpoint the origin. Power rose from a well deep inside her. A powerful place, one connected to everything and nothing at the same time.

She wanted to take the time to explore. To turn inward instead of away as ribbons of light blazed inside her mind before swelling out to surround her, creating the shell she stood inside. Another time, perhaps. Right now, she had more immediate concerns. She was too busy running.

Elbows and knees pumping, Truly propelled the sphere through toothy crevices, racing along crooked trails created by tall standing stones. While a pack of snarling Hyraxes attacked the outside of the ball. Clawing, biting, trying to maul their way inside, animals the size of lions leapt from high ledges and low hollows, hurling their bodies at the magical-fueled shield surrounding her.

Each collision jolted her.

The sphere veered left only to hurtle to the right, skipping over rough ground, slamming into the sides of tall towers. Knocked sideways, she hit her knees, then clambered back to her feet. Forward momentum was a must. The faster she moved, the more power the sphere gained, outer shell toughening, becoming harder as snarls echoed. Huge paws slammed into the ball. Lethal-looking claws shrieked against the hard surface as Hyrax after Hyrax attempted to slice its way inside.

Not that she could see much beyond the slime.

The sphere might be smooth on the inside, but it was sloppy on the outside, throwing blue liquid in wide arcs, like mud off monster truck tires. Messy conditions that made it difficult to navigate, but it wasn't all bad news. She was still breathing. Hadn't been torn apart or eaten yet, so no matter how challenging the terrain, she considered it a win so far.

A pair of glowing eyes flashed in her periphery.

Wet fur smeared with blue hammered the side of the sphere.

Truly braced as she skidded sideways. The ball slammed into a standing stone, sending her sprawling. Her forward progress slowed. She struggled to get up and, planting her hands against the curved wall, pushed forward. The slimy surface under the sphere bit against grainy sand as she sped up again.

Standing on top, Hyraxes went flying.

Feeling like a hamster on a wheel, Truly bared her teeth and kept going. She fell again. And again. More times than she cared to count, but refused to quit running. The outer shell continued to shed. Arching splashes flew off the outside like blue paint as she rolled. Thick slime sprayed across stone like blood spatter, leaving shimmering tracks in her wake.

Finally, some good news.

The sphere might be strange, but at least, it acted as more than just protection. The spray off its outer shell served another purpose. A messy trail was easier to follow than a subtle one. No guesswork or expert skill needed to track her and...

Westvane wouldn't be far behind.

Up on her toes, she whirled around a sharp corner. It wouldn't be long now. Glancing up, she tried to see through the sloppy exterior. The shimmering sphere revolved around her. She caught a glimpse of red rock, heard the clang of striking claws, but —

No Westvane yet.

His absence, however, didn't mean he'd abandoned her. He was there. Somewhere. Lurking above, searching for an opening, tracking her progress. All she needed to do was stay the course until he reached her.

Light sliced between two standing stones.

Truly leaned right, aiming the sphere at the opening. Too narrow, perhaps. Not enough room for the ball to squeeze through, maybe. Could end up being the wrong decision, but at this point, she didn't have a choice. She had become a living, breathing example of the slogan "do or die," so despite the uncertainty, she ran toward the narrow fissure anyway.

The standing stones rose labyrinth-like around her. The slice of light glowed ahead of her. The gap between the rock walls narrowed even further.

Pace furious, Truly aimed the ball at the light-filled hole. The sphere slammed into the break between boulders. Rock exploded like a starburst. Shards of shrapnel rained down. Rock badgers roared in pain. The air inside the sphere heated as glass-like walls shrank inward, brushing the sides of her shoulders.

Tumbling like a pinball, she pedaled her legs, forcing the magic to bend as the Hyraxes regrouped.

Claws and teeth ripped at the outer shell.

"Truly!"

Looking up, she saw him through spinning blue muck. Feet planted. Stance aggressive. Wings folded. Twin swords undulating with black flames, Westvane stood on the edge of the last tower.

"Westvane — get me out of here!"

"Move your ass, princess. Roll clear of the rocks!"

Baring her teeth, she snarled at him. Great suggestion. In no way helpful, given she was already throttled up, at maximum capacity, fighting to move the sphere forward.

"I'm stuck!"

Truer word had never been spoken.

She *was* stuck. Stuck inside a ball. Wedged in a crevice. Trapped by magic she didn't understand as Westvane yelled more impossible instructions, and rock badgers attacked, beginning to tear the sphere apart, leaving her vulnerable to the swipe of razor-sharp claws.

26

I ALWAYS DO

Too far away to help, Westvane watched Truly struggle inside the sphere. He willed her forward from his position atop the high cliff. She was mired in mucky sand. Slipping on blue slime. Wedged between rocks as Hyraxes continued ramming the shell protecting her deeper into the crevice.

Twin swords in hand, he ran along the ridge. His focus jumped between Truly and the soaring stone arch above her, searching for weakness in the structure. Not much there for the Hyraxes to exploit. Rock cantilevered above her, thick slabs forming a doorway wide enough for one person to walk through, but not for the sphere. His eyes narrowed on the tower tops. Solid enough. The beasts would have to go up and over to attack from multiple vantage points.

Leaping from one stepping stone to the next, Westvane made a few rapid-fire calculations. The delay cost him. He wanted to charge to the fray. He wanted to intervene. He wanted to get between her and danger. Nobel sentiments. A warrior-worthy goal. Almost altruistic. He hardly recognized himself or the need that drove him anymore.

Not that it mattered. Nothing *mattered* unless she *moved.*

Out of the line of fire. Out of the kill box. Out of his way long enough for him to go to work.

Dropping in behind the Hyraxes wasn't a good idea. The entire pack prowled inside the chasm, pacing, snarling, each waiting their turn to attack. Landing in that mess would get him nowhere. Hyraxes would die, sure, but so might he. He was durable, but not invincible. Even with Montrose at his back, fifteen against two weren't good odds.

"Truly!"

Baring her teeth, she shoved against the inside of the sphere wall. The ball churned forward, moved an inch, then stopped. Her feet slid against the curve as she tipped her head back and glared at him.

Magic pulsed in the air around her.

Fierce, shimmering blue eyes met his. "I'm trying!"

"Try harder!"

She screamed in fury.

He vaulted off the cliff edge. Halfway down, he twisted into a backflip. Wind dragged through his injured wings. Rotating flaming blades in his hands, he beat back the discomfort and landed on the grassy plain abutting the rock field.

"Use your mind," he growled, moving forward to help her. "Change the shape of the ball. Shrink it."

"Stop criticizing!" A rock badger slammed into the sphere. Truly lost her footing, landing hard on her knees. "You come in here and try this!"

Westvane bit back a smile. Goddess, she was something. Such a fierce little thing, and as much as it chafed him to admit it, he admired her spirit. Enjoyed the fact she wasn't afraid of him. Even in the middle of a life-and-death situation, she spoke her mind, standing up to him when no one else dared. Was she annoying? Yes. Did she irritate him most of the time? Without a doubt. But she was also brave and smart, and despite his tendency to dislike everyone, he couldn't dislike her. He respected her never-say-die attitude too much.

Shifting to his left, he reassessed the situation and his next move. Montrose appeared at the top of one of the stepping stones. Westvane tipped his chin. Fangs bared, the gargoyle nodded and, leaping from one stone to the next, positioned to defend as Westvane spotted what he needed — an opening into the one-sided battle.

His nose flared as he ramped into a run. He couldn't go through, so he'd do the next best thing — go up and over. If he used the side wall as a launch pad, and Montrose engaged from above, he might be able to create confusion. A few seconds, enough time to surprise and scatter the Hyraxes. The instant he entered the fight, the pack would turn on him, allowing Truly a clear avenue of escape.

At least, he hoped. He couldn't be certain. The pack was hungry, frenzied by the hunt, the scent of Truly's magic like chum in open water.

Tucking his wings, he sprinted toward the arch. The toes of his boots dug in, leaving divots in the grass. The smell of loam swirled as he searched the side wall for an adequate foothold. There. Right there. A couple feet above Truly and the sphere.

About to leap over the sphere, he looked at her.

Crumpled, dented along both sides, the sphere shimmered, changing color, moving from blue to purple, then gold, only to shift back again. The light show blinded him for a moment. Narrowing his eyes, he minimized the glint and —

A hole opened on the side of the sphere facing him.

Breaking stride, Westvane put on the brakes. Blue shimmer covering her skin, Truly stuck her arm through the opening. Her hand stretched out toward him. Feet sliding across dew-soaked grass, he opened his wings. Angling the feathered tips, he slowed his forward progress and spun to one side. His back thumped against the stepping stone. Shoving both swords into one hand, he grabbed her wrist and yanked.

She flew head-first out of the sphere. The ball popped like an air bubble. A loud *crack!* eclipsed the howl of Hyraxes. Slime sprayed over her, all over him, splattering the ground, painting the area with blue ooze.

Rock badgers clamored through the gap. Paws slipping on the goo, the beasts fell over one another, landing in a pile as he tossed Truly out of the way.

Her feet left the ground. She landed somewhere behind him. Not that he bothered to look. He was too busy attacking. He heard the thump, though — and the creative cursing that followed — as he swung his swords. Catching a rhythm. Driving the pack back. Striking at the few already through the breach. The flaming tips cut through fur, severing muscle and bone. Hyraxes' blood sprayed across his hands, chest, and arms.

He paid no attention.

And felt no remorse.

He would've preferred to leave the pack alive, but it was too late to change tact now. Instead of retreating, he made death his friend. In truth, he'd never lost contact with it. The ability to kill came when called, rising up, taking over until he became a harbinger, deliverer of death.

Somersaulting off a tower, Montrose landed behind him.

"Get her to safety," he snarled, moving deeper into battle.

The gargoyle didn't listen. Claws raised, fangs bared, he moved into position, determined to help Westvane defend. "Nowhere to go. We make our stand here."

"The forest," Truly said, breathing ragged, voice weak. "We go into the forest."

"No," Montrose said, grabbing a Hyrax by the head. With a violent twist, he snapped the beast's neck. Whipping around, the gargoyle threw the carcass like a shotput, knocking rock badgers back into the crevice.

Westvane grunted in approval.

Excellent aim. A definite asset in a fight.

Angling his sword, Westvane stabbed and sliced, killing one Hyrax after another. He heard a rustle behind him. Kicking a beast off the end of his blade, he caught movement in his periphery. On her hands and knees, Truly struggled to her feet. Exhaustion made her sway. Her knees buckled, leaving her slouched in the short grass, angry shadows of Weeping Hollow rising behind her.

"Yes, the forest," she said, face drawn and pale. "It's the only —"

Static electricity sizzled through the air.

A flurry of wings flapped as multiple feet thumped against turf.

"A likely plan," a deep voice said, spiraling across the grassy knoll between forest and stones. "But I wouldn't advise it."

Sensing the pulse of power, the pack of Hyraxes retreated into the labyrinth. Not fast enough. One moment the archway between stones stood open. The next, it slammed shut as magic spilled into the void. The heated wave cut the last rock badger in two — front half inside the ravine, rear end twitching on the short grass outside it.

Rotating the swords in his hands, Westvane turned to face the new threat. What he saw didn't shock him. He knew that voice... and wasn't surprised by what followed. A contingent of the queen's guard, wings spread wide, landing on the plateau to his left.

The smell of sweet grass rose as their feet touched down.

His eyes narrowed on the leader. "Priestly."

"Westvane." Hair on his head as tawny as the feathers on his wings, Priestly bowed in greeting. "Good to see you again, my friend."

His eyes narrowed. The greeting should've warmed him. It left him cold instead. "Should've known she'd send you."

Priestly's mouth curved. "Yes, you should have."

"Thought you were done playing fetch for the witch."

Calm. Controlled. Never one to take the bait, Priestly raised a brow. His green eyes sparked in amusement. "Wings, Westvane, really. Such a surprise. Is the queen aware you have them? Or have you denied her the pleasure of knowing you're one of us?"

"One of you," Westvane said, his voice the lethal kind of melodic. The taunt was a good one. He'd never been *one of anything*. Alone. Apart. Reviled. No group had ever wanted to claim him. "Won't happen."

"It could." Watching him with predatory interest, Priestly folded his wings. He made a show of it, the multitude of golden feathers fluttering. "If only you would accept —"

"Never. I will *never* wear her collar." Nostrils flared, he spat on the ground between them. "Why are you so eager to?"

As intended, the barb hit its mark like an arrow.

Priestly flinched. "We could be friends again, you and I."

The bastard's words were softly said. The invitation, however, landed hard.

Westvane stifled his response. No need to answer. He knew Priestly was right. They could be friends... if he wanted them to be. They'd grown up together on Eckizbad Island. His mother imprisoned inside unforgiving fortress walls, Priestly's father one of the guards. They shared history. Had once been inseparable as young males, playing together in dark corridors and long hallways even though it had been forbidden.

The silence — all the things left unsaid — grew between them.

A muscle twitched along Priestly's jaw. "Have it your way."

"I always do."

"Don't I know it," he said, a note of something in his voice. Sorrow, maybe. Regret, perhaps. Not that it mattered. "Give me the Door Master, Westvane. Do that, and I'll let you live. I have no quarrel with you."

Tightening the grip on his weapons, Westvane shifted, moving like a sidewinder. "What makes you think I don't want the fight?"

Priestly smiled, a true one, humor tinged with anticipation as he conjured his own swords, prepared to give Westvane what they both wanted.

LIVE TO FIGHT ANOTHER DAY

The clash of swords rang across the plateau. Each strike raged against the quiet, bouncing off stone, only to boomerang and lash the trees edging the woods a hundred yards away. Muscles aching, so tired she couldn't stand, Truly glanced at the forest, then back at Westvane. Weapons blazing, he attacked. Movements precise, Priestly defended. The raging cacophony hurt her ears while fascinating her at the same time.

She'd never seen anything like it.

Warriors locked in mortal combat. It wasn't play-acting. It wasn't a movie set. The fight was real. Westvane's intent was clear. He planned to kill Priestly. Probably by slicing him in two.

Curling her hands in the short grass, she watched Westvane drive his opponent back, and wished she had her camera. Wrong thought, maybe, but the battle was beautiful. Gritty and undeniable. Each forceful swing. The answering parries. Fire blades held by skilled hands — one flaming black with tendrils of gray, the other blazing white and gold.

Unable to look away, she stared, almost positive recording the battle for posterity was the right thing to do. History would demand it. The better angels inside her head said *"not a good idea."*

No matter how mesmerizing, the fight needed to stop. Now. Before the worst happened, Westvane won, and Priestly ended up one head shy of a body.

Truly could see the shift happening. The fight looked balanced, but it wasn't. The longer it went on, the more evident it became Westvane was toying with him. A master playing with an apprentice, he moved Priestly around like chess pieces on a board. Without compunction or mercy. Sheer will imbued with lethal intent.

The black flame of his blades flashed.

Priestly's defenses weakened. A hole opened in his guard. Instead of taking advantage, Westvane paused, shifted, allowing him to recover before going on the offensive again. It was only a matter of time. The instant Priestly faltered, the guards at his back would move in. Surrounded them. Attack from all directions, overwhelm Westvane and take her.

Truly refused to let it happen.

Westvane needed to prove his superiority? Fine. He'd done that, but now, it was time to back off and regroup. Abandon stubborn pride and live to fight another day.

Gathering her last scrap of strength, Truly searched for Montrose. She found him less than three feet away. Arms crossed, gaze riveted on the duel, he stood guard, ready to move, wanting to enter the fight. Not that he dared. Westvane would skin him alive if the gargoyle intervened. The Assenta wanted to make a point, and he didn't need anyone's help to hammer it home.

"Rosy," she said, her voice so weak she worried he wouldn't hear her.

He glanced at her from the corner of his eye.

"Get ready."

"Don't intervene."

"We can't stay here," she rasped. "I'm going to move. Be ready."

"Triple," he growled in warning.

"It's not going to end well." Gritting her teeth, she pushed onto her knees. Her muscles shook. Her vision blurred. Battling through the pain, she squared her shoulders. "Westvane's fixated. Too stubborn to stop. He isn't thinking straight."

The clang of magical swords raged.

Montrose cursed under his breath. "Your plan?"

Palms pressed to her thighs, she narrowed her focus. *Concentrate.* She needed to concentrate. One lesson the sphere had taught her — if she could imagine it, she could manifest it. She hoped the theory was right. Prayed the magic answered when she called. With weakness invading and her body aching, she couldn't be sure, but...

She'd know in the next few seconds.

"Just be ready to retreat," she said, building an image inside her mind.

"To where?"

"The forest."

"Triple —"

"Be quiet. Get ready."

She whispered the instruction and hunted for magic. An answering burn sparked, humming a melody, rising in volume until her ears buzzed and her body burned. Remnants of slime left by the sphere contracted. Minus the blood and dirt, ribbons of blue liquid ran into rivulets, amassing into a large pool around her. Dipping her fingertips into the stream, Truly wove wet fibers together, giving it shape and form.

"Holy shit," Montrose said.

"Westvane," she murmured, seeking, reaching, warning him.

Keeping himself between her and the queen's guard, he growled at her.

A form of non-verbal communication. Something Westvane excelled at delivering. His body language said more than most people's words. Truly understood what he meant. She picked up what lay in his undertone. He wanted her to butt out, preferably while staying silent.

She huffed. Not going to happen. The rabble behind Priestly was growing impatient. And Priestly? A pang of anxiety hit her as she watched the blond guard. He was weakening, trying to hold the line and save face, so...

No way would she do what Westvane demanded.

She needed to get herself, him, and Montrose clear before things went sideways, and they ended up dead.

"Westvane."

He grunted.

"Don't argue," she said, gathering the liquid strand in her hands. "When I say so, duck and dodge right."

Slamming through his opponent's guard, he punched Priestly in the face.

Truly took that as agreement, counted off the seconds, then whispered, "Now!"

Ducking beneath the zing of a blade, Westvane spun to his right.

With a sharp exhale, Truly threw her hands up and lashed out. Ribbons of blue liquid formed into what she imagined in mid-air. Wide, long, thick, the tendrils crisscrossed, weaving into a net before attacking the queen's guard. The contingent cursed, then flailed, fighting to break free of the sticky web. Heavy blue fibers flexed. The net contracted, tarring feathers, tangling wings, putting on pressure. One by one, the queen's guard fell, knees buckling until each lay belly-down on the ground.

Immobilized by the net, Priestly cursed at Westvane.

Twin swords still flaming, Westvane turned to snarl at her.

"Stop being an idiot," she said... or at least tried to, but ended up rasping, "Move it."

The order leaked out of her as she listed sideways. Her stomach pitched. Her vision tunneled. Doubled over, Truly dry-heaved into the grass. The thump of footfalls rushed toward her. Someone yelled something. A second later, large hands yanked her off the ground. More rapid footsteps. Terrain whirled as head bobbing on her shoulders, she struggled to stay conscious.

"Westvane," she whispered.

"Shut up," he growled, towing her behind him.

She blinked up at him... and realized two things at once. First — sword in one hand, the other fisted in the back of her shirt, he was running full tilt, dragging her behind him across the plateau. And second, he'd just entered the cool recesses of Weeping Hollow, a forest everyone feared and no one dared to go.

THE FOREST WASN'T SAFE

He wanted to throw Truly into the nearest ravine. Grabbing her under the armpits, Westvane heaved her over his shoulder instead. Tossing an unconscious Door Master into a gully wasn't the most honorable thing to do. When she regained consciousness, however, all bets were off.

She'd intervened. Again.

Getting between him and his target seemed to be a running theme with her.

He wanted to blame her. Hell, he *did* blame her, but her budding power couldn't be denied. The sticky net had been a stroke of genius. He'd never seen anything like it. Neither had Priestly. The look of shock on his childhood friend's face — priceless. The satisfaction of seeing him and the queen's guard pressed to the ground, wings tangled, swords mired in blue goo? Almost worth the aggravation of not getting the fight he wanted. No, correction — *needed*.

Wiling away hours — days, weeks, months — inside his cage, he'd dreamed of crossing blades with Priestly for years. Longed for a confrontation with a member of the Azlandian warrior rank. Part of a select few, Priestly was a respected member of the Queen's Court. The bastard sat at the High Table, advised the council, a group that enforced the status quo — the laws that bound the majority Azlandians to a lifetime of servitude.

He knew his ex-friend. Strong. Stubborn. Smart. Priestly possessed a mind of his own, was able to defend his views, even as Lyonesse brainwashed everyone around her. Which was why he'd needed the fight. Testing Priestly was an integral of his plan.

Despite his political leanings, Priestly might be amenable to a changing of the guard. An ally in the fight for equality in Azlandia, instead of standing in opposition to change. If his intel proved true, Priestly could be the lynchpin — the inside man Westvane needed to dismantle the systemic discrimination plaguing his world.

A long shot, all things considered. A dangerous game that would no doubt end in his death, but...

Worth a try to set things right.

And Truly had ruined his chance.

Carrying her like a wounded soldier, he adjusted his grip, bouncing her into a more comfortable position. Stubborn Door Master. Total pain in his ass. Truly needed to start trusting him — and stop insinuating he was an idiot. He knew what he was doing. At least, he had five minutes ago — goading Priestly, manipulating with skill, angling for an eventual discussion. Now, however, half a mile inside Weeping Hollow, he wasn't sure of anything anymore. Other than the fact he shouldn't be here.

No matter what Truly thought, the forest wasn't safe.

Crooked and angry, trees creaked as he strode past, branches bobbing, gnarled fingers reaching out to touch their neighbors. One limb swayed into the next, delivering a message, spreading the news intruders travelled inside hallowed terrain.

Interlopers, giant pines whispered. *Unwelcome,* ancient sequoias and bent beeches replied.

Heaving with magic, humid air slithered against his skin.

Fine hairs on the back of his neck rose.

Westvane scanned the shadows, hunting for monsters in the dark. He felt the eyes. Knew something unholy hid inside the gloom, watching, waiting, ready to pounce as he moved between enormous trunks and jumped over downed logs. Montrose kept pace, running to his right, tension radiating like sweat from his pores.

He should not be here.

Wrapping his arm around the backs of Truly's legs, he conjured a sword. Black flames bit along the blade, flickering blue, spinning to gray. The pool of illumination ate through shadow. The iridescent glow of eyes gleamed in the sword-light.

Surrounded. He was *surrounded* and...

Westvane realized his mistake.

His sword made him a target. Firelight from the blade, a perceived show of aggression. Something the creatures hidden in the dark wouldn't view as a peace offering.

Montrose hissed. "Westvane, put that ou —"

He snuffed the flame. The sword dissolved in his hand, leaving him weaponless, vulnerable as snarls rumbled through the quiet.

Air thickened.

The trees around him lashed out. Thick branches curled around his ankles, then whipped him off his feet. He lost his hold on Truly. Hanging upside down, he cursed as she fell. Eyes still closed, arms and legs akimbo, she hit the ground. The thump reverberated. She didn't move. Didn't flinch. Instead, she tumbled over rough ground, leaving him swinging upside down, unable to help as he watched her disappear over the edge of moss-covered rocks.

TRULY SURFACED like a submarine through water. Slowly, looking through acute amounts of wavy blur. She blinked, battling mental fog, wondering at the strange pendulum motion. She kept swinging forward and coasting back, swaying in time to what sounded like footsteps.

Narrowing her view, she reached for focus. More information arrived, giving her bits and pieces of a jagged puzzle. Her body ached. Her palms and fingertips burned. Pressure beat against her temples, making her realize her hair swung loose, something rough pulling at the wet strands, tugging at her scalp.

Swallowing past a bad case of dry mouth, she fought to clear her vision. Flashes of detail pierced through the haze. Odd-shaped shadows. The rough texture of tree bark. Dead leaves below her, leafy green ones in full foliage above her, the visual scatter lit by an odd light. The moon, maybe? She frowned. No, not moon-glow. The luminescence was too yellow, ochre blended with buttery hues, not white or pale enough to be coming from the sky.

The strange swaying continued.

Battling to get her bearings, she concentrated on the motion and took another round of inventory. Body sore. Mind woolly. Exhaustion beating down her door. It felt as though she'd tucked into a bottle of tequila. The good stuff. Which didn't make sense. Last thing she remembered, she —

She jolted as details came flooding back.

"Shit."

More croak than coherent sound, the utterance garnered attention. Pressure tightened around her ankles. A lifting motion jacked her upright, making her realized she hung upside down and —

Something grunted at her.

A second later, she saw what held her — a one-eyed monster, made entirely of tree bark. Though, *one-eyed* might be inaccurate. The creature didn't have an eye, exactly. More like a round hole in the center of what she assumed was its face, the aperture aglow with yellow light.

Truly jerked in its hold.

With another grunt, it raised her higher.

She sucked in a shaky breath. Which hurt... a lot.

Her gaze even with its gaping yellow eye, she brushed the discomfort aside. No time to sit with the pain as the bark monster tilted her one way, then the other, studying her as though she was some kind of strange specimen.

Afraid to move, she took shallow breaths.

The monster continued to stare.

Moving nothing but her eyeballs, Truly returned the favor. Branches rose, some thick, others thin, wrapping like armor over its shoulders, crisscrossing behind its head. Bark dipped and rose on its torso, curling into waves at the edges. Leaves sprouted from the tangle, undulating, making it smell like Spring and newly fallen dew.

Blood rushed to her head. Her temples began to pound. She waited, tense — for it to shake her, raise a wooden fist and hit her... or do anything at all. Nothing of the kind happened. Silence expanded. Seconds ticked past. Time full of intense study as she looked at it, and the monster looked back.

Freaked out, not knowing what else to do, she greeted it. "Hello."

"Turnbolt," it rumbled through no mouth at all. The thing didn't appear to have one. Just a ropy, bark-covered face with the single light-filled hole for an eye. "Finally, a Turnbolt."

Well...

At least that was a familiar refrain.

Her house had said the same thing. Exact phrase. Making her wonder — was Weeping Hollow, enemy to Westvane and all other Azlandians, a friend to her? A safe haven, in the same way the Victorian on Isadore Street turned out to be?

Truly chewed on the inside of her lip. Could be true. A solid working theory, given the creature hadn't killed her yet.

"My friends," she said, testing the waters. "I need to know wh —"

With another grunt, it flipped her upright.

Her head snapped back. Pain streaked down her spine.

Grimacing, she cupped the back of her neck with one hand. With the other, she grabbed the bark monster, holding onto a branch, before she went flying over its shoulder. Perched safely in its grasp, she glanced down. Her stomach dipped. She shouldn't have looked. The thing was tall, which meant she was a long way up. She already hurt all over, and taking another tumble, wasn't on her list of things to do. Survival, however, sat right at the top, and if she could avoid more bruises while accomplishing that, all the better.

The creature lurched on.

Truly rode in silence, reshuffling her deck as she tried to figure out how best to proceed. Her first priority needed to be Westvane and Montrose. She'd already searched the forest. Neither of her friends were behind her, being carrying through the brush by other bark monster brethren.

"What's your name?" she asked, staring at its profile.

The creature grumble-growled and, with a flick of its tangled wooden fingers, kept walking, navigating through dense shadow and forest murk.

Settled in the crook of its arm, she hung on, struggling to see in the dark. Thick canopy overhead. Slices of moonlight. Pale patches of light dominated by deep gloom. Enormous trees everywhere. Mossy vines dripped from thick branches. No clear path in front of her, but the creature knew where it was going. It moved with an easy gait. Long strides neither fast or slow, just steady and even.

The thump of its footsteps crunched over downed branches, making her senses hum. She listened harder, paying attention. Subtle, but... a cacophony of sound broke through the quiet. Too much noise. More than one set of footsteps kicking up the musty smell of old leaves and rotting wood.

She glanced around the creature's tangled crown of branches and sucked in a choked breath. The thing wasn't alone. A platoon of bark monsters broke from the shadows, falling in line behind their leader. Moving in time, like a military unit, she saw a dozen, but knew there were more, striding with purpose passed towering trees and jagged bluffs.

Heart in her throat, Truly returned her gaze to the creature who carried her. "Your name?"

A series of clicking sounds came at her.

Truly frowned. Maybe it wasn't fluent in English. Maybe it possessed a limited vocabulary. Or maybe, it was following orders by refusing to give her any information. Could be his one-eyed comrades had already killed her friends.

Twisting in its grasp, she yelled, "Rosy! Westvane!"

Her shout echoed through the woods.

Grabbing her ankles, the bark monster turned her upside down again. She swung out to the side like a pendulum. Arms flailing, feet imprisoned, she pumped her knees, struggling to break its hold. The creature's gnarled wooden fingers lengthened, snaking up her legs and —

"It's alright, Eblin," a woman said. Perfect English. Hint of a British accent. The voice's owner standing somewhere behind her. "Put the Door Master down and return to patrol. I will take it from here."

More clicking noises.

A moment later, Truly hit the ground. Air left her lungs as dry leaves flew up around her. Coughing, she flipped over. Knees churning up dirt, she spun around and spied the woman standing six feet away. Taking a moment to steady herself, Truly drew a much-needed breath and studied her. Dressed in a white robe. Hands tucked into wide, bell-shaped sleeves. Dark skin glowing with vitality. Long gray dreadlocks spilling over her shoulders. The face of an angel, without a single blemish or wrinkle.

Truly frowned. "You're human."

"Indeed, I am." A soft smile played over the woman's face, making her even more beautiful. "Welcome to Weeping Hollow, Truly of the House of Turnbolt. I am Azalea, leader of the Human Legion. I am so very pleased to meet you."

"I don't understand."

"I know."

"My friends."

"All will be seen to in time." Another cryptic smile. This time, though, it reached her eyes. "Now, up, child, and follow me. I have much to tell you."

Pushing to her feet, Truly looked over her shoulder. She watched the bark monsters retreat, disappearing into the gloom. *Questions.* She had so many questions. Azalea intimated she held the answers, but...

Did she really?

Her eyes narrowed on Azalea's back. Friend or foe? A hinderance or a helping hand? Or was her friendliness a trick — a trap, misdirection designed to put her at a disadvantage?

A distinct possibility.

Nothing in Azlandia was ever what it seemed.

Everything corkscrewed, tumbling down twisted paths into even more unknowns. But as she followed the leader of the Human Legion (whatever that meant), her senses twitched. *Answers. True understanding.* A chance to possess what she needed to keep herself and others safe. A wealth of knowledge within easy reach, at her fingertips.

The allure was too tempting to resist. So instead of making a break for it, Truly walked along the winding path in Azalea's wake, stepping over thick roots and around stones, gaze scanning, on high alert, the need to know a living thing inside her. Maybe if she dug deep enough, understanding would come, and she'd never be outmatched again.

A worthwhile goal.

But first...

Westvane.

And Montrose.

Instinct warned her neither was safe inside Weeping Hollow. The forest spirit didn't want her friends here. Which meant she must find them, and do it fast. Before the malevolent being who protected the woodland took its toll and ended their lives.

29

BEWITCHING ARMS OF THE UNKNOWN

The pain came in waves, like splashing acid being poured over open wounds. Westvane rolled in the current, struggling to tear away from the straps holding him down. The ropes should've been easy to break. He was strong, smart, able-bodied... practically indestructible.

Or so he'd been led to believe.

The agony, though, told a different story.

Swimming in anguish, Westvane forced his eyes open. Absolute darkness, nothing but black spiraling into black, despair so dense he couldn't find his way out. Self-preservation jabbed at him. He flexed his hands, trying to move his arms. Thin bands tightened around his wrists, crisscrossing his body, securing him with gentle tugs. Hushed voices whispered around him, tones soothing with tender persuasion, beguiling him, lulling him toward relaxation.

His eyes drifted closed.

He shouldn't feel this way — compliant and non-combative. The idea was foreign to his nature. An insult to everything his mother made him, and all she hoped he would become.

The thought drifted, floating away before he could catch

hold. Beguiled by the spell, he sank deeper, hovering on the edge of consciousness. Eastbrook nudged him. Poking. Prodding. Ruffling his feathers against his cheek. A beak tugged at the ends of his hair.

His eyes opened and closed again.

Arching, shifting, digging his heels into mucky ground, Westvane wriggled side-to-side. Eastbrook was right. He couldn't stay here, in softness and comfort. He must fight his way free. Find a way out, but as he twisted against his bonds, the beguiling voice came again, washing over him like warm water. The darkness thickened. His mind loosened, and he drifted, away from all he knew, into the bewitching arms of the unknown.

30

POSITIVELY MEDIEVAL

Catching the toe of her boot on a raised tree root, Truly stumbled sideways on the uneven trail. Her arm flew out to stop her fall. Her palm landed on a huge tree trunk. The rough bark scraped across her cuts and bruises, causing her to push off too fast and lurch to one side.

Her knee bounced off the ground.

With a hiss, she righted her balance, coming to an awkward stop at the bottom of a ravine. Doubled over, she looked uphill. She scanned the top of the rise, plotting her trajectory up the slope. Near the crest, Azalea turned to wave her on before disappearing over the other side.

Truly pushed upright, loose soil shifting beneath her feet as she began her ascent, following a woman she didn't know deeper into Weeping Hollow, a place Westvane and Montrose insisted tortured and killed people.

The gamble was a big one, given the stakes. Her friends' lives hung in the balance. Trusting Azalea, following her instincts, might get them all killed.

Climbing over a moss-covered log, she sliced between two enormous trees. Her feet slipped again. She grabbed an outstretched branch, pulled herself up, and forged on, even as she shook her head. Was she making the right decision? Or a huge mistake?

Her intuition was a powerful tool. She listened to it often, going with her gut, feeling her way through situations most of the time. Analytical people thought her approach to life qualified as *nuts*. Other intuits got it, understanding how she knew the path she took was the right one without looking at hard data. Now, though, she would've given anything for a spreadsheet. For a list of pros and cons. Anything that might land her in the vicinity of absolute certainty.

Instead, she began questioning everything in detail. Her choices. The direction she hiked. Along with her own goddamned mind.

As awful thoughts plagued her, worry gnawed on her. What if her friends were already dead? What if nothing she did now could save them?

"Shit," she whispered, her throat tight, each breath coming hard as she crested the hilltop.

Thick woods thinned, opening up into a clearing along the ridgeline. Deep gloom lifted as clouds drifted and the moon came out to play. The shine settled like a blanket over the trees, painting bright green leaves with a silver brush. Old-growth trees with wide canopies swayed above her head, creaking in welcome... or was it warning? More questions. Another thing to worry about, as the smell of pine sap drifted and a brisk breeze cooled the sweat on her skin. Inhaling through her nose, she breathed in the forest scents and...

Picked up another.

Magic. Powerful. Potent. Different than hers, but also the same.

Watching Azalea traverse the zigzagging trail below her, Truly scanned the valley from her vantage point on the bluff.

Her gaze snagged on the soft glow of faraway streetlights, then moved on to trace rooftops and roads. Civilization in the form of a village. Pretty and picturesque. Still and silent. At peace with the knowledge it sat nestled in the center of Weeping Hollow's palm.

Her eyes narrowed, trying to get a better sense of it from afar. Large town? Or tiny hamlet? Single-story huts lined narrow streets. Angled roofs sloped to pointed eaves, some tall and peaked, others low-pitched and less-inspired. The ones she could see possessed nice-sized yards, wattle fences demarcating the space between homes. Looked like a spiral layout, streets circling, one rounding into the next, forming the shape of a Nautilus shell.

Her mouth curved.

Fibonacci would've been impressed with the precision.

Even the trees fell into the line, respecting the obvious mathematical equation.

At the shell's center, however, stood an outlier. The singular anomaly — a statuesque timber-beam building surrounded by green space, fronted by a town square. A place people gathered to socialize. Large enough to host a marketplace.

Hours spent studying Art History allowed her to frame the scene. Her first thought — thirteenth century Norway. Viking revival with a hit of feudal lord. A throwback to the days before the invention of modern comforts. Truly shook her head. The place looked positively medieval.

Finding Azalea in the dark, Truly started down the hill after her. Her pace was fast, her stockpile of questions multiplying with every step. Hopscotching over a collection of flat-faced rocks, she continued her pursuit. She caught up with Azalea at the bottom of the slope, slowing to walk shoulder-to-shoulder with her.

"What are they?"

Azalea glanced at her. "Who?"

"Eblin and his ilk."

"Sentries," she said. "Protectors of Weeping Hollow."

"They don't like magic-wielders?"

"No." Approaching a tree, Azalea veered left around its trunk.

Truly went right, rejoining her on the other side. "But I'm a magic-wielder."

"Not one Eblin considers a threat," Azalea said, skirting a large boulder blocking the trail. "Your magic is drawn from the *Ecotone*. It isn't divisive. It seeks to heal, instead of divide. The magic you wield is powerful, but it's also gentle and kind. You have the ability to knit worlds together."

"And the Electi?"

"War mongers. Selfish and greedy."

The path widened, then forked, becoming less rough underfoot.

Azalea walked to the right.

Stepping over the gnarled knuckle of a tree root, Truly stripped the elastic band from her hair. Focused on her companion, she raked the strand away from her face, retying her ponytail. "From what I've heard, the Electi don't treat Assentas and Croppers well."

"They never will," she said. "Which is why the Mirror Kingdoms always have, and always will, need a Door Master. One who is human, not of this world, able —"

"To be objective and fair?"

"Precisely," she murmured. "You may not govern here, but you have a voice. A strong one. You determined the health of our world. With the *Ecotone* open, Azlandia is breathing again. The air smells sweeter. Things long dormant have begun to grow once more."

"It's been less than two days."

Azalea's mouth curved. "We move fast around here."

"The speed of light moves slower," Truly muttered, throwing her a sidelong look. "About my friends?"

"Dog with a bone."

"What?"

"Dog with a bone," Azalea repeated, shaking her head. "You need to let that go, Truly. Your companions are lost to you now."

Her chest tightened.

"They're not dead," she said, refusing to believe it.

Azalea had to be lying. How she knew, Truly wasn't sure, but with her intuition clanging, she made an educated guess. Weeping Hollow wanted to keep its secrets, and Azalea was here to ensure the spirit who called the forest home got what it wanted.

Truly, however, didn't care what Weeping Hollow wanted. She needed her friends returned to her — hale and whole. She might not know Westvane well, but Montrose was a different story. Three months of him being a jerk. Three months of squabbling with him on the phone and inside Montrose & Brim. Three months of coming into her own after feeling lost for so long. All of which her grouchy gargoyle-of-an-ex-boss had allowed. In truth, Montrose had encouraged it — and her — every step of the way, cracking through her hard shell to drag her out into the real world. So...

Whether Azalea and the Hollow liked it or not, one thing must be made clear — she wasn't leaving without Westvane and Montrose in tow.

"You should know something, Azalea," Truly said, tone even and icy. Allowing fear to lead wouldn't get her anywhere. Not here, inside a place where a forest spirit ruled. "About Westvane —"

"His kind is not welcome here."

"I'd understand that if he were an Electi, but —"

"He is," she said. "He has wings, commands magic and —"

"He's also half-Assenta," she said, using instinct as her guide to direct the thrust of her argument.

Azalea stopped walking. Her face paled in the moonlight. "He's a hybrid?"

"Yes."

"Born of royalty?"

Truly had no idea. Westvane hadn't talked much about his parents. But if agreeing helped get him back in one piece, she wasn't above sharing what little she knew... or lying through her teeth. "His mother was executed by Lyonesse. His father —"

"Gods," Azalea whispered, staring at her in horror. "He could be the one."

Truly blinked. "The what?"

A good question. One in need of an immediate answer, but...

Azalea was already gone. Long robes kicking up behind her, she sprinted down the hill toward the village. Dark brown eyes flashed as she glanced over her shoulder and shouted, "Come on, Truly! We must reach him before it's too late."

More worried about her friends than ever, Truly didn't hesitate. She raced after Azalea, a single thought running on repeat inside her mind.

Azalea's reaction didn't bode well for Westvane.

And as she sped down the path, swerving around trees, jumping over rocks, and skidding across dead leaves, she started praying. Please God, let her reach him in time. Before whatever damage Weeping Hollow had done became irreversible, and she lost him forever.

31

BELLY OF THE BEAST

A step behind Azalea, Truly reached the edge of the village. It'd been a rough, downhill run, but as she dashed passed stone monoliths and onto a cobblestone street, she ignored the hitch in her side, along with the pain. Sore muscles and burning lungs were the least of her problems.

All that mattered was keeping up with Azalea.

No easy feat. For a senior citizen, the woman could flat-out run.

In full gallop, she timed her strides, staying close, following while fighting the urge to take the lead. Azalea turned left between two houses, into an alleyway, toward a dead-end. Truly slowed. Her companion didn't.

With cat-like grace, the woman hitched up her long skirt and leaped over the wooden fence blocking the lane. The second her feet landed, she took off across a backyard. Lights flickered. An odd buzz hummed across the lane. Humid air stirred and darkness shifted. Leaping over a row of thick curling vines and pumpkins, Truly watched in amazement as what she assumed were streetlights took flight.

Hummingbirds.

Everywhere.

Hundreds and hundreds in flight, bodies glowing like fire-flies. The hum of tiny wings increased. Soft shine radiated, then expanded and flew ahead, lighting her way in the dark.

She tore her gaze away from the living lights as Azalea upped the pace. Breathing hard, Truly stayed on her heels, weaving around yard furniture, ducking beneath clotheslines, trampling through people's gardens. She crashed through a hedgerow, came out clean on the other side, and looked both ways. She caught a flicker of movement at the end of the path.

With a curse, Truly turned right and kept running. Azalea's mad dash signaled disaster. The harbinger of bad things to come. Things Truly didn't want to contemplate, but...

Was she already too late?

If she wasn't, would she reach him in time to help?

Fear tightened its grip, shortening her breath, making it diffi-cult to run. Truly pushed herself harder, forcing her muscles to work as she sprinted alongside a cathedral-like building. Trees stood on either side of the road. The huge canopies grew up and curved inward, creating a leafy tunnel. Hummingbirds flew into it, illuminating the structure of twisted branches from under-neath, allowing her to see Azalea.

"Almost there!" Azalea yelled without looking back.

Thank God.

Reaching the end of the tunnel, Truly skidded into the town square. A large well stood at its center. An intricate arch curved over the well's mouth, a bucket-and-pulley system attached to a hook anchored in stone.

Doubled over, breathing hard, Azalea stood beside it.

Truly slid to a stop beside her. Palms planted on the granite lip, she leaned in, trying to catch her breath as she glanced side-ways at Azalea. "Where is he?"

Wiping the sweat from her forehead, Azalea pushed up

from her crouch. One hand pressed to her chest, she pointed to the well with the other. "In there."

"Are you serious?" Anger rippled through her. Dread rolled in on its heels as Truly looked into the inky surface of the water. "You drowned him?"

She shook her head. "He's in an air pocket... at the very bottom. You must go down and get him."

"What the —"

"No time to explain."

"Do it anyway."

"Truly —"

"Give me the condensed version."

"Weeping Hollow feeds on magic. It eats magic-wielders alive."

Her brows collided. "Alive? What do you mean *alive*?"

Azalea didn't answer the question. She veered off course instead. "As Door Master, you may be the only one who can save him. The forest spirit has accepted you. If you're lucky, it will allow you to enter the well and bring him out."

Terrific. Lovely. Perfectly horrible. Just what she didn't want to hear. "But not you?"

"No," she whispered, anxiety in her tone. "You must be the one to go."

"But, how?" Pressure increased behind her eyes, making her head ache. "It's full of water."

"Only for a few hundred feet," Azalea said. "Get in. The bucket is large enough. You'll fit, so will Westvane. Go down, grab him, and come back up."

"You're crazy."

"If you want him to live, you must do as I say." Azalea's gaze tunneled into hers. "Trust me, child."

Truly swallowed past the knot in her throat. The last thing she wanted to do was climb into the bucket, but she couldn't leave Westvane. If she refused to go, he died. If she stayed, prioritizing her own safety, she'd never forgive herself for not trying.

Cursing under her breath, Truly grabbed the edge of the bucket. "If you're lying to me, Azalea, I'll —"

"I would never do you harm, Truly." Expression earnest, Azalea flexed her hands on the crank handle. "A dry space exists below the waterline. You'll find him there."

"What about Montrose?" she asked, climbing into the bucket.

"We'll deal with him after you retrieve the hybrid." Releasing the locking mechanism, Azalea cranked the lever one full rotation. Steel teeth rasped against the metal disc. The bucket dropped toward the surface of the water. "Hold your breath."

"Super advice — thanks," she said, sarcasm biting as she glared at Azalea.

Azalea continued to turn the crank.

Cold water washed over her feet.

A hummingbird left its perch on the spire rising above the well. A soft puddle of light spilled around her as it settled on her shoulder. Truly looked from her tiny companion to the waterline.

Now or never.

Speak, or forever hold her peace.

Taking a deep breath, clinging to wooden sides, Truly settled onto the balls of her feet in the middle of the rectangular bucket. Crouched low. Heart hammering. Unease rising as water washed over her waist. Deep breath in, long breath out. Catch and release. One inhale followed by the next exhale. Water touched the bottom of her chin.

A second hummingbird joined her.

Soft wings brushed against her cheek.

She looked at Azalea.

Azalea held her gaze. "Be brave, Door Master. I'll be here when you bring him up."

Truly nodded, closed her eyes, and taking one last fortifying breath, descended into the belly of the beast.

32

TINY BUBBLES

The water was cold. And getting colder by the second.

The rapid descent didn't help. Something about her plummet into darkness wasn't natural. The bucket acted like an elevator, conveying her down, instead of allowing her to sink like a stone. Holding her breath, Truly ignored the burn in her lungs and tapped into the strange sensation.

Power slithered up from down below. The magic hissed, warning her to return to the surface as the chill deepened and water swam over her skin. The wet fingers tumbled around her like mini-cyclones, grasping at her clothes, pulling at her hair, needling into her skin until numbness set in.

Shivering in the dark, Truly clenched her teeth, gripping the wooden lip of the box as a cross-current battered her. The bucket swung toward the side of the well. Tiny air bubbles streamed past, swirling through faint light as hummingbirds walked the tops of her shoulders. Tail feathers aglow, the matched pair switched sides, changing the angle of illumination.

Truly stared into the abyss. But even with the humming-birds' help, she couldn't see much. Darkness driven by unnatural forces crept in from the outer well walls, cannibalizing the light until indistinct lines faded into blurry shapes.

Balanced on the balls of her feet, Truly descended deeper into the darkness. She glanced over the edge. Her hair streamed into her face. Wiping the loose strands away, she squinted into the on-coming flow. The hummingbirds shifted. Small talons dug into her shoulders as the glow around each brightened, eating through the gloom, and still...

Nothing but a gaping abyss below her. Total darkness. Pain beating on her chest, Truly closed her eyes. God. She hoped Azalea was right. Though to her, it seemed impossible Westvane lay at the bottom of the well. Trapped beneath unknown amounts of water. Injured by Eblin and his sentries. Being made a meal of by a powerful forest spirit who didn't want her to find him.

Dread pooled in the pit of her stomach.

Bile touched the back of her throat as she opened her eyes. *Please, let him be alive.* The silence plea echoed inside her head. But even as Truly clung to hope, she forced herself to face the facts. She might be too late. For all his strength and skill, Westvane might already be dead.

Wielding her intuition like a weapon, she tapped into the cradle of her own power, reaching into the magical library that lived inside the *Ecotone*. Her mind ran through miles of ancient corridors. Books flew off shelves. Pages flipped. She absorbed the written word, tucking the knowledge away as understanding rose.

The spirit that protected Weeping Hollow was unforgiving. A vengeful spirit without conscience, showing no mercy to those it considered a threat. After her encounter with Priestly and the queen's guard, Truly couldn't blame it. Lyonesse was cruel, brandishing the magic she commanded without caring whom it hurt. Taking their cue from her, her followers acted in accordance with her wishes, beating down anyone who opposed her.

Not surprising.

Systematic oppression thrived in a vacuum. Those in authority liked the status quo — the less awareness and more control, the better. The dominant caste in Azlandia was no different. As with most authoritarian regimes, inequality and abuse ran rampant inside a framework of *us versus them*. Privileged classes always resisted change. Equal rights for all required an even playing field, but also, true acceptance. A fact Lyonesse knew.

If the collective's focus shifted toward fairness, the perks the Electi enjoyed as the ruling class would disappear. Her iron grip on Azlandia, her insistence on the old ways supported by cruel laws, ensured the people stayed in line, and she remained in power.

Tried and true tactics for a dictator.

Azlandia might be a new world to Truly, but the story unfolding inside it was as old as time. Which made Weeping Hollow's reaction to magic-wielders understandable. If she was the forest, Truly wouldn't want Electi on her turf either. That didn't mean, however, that she wouldn't challenge the entity who called it home. Try to make the woodland spirit her friend, instead of keeping it a wary ally. If she succeeded, Weeping Hollow would become a sanctuary. A place for her to revisit and rest each time she crossed the *Ecotone* and —

The bottom of the bucket banged into something.

A thump swirled in the heavy current around her. Wood twisted, bowing underfoot as a vortex opened beneath her. Water raged upward. The violent tornado clawed at her hair and clothes, tossing her overboard. Truly grabbed one of the ropes, fighting the pull as the whirlpool banged her against the wooden side, trying to tear her away.

The stream of water reversed, funneling toward the top of the well.

Water drained away. Gravity grabbed hold, slamming her into the bottom of the bucket. Rough rope rubbed her skin raw. Pain ghosted up her arm. Rubbing the sore spot, Truly blinked water out of her eyes and looked up. The surface rippled above her. Fresh air instead of cold water rolled in to surround her. Flipping onto her side, she sucked in a choked breath. Her lungs spasmed as her ribcage expanded. Couching, inhaling hitched breaths, she threw the rope aside and sat up.

Hummingbird wings buzzed as her companions took flight.

Light spread through the cavernous space.

Shifting to her knees, she peered over the side. Uneven stone walls. Stalagmites rising like jagged teeth from the floor. A cave at the bottom of a well, the perfect place for the forest to make a meal of someone.

Still coughing, Truly climbed out of the bucket. Her feet slipped on mucky ground. Her knees buckled, and she folded in half, stifling a groan as her body protested the movement. Battered. Bruised. Nearly drowned by a magical well. No wonder she hurt everywhere.

Kneeling in the mud, she watched the hummingbirds flit around the cave, shining light in dark corners, and forced herself to stand up. Tiny wings vibrating, one hovered over a stalagmite and —

Truly sucked in a rasped breath.

Westvane — lying prone, face up, limbs thrown wide. Battered black feathers lay like corpses around his body, as though each had been ripped out by the root from his wings.

"Westvane!"

Her shout echoed across the cave.

He didn't move.

"Damn it." Gritting her teeth, she climbed between two rocks, making her way toward him. "Westvane!"

No movement. Zero reaction. Not even a twitch.

Rounding a stalagmite, she slid through a crevice. Halfway through the narrow opening, she reached out and grabbed the toe of his boot. Wedged in the gap, she shook his foot. Still no reaction. With a curse, she wiggled between the jagged stones — boot soles slipping on fallen feathers — to reach his side.

She dropped to her knees beside him.

Dead. Was he dead? Was she too late?

Fear clogging her throat, she reached out and placed her palm on the wall of his chest. No up and down movement. She checked his pulse. Nothing there either. With a curse, she stacked her hands and pressed down on his chest. Once. Twice. A third time, over and over... again and again. A sob escaped as she continued giving him CPR. Trying to revive him. Praying she could get his heart started and Westvane breathing again.

33

TAKE A DEEP BREATH AND HOLD IT

Someone was pounding on his chest. Fists rained down. Forceful. Steady. The rhythmic beat pressed down over his heart. Odd mutterings followed each compression, strange accompaniment to the hard hammering. Westvane's first thought — annoying. His second — no one touched him without permission. And he never extended the invitation.

Whoever owned those fists was going to die.

The muted utterances came again.

"One, two, three, four, five. If you wake up, I'm going to kill you," the voice said. "One, two, three, four, five."

More hard compressions against his sternum.

Floating inside his own mind, Westvane reached for focus. His brain glitched, flickering in warning. He tried again. Clarity flashed bright, then faded, leaving him drifting in soupy mental fog. He urged his body to move. Nothing. His muscles felt frozen. Even his fingertips refused to twitch.

His heart turned over in his chest as frustration collided with alarm. Not good. He needed to move. To get out from under whatever held him down in order to get mobile. Staying stationary wasn't an option. His enemies would find him. The queen would —

The voice muttered, tone rising as the pressure increased on his chest.

Searching for a lifeline, Westvane grabbed hold. To the feel. To the sound. To the pain as someone struck him over and over, dragging him up to the surface of his own mind. Synapses firing, he clung to the voice, using the sharp tone to break free of the cerebral undertow.

"Goddamn it, Westvane. Wake up! One, two, three, four, five. You're supposed to be my guide over here. How am I going to save Montrose, avoid the stupid queen, or find Brim inside the House of Scholars if you're both dead? One, two, three, four, five. Tell me that much, you stupid jerk. Come on, tell me. How, huh?"

A pointy elbow jabbed him in the ribs.

"And let's not forget about the Wendigo. It's still out there. He's probably eaten half of Philadelphia by now, and where am I? Here, at the bottom of a well, trying to save you." A huff. Sounded like disgust. A sob hitched to an inhale. Sounded like panic. "One, two, three, four, five. Get up! I need you to get up. I'm not doing this, saving... I don't know... the world, you and whoever else... all by myself."

Palms slapped against him.

The sharp sound tunneled into his head.

A jolt rammed through his veins. The zap electrified his muscles. His fingers twitched. Westvane exploded into awareness. He sat up and, lightening quick, caught the hand swinging toward him. "Stop hitting me."

"Westvane?"

He blinked away the remanence of haze. "What are you doing?"

"Thank God," Truly whispered. "You're back."

"Where are we?"

"Weeping Hollow, in the bottom of a well."

Sitting on his ass, he stared at her, not understanding.

She clarified. "It's trying to eat you."

His brows collided. "What?"

"The forest is trying to eat you," she said, as though the explanation made perfect sense — and she didn't sound like a lunatic. "It doesn't like the Electi. Magic of any kind, really."

"I'm not an —"

"Half." Kneeling in the muck beside him, she grabbed his arm and pulled, trying to force him to his feet. "You're half Electi. Apparently, the Hollow doesn't discriminate in its dislike."

He scowled.

She yanked on his coat. "We need to get out of here. Can you walk?"

Could he walk?

Westvane frowned. He didn't know. Pain drilled deep, infecting his muscles, gnawing on his bones. The worst of it, though, knifed along his spine and down the back of his thighs. He glanced over his shoulders. His stomach dropped. His wings were gone, nothing but bloody stumps, black feathers strewn like fallen soldiers around him. Ragged and moth-eaten, his leather trench gapped open at the back, exposing raw skin scorched black underneath.

Gritting his teeth, he reached for Truly. "Help me up."

She didn't hesitate. Throwing his arm around her neck, she used her legs to pry him off the ground. Torn to shreds, the back of his pants fell away. The skin on his ass and legs peeled off, leaving part of him stuck to the stone floor.

Agony laced him.

Baring his teeth, Westvane beat back a roar.

"Okay?" she asked, readjusting her grip on him.

Leaning on her, he forced his feet to move. Each step brought more pain. Bile burned the back of his throat. Fighting his gag reflex, he rasped, "Where... where?"

"The bucket." Struggling to stay upright, Truly grunted beneath his weight. She moved him forward, steering him around rock formations, across a cavern. "We need to get into the bucket."

His vision wavered.

Squinting through the blur, Westvane tapped into the mercurial force underpinning his power. Volatile, temperamental, it never failed him. Was always swimming beneath his surface, ready and waiting, desperate to be used. But as he reached for the magic, something strange happened. His senses didn't sharpen. His vision remained flat, hampering his ability to see in the dark. The predatory instincts he relied on (and under the circumstances, obviously took for granted on a regular basis) failed to arrive, showing him nothing but dark corners and shifting shadows.

So forget about the bucket.

He couldn't see five feet in front of him, never mind navigate his way toward safety. Which made him helpless.

He was *helpless*. Unable to fend for himself. Forced to rely on another. At a woman's mercy, just as his mother had been all those years ago. All of a sudden, it struck him, and he understood — the vulnerability, the inescapable quality of it, the raw, deafening roar of unfairness. What most Azlandians must feel and endure every day.

Even as a child, he'd never been weak. His mother had seen to it. His experiences in Eckizbad prison and the Parkland had honed him to a lethal point. Made him strong, but also arrogant and selfish, allowing him to wall off the outside world and self-isolate, keeping others at a safe distance in order to protect himself. But as Truly steered his path across the cave, Westvane acknowledged a truth he never wanted to before.

Friendship was important, invaluable in so many ways. Loyalty to one's tribe was paramount. Being part of a team meant everything, and as he leaned on the Door Master, he realized something else.

Alone in the world didn't need to mean family-less. Sometimes, when left with no other option, a warrior simply needed to build one of his own.

"Truly."

Breathing hard, she propelled him across uneven ground. "Yeah?"

"Need to know something."

"What?"

"Why does he call you Triple?"

"Rosy?"

In too much pain to give her a full answer, he grunted. "You really wanna talk about this *now*?"

"No better time."

"You're nuts," she said, sounding irritated.

"Well?"

She made a sound of frustration. "You ever heard the expression *double trouble*?"

Westvane shook his head.

"When I first started working for Rosy, he always said, '*You're double the trouble and triple the threat.*'"

"And Triple stuck."

"Yeah. Annoys the crap out of me, but —"

"Montrose calls you that anyway."

"Yeah."

"Tell him to stop."

She huffed. "Brilliant suggestion, bozo. Why didn't I think of that?"

Her snarly tone tickled his funny bone. Unable to help it, Westvane laughed. Goddess, she was prickly. Beyond stubborn. So fierce, he couldn't help but admire the way she moved through the world — unapologetically, with a tenaciousness that matched his own.

"Truly —"

"I don't want to hear it."

"If I die, you need to —"

"You're not going to die."

His temper ignited, helping him stay on his feet. "Quit interrupting me."

"Then stop saying stupid shit."

"I'm trying to tell you —"

"Shut up, Westvane. Now is no time for epiphanies," she said, shoving him forward. "Get in the bucket."

Arm around her shoulders, hand fisted in her coat, he swayed and, vision wavering, stared at the bucket. Large. Wooden. Thick ropes attached to it. Looked sturdy, strong enough to carry his weight.

Bracing for the pain, he grabbed the edge and planted a knee on the lip.

Truly shoved him from behind.

He toppled inside, hissing as he hit the bottom.

Truly climbed in after him, and crouching behind his bent knees, grabbed the rope attached to the top of bucket.

She met his gaze. "When I say *now*, take a deep breath and hold it."

Westvane nodded. He didn't have much more in him. The journey across the cave had hurt. Hitting the bottom of the bucket had felt worse. And as he looked up and saw water rippling overhead, he knew whatever came next wasn't going to be any better. Now all he needed to do was hope he held his breath long enough to survive the ascent back to the surface.

34

DEAD IN THE WATER

The bucket moved slower going up than coming down. Westvane's fault. He was a big guy, huge by human standards, no slouch when measured by an Azlandian yardstick either. The fact he fit in the bucket at all counted as a minor miracle.

The kind she appreciated right now.

Even so, Truly prayed a bigger one hung on the horizon. One that moved her into warp speed. She needed to reach the top of the well soon. Her lungs weren't holding up. Pain, worse than before, burned inside her chest. She was running out of air. Running out of time. Running out of hope while water swirled and the chill took chunks out of her willpower.

Palm pressed to her breastbone, she glanced at Westvane. He wasn't faring any better. Under normal circumstances, the well wouldn't have fazed him. He'd have spiraled up to the surface without the bucket's help, then stood in the moonlight and snarled at the forest, disgusted by its attempt to kill him.

In the weak light thrown by glowing hummingbirds, Truly couldn't see a hint of his usual arrogance. The Slayer's brashness was long gone. He was struggling to hold on. She felt his pain, sensed his weakness, saw the awful burns on his body and what the Hollow had done to his wings. Now, she was forcing him to hold his breath, pushing his limits, adding insult to injury.

Come on.

Come on.

Gripping the frayed edge of Westvane's coat, she reached up. Her hand found the rope attached to the bucket. She yanked, trying to speed their ascent. Her efforts didn't make the bucket move any faster. Lungs burning, stomach churning, she looked up. Water streamed over her as she peered into the darkness, desperate for a glimpse of light above her.

Stone walls whirled past. Well water rippled and flowed. Cold needled into her skin, drilling into her bones and...

There. Just there. Beyond the blur, a glimmer reaching through the gloom.

She shook Westvane.

His eyes cracked open.

"Almost there," she mouthed.

Black eyelashes nothing but dark slashes against his pale face, he nodded. The movement hardly signified. More flinch than actual acknowledgement, but at least, it was something. An indication he was still alive.

The glow widened, brightened.

Truly glimpsed the shadowed slash of a straight line. Seconds later, the bucket broke the surface of the water. Half submerged, listing to one side, she grabbed the wooden side to keep the box upright. Sucking in a raspy breath, she blinked water out of her eyes and searched for Azalea. She found her at the edge of a gathering crowd.

"Got him," she said, the words scraping the back of her sore throat. Truly cleared the rawness away, but... God. She sounded terrible, like someone who'd spent years smoking three packs a day. "He's hurt."

Her brow furrowed, Azalea stepped up to the well. Those gathered behind her followed, crowding in like looky-loos, curious and clustered, wanting to see an injured Slayer.

"How bad?" Azalea asked, peering inside the bucket.

"It isn't good." Climbing onto the stone ledge, she dragged the bucket closer to the side wall. Droplets splattered over the ground. Wood bumped against stone. Westvane snarled. The group jumped back. "I need help hauling him out."

The looky-loos beat a fast retreat.

Azalea wrung her hands. "No one will —"

"I don't care that you're afraid of him," she said, keeping her gaze level and her tone firm. "Here's what I need, and you're going to give me — someone to help lift him out, a warm place to stay and —"

"A hut has been prepared for you."

Truly nodded. "Thank you. Do you have a doctor here?"

"A healer," Azalea said, eyes on Westvane, face white with fear.

"Get her."

"Him."

"Whatever. Just bring him to me," Truly said, worry eclipsing patience as Westvane shivered, shaking the bucket, making water slosh. "And while you're at it, bring Montrose to me as well."

"Who?"

"My gargoyle."

Azalea opened her mouth to reply.

With a slash of her hand, Truly cut her off, gaze bouncing over the crowd. Her attention landed on two shaggy looking... she frowned, trying to figure out what species the two creatures standing at the back of the throng belonged to — Sasquatches,

Yetis, relatives of Chewbacca? All pretty good guesses, given the duo possessed thick white fur sticking up at odd angles. Head and shoulders above the rest, the Yetis looked strong, calm, less afraid than the others. She made a split-second decision and drafted both into her make-shift army.

She pointed at the shaggy pair. "You two — I'm gonna need your help."

Grunting in unison, the Yetis lumbered toward her, approaching with caution as they moved through the crowd. Breathing a sigh of relief, Truly helped moved Westvane from the bucket onto a cart someone rolled alongside the well.

Westvane growled.

The on-lookers gasped.

Truly ignored their fear and, crouched on the wagon bed, wrapped Westvane in blankets

"Hold on, Westvane." Brushing aside his hair, Truly laid her hand on his forehead. Hot to the touch, the sharp rise in his temperature a direct contrast to the shivering. She checked his pulse. Strong despite his clammy skin. "Hold on. We'll be safe and warm soon."

Unconscious now, Westvane didn't answer.

Her chest tightened as panic clawed through her.

Taking a deep breath, Truly controlled the emotion. Freaking out now wouldn't help anyone. Least of all, Westvane. She must reach deep and smooth her upset. Too many eyes watched her. Too many eyed Westvane with a combination of mistrust, disgust, and fear. Voicing her concern for him wouldn't get her far. Or get her friend what he needed.

A show of strength — of assured command — would produce better results in the long run. But as the Yetis pulled the cart away from the well, away from the town center into a side street, the relief she should've felt didn't come. Dread hammered her instead as Westvane struggled to breathe.

Air rattled in his chest. Each labored inhale a sure sign he'd spent too much time in the belly of Weeping Hollow.

Too long for him to make a full recovery?

Truly didn't know. Westvane was in bad shape. She didn't understand Azlandians well enough to know how fast one healed. Had no idea how long it would take for a hybrid like Westvane to recuperate. But as the cart swayed, progressing down cobble-lined streets, she prayed he made it through alive. If he didn't, she was dead in the water. A sitting duck set adrift in a foreign world before she'd learned to tread water, never mind swim.

WHISPERING WOKE HIM UP. Two distinct voices, and an odd clicking noise. He listened closer. Truly's distinct accent, for sure... along with a second person's. Deeper voice than the Door Master's. Hushed and husky, stress vibrated in the other woman's undertone, an argumentative quality layered on top. His senses contracted, laying down a grid. The gossamer threads spilled into the room, expanding around him. He pulled on the strings, sending each out to explore the outer edges of the room.

Standing fifteen feet away, the pair were trying to be quiet... and failing miserably.

His hearing was keen, so sharp he detected the slightest sound.

Staying still and silent, Westvane took stock of his surroundings without opening his eyes. Warm air. The crackle of a fire burning nearby. Soft cotton under him, softer blanket over him.

He shifted on the sheets.

Belly down. He was lying belly down, head on a pillow, arms flung over his head, feet hanging off the end of the bed.

The quiet argument continued.

"I have to go," Truly said.

"Not a good idea."

Boots scraped over stone. Predatory instincts alive and well, he picked through the noises. Truly planting her feet. The rustle of her jacket as she crossed her arms. The scent of determination swirling in the air around her, joining the smell of burning wood and ash.

"I can't leave him there."

"We can't get him down," the unknown woman said. "What makes you think you can?"

"Have you tried asking nicely?"

A huff, full of disgust, streamed across the room. "It's pointless, Truly. The forest spirit won't let him go."

Westvane cracked one eye open.

Blurry vision greeted him. He blinked to clear the unwanted interference. His surroundings came into sharper focus. One-room cabin. Fireplace on the far wall, the bed he lay in opposite it. Stone floor, thick rugs, two wide-back chairs in front of the hearth. Truly and a dark-skinned woman standing across the room, facing off against the backdrop of a wooden door.

Chin leveled, Truly stared her down. "Just show me where he is. I'll do the rest."

He pushed up onto an elbow... and regretted it immediately. The movement set off a chain reaction. Pain exploded beneath his skin. Nerve endings screamed in indignation. Fisting his hands, he breathed though the anguish and, with supreme effort, refocused.

"It won't work. I've tried everything."

"You haven't tried *me*."

Drawing her white-gray dreadlocks away from her youthful

face, the woman shook her head. "Your magic doesn't work here. It's a dead zone."

"I know," Truly said, taking a half step closer, posture moving from stubborn to beseeching. "But that doesn't mean my way isn't worth trying."

The woman pursed her lips, denial in the lines of her body.

Westvane swallowed past a bad case of dry mouth. "What's going on?"

Truly whirled in his direction.

"You're awake," she whispered, coming unstuck, moving toward him from across the room. "How do you feel?"

He ignored the question, gaze bouncing from the stranger, back to her. "What's going on?"

She reached his side and, without permission, set her palm to his forehead. "Rosy's stuck."

Batting away her hand, he rolled, levered himself upright, and swung his feet over the side of the bed. The blanket fell to his waist, grating over raw, bare skin. A growl escaped between his clenched teeth. "Where?"

"No," Truly said, tone sharp.

"What?"

"Don't get up. You need to rest. Your back is still —"

He scowled. "Where is he?"

She sighed. "I'm trying to find out."

"I'll take her," the woman said, a tremor in her voice.

Westvane glanced her way.

Spine pressed against the door, the woman was trying to flee his presence while standing in the same room.

"I'll take her." Wide-eyed, face white with fear, she reached behind her. Her nails scraped over wood in her frantic search for the door handle. Her horrified gaze moved from him to Truly. "I'll take you. Now, if you want and —"

"Okay. Let's go, Azalea." Grabbing his wrist, Truly swung

his arm around, forcing him back onto the mattress. With a curse, he collapsed against the sheets, the pain so intense he thought he might throw up. "You — stay here. Rest, sleep... whatever."

"Truly," he rasped, watching her walk toward the door.

"I mean it, Westvane. Don't move a muscle." Tossing him a warning look, she pointed at the bed. "I'll be back soon."

He opened his mouth to order her to wait for him.

The door slammed behind her before he got the objection out. He clenched his teeth. Such a bossy little menace — and a total pain in the ass. He should let her go. Allow her to walk into whatever danger awaited her out there... in the murderous, magic-hating forest that tried to eat him. *Eat him*, for the love of Azlandia. Powerful mage or not, the new Door Master needed her head examined.

Still, he could no more leave her to whatever idiocy she planned than cut off his own arm. Truly might be crazy, but as a member of his team, he refused to let her go alone. She'd get herself killed, and Montrose roasted right along with her.

Breathing through the pain, Westvane slid his legs over the side of the bed. Mattress springs creaked. His bare feet hit the floor. He glanced around the room, searching for his clothes. He needed to get dressed and on the trail. Before her scent faded. Before she ended up buried in a ditch, hung in a tree, or burned at the stake.

Whatever.

The method of execution didn't matter. Keeping her alive in Weeping Hollow, in a forest hell-bent on murder, however, mattered a whole lot more to him than it should.

35

TRIAD OF POWER

Gloom danced between towering trees, throwing long shadows over the front steps of the cathedral. Standing on the edge of the town square, at the entrance to a trail, Truly stared into the forest. Fat vines snaked over and between damp branches. Thick trunks covered in Irish moss. The scent of savagery in the air.

How she knew what savagery smelled like, Truly didn't know. No time for her to care either as awareness prickled through her. She narrowed her line of inquiry, focusing inward instead of out, relying more on magic than her five senses. Information drifted on the breeze, informing her the woods teemed with hidden danger. The kind of wild animals people on her side of the *Ecotone* had never seen, never mind encountered.

Stepping onto the path, Truly tried to tamp down her apprehension. Problem was, she possessed an excellent imagination. Deep shadows slicing between heavy, knotted trunks lent credence to the legend growing inside her mind. Nothing good lived inside that stretch of forest. The odd mix of old growth oaks, stoic redwoods, and giant sequoias made a serious statement: *Enter at your own risk.*

The wind picked up, whistling between twisted branches. She stifled a shiver as more scents kicked up. The smell of wood bark, wet grass, and marshy ground. Dank. Fragrant. Almost pleasant, if it weren't for the caustic curl of magic hanging heavy in the air.

An ethereal quality roped between the trees like Christmas lights. A faint wink here, a shimmering twinkle there. The effect was mesmerizing, urging her forward while simultaneously making her want to turn around and go back. An illusion cast by a malevolent spellbinder? A warning to ensure she stayed away? An enchantment cast to lure? She didn't know. Couldn't tell if what she saw was real or imagined.

No doubt the forest spirit's intent.

Staying on the flagstone path, she walked deeper into the woods. Just before she rounded the first bend, Truly paused to look over her shoulder. "Are you coming?"

Back to wringing her hands, Azalea shook her head. "I've already been. The forest no longer wishes to hear from me. Maybe you'll have better luck."

Truly hoped so. Otherwise, she'd never get Montrose back.

She scanned the trail ahead, where uneven cobblestones swerved behind an oak.

"Stay on the path," Azalea called. "Do not step off the stones."

"Why?"

"The Scions will be watching. If you step off the stones, you become fair game."

"Scions? What are —"

"Never mind. Just stay on the path," Azalea said, backing away, leaving her standing alone on the pathway. "When you come to the fork in the trail, go left. Your friend is not far beyond that point."

Truly nodded. "If I'm not back in an hour, send someone after me."

She heard Azalea agree, but didn't look back. Squaring her shoulders, she walked on. Slowly at first, then faster as nerves got the better of her, pushing into her a jog. Time was of the essence. So was getting out the woods. Nothing about the forest said *peaceful*. She sensed the churn of violence beneath the surface beauty. Weeping Hollow was waiting for her to step wrong, make a mistake, giving it an excuse to strike. Which meant her mission had just moved from urgent to surgical. She needed to be precise — get in, retrieve Montrose, retreat to safety even faster.

Rounding the bend, she dipped beneath a low-hanging branch. Her boot soles slid across wet stone. She adjusted her balance, and stepping with care, headed down a sharp incline. The farther she travelled, the rougher the trail became. Thin slices of moonlight lit the way, helping her see the stones demarcating trail from rambling undergrowth.

The path dipped into a shallow valley.

Truly ran up the other side of the hill and around another bend. A scuttling sound erupted around her. Her gaze snapped left. She scanned the woods on both side of the path. Nothing yet, but she knew they were out there. Watching. Waiting. Beady gazes on the trail edge, hoping she'd step wrong and —

A wave of loud rattling rumbled over the rise. Bright light painted rough tree trunks. A second later, she saw them — hundreds of them — hard, blue scorpion-shaped shells glowing in the dark. *Scions*... some big, some small, bladed dual claws snapping, tails with black stingers curled over their backs. Legs clicking together, the swarm rushed both sides of the path.

Her gait faltered. She stumbled sideways. With a curse, she scuttled backwards before she stepped off the stones. Afraid to move any further, Truly stood close to the edge of the trail, boots planted on flagstone, waiting for the army of Scions to attack. A second wave scrambled over the rocky rise to join the first.

She blew out a shaky breath. Surrounded. She was *surrounded* on both sides. Nowhere to run. No place to hide, even if she managed to get there.

So tense her muscles hurt, she watched the swarm organize, arranging into lines that reminded her of military formation. In order of rank and size — biggest Scions in the middle at the front, smaller ones fanning out from their sides, until the contingent formed a half moon.

Strange, but no doubt effective.

And yet, once in formation, none of the Scions moved toward her.

She stared at them.

Beady eyes stared back at her.

With a quick hop, she jumped to the center of the path. The movement caused a flurry of excitement. Claws snapped together like bladed teeth, the rhythm like a drumbeat. Stingers began to swing like pendulums as Scions surged forward, legs scuttled over rock, violent sound echoing through the forest.

She froze, waiting to be swarmed and eaten.

Five feet from the edge of the flagstones, the Scions stopped and, with a quick rearrangement, fell back into formation.

Testing the waters, she took a step forward.

Scions bristled. Powered by the group's agitation, blue shells glowed brighter. Truly shuffled forward, fingernails biting into her palms, then took a few tentative strides. The swarm scuttled sideways, moving as one, keeping pace in proper formation.

Creepy. Also, impressive.

Staying in perfect alignment couldn't be easy while on the move. But like a single-cell organism, the Scions worked like a hive, communicating without difficulty, maneuvering over rough terrain as a unit, following her progress while maintaining a strict boundary.

Thank God for Azalea. She'd given her solid advice.

One eye on the Scions, the other on the trail, Truly upped the pace. The flock of calamity continued to follow. Ignoring her hard-shelled companions (difficult given the noise), she stayed on the path. Her feet beat across stone. Shadows deepened. Scions scuttled around huge trunks, over mossy logs, and under thick brush. The scent of rich earth and running water reached her.

Flagstone forked into two separate trails.

As instructed, she veered left, ran down another hill and —

Heard Montrose before she saw him.

Listening to him curse, she followed the sound of his voice. After a minute or two, the trail widened into a clearing. Flagstone stopped at the edge of a circle with a floor made out of bricks. Some large, some small, all hand-painted by someone, laid out in a pattern both beautiful and ancient.

Scions scrambled up to the mosaic edge. Thousands deep, the horde surrounded the clearing with living light, jockeying for position.

"About fucking time!"

The yelled complaint made her look up.

"Wow," she said, spotting her ex-boss.

"Yeah," Montrose snarled back from his prison cell.

Suspended in the air, the odd enclosure was made of... well, she didn't know. The structure looked alive. Thick vines comprised of bark — or maybe, snakes — slithered around Montrose, trapping him inside...

She frowned up at him. "What is that?"

"A living cage."

"A *what?*"

"You want to me to explain — right now?" Montrose threw

up his hands in frustration. His razor-sharp claws flashed in the glow of scions. "Seriously?"

"Maybe not," she murmured, staring at her friend.

Walking underneath the cage, she turned full-circle. No door, which meant no key. No rope attached to the top of the living cage, which meant no way to cut him down. From what she could see, the cage grew directly from the branch above it.

"Okay." Truly pursed her lips. "Well..."

"Get me down," Montrose said, clawing at the vines.

His fist smashed through the barrier.

Another twisting, wooden bar grew in its place, repairing instantaneously.

Montrose threw another punch.

"Stop it, Rosy. You'll never get out that way," she said, following the branch to the trunk. Scion crawled around its base, surrounding the tree beyond the monoliths standing at the edges of the brick patio. "Give me a second to figure it out."

He growled at her.

Truly ignored him and listened to the forest instead. The scuttle of scions sank beneath the wave of concentration. The woodland hummed. She tapped into the whisper, into the vibration beyond the monoliths, aligning herself with the presence she sensed beyond the clearing. Preternatural heat invaded her veins. Simmering. Bubbling. Burning through her as intuition spiked. Her senses opened. Her focus narrowed and...

There. *Right there.* The spirit who protected Weeping Hollow — invisible to the naked eye, but perceptible to her — stood beyond the monoliths, watching her, waiting for an introduction.

Using instinct as her guide, Truly hit one knee and bowed her head. Carried by an ancient knowing, words spilled into her mind and, all of a sudden, she knew what to say.

"Spirit of the Hollow," she said, her tone respectful. "I am Truly, Master of Doors, Protector of the *Ecotone*."

Light taps traced her temples. A warm drift brushed across the tops of her cheekbones. Perception unlocked, creating a channel inside her mind. A buzzing hum slipped through the fissure. A low voice echoed inside her head as mind-meld took hold. *"Welcome, Truly, Master of Doors, Protector of the Ecotone."*

"Ancient one," she murmured. *"I have a request."*

"Ask."

"Release my friend."

"No."

"I need him," she said. *"I need him to do what must be done."*

"You took the other."

She frowned at the painted bricks underfoot. *"Westvane?"*

A rasping sound rolled in from edge of the clearing.

Fine hairs stood up on the back of her neck. Keeping head bowed, Truly peeked over her shoulder. In nothing but a blanket and bare feet, Westvane stood five feet behind her. Although *standing* might be too optimistic a term. Pale-faced and sweating, he looked ready to fall over. The idiot. He was healing, but still injured. No way should he be running around in the woods.

"You just can't help yourself, can you?" she asked softly, struggling to maintain her mental connection with the Hollow.

He swayed on his feet. "Truly, are you —"

"I'm fine. You are not." She glared at him, worried he really might fall over. How could she want to rip his head off and be concerned about his welfare at the same time? A conundrum. An annoying one that required further investigation but...

Another time. Right now, she had bigger fish to fry.

"Take a knee, Westvane."

He opened his mouth to argue.

Worried about disrespecting the Hollow, she pointed at the ground. "A knee, Assenta."

The formal redress did the trick. Folding forward, Westvane knelt. He winced as his knee touched down on brick, but held steady.

"*One.*"

The word came through mind-meld, tapping across her temples.

Truly shifted to face forward again. "*What does that mean?*"

"*One or the other,*" the Hollow whispered. "*Choose, Truly, Master of Doors, Protector of the Ecotone.*"

Comprehension bloomed.

Truly tore the pedals off the rose, refusing to accept the ultimatum. "*No. I need them both.*"

A pause.

A shift as the Hollow moved more fully into her mind.

Holding steady, she didn't fight the intrusion. Truly dropped her mental shields instead. She might be a new Door Master, still unclear about her responsibilities, but every hour brought more insight. The forest spirit needed to understand. The stakes were too high to remain stubborn and uncooperative. So instead of fighting, she opened up and shared her hopes, her dreams... all the things she wished to accomplish in both Earth Realm and Azlandia.

"*Three in one.*" Fog rolled into the clearing, frothing between tall monoliths, over mosaic-laid brickwork. "*Triad of power.*"

"Yes," she said, confirming the coalition. "*Please release him. Let us go in peace.*"

The Hollow hesitated.

Fog-filled fingers caressed her cheek as she felt the forest spirit retreat. The presence inside her mind withdrew. Sucked out by invisible threads, the mist exited the clearing. Scions scurried over the hill and disappeared from view. The wreathing vines imprisoning Montrose opened. Without warning or mercy, the cage ejected him, throwing him head-first toward the ground.

36

FOREVER YOUNG

Gargoyles snored. Worse than bulldogs.

A miracle by all accounts, but the noise didn't keep Truly from sleeping. Exhaustion had long set in. She'd been tired for days. For months, actually, given her nighttime gig as Montrose's eyes, ears, and purveyor of sleazy photos in Philadelphia.

The thought opened her eyes. Slouched in one of the high-backed chairs in front of the fireplace, she stared at the rough, timber-beam ceiling.

Philadelphia. Her job at M&B.

It felt like years, not just days, since she'd crossed the *Ecotone*, leaving home behind. Nothing approaching normal had happened between then and now. But then, normal always ended up being a matter of how a person chose to look at things. Divinity lay in the details. A matter of personal perspective, more photoshopped reality than unvarnished truth.

She lived inside a new normal now. One that included sharing a rustic cabin with a hybrid Assenta warrior and a foul-mouthed gargoyle.

Blowing out a long breath, she shifted in the chair,

straightening her legs to prop her sock-clad feet on the hearth-stone. Sore muscle stretched. Tendons lengthened. She nearly groaned in relief. She swallowed the sound at the last second, afraid of waking Westvane and Montrose. No sense disturbing the pair. Both were out — Westvane lying belly-down on the bed, head turned away from her, Montrose splayed flat on his back on the floor beneath the kitchen table, claws twitching, snore constant... and almost as loud as a chainsaw.

Tuning him out, Truly listened to the crackle of the fire, then pushed the blanket aside, and stood. Her back complained as she straightened. She rolled her shoulders, working out the twinge, and realized she felt alright. Better than she had in a while. Less anxious. More focused. Or...

Turning her head to one side, she cracked her neck.

Maybe that wasn't it. *Less anxious* didn't make the grade. More awake seemed a better fit. More settled and alive too, less oblivious to the world around her.

Something had happened while chatting with the Hollow. The channel inside her mind stayed open after it retreated, leaving her plugged into a powerful outlet. Now, her senses hummed. Her magic flexed. Her ability to tap into the stream electrified. The pulse sizzled through her, amplifying every-thing — sight, sound, touch, taste, and scent — making her more aware of her surroundings.

Faint footstep approached the cabin door.

She caught the scent of perfume, the musk of thick fur and...

Azalea. Accompanied by a group of Yetis.

Grabbing her boots off the floor, Truly tiptoed across the cabin. She skirted the end table sitting by a low-backed couch. Moved around the kitchen table (and Montrose), avoiding the mismatched wooden chairs scattered around it. Footfalls cush-ioned by a smattering of area rugs, she reached the front door.

Cool metal brushed over her palm. The latch clicked as she turned the door handle.

The snick sounded loud in the quiet.

With a silent curse, she glanced over her shoulder.

Undisturbed by the noise, neither of her bunkmates moved.

Releasing a measured breath, Truly pulled the door open. Slowly. An inch at a time. Her gaze riveted to Westvane. Montrose wouldn't care if she snuck out for a minute. Westvane wouldn't be as understanding. The Slayer would lose his mind. Again. Like he had trailing her down the path after Montrose hit the ground inside the clearing.

The crash had echoed through the forest. Westvane hadn't missed a beat — or bothered helping the gargoyle off the ground. Top of mind for him had been lecturing her. He'd gone on and on about safety and the importance of having him at her back on the way back to town.

Truly frowned at him over her shoulder. Difficult to argue with him. He might have a point. Rushing into the forest to save her ex-boss landed squarely in the column of "hasty decisions." Even so, in the end, she'd made the right play. And honestly? Westvane could've cut her some slack. Maybe even given her a pat on the back for a job well done. Or at least one for not getting killed.

Didn't happen.

Which made escape from the cabin without him noticing all the more necessary.

He'd have more to say if she left without him, but... whatever. She wouldn't go far. Would stand right outside the door and greet Azalea, if only to keep an eye on her friends.

Neither was one-hundred percent on the physical front. Montrose worried her less than Westvane. Though his injuries were healing, he wasn't close to one-hundred percent yet. The skin on his back looked almost normal, nothing but a tinge of pink where blisters and raw skin had been. The loss of his wings, though, concerned her.

The bloody stumps had disappeared, leaving the smooth expanse of his bare back. No regrowth of skeletal structures, no sprouting of dark feathers, making her wonder if the Hollow had succeeded in eating them. Were his wings really gone? Was their absence a permanent thing for him now?

Truly shook her head. A worry for another day. Right now, she needed to hear what Azalea came to say and figure out next steps.

With one last glance at her friends, Truly slipped outside. Closing the door gently behind her, she stood on the stoop and tugged on her boots. "Azalea."

"Evening," she said, latching the garden gate behind her.

The greeting tuned Truly into the time. She glanced at the sky. Dusk was falling, encouraging stars to bloom. She tipped her chin at Azalea. "You need something?"

She shook her head. "I came to tell you a meal is being prepared for you and the others."

The news made Truly's stomach rumble. "Kind of you. Thanks."

"Once you eat, I'm assuming you'll leave."

"Probably a good idea. We've been here too long as it is," she said, attention drifting to the Yetis milling around beyond the low garden wall. "We were chased into Weeping Hollow by the queen's guard. We need to move on before Priestly tracks us."

"No need to worry about that."

"Why?"

"Time stands still inside Weeping Hollow," Azalea said. "The clock stopped the second you stepped foot inside the forest. The moment you entered the Hollow will be the same one you exit it."

"Exactly the same time?"

"The Electi will be precisely where you left them. In the same state, as well."

So, pinned to the ground, fighting to break free of her net. "Nifty trick."

"The advantage of living here. No one ages. No one gets sick. Disease doesn't exist in the Hollow."

Interesting.

Also... a little weird.

Her gaze roamed Azalea's face. Youthful. No wrinkles in sight. Other than the mix of white and dark gray in her dreadlocks, the woman didn't look a day over thirty.

Curiosity got the better of her. "How old are you?"

"Ninety-one."

"Wow."

Azalea chuckled. "Forever young."

"But only if you stay inside Weeping Hollow."

"Small price to pay. It's beautiful here. Safe. Simple. Abundant amounts of fresh water. Food is plentiful," she said. "But don't go telling anyone on the other side of the *Ecotone*. We'll be overrun by humans in search of the fountain of youth."

"All the diehards."

"Exactly," Azalea said, glancing toward the darkening sky. "What's your next destination? Home?"

Truly shook her head. "Ipsalar."

"The city?" Her newfound friend frowned. "Not a great idea, Truly. Lyonesse and those who sit the High Table call Ipsalar home. The royal palace rests on Temple Hill, carved into the mountain side, above the city."

"Montrose told me, but I need to visit the Hall of Scholars." She leaned back against the door, shuffling through information she already possessed, identifying what she'd yet to learn. "You mentioned a prophesy earlier... something about *the chosen one*. Do you —"

"No," Azalea said, shaking her head.

"Why not?"

"I shouldn't have said anything. It's nothing but a rumor. Most scoff, insisting it's false hope for a better future, one that will never exist. Others —"

"Believe it."

Azalea nodded.

"Well, either way…" Chewing on the inside of her lip, her attention drifted to the rose bushes abutting the garden gate. "Instinct tells me I'll find the answers I'm looking for there."

"No better place to find them," Azalea murmured. "I've heard about the great hall. It's said there are so many books, it would take a hundred years to count them all."

Truly didn't know whether to be encouraged by that or not. Once inside the hall, she wouldn't have a lot of time. The information she sought might be specific, but she must locate it fast. Before the queen caught on and unleashed Priestly again.

"It's a risk," she said, one worth taking if she got what she needed from Brim.

"A big one."

Truly shrugged. "So, supper?"

"Anytime now. Ah," Azalea said, gesturing behind her. "Here they are."

Truly looked in the direction she pointed. Two tall shadows approached the others milling around on the street. Lumbering gait. Enormous paws carrying baskets. Matted fur sticking up like crowns on top of shaggy heads

Truly mouth curved. "Yetis, right?"

Azalea nodded. "They were happy to oversee the preparation of your meal. It's their way of saying thank you."

"Why would they need to say —"

"Some of their friends and family members are trapped in Earth Realm, on the wrong side of the *Ecotone.*" Reaching out,

Azalea squeezed her hand. "Once you reopen the bridge, their kin will be able to return home."

Truly blinked. *The bridge?* What bridge? Also... how, when, and where was this supposed to happen? "Azalea —"

"Don't worry so much, Truly," she said, picking up on her confusion. "You'll figure it out. Everyone will remain patient while you do. We all know you're young and have no mentor. But when you get back home, spend some time in your library. I don't know what section the book will be in, but it's there. Find and study it. When you're ready, the bridge between the Mirror Kingdoms will make itself known."

"Terrific," Truly muttered, something else to be stressed about.

After listening to Montrose, she knew some Azlandians had been trapped in Earth Realm when the *Ecotone* closed. Her ex-boss been separated from Brim for twenty-seven years. But the awareness hadn't transferred to those missing loved ones in Azlandia.

The Yetis didn't bother with the front gate. Without breaking stride, the pair stepped over the fence onto the front walkway.

"I'll just go..." Truly pointed to the door behind her. "Wake them up."

"Sure." Azalea gave her another squeeze. "Enjoy your meal. Meet me in the town square when you're done. I'll show you the best way out of Weeping Hollow."

With a nod, Truly opened the door and re-entered the cabin.

Sitting on the edge of the bed, hands gripping the mattress, bare feet planted on the floor, Westvane scowled at her.

"Supper's here."

He grunted.

Montrose shot to a seated position. A thump echoed as he smacked his head on the underside of the table. "Fuck!"

Biting back laughter, she watched him lean sideways. Gray fur sticking up at odd angles, bright blue eyes met hers from under the wooden edge as he asked, "What's for dinner?"

"No clue," she said, exasperation in her tone. "I might be a Door Master, but I don't have x-ray vision."

Montrose snorted. "Prickly."

"Well, you're annoying."

Westvane huffed in amusement.

The Yetis set the baskets on the floor inside the door.

She nodded at the pair. "Thank you."

The furry duo growled in answer, turned and left.

"Smells fucking fantastic," Montrose said, nose twitching.

Truly rolled her eyes. No sense admonishing him for his language. Nothing she said would make him behave.

Grabbing the woven handles, Truly dragged the baskets further into the cabin and closed the door. Hurdle one-thousand-fifty-seven down, a billion more to go. Next obstacle up — Ipsalar.

She needed to find a way into the Hall of Scholars. Having her magic return — along with her ability to open a door and transport them out of Azlandia — sounded like a good idea too. Otherwise, she'd end up trapped in a city the queen knew well with few avenues of escape.

Heaving the baskets onto the table, Truly flipped the wicker tops open and set out the food while rearranging the things on her to-do list. So many items, too few solutions. With a sigh, she shelved her worries (along with potential catastrophes), deciding to tackle the problems later. After she enjoyed a good meal... and listened to Westvane lecture her some more.

37

SPIDERS AND THE DARK

Boots planted in front of a cave, Truly saw the next challenge clearly. She understood the danger. Difficult not to, given it stared her in the face. The dark hole didn't inspire confidence. She'd never wanted to go spelunking. Now, as she studied the yawning mouth cut into the side of a jagged cliff face, she wondered (not for the first time) whether she'd lost her mind.

Or had a death wish.

Seemed a pretty good bet she might be suffering from both afflictions.

Leaning forward a little, she peered into the narrow opening. Five feet across, dark as pitch, light from the torches didn't penetrate far. Another round of apprehension skittered through her. Goosebumps spiked on her skin. She rubbed the outside of her arms, attempting to rub away the fear.

A huge task.

She didn't like tight spaces. And the cave looked way too *tight.* Beyond the entrance, the floor slanted down, chiseling through solid rock to ravine deep underground. Her stomach pitched as she imagined a series of wormholes, unending tunnels leading to things that wanted to eat her in the dark.

Standing to her left, Westvane started toward the entryway. "Ah..."

He paused to look behind him. "What's wrong?"

"Apart from everything?"

He sighed.

Truly took a step back as the heebie-jeebies set in.

Looking toward Azalea, she asked, "You're sure there's no other way?"

"Well, yeah," Azalea said, twisting her lips to one side. "Of course, there is."

Truly's eyes narrowed on her.

Azalea lost the battle and smiled. "But you'd have to traverse the densest part of the forest and —"

"No fucking way." Tufted ears swiveled, then flattened, making Montrose look like a pissed-off wolverine. "No chance in hell I'm doing that again."

"I've made peace with the Hollow, Rosy. It'll let us walk through it safely."

"Triple," he said, a rumble of warning in his tone.

Truly pursed her lips. She didn't want to go in there. Would rather cut off her own —

"Traversing the Hollow will add days to your journey." Angling her torch higher, Azalea tipped it toward the cliff face. "The cave system folds time. It will not only get you there by morning, but take you right up to the city walls."

Score one for the cave.

She didn't have days to waste. Arriving at, sneaking into, then back out of the Hall of Scholars trumped claustrophobia. Getting back to Philly fast mattered, too — before the Wendigo ravaged the entire city.

Westvane raised a brow. "Ready?"

Squaring her shoulders, Truly nodded.

"Stay behind me. Right on my heels." Dark eyes riveted to her, Westvane stopped in the mouth of the cave. She assessed his physical state, searching for signs that his injuries still bothered him. He looked pale, no wings, the tattoo of Eastbrook on his neck light gray, instead of the usual jet black, but other than that, he seemed fit as ever. "I'll lead us through safely."

"I don't like tight places." She chewed on the inside of her lip. "Or spiders."

"Spiders?" Montrose asked, sounding incredulous. "You went head-to-head with the queen's guard, and you're scared of *spiders?*"

"That, along with anything big enough to eat me in the dark."

Amusement sparked in Westvane's eyes. "I can see in the dark."

Truly blinked. "Finally, some good news."

Stepping around her, Montrose threw her a disgruntled look.

She flexed her fingers, resisting the urge to punch him. "Can you conjure your sword and shield?"

Westvane shook his head. "Not yet. My magic has yet to return."

She heard the words, but tapped into the undertone. He didn't sound confident. Was doubting that his magic — and his wings — would ever return.

"Westvane —"

"Time to go, princess," he said, brushing her concern aside. "No more stalling."

Her grip on the torch handle tightened. A magic-crippled Assenta. A wary Door Master. An impatient gargoyle. Not the best combination, given her magic still hadn't sparked. No matter how hard she hunted, the doors inside her mind remained silent and dark. The stillness so profound, she chafed at the strangeness of it. She hadn't been a Door Master long, but the absence felt wrong, as though a necessary part of her had been amputated.

Now, she experienced the phantom pains, yearning for a part of her she hadn't realized she possessed until days ago.

"What if —"

"I have my fists, Truly."

Montrose chimed in. "And my claws work just fine."

All right, then. No time like the present.

"Go," she said, gathering her courage. "I'll follow."

"About time," Westvane murmured, entering the cave.

Unable to help it, Truly rolled her eyes. Raising her torch higher, she put her feet in gear, moving forward while looking back. She mouthed "thank you" to Azalea.

The woman tipped her chin. "I'll see you again someday."

One could only hope.

Staying on Westvane's heels, she followed him into the cave. Darkness closed around her. Musty air drifted as light from her torch cast shadows across uneven ground and craggy walls. The sound of trickling water and the scent of decay kicked up. Truly drew a fortifying breath. No turning back now. She was in it, entering a dangerous place populated by unknown creatures. Nothing to do now but pray the subterranean warren spit her out the other side, with all her limbs attached.

ROCK SCRAPED across his back as Westvane squeezed through a narrow crevice. One of many he'd navigated in the last few hours. Unlike those other times, though, he grunted in discomfort. The pain was starting to get to him. So was the fact his magic had yet to return, driving concern deep as his strength ebbed with every step he took.

Not that he would voice the concern. Or admit he felt sick to his stomach.

The gargoyle's reaction to his rapidly deteriorating state didn't worry him. Montrose could look after himself. The idea of letting Truly down, though, made his skin crawl.

The thought caused old habits to rise hard.

He wanted to say *screw it* and scrap the plan. Truly wasn't weak. As a Door Master, she could fend for herself too. She'd manage without him. Find a way through. Return to Earth Realm and deal with the Wendigo while he travelled across Azlandian, rallying other Assenta to his cause.

An army of hunter-killers wouldn't be difficult to mount. The war with Lyonesse and the ruling class would arrive on its heels. With a little time and a lot of effort, justice would be served — and centuries of wrongdoing would be righted.

Azlandians would gain their freedom.

New laws would be written.

Equality would become a mainstay in Azlandians' lives. Acceptance the rule instead of an exception.

But even as temptation urged him to go his own way, the idea of leaving Truly behind sat like a stone in his gut. He'd given her his word. A novel experience for him. A strong move in the direction of regaining his honor. One he was loathed to give up. The new-found sense of duty refused to let him. Pride chimed in, then dug down, infusing his muscles and invading his bones.

Despite the pain, his growing weakness, and the heavy task of freeing his fellow Azlandians from the yoke of a tyrannical queen, he couldn't abandon Truly. He must keep his word. Hold the line. Watch over her while she developed into a powerful mage, strong enough to stand with him when he ousted Lyonesse from the throne.

Emerging from a ravine, Westvane navigated a sharp turn on the narrow trail. Jagged rock face on his right, a sheer drop on his left. Single file only. A blessing right now. With Truly and the gargoyle behind him, he didn't have to look at them. *Look* at her, and worry she'd read his mind. At full strength, she could do it — cherry-pick the fact he'd toyed with picking up the pace and leaving her behind.

The idea shouldn't bother him. What Truly thought of him shouldn't mean anything, and yet...

Somehow, it *did*.

Westvane scowled. His reaction was maddening. Confusing. Annoying. None of what he felt made sense, but the truth of it was — her opinion mattered.

Raising his torch higher, he examined the narrow path ahead. More bridge than ledge, the trail continued onto a narrow stone overpass. Not too long a span, but as the wall dropped away on the left side, so did the sense of security. The shift in terrain would tweak Truly, and she was already spooked enough.

Stopping where the cliff wall ended and the bridge began, he glanced over his shoulder. He clenched his teeth to keep from laughing. Freaked out, she stood right behind him. Practically breathing down his neck, her tension so thick it burned around her like an aura, pricking against his skin.

"Princess?"

"Yeah?"

"Relax."

"Easy for you to say," she said, voice full of strain. "You can see in the dark. I can barely see a foot in front of me."

Leaning forward, he peered into the gully. Deep. Dark.

Even with his night vision sparking, he couldn't see the bottom. "So, here's the thing..."

"Oh, God. What now?"

"There's a bridge ahead."

"What kind of bridge?" she asked, trying to look around him. He widened his stance to block her view. She didn't need to see it before she crossed it. Sometimes ignorance was bliss. "Rope or stone?"

"Stone."

"That doesn't sound too bad."

"You haven't seen it yet, Triple," Montrose said from behind her. "Narrow, Westvane?"

"It isn't wide."

"Railings?"

"No." Nudging a pebble off the cliff, Westvane counted off the seconds.

He reached thirty before the stone hit bottom of the ravine.

A long, long way to fall if Truly lost her footing. He wasn't worried about Montrose. Gargoyles were excellent climbers. Tough hides, sharp claws, hard heads upped the rate of Montrose and his species' survival.

"Two options, princess."

"Hit me."

"I carry you on my back or —"

Truly scoffed. "Next."

"You gut it out," he said, relieved she didn't want his help. With his strength waning, carrying her would cost him.

"Go, Westvane. I'll follow."

"If you feel your balance falter, get low. Drop to your knees and crawl, if you need to," Montrose said. "No joke, Triple."

She nodded, then tapped the back of his shoulder. "Go, Westvane."

"Wait until I reach the middle, then follow me across."

She didn't answer.

He didn't wait for her response.

Inching forward, Westvane stepped onto the bridge, hoping the structure was strong enough to hold his weight. One sliding step at a time, he worked his way across. When he reached the center, he looked back at Truly and Montrose.

"Slow and steady," he said, waving Truly onto the bridge. "One at time."

Truly took a deep breath, then struck out. She copied his movements. Torch hand forward, the other one back, she shuffled across stone, eyes on the ground in front of her.

Six feet from the cliff edge, she wobbled.

"Don't look down," Montrose growled.

"Rosy," she whispered.

"Yeah."

"Shut up."

The gargoyle snorted.

Westvane bit down on a chuckle. A completely inappropriate reaction. He ought to be worried about her falling, not amused by her spirit.

An impossibility.

Her bold approach to life — the courage she showed — was difficult to ignore. Keeping several feet between them to ensure equal distribution of weight, he surveyed her progress, thankful she couldn't see beyond the pool of light thrown by the torches. If she knew how many spiders watched her — from webs strung in high corners, translucent threads hanging inches from her head — she'd freak out and fall.

Plunge to her death.

Screaming about spiders the whole way down.

A bad outcome. A dead Door Master would put a crick in his plans.

Aware rushing Truly wouldn't help, Westvane tried to be

patient. He wanted out of the cave system. Time might stand still inside the Hollow, but that didn't mean it was on their side. His former childhood friend wasn't stupid. Priestly possessed strong magic, and an even stronger mind. The instant Truly's net forced him to the ground, he'd have reached out to Lyonesse, using Electi mind-meld to raise the alarm. Now, the faithless witch would be roaming, searching, listening for the cosmic ticks that signaled their exit from the forest, giving their position away.

Under normal circumstances, he'd relish the opportunity to put Lyonesse in her place. Not tonight. Not right now. Truly owned all his focus. The second she came into her own, however, he'd unleash her inside Azlandia and bring the queen to her knees.

Reaching the other side of the bridge, he sidestepped and waited for Truly to reach him. As she came within grabbing distance, he reached out. She latched onto his hand. He pulled. Arm outstretched, her feet slid across stone. The rasp of her boot soles echoed. With a grunt of discomfort, he put his back to the wall, drawing her in front of him.

She shuddered. The torch wobbled.

Wrapping his hand beneath hers, he took it from her, then turned and rammed the handle between two stones above his head. She flexed her fingers and shook out her hands. The sound of footfalls came from the other side of the bridge. Without a care in the world, Montrose sauntered the rest of the way across.

Her eyes narrowed on the gargoyle. "You bother me."

"Don't be a hater," Montrose said, smile bright, sharp fangs bared.

Ignoring the byplay, Westvane yanked the torch from the fissure. He handed it back to her. Truly accepted the flame, looking up the trail as he stepped around her. Footfalls heavy, he headed into another gully. Weakness dogged him the whole way. Pain set in harder, cramping his muscles, gnawing at his lower back, making his head hurt and neck ache.

Battling fatigue, Westvane paused at the bottom to catch his breath.

"You're such a liar." Following his example, she wedged her torch between two rocks and dipped beneath his outstretched arm. Planted in front of him, she peered up into his face. "We should've stayed in the cabin longer. You're hurting."

"Staying wasn't a good idea," he said. "I need out of the Hollow."

"Does it still have its hooks in you?" she asked, wiping the sweat from his brow with her shirt sleeve.

"It hasn't quite let go."

"Pain or —"

"Pain I can handle," he said, wanting to be stubborn, knowing honest was best. "My head's fuzzy and my muscles are sore. My energy is flagging."

Lifting a leather strap over her head, Truly uncorked the wine skin. "Drink this."

Without objection, Westvane took it from her. His head tipped back. Cold water cut with lemon streamed into his mouth and flowed down his throat, soothing dry patches.

"You need sleep, Westvane."

Hopping over a large rock, Montrose landed behind her. "We need to get the hell out of here. Too many eyes."

"Eyes?" Truly tensed and looked around. "We're being watched?"

"Never mind," Westvane said, throwing a warning look at Montrose. She didn't need to know about the spiders... or the more vicious creatures that called the underground enclaves home. "Break's over."

Gaze scanning the uneven walls, Truly drew a shaky breath. "Have I mentioned how much I hate being underground?"

"Only fifty times," the gargoyle said.

"Rosy?"

"Yeah?"

"Shut up," she said, the comment by rote as she glanced at him. "How much farther do you think?"

Nose pointed toward a ceiling, Montrose sniffed. "The air's thinner."

"What's that mean?"

Dropping his hand from the wall, Westvane rolled his shoulders. Muscles protested the pull. He ignored the discomfort and examined the cave. Dome ceiling. Larger than the others he'd traversed so far. And fifty yards away? A firepit, blackened stones set in a circle. An encouraging sign — one Azalea had told him to look for as a marker along the path.

He scanned the other side of the cavern and...

Hell.

He'd almost missed the guide posts.

Cut into the bedrock, disguised by staggered stones, a staircase climbed the opposite side of the cavern. He raised his torch higher. The charge in the air reacted to the flame. Tiny bolts of lightning blazed into a ball above his head.

"Static electricity," Truly said.

Westvane nodded. "We're close now."

Her gaze tracked to the steps. "To what?"

"To the place Azalea said bends time." He studied the rise of stairs, focused on the spot the treads disappeared behind a rock formation. Scenting the air, Westvane breathed deep. As he filtered through each smell, a tinge of *something* came to him. "Heads up. We're not alone."

"What is it?" Truly asked.

He raised a brow. "Do you really want to know?"

"Terrific," she muttered, reading him without effort. "More monsters — just what I wanted for my birthday."

Westvane turned to her. "It's your birthday?"

"A month ago."

"Could be worse," Montrose said. "The spiders could be attacking, instead of watching."

Westvane snorted in amusement.

Truly scowled. "Am I allowed to kill him?"

"No," he said, shaking his head.

"Later?" she asked, hope in the question.

Westvane's lips twitched. "I'll think about it."

Unfazed by the threat, Montrose chuckled.

Glaring at the gargoyle, Truly started toward the stairs. He outpaced her, taking the lead, jogging between boulders and around jut-outs, picking his way across the cave. The tap of footfalls echoed under the crooked dome, making an already tense group tenser. So much for fleet of foot. The noise announced their presence, decimating the element of surprise.

An advantage he would've liked to keep until he knew what kind of creature lay in wait along the path.

At the bottom of the stairs, he paused to look up. A steep climb. A narrow entrance between rock walls at the top. Enough space to walk through single file. Disadvantage stacked on top of another stumbling block. The structure left little room to maneuver. And without his sword and shield? He risked walking into a battle unarmed.

Westvane smelled the danger. He sensed it seething on the other side the opening. Lying in wait for him. And yet, he didn't hesitate. Shifting into high gear, he ignored the weakness plaguing him and took the stairs three at a time.

Surprised by his sudden move, Truly hissed, "Westvane!"

He didn't bother to turn around. Or look behind him. He needed to reach the doorway first. She was a Door Master. He was her shield, the one who would ensure she stayed in one piece — no matter the threat. But as he reached the halfway point, sprinting toward danger to keep her safe, he wondered for the first time whether he was strong enough.

Strong enough to meet the challenge.

Strong enough to snap Weeping Hollow's spell.

Strong enough to defeat the next monster. Or if whatever lay beyond the breach would finally be the death of him.

38

TOTALLY GONZO

R amping into a run, Westvane took the stairs four at a time.

Gaze glued to his back, Truly frowned. "What does he think he's doing?"

Right behind her, Montrose grunted. "His job."

"He's crazy." Hopscotching over rocks, she leapt to the bottom tread and started up the steep rise. Damp air sawed in and out of her lungs. The violent staccato of her feet on stone echoed as she raced after the maniac leaving her behind. "Totally gonzo."

"Assenta warriors usually are," Montrose muttered, keeping pace behind her.

"You're one to talk." She cursed as she lost sight of the lunatic in question. Gritting her teeth, she kept going, but... utterly hopeless. She'd never catch up. Mere hours after suffering a terrible injury, and Westvane still managed to outrun her. "Rosy —"

"Forget about it."

"You have to go after him."

"No."

"He's not okay, Rosy. He needs help."

Montrose shook his head. "I stay with you."

Heart hammering the inside of her chest, Truly glanced at him over her shoulder. "I'll sidestep. Get out of your way. Just —"

"What do you think he'll do to me if anything happens to you?"

Excellent point. One she needed to concede.

Westvane would kill her ex-boss-turned-gargoyle. Rip him limb from furry limb, then feed him to Hyraxes if something happened to her.

Her boot caught the edge of a tread. Momentum threw her forward. Arms pinwheeling, Truly tripped up three steps before righting her balance. "He's going to get himself killed."

"Not your problem."

"Of course, it's my problem!" she rasped, half-turning to run sideways up the rise. "He's my friend."

"Typical," Montrose grumbled. "Only you could make friends with a Slayer."

"Rosy!"

"You wanna help?" Reaching out, he grabbed her biceps and shoved, propelling her upward. "Run faster."

Throwing him a killing look, Truly faced forward, and pumping her arms and legs, launched herself up the stairs. Air sawed in her lungs. Her chest started to hurt and...

God. Seriously. If the craziness went on much longer, she was signing up for cardio classes. Or joining a running club. If she didn't, Azlandia would chew her up, spit her out, then grind her into dust.

Truly huffed as she reached the first landing. Gritting her teeth, she whipped around the narrow space. Whom was she kidding? Westvane's side of the *Ecotone* was already kicking her ass, making her feel inadequate. Unable to do what a Door

Master should be able to do — back up one of her teammates, an Assenta who took his job so seriously he kept putting himself in danger to protect her. The thing Westvane had yet to grasp was — she felt the same way about him.

She didn't want him in the line of fire alone. Teammates worked together. Family stuck together. Friends backed each other up. And as strange as it seemed, in a short amount of time, Westvane had become all three.

Which made his sprint up the stairs (towards almost certain death) annoying. Though she had to admit Montrose was right. Westvane's predatory nature dictated the play. He needed to be first into the fray. Being a warrior was embedded in his DNA. As much as she wanted to shield him, standing in his way wasn't the right approach. Preventing him from engaging would only piss him off. Helping him, however, remained on the table, along with the full complement of weapons at her disposal.

First things first, though. She needed to catch up.

Rounding a turn, she pushed harder. Her legs pumped. Her arms swung, one hampered by the heavy torch as she took the stairs two at a time. Movement flashed up ahead. She caught sight of Westvane a second before he disappeared again, between two statues, into an opening along the cave wall.

Her gaze narrowed on it. Looked like a doorway. Tall. Narrow. Smooth stone jambs marked with symbols, rising to meet an arched lintel. Chiseled into the rock, engraved letters painted gold shimmered in the torchlight. The closer she got, the more details came into focus. Elaborate mosaic floors set at the feet of two stone-faced phoenixes. Huge statues carved by a master hand, with what looked like hieroglyphs carved into the stone bases. *Hieroglyphs. Pictograms.* The mode of writing used by ancient Egyptian civilizations. Which begged a question — what were they doing deep in a cave system on this side of the *Ecotone*, far from shores of the Nile and North Africa?

She scanned the archway again, picking up more details. The carvings and symbols, the nod to Egyptian culture, seemed undeniable, but... was that assumption really true? Or had the tenets of ancient Egyptian society originated here, in Azlandia, a place rooted in magic and shrouded by mystery? The urge to stop long enough to carbon-date the statues prickled through her as she started up the last rise of steps.

Her attention bounded to the towering uprights flanking the entrance. More hieroglyphs chiseled in stone. More intricately laid mosaic tile and —

Something slid over the floor beneath the archway.

She dodged around an outcropping, trying to get a better look and...

Fingers.

Truly frowned. No, not fingers — *tentacles*.

Long and thick, slithering like snakes, moving with purpose. Dragging over the floor, beneath the tall doorway, following in Westvane's wake.

Alarm clawed through her. Muscles contracted around her bones. Air rasping against the back of the throat, she crested the top step and...

Sensation sizzled through her, popping like fizzy bubbles against her skin.

She felt Weeping Hollow's grip loosen as she sliced through the invisible barrier marking its boundary. One finger at a time, the forest spirit released her. Perception shifted. Her senses opened. Light sparked through her, smoothing out fear as magic coalesced in her veins. She felt the sparkling rush, embraced the power, eclipsing pain, and entered a state of *flow*.

Cold air heated around her.

The jumble inside her head cleared.

Mind and body in sync, her breathing even out as she

moved with unnatural speed, nothing but the monster and reaching Westvane in her frame.

"Fuck," Montrose rasped, sprinting now to stay close to her.

Truly didn't slow.

Her vision flickered, shifting to something unknown as magic forked like lightening through her veins, changing her alchemy, allowing her to see in the dark. Night became day. Dropping the torch, she left Montrose behind, and gaze locked on the doorway, lunged over the last step.

An unholy hiss rippled through the quiet.

Westvane cursed.

Truly sprinted past the towering statues, beneath the archway, into an antechamber of some kind. More steps down. More statues standing guard. Ignoring the display, she vaulted over the stairs. As her feet slammed down on colorful tile, she took a snapshot — massive, man-made chamber, gold and silver sculptures everywhere and —

Westvane, dodging, weaving... battling a giant octopus in the center of the room.

39

BLACK BLOOD, DEAD OCTOPUS

Fast reflexes kept him upright. A keen sense of self-preservation did the rest.

Ducking beneath barbed tentacles, Westvane pivoted, evading the coil of multiple arms at once. Slanted eyes with round pupils narrowed on him. The giant Earth Octopus slashed at him again. His feet left the floor. Rotating into a somersault mid-leap, he spiraled between the lash of powerful limbs.

The sharp teeth embedded in the suckers on its tentacles raked over the floor. A scraping shriek echoed through the chamber.

The fine hairs on the back of his neck stood on end.

He was in trouble — weaponless while an Azlandian apex predator tried to flay him alive. He needed to think fast and move faster. If the Earth Octopus managed to grab hold of him — game over. He'd be cut to ribbons seconds before the monster moved in for the kill, then made a meal out of him.

A thump sounded behind him.

Footfalls rapped across the stone floor.

The creature shrieked, tentacles arched, readying another attack.

"Truly!" he yelled, leaping sideways to avoid its arms. "Get down!"

A tentacle swung toward her.

Blue eyes aglow, she ducked beneath the snaking thrust, then flexed her fingers. One of her knees landed on the mosaic tiles. Swinging beneath another swipe, she cocked her elbow and punched her fist down. Magic detonated around her. A long staff formed in her hand. She hammered the base into the floor. The hard rap rocked the chamber as the scepter exploded with light. Quick strike lightning. Alive with electricity. A second staff appeared in her other hand. Shouting his name, she whipped the weapon over her head, then let go.

Ablaze, energy crackling from the tip, the staff whirled toward him.

Vaulting between slashing tentacles, he snagged it out of mid-air. Heat fused it to his palm. The head of the scepter spun. Mid-rotation, three blades sprang from the end. Westvane bared his teeth on a snarl. Excellent. Powerful magic staff — check. Razor-sharp electric blades crackling with lightning — absolute perfection.

Controlling the flip, he landed on the balls of his feet. One second spilled into two. Westvane attacked, swinging the staff like a club. Electrified blades bit. The Earth Octopus reared as he sliced through its tough hide and thick flesh. The lethal tips spun. Chunks of octopus flew. Westvane struck again. And again. Angling the weapon. Doing maximum damage. Avoiding the vicious swipe of tentacles as the monster attacked.

Black blood spattered over him, spraying the statue behind him. The beast roared. Half a tentacle hit the floor.

Westvane growled in appreciation. One down, seven tentacles to go.

Drawing strength from the specter, he dodged and struck over and over, showing no mercy. Lightning cracked from the tip of the staff as he hammered the beast, forcing it to retreat as Truly attacked from the other side.

Footwork perfect, wielding her weapon like she'd been born to it, she parried and thrust, moving in concert with him. Dipping beneath one tentacle, she hacked at another, avoiding the deadly needles, distracting the Earth Octopus while he shifted into its blind spot.

Sheer genius. Great teamwork with just the right amount of luck.

Seeing his opening, Westvane rotated the staff. Magic burned across his palm as he threw it like a javelin. Bolts of electricity arched across the antechamber. Death-dealing blades sank into the beast's soft underbelly. The Earth Octopus flailed. Sharp needles raked the side of his head. Blood ran down his temple. As it dripped into his eye, he dodged and, with one last thrust, kicked the end of the scepter. The staff sank deep, cutting through muscle to reach its spinal cord.

Tentacles rippled in distress.

The creature teetered and collapsed, becoming a gelatinous blob on the stone floor.

Breathing hard, Westvane backpedaled, putting distance between him and it. "Truly?"

"Here," she said, from somewhere on the other side of the dead octopus.

"You good?"

"Is it dead?"

"Yes."

"Then I'm good."

Westvane huffed and, avoiding twitching tentacles, rounded the room toward her. His lips curved when he spotted her. Covered in black blood, sitting beside a statue of a sea goddess, ass planted in a pile of gold coins, she stared at the Earth Octopus. An expression of horror — or maybe, something more aptly described as disgust — lined her face.

"Are you going to throw up?"

She wrinkled her nose. "I'm thinking about it."

He studied her. Blue eyes still shimmering. Fading lightning staff still gripped in her hand. "Your magic's back."

"Fully juiced," she said, rolling to her feet. Gold coins tumbled, rolling down the pile and across the floor. "You?"

Cracking his neck, Westvane took stock. Solid in his skin, stronger, but... the absence of his wings was telling. "Not quite, but it's coming."

With a nod, Truly flicked her hand. The scepter shrank, reabsorbing into her palm as she looked around. "Where's Rosy?"

"Over here." Montrose's quick reply echoed across the chamber.

Following his voice, Truly walked to her left. She kept to the perimeter of the room, stepping over chunks of octopus, gaze searching. He stayed right behind her, scanning the space, visually investigating the nooks and crannies, alert to the possibility of another attack.

One never knew.

More than one Earth Octopus might call the subterranean cave system home.

On her heels, Westvane rounded the last curve. The gargoyle came into view. Fur matted with sweat, black blood dripping from his claws, he stood on a landing beyond a short rise of stairs. An entrance shaped like a hexagon rose beyond him. Glowing green, the space between the stone jambs undulated, tiny threads stung tight across the rippling surface.

Jogging up the stairs, Truly stopped next to the gargoyle. "Is that it?"

Montrose nodded. "The time warp."

Head tipped back, she studied the structure. "You go first."

"What?" Ears flat against his skull, Montrose frowned at her. "Why me?"

"Westvane killed the octopus. I provided the weapons," she said, eyes dancing with mischief. "Least you can do is be the first to step inside."

His ears swiveled to face front as the gargoyle growled, "Three months — three months of putting up with your shit. This is what I get. Pain in my ass. That's what you are... have been from the start."

Truly grinned, white teeth flashing through the grime on her face.

Westvane shook his head.

With a sigh, Montrose accepted his fate and strode toward the time warp. The green glow began to bubble. The strings inside the device spun, funneling into a vortex. The loud hum shook the antechamber. Dust filtered down from high columns ringing the room as wind gusted and the gargoyle stepped inside.

Bright light pulsed, obliterating the gloom.

A popping noise. A quick flash and...

Montrose disappeared.

"My turn." Taking a deep breath, Truly took a different approach. Instead of walking in as the gargoyle had done, she ramped into a run and sliced into the glow. A second before she vanished, she looked over her shoulder and yelled, "You coming?"

Westvane stared at the spot where she disappeared. He inhaled deep, held the breath until his lungs began to ache, then exhaled hard and started the countdown.

One. Two. Three...

Go.

With one last glance at the dead octopus, Westvane stepped into the distortion, praying the time warp dropped him, not only safely, but in the same location as the irksome Door Master he'd sworn to protect.

40

A MILLION PIECES

Truly wished she'd paid more attention in school. If she had, the science-rooted menace holding her in its grip would've made more sense. Calculating the angles, understanding the laws of physics, seemed important right now. A skill that would increase her chances of making it out alive. But had she paid attention? No, of course not. She'd been too busy doodling in her textbook to listen to Mr. Armitage talk about, well... whatever he was attempting to teach her.

Now she was paying for it. Being hurled down a corkscrew inside a space-time continuum at the speed of light. With no idea how to control her wild flight down the tunnel.

Azalea had done her best to explain.

Truly thought she understood.

Nothing prepared her for the reality.

The mind-blurring velocity turned her inside out. She was being pulled and pushed at the same time. Millions of cosmic threads stretched her thin. Half moved one way, half went the other, whipping around corners, only to fling her out the other side. She felt like an astronaut without a space suit. Weightless.

Exposed to the elements. Stardust clogging her lungs. Any moment now, she'd implode, end up in fragments, smeared along the interior of the corkscrew.

Not part of the plan — hers or anyone else's.

Being torn into pieces — and jettisoned as human confetti — defeated the purpose of entering the vortex in the first place. Dead on arrival wasn't part of the deal. Montrose would never forgive her. And Westvane? The mangled parts of him would no doubt rally, putting what remained of him back together long enough to kill what little remained of her.

Truly closed her eyes as the tunnel twisted into another spiral.

Her body spun the opposite way. She bumped into the side wall. Pain blazed up her side, jabbing her in the ribs.

Curled in a ball, knees to chest, she pressed her face to the tops of her thighs. Bright colors blazed across the smooth walls. The strobing effect pierced through her closed lids, stabbing into her skull. Her head started to ache. She gave voice to her frustration, and baring her teeth, screamed at the time warp.

She wanted the corkscrew to let her go. Spit her out. Allow her to abandon ship. Or simply throw her overboard.

Anything. Everything. Just as long as the world stopped spinning.

The tube raced on instead, spiraling into space. Her stomach pitched. Her mind continued to scream. She tucked in tighter, caving in, heaving out, trying to go with the flow. Fighting the violent flight wouldn't help. She was a part of it now. No way out as the strings pulled and the velocity increased. The air thinned as the tunnel burned hotter. Bile sloshed up the back of her throat. The time warp was too much — too much speed, too long of a trip, too much heat for her to handle. And still, the whirling corkscrew blazed, making sweat bead on her skin.

Individual droplets evaporated, only to be replaced by more, sucking water out through her pores. Thirst set in. Dizziness followed. Truly sucked in a desperate breath. She couldn't get enough oxygen. Every breath felt thin, and her lungs hurt from working too hard.

Hollowed out, Truly peeked from between her bent knees, trying to see ahead of her. A mistake. She made a terrible mistake trusting Azalea.

The woman didn't know what she'd been talking about. Had she left Weeping Hollow once since arriving in Azlandia? Had she ever traveled inside the time warp? Did she understand the laws of physics? Seemed a good guess to assume *no*. Azalea lived happily inside the Hollow, content under the canopy of protection the forest provided. No reason for her to leave, and, given that incontrovertible fact, Truly wondered if —

The mind-bending velocity slowed.

Punishing heat dropped away. Fresh air rolled in to replace it.

Truly inhaled a raspy breath, filling her lungs as vapor blew in around her. Surrounded by cool mist, she slid through time, suspended in animation before crashing into a barrier. The surface funneled outward. A whirlpool swirled around her. Water splashed as she broke through the other side.

Flipping end over end, she searched for a point of reference. Greenery blurred into an undefinable landscape, tumbling with her — green, then blue, splotches of brown and —

An arm snapped around her waist.

She slammed into someone. He grunted. The collusion lifted both of them off the ground. Tangled up with a big body, Truly started tumbling again. Controlling the spin, he tucked her into the cove of his arms. The frayed lines of her brain uncrossed. Realization struck — Westvane. What was happening? She'd entered the time warp before him. How had he made it out the other side before her?

The pitch and roll came to a rocking stop.

On top, spine pressed to Westvane's chest, she stared up at blue sky. "How am I not dead?"

With another grunt, Westvane shifted her to the side. As she settled on grass, he frowned at her. "What took you so long?"

Working moisture back into her mouth, she shook her head.

His brows collided. "You look like a drowned rat."

"I feel like one. That thing is awful."

Crouched beneath a tree clinging to the cliff edge, Montrose glanced over his shoulder. His gaze raked her, then returned to the view. "Got us here in one piece, didn't it?"

"Close call," she said, deciding to hold a grunge. "I'm pretty sure it tried to kill me."

"Smooth sailing for me," Montrose said from his perch.

She looked at Westvane.

"Same," he said, dark eyes full of laughter. "You're the only one who got a rough ride, princess."

It figured.

The Hollow hadn't been happy when she'd taken both Westvane and Montrose away. Maybe her rough ride through the vortex was the forest spirit's way of paying her back for a lost meal. Not that it mattered. Truly didn't have it in her to complain. Her companions appeared none the worse for wear, she was still alive, so... moving on.

Planting her palms in the grass, she rolled to her feet. Sore muscles protested. She ignored the aches, lifted the water skin over her head, and after uncorking it, took a long drink. Extending his arm, Westvane flicked his fingers. She handed it to him, then limped over to see what held Montrose's attention.

Shuffling sideways on the balls of his feet, he made room for her between him and the base of the tree.

Her gaze swept the valley. "Wow."

"Ipsalar," he said, gesturing to the urban landscape. "The White City."

"Your home."

Montrose nodded.

"You haven't seen it in a long time."

"Over two-and-a-half decades," he whispered, focused on the city. Surrounded by forest, Ipsalar's tall towers and thick walls rose from the valley floor, white stone shimmering in the glow of a rising sun. "Too long."

"Brim's there?"

"See the green dome?"

Her eyes roamed until she found the tallest structure in Ipsalar.

"Made of jade. Stands for wisdom, justice for all." Unshed tears in his eyes, Montrose met her gaze. "She lives there, under that dome, inside the Hall of Scholars."

"Home at last."

"At long last." His throat worked as he swallowed. "Thank you, Triple."

"No need. You more than earned it," she said. "Gave me a job. Kept me safe when it counted."

A gleam replaced the tears in his eyes. "Not easy keeping you from trouble."

She wrinkled her nose, playing along, understanding his need to lighten the mood. He disliked showing emotion. He'd never been a touchy-feely kind of gargoyle.

Punching his shoulder, she shoved him off balance.

His butt hit the dirt. "Fuck, Triple."

With a grin, she stood and glanced at Westvane. "How's our timeline?"

"Holding," Westvane said, tossing her the water skin. "For now. But we need to move."

Probably a good idea.

Priestly and the queen weren't stupid. The pair might be behind a step now, but wouldn't be for long. The time warp packed one hell of a wallop. The energy it emitted wouldn't go unnoticed — or be ignored.

"All right, then," she murmured, onboard with moving fast. "What's the play? How do we get into Ipsalar undetected?"

"*We* don't."

Truly frowned at Westvane. "What do you mean?"

"We're not going with him."

Alarm bells clanged inside her head. "Hang on a —"

"Slayer," her ex-boss growled.

"It's the right play, Montrose," Westvane said, holding the gargoyle's gaze. "We go our separate ways here — you, into Ipsalar, Truly and I back to Earth Realm."

"But..." Her protest arrived on a rasp, sounding weak. "I can't leave him here. Alone. I can't —"

"The Wendigo is loose, Truly. The longer it is, the more damage it will do. Humans will die if we don't return soon." Setting his hand on top of her shoulder, Westvane squeezed.

His gentle touch surprised her. Unbalanced her. Made her reshuffle her mental deck.

Intentional on his part? Maybe, but she didn't think so.

He wasn't trying to manipulate her. Strange as it seemed, Westvane meant to reassure, to calm and soothe. A huge deviation from the normal rough-and-tumble. At least, for him. One she appreciated, and if it wasn't so important, she would've given him what he asked without argument.

"You don't understand," she said, palming his wrist to prolong the connection.

Dipping his head, he brought his face closer to hers. "Explain it to me."

"I need to meet Brim and get into the archives. There are things I need to know. Things she might —"

"What things?" Montrose asked, nudging her.

"Azalea mentioned a prophesy, something about the *chosen one*, next ruler of Azlandia. The one meant to lead this land into a new era. One of equality, prosperity, and —"

"That's you, Truly," Westvane said, frowning.

"I don't think so."

"Princess —"

"Maybe in Earth Realm, but not here. I can't explain how I know. It's instinct, total gut reaction, but I'm not *the chosen one*. Nor am I meant to be, not for the people of Azlandia." Opening her senses wide, Truly sank deep into her own knowing. A place that felt foreign, yet true and right. Seeing the confusion on her friends' faces, she tried to explain what she couldn't yet prove. "I may have been slow arriving at the party, but I know who and what I am now. As a Door Master, my role is defined. It's never been in question. But this?"

Flicking her hand toward the high walls of Ipsalar, she shook her head. "This is something else. A vital piece of the puzzle we may need down the line. Information Lyonesse is guarding. A secret she fears, something so important, so dangerous to her it has the potential to —"

"Start an uprising. The people will rebel. Raise an army and go to war against her," Westvane said, finishing her thought.

"I'll get it." Rolling his shoulders, Montrose stared at The White City. "Go home, Triple. I'll get the information you need."

"How —"

"I'll knock." Sharp fangs flashed as he smiled at her. "You've got, like, a thousand doors inside your head or something. You'll hear me when I start banging."

She didn't like the idea at all. Hadn't expected it, although, she should've been prepared. She knew Montrose longed to go home. He'd waited decades to come back. Only made sense he'd want to stay upon his return. Somehow, though — somewhere along the line — she'd convinced herself the three of them were a team. She belonged with them, and they with her, no matter the obstacles set in their path.

Her throat tightened. "You'll be alone, Rosy."

"This is my home, Triple. My mate is here. I'll never be alone in Ipsalar."

Hating it, but knowing it was the right thing to do, she made it easy for him. No goodbye. No hug. Holding her tears at bay, she tipped her chin, giving him a smile. "See you on the flipside?"

"Count on it." Clucking her under the chin with the smooth side of a claw, he turned and began walking along the bluff. "Later, Assenta."

Westvane grunted in return.

Truly watched her ex-boss-slash-new-friend leave her behind. It felt wrong to let him go. She did it anyway, knowing what he needed from her, giving it without reservation.

"This totally blows," she said, watching him reach the trailhead.

"In my experience, most things do," Westvane said softly.

Seconds ticked passed in solidarity, in stillness and silence as she stared at the spot Montrose disappeared behind the bluff.

"Time to go, princess."

Grief clogged her throat.

Pressing her hand against her breastbone, Truly breathed through the pain, dragged her gaze away, and did what Westvane expected. What she been born to do and made to be.

Widening her stance, she closed her eyes. A spark appeared in the darkness in the back of her mind. She coaxed it to life, commanded the flame, bending the magic to her will.

A frame made of fire spread in her mind's eye.

Truly opened her own and, without looking at Westvane, walked across the clearing, pushed the door hovering above the grass open, stepped over the threshold, and heart aching, left Azlandia and Montrose behind.

FIND THE GARGOYLE

The updraft played in her feathers as Lyonesse angled her wings and swung into a holding pattern above the clearing sandwiched between two bluffs. One revolution turned into two, then spun into another. Gaze locked on the Electi warriors trampling the grass below her, she surveyed the mood on the ground.

Strong vibrations rode the morning wind, strings taut in the sunlight, tempers flaring hot, patience at an end. Snug and warm inside a cloaking spell fed by her magic, she spread her wings to slow her flight, then hung in mid-air to soak in the atmosphere.

Angry.

Frustrated.

Murderous. Priestly wanted to kill someone.

From what she could see from her altitude, his entourage stood off to the side, backs to the bluff, giving him a wide berth. All the time and space he needed to cool his anger.

And her personal guards?

Her lips curved. The entire contingent refused to go anywhere near him. Instead of landing in the clearing, her warriors perched on the opposite cliff top, removed from striking distance, wings folded, looking down, waiting for her to land first.

Bad mood rising.

An advantage to her, given the way Priestly wore calm like armor. Not much ruffled his feathers. The warrior was unflappable, but... not today. His temper and competitive drive were on display. The sight encouraged her. He might not like doing her bidding, but he wouldn't balk when she gave him his orders now. He'd been sufficiently provoked. Would stop at nothing to chase down and eliminate the threat to his honor.

No need for her to convince him of the mission. All thanks to the Door Master she wanted dead, and in a satisfying twist of fate, Priestly now wanted impaled on a stake.

Amused by his temper, Lyonesse folded her wings. Wind played in her hair as she dropped out of the sky. Her feet slammed into the turf. Bits of grass, rock, and loam exploded into a ring around her.

Priestly spun to face her. His noses flared. "Done circling like carrion?"

The sharp insult struck.

Lyonesse steeled herself, then smoothed her expression, refusing to let him get under her skin. Now was no time to take offense. And laughing at him while he frothed at the mouth? A terrible idea, one unworthy of her. Stoking his anger, picking apart his pride, made for a more enjoyable game.

Settling her wings, she ran her gaze over him. Such a beautiful specimen — strong, striking in appearance, iron-willed. The kind of warrior she'd choose to father her children one day if fate spun the way she wanted. Westvane would've done too, but his inferior bloodline — the ruination of his genes — made that impossible. When she bred, it would be to a pure-blooded

Electi, someone of stellar lineage, a male of sound body, mind, and spirit.

"You seem out of sorts, Priestly," she murmured, poking at him. "Something happen I should know about?"

A muscle ticked in his jaw. "You already know."

True. But what better way to remind him of his failure than by forcing him to voice it. "Tell me anyway."

"Little witch pinned me to the ground. Interrupted my fight with Westvane."

The news flattened her good mood. *Immobilized? Fight with Westvane?* Lyonesse frowned. Seemed as though Anckar missed relaying some of the more pertinent details of Priestly's encounter with the Door Master.

"Do you know how long I've waited to cross swords him?" Golden eyes glowing with fury, Priestly snarled, "Do you?"

Processing the information, Lyonesse shook her head.

"Meddling little witch."

Lyonesse took a step toward him. "Priestly —"

"She's strong." Ignoring her, he paced in a circle, stopping in front of the lone tree clinging to the cliff side. "Much more powerful than the last."

"Stronger than Herron?" Lyonesse clenched her teeth. Saying the name of the former Door Master aloud offended her. It left the worst taste in her mouth. "You're sure?"

"I saw it with my own eyes. Untapped magic. Formidable. Strongest I've ever seen." He scowled. "Not that she knows how to use it yet."

Well, finally. Some good news.

His scowl so black it scorched the air, Priestly kicked a raised tree root. "And Westvane."

"He was with her?"

"He protected her."

"The traitor," she said, fisting her hands so tight her nails cut into her palms. "Nothing but flesh and filth."

"Not the worst, or the least of it."

Her gaze narrowed on Priestly. "What could be worse than that?"

"He commands magic, Majesty. Has black-feathered wings. Fully fledged," he said, his unease mirroring her own. "He's an Electi — one of us."

"No, he isn't," she said, hissing at him. "Tainted blood runs through his veins."

"Only makes him stronger. Electi magic and Assenta strength combined. He's more dangerous than ever. You should've killed him when you had the chance."

She knew that, but...

"My father loved him. I made a promise."

"One you must break now." Watching her with shimmering golden eyes, Priestly exhaled long and slow. "Something else too."

Azlandia help her. There was more?

She raised a brow, telling him to continue without saying a word.

"A third travelled with them."

"A third?"

Pushing away from the tree trunk, Priestly walked toward her. She sidestepped, letting him pass as he gestured to a set of tracks on the ground. "By the scent of it... a gargoyle."

"Male?"

"Yes."

Her head snapped toward Ipsalar and the House of Scholars. Eyes on the jade dome in the distance, she put two and two together. "Did they split up? Or is the witch in Ipsalar? Are she and Westvane —"

"The gargoyle went into the city," Priestly said, pointing to the lone set of tracks on the trail that disappeared over the bluff edge. Turning the other way, he pointed to a depressed patch of grass near the base of the cliffs. "Westvane and the Door Master went back to Earth Realm through a door."

"So, out of reach for the time being, but..." she trailed off, turning all the information over in her mind. The trio had travelled together, in Earth Realm and across Azlandia. Each protecting the other, forming an alliance of some kind. Stood to reason, if she threatened one, the other two would come running. "Find the gargoyle. Tear Ipsalar apart if you have to, Priestly, but find him."

Boots planted at the trailhead descending into the valley, Priestly glanced at her over his shoulder. "And when I do?"

"Bring him to me," she said, voice soft with the threat of violence. "He'll make excellent bait."

One way or another, she'd sink her nails into the new Door Master.

After that, she'd turn her wrath on Westvane.

Priestly was right. She never should've honored her father's dying wish. Last requests belonged to fools, and compassion was a waste of time. Keeping Westvane alive had been a mistake. Pure folly, an error in judgement she would rectify in one of two ways. Either she'd recapture Westvane when he returned to Azlandia after neutralizing the Wendigo. Or she'd get him by setting a trap. One baited by an injured gargoyle in need of immediate rescue.

Either scenario would work.

All she need do now was wait to see which one the universe granted her. A queen, after all, required her pleasures, and the manner in which she eliminated enemies had always been her preferred form of entertainment.

42

BAD MOJO

The trip across the *Ecotone* was uneventful. No sea serpents this time, just vast stretches of open water and distant mountain peaks as she crossed the expanse between the Mirror Kingdoms. Soothing air currents tugged at her. Pure energy enveloped her, stroking along her spine, soothing cords of frayed nerve endings. Sore muscles relaxed. Jumbled thoughts aligned into a focused stream as she pictured the inside of her house.

Holding the image of the old Victorian inside her head, she allowed a door to form in her mind. Sparks flew. An archway streamed into view, following the curve of a round-topped door. Relief winged through her as she pushed the door into Earth Realm open and stepped over the threshold, back into the hallway inside her new home.

With a long exhale, she stood still, both feet rooted to the floor, feeling the relief. Huge, crystal-laden chandelier sparkling above her head. Wood paneling of the entryway polished to a high shine. Familiar area rug underfoot. *Details* — all the little details came to her, making the safe landing on her side of the *Ecotone* seem like a miracle.

Particularly since she hadn't known if she was going in the right direction.

All she'd done was picture the house, hoping to land somewhere she recognized. The *Ecotone* had done the rest, directing her path, sending her where she wished to go — home.

Right into the clutches of a scowling Earl.

Truly sighed. Shit. She'd forgotten about Earl. How the Mantipede slipped her mind, she didn't know. The creepy-crawly half of him was difficult to forget... and even harder to ignore.

"Hey, Earl." Moving out of the vestibule, Truly strode into the central corridor.

"Where have you been?" Arms crossed, eyes narrowed, Earl tapped a number of his feet against the wooden floor. "Thought you'd be back for supper. I've been waiting two days."

"I ruin the soufflé or something?"

The sarcasm didn't go over well. It never did with Earl.

"Two *days*, girl." His frown became more pronounced. "Almost three now."

"Worried about me?"

"Still got the Slayer with you?" he asked, blocking her from entering the kitchen.

The tapping of multiple feet announced his agitation. The spatula he held spelled bad news if she didn't answer fast.

Too tired to play games, she nodded.

His frown smoothed out.

"You really shouldn't call Westvane that, Earl."

He shrugged. "Don't care about him, care about you."

Nice.

A compliment. Not a bad way to come home after two long days of fighting to stay alive.

"Where'd you get the hat?" she asked, using distraction to

take him off course. Always the best strategy when Earl sank his teeth into something.

A gleam in his eyes, he straightened the chef's hat on top of his bushy hair. "Closet. I made myself at home."

"Good," she said, glad he had, but... "Though, gotta say — you don't have to cook or clean to live here."

"I don't see to the cleaning." Earl's feet shuffled like dominos, cascading over the floor runner. "House cleans itself."

Well, that figured. The instant she stepped inside the place, she'd known it wasn't normal. Shut up for years and yet, the interior had been unnaturally tidy. An anomaly, just another in a long line of them after meeting Minador. Century-old homes usually needed a lot of work. Most were money pits. The fact hers wasn't both pleased and annoyed her.

She'd wanted a project. A place to call her own by putting her stamp on it. What she'd gotten instead was magic.

"Good to know, Earl, but no matter what, you're welcome here. No need to earn your keep by cooking," she said, eyes on Earl, focused on the open door behind her.

Sensing movement, Truly walked further into the hallway. A shadow fell across the threshold. The *Ecotone* flexed. The silhouette shifted, the magic-driven glow dampening as Westvane appeared in the doorway.

Black eyes alert, he scanned the interior, saw her, and stepped into the house. The second he cleared the threshold, she closed the door behind him with her mind. No need to repeat mistakes. She didn't want anything else unsavory escaping from Azlandia into Philadelphia.

"You hear me, Earl?" she asked, driving her point to the Mantipede home. "No need for you to —"

"I'm not earning my keep, girl. I'm taking care of you. There's a difference, you know? And honestly, numb-nuts there..." Brandishing the spatula, he pointed the silicone tip at

Westvane. "... needs all the help he can get when it comes to you."

She snorted in laughter. *Numb-nuts* — seriously? Earl must have a death wish. One that would come true if he continued to call Westvane insulting names to his face.

Truly glanced at Westvane out of the corner of her eye.

Citrine light firing in his gaze, he scowled at Earl.

Racking her brain for a way to smooth over the insult — and keep Earl alive — she watched him searched the hallway behind her, looking for something.

When Earl didn't find it, his attention snapped back to her. "Where's Montrose?"

Her heart sank. Her nose started to sting as tears threatened. She locked the waterworks down, refusing to acknowledge how much she already missed the bad-tempered gargoyle. No matter what Montrose said, leaving him behind felt wrong. As though she'd abandoned her friend in the middle of a battle, instead of protecting his back.

She cleared her throat.

Earl frowned. "What?"

"Montrose stayed," she said, the admission tasting like sour milk in her mouth.

Earl blinked. "Stayed?"

"Behind."

Earl nodded as though the bombshell she'd just dropped made perfect sense. "Bound to happen. He wasn't going to stay forever. He belongs in Azlandia, Truly."

"But not you," she whispered, worried he planned to leave too.

"Now, I'm what you'd call a long hauler. Never plan on leaving." Patting the crown of her head, Earl offered awkward, but well-intentioned support. "Let Rosy go, girl. Be happy for him and be on about your business. Getting on with it — best medicine around."

"Right." Sound advice. Now all she needed to do was make herself believe it. "Now, about you slaving away in the kitchen."

He huffed. "We back to that?"

"Leave him be, princess." Footfalls silent, Westvane brushed by her on his way to the kitchen. "He wants to feed you? Let him."

"Well, now." Crooked teeth flashed through his bristly beard as, multiple feet pitter-pattering, Earl grinned, then scurried out Westvane's way. "Good to see you back."

Westvane grunted. "Got a monster to catch."

"About that," Earl said, turning serious eyes on her. "Gotta bring you up to speed. Some things are happening in the city."

Oh, boy. Here she went again, jetting head-first into crazy. "What things?"

"Bad mojo, girl, bad mojo."

Dipping his head beneath the lintel, Westvane disappeared into the kitchen. His disembodied voice rolled out into the hall. "Tell us while we eat, Earl."

"Good, good. Understood." Raising the spatula, Earl sliced the utensil through the air like an expert swordsman, then wheeled his lower half around and creepy-crawled after Westvane. "Come on, girl. Time's a-wasting. You got a meal to eat, then places to go."

Truly sighed.

Her life just kept getting weirder and weirder.

Not that she balked at the promise of food. She was hungry, and a delicious smell wafted through the air. Earl had been up to good things in her absence. And despite her not wanting to take advantage of him, she admitted having Earl around wouldn't be a hardship. She liked him. He liked to cook, which meant (much as it pained her) Westvane was right.

No sense arguing the point.

She'd lose.

Earl would win, and she'd end up right back where she started... standing in a gorgeous kitchen, inside a house that belonged to her, wondering what Earl had to report, and what kind of trouble Westvane planned to toss her into next.

43

UNSAVORY SKILLS

Thick branches creaked above her head as Truly trailed Westvane down a deserted street. He strode right down the middle, boot soles quiet against a single yellow line. She chose a different tack, sticking to the sidewalk, obeying traffic laws, even though she planned to break a much bigger one in short order.

Truly thought about educating Westvane about the rule of law.

She didn't bother.

Dusk had fallen, deep shadows along with it. No one was around or out for a late evening stroll. The houses along the one-way street sat snug in landscaped yards, the people inside settled for the evening. Every once in while she caught movement behind diamond-paned windows. A light would go on, others would go off. Big leafy trees kept the peace, marching along the sidewalk, blocking the view, acting like a bulwark against the outside world. Even if someone looked out a window, no one would see him.

Or what she was about to do.

Scanning the street, she evaluated the vehicles parked curbside.

"No way I'm stealing a car from here," she mumbled, mostly to herself.

Westvane and his supersonic hearing picked it up. "Why not?"

"Too close to home." Her eyes jumped from a low-slung Mercedes to an SUV, then moved on to a pickup truck. Lots of bling. Monster tires. Too showy. No way she was breaking into and stealing any of those. Rolling through Philly with Westvane made her conspicuous enough. "We need to go farther afield."

Westvane gave her a strange look. "You do realize your house is invisible."

"Invisible?" Another slice of startling news. Truly stopped beneath the outstretched arms of a big oak tree. Really, it was getting old. She ought to be used to surprises by now. "What do you mean — invisible?"

"Humans can't see it."

"But..." She frowned. "I have an address."

"Not one that exists in human databases."

Well, there went the possibility of meeting her new postman.

"Safer for you. The Yeomanry can't attack what they can't find." Parallel to her position on the sidewalk, Westvane glanced up through the maze of branches, his gaze on the rising moon. "And Azlandians who require an audience with you can visit without drawing notice."

An audience? "I'm not the Queen of England, Westvane."

"No, you're much more important."

"You need to stop."

"What?"

"I can't handle any more surprises right now."

Dragging his focus from the sky, he looked at her from the

corner of his eye. "Can't help you there. Until you learn what you need to, surprise is part of the game."

"Figures."

"Stop stalling," he said, gesturing to the line of vehicles. "Pick one."

"I want my baby."

"Who?"

"My 'Cuda."

He grumbled something under his breath. "We spoke about this."

"You did. Doesn't mean I agreed." Liberating her girl from the PPD's impound yard ought to be priority number one.

"Truly."

"All right, all right."

Making it clear she was doing it under protest, she started walking again. She took inventory, tracking both sides of the street. She needed something fast with clean lines, nothing too flashy. She wanted to fly under the radar. The last thing she needed was cops on her tail.

Halfway down the block, Truly spotted it — a low-slung El Camino. Rusted in spots, scratched and dented in others, at a guess, circa the mid-1980s. Perfect. Big engine. Tinted windows. A bucket in back to toss the Wendigo after Westvane trussed it up.

Stopping beside it, she checked both sides of the street. "Keep an eye out."

Westvane nodded.

She slipped her kit from beneath her leather jacket. A pro at getting into cars, she handled the tool with ease, sliding the bar between the window and the rubber seal. A quick thrust down, a quicker jerk up and...

The lock clicked as the door knob flipped up.

Thanks for the unsavory skills, Rosy.

Shoving thoughts of the gargoyle aside, Truly palmed the handle and pulled. Hinges groaned as the heavy door opened. She slid inside and, reaching over the center console, unlocked the passenger side.

With one last look around, Westvane moved the seat back, folded almost in two, and crammed his frame inside. "I think I should drive."

"Do you know how?" she asked, yanking wires from under the steering column.

"I've seen you do it," he said, closing his door quietly to keep from alerting the neighborhood. "Couldn't do much worse."

She grinned. "The person who steals the car gets to drive it."

"Is that an Earth Realm rule?"

"Totally," she said, lying to keep him out of the driver's seat.

He threw her a disbelieving look, but left it alone. Thank God. Letting him drive would be a disaster. He'd no doubt run over whatever got in his way, people included.

Fiddling beneath the steering column, Truly twisted two wires together. The big V6 rumbled. She hummed in satisfaction. Never let be said Montrose hadn't taught her anything useful. "Where to first?"

"Downtown," Westvane said, dipping his head down to look through the windshield. "Where the riot is taking place."

Right in the thick of it.

Earl's intel jived with the news stations. Three straight nights of chaos in downtown Philly. Some people protested police brutality. Some governmental over-reach and systematic abuse. Others looted, breaking glass store fronts, starting fires, clashing with protestors. Now, what started as mostly peaceful marches had grown into a full-blown riot. One that continued to spiral out from the downtown core to engulf entire neighborhoods. Stood to reason. Made perfect sense. Wherever the Wendigo went, rage, hatred, and violence erupted.

She'd learned more about the Wendigo in the last hour than she ever wanted to know. Earl had regaled her during supper, informing her the assassination of the Austrian Archduke Franz Ferdinand — an event that started the sharp downward spiral into WWI — just one example of the kind of chaos the Wendigo was capable of unleashing.

Pulling onto the street, Truly glanced at Westvane. "Will you be able to capture it?"

"Need to find it first."

"But when we do —"

Westvane cut her off with a glance.

The intensity in his gaze said it all — fierce, brutal, unbridled violence unhidden. Yes. He'd be able to cage the Wendigo before sending it howling back to Azlandia. But as Truly turned out of the neighborhood, worry swept through her. Westvane's abilities might not be in question, but the amount of carnage he left in his wake was a serious concern. So, the question needed to be asked — how far was too far? How many innocent people would be hurt before the night ended?

"Okay, so…"

"What?"

Mentally girding herself, she buckled her seatbelt in place. "We need a game plan."

"I have one," Westvane said, ignoring his own seatbelt.

"And that would be?"

"For you to stay out of my way."

"Westvane —"

"When I need you, princess, I'll let you know."

His tone brooked no argument.

Truly didn't like it, but tamped down her counter-argument. He was focused, on mission, an Assenta warrior with one thing on his mind — the *hunt*.

She wouldn't be able to shift his strategy. Not now. When he had a job to do.

What he failed but needed to understand was, as Door Master (and a resident of Philadelphia), she had a mission too. A little daunting to go up against him, but as she drove downtown, Truly made a decision. She'd do what he asked and stay out of his way... until it became clear she couldn't anymore. The Wendigo was his problem. Protecting innocent people, keeping Westvane from leveling the city she called home, had just become hers.

TRULY REMAINED uneasy the entire way downtown.

Operating a motorized death-trap, driving through angry crowds, wasn't as easy as it looked. From his position in the passenger seat, Westvane tapped into her tension. The Door Master didn't like what she was seeing.

The people of Philadelphia weren't fooling around. Throngs of humans stood on every street corner. More marched, rising and falling like waves along wide boulevards, streaming down sidewalks, past the brick buildings acting like bulwarks on either side of the street.

Mob mentality.

Hive mind.

The crowd jostling the car suffered from both maladies.

The Wendigo had been more than just busy. It now presented a clear and present danger. One Westvane would've preferred Truly sit out. Instead, she sat in the driver's seat, cursing under her breath, trying to find a clear path through the heaving mass while he rode *shotgun*.

Weird colloquialism.

He didn't even have a shotgun. Though, as he understood it, humans liked idioms and ignored the literal, enjoying all manner of odd sayings. *The stranger, the better.* Earth Realm ought to adopt the slogan as their new planetary anthem. Write the lyrics. Hammer out a melody. Sing the song until everyone caught the fever. Maybe the rabble, carrying banners and hand-made signs, buzzing like angry bees toward the city center, would sing-shout it while on the march.

Not an outlandish assumption given the sheer number on the street.

"We need to get out of here," Truly said, scanning left, then right, searching for a way off the main boulevard as people swarmed the vehicle. "Find somewhere to park away from the crowds."

Westvane agreed. "Walk in from the perimeter."

"Blend into the crowd." Turning the wheel, she crept forward, doing her best not to hit anyone. "You think you can do that?"

With a snort of disbelief, he cranked his window down. "No. I want them to see me coming."

Her brows drew together. "Why?"

"The sooner they see me, the faster they'll get out of my way."

She eyed him. "You'll scare the bejeezus out of them."

"Good."

"And if there's a stampede?"

"Their problem, not mine."

"Westvane," she said, tone low with warning. "You're not allowed to kill anyone here."

"If someone's stupid enough to get in my way, I'll give them what they deserve."

She opened her mouth to lecture him.

He cut her off by leaving his seat. Sliding his upper body out the open window, he perched on the steel frame and, head and shoulders above the crowd, looked for an opening big enough to get the car though. He spotted one less than ten yards, a clear path between two tall apartment buildings.

"To the right, princess."

"A street?"

He nodded. "No barricades."

She turned the wheel, nudging people with the side of the vehicle.

People banged on the hood, yelled, calling the Door Master names.

Westvane lost his temper. Hopping up, he planted his feet on the window ledge. Baring his canines, he snarled at the offenders.

A collective gasp rose, riding thick autumn chill.

Humans recoiled, then scattered.

Truly sighed. "Subtle, Westvane. Real slick."

"Now, Truly."

Listening for once, she drove through the hole. Two tires up on the sidewalk, two rolling on asphalt, she wheeled onto the side street. A few stragglers jumped out of the way. The group shouted at her. She accelerated. The engine rumbled. More yelling. Truly didn't slow down. She gunned it instead, speeding toward two pillars near the end of the narrow avenue.

Worried about getting hit, Westvane shifted onto the rooftop. Steel dimpled beneath his feet as she drove between the uprights.

Concrete grazed both sides of the car. Metal screeched. Sparks flew.

Truly roared around the next corner. The back end swung out. The car rocked and lurched forward. The smell of burnt rubber on asphalt and the faint tang of smoke wafted into the air. Westvane jumped into the truck bed behind the driver's seat, and hitting his haunches, hung on as Truly swung the vehicle into a one-hundred-and-eighty-degree turn.

The back end whipped around.

The car slid sideways, then came to an abrupt stop. Momentum threw him backward. He landed on his ass next to the tailgate.

Grunting in discomfort, Westvane looked over the side of the car. Both tires an inch from the curb. In perfect parallel. Westvane stared at the concrete lip. Incredible. Certifiable. One-hundred-percent crazy. She'd brought the vehicle to a screeching stop between two parked cars.

The driver's door swung open.

Truly stuck her head out and grinned. "Not bad, huh?"

He scowled. "Next time, I'm driving."

Exciting the car, she slammed the door behind her. Hinges shrieked. She leveled her blue eyes on him. "Try it. See what happens."

"Whatever," he muttered, stealing one of her favorite words as he hopped out of the back. His boots touched down on concrete. Tipping his head back, he breathed deep. Cold air filled his lungs. The scent of oranges and ash tickled his senses. "The Wendigo's here."

"You can smell it?"

"It's faint, but the beast is with the crowd. East of here."

"Closer to downtown," she said, gazing up at the buildings surrounding them. "We'll keep to the side streets, walk a parallel route, stay out of the crowds."

"Don't trust me?"

She pursed her lips, twisting them to the side. The look in her eyes, the expression on her face, shouted *no*. Wise of her. He refused to be contained. Or bossed around by a stubborn Door Master, no matter how powerful her magic.

"From what Earl said, the protest is in and around Ritten-house Square."

Predatory interest rose, then narrowed. "Rittenhouse?"

"It's a park in Center City. An historical district." Raising a brow, she glanced at him sideways. "Wouldn't hurt to have eyes in the sky. Is Eastbrook around?"

At the mention of his name, the raven blinked his eyes, making his skin sting. Boots planted on the sidewalk, Westvane stayed silent and waited. Eastbrook's choice. Weeping Hollow had nearly eaten the bird right off the side of his throat. He wouldn't blame his feathered friend if he decided to sit this one out, instead of entering the fray.

The itch on the side of his neck intensified.

Westvane breathed deep. Magic burned in his veins as ink swirled across his neck. Soft plumage brushed his cheek. With a low caw, Eastbrook materialized fully formed, sharp talons curved around his shoulder.

"Hello, handsome," Truly said, smiling at the raven.

Eastbrook chuffed, greeting her like an old friend.

Drawing a fingertip over Eastbrook's head, Westvane shrugged, telling him to take flight. The raven obeyed and leaped skyward, adding another pair of eyes to the hunt.

He watched his friend soar, then turned his attention to Truly. "Listen, carefully."

"You lead, I follow, right?"

"You get me to Rittenhouse Square, then back off," he said, issuing instructions, not wanting her anywhere near the Wendigo. "The second I lay eyes on the beast, the hunt begins, and I'll be gone. Stay down range. Follow at a distance. When I need you to open a door, I'll call."

"Sounds good," she said, agreeing with him, making him suspicious.

"I mean it, Truly. Stay out of my way."

"You said that already."

"Bears repeating."

"Won't be a problem, Westvane." Leaving him standing by the car, she jogged across, then down the street. He caught up with her as she turned into a narrow alleyway and ramped into a run. "I'll stay out of your way, as long as you stay out of mine."

Westvane bit down on a curse.

Exactly what he feared. Truly had an agenda of her own. Bad news. Her skill at finding trouble was fast becoming legendary, which meant he was once again in unchartered territory. Glaring at the back of her obstinate little head, he made a split-second decision.

His plan needed adjusting.

With her running rampant, he'd be forced to fight on two fronts. The first battle — hunt, capture, and re-cage the Wendigo. Challenging enough on its own. The second, however, would be even more difficult — keeping Truly from sticking her nose where it didn't belong. Given her luck, she'd get it lopped off, or worse, get herself killed.

A serious problem.

He needed Truly to remain in one piece, hale, whole, able to open doors at will. Now, and in the future. If the execution of tonight's plan went sideways, Lyonesse would be waiting when he returned the Wendigo to Eckizbad Prison. The worse possible outcome. A scenario that not only put him in the queen's crosshairs, but ensured Truly ended up a sitting duck, vulnerable to whatever violence the faithless witch and Priestly had planned.

44

DON'T LET GO

The crowd thickened on Walnut Street.

Standing on the corner, surrounded by people taller than her, a block from Rittenhouse Square, Truly glanced over her shoulder. Right behind her, Westvane wore a scowl that would scare motor oil out of an engine.

Nothing new. He almost always conveyed displeasure when he looked at humans. Though, *displeasure* might be too tame a word.

His expression gave nothing away, but she'd learned to read him. He wanted to kill someone. Brandish his lightning sword. Conjure his smoke shield. Slam both into multiple human heads. The nasty gleam in his eyes clued her in, which was how she knew he'd truss her up, stash her some place safe, and leave her behind if she got in his way.

"Can you see a way through?" she asked, trying to distract him from committing murder while she took advantage of his height. And Eastbrook. Maybe the raven could find a path through all the people.

Someone jostled Westvane from behind, pushing him into her.

His nostrils flared. His eyes grew blacker. Citrine light sparked in their depths as the air around him cooled. Frost touched the top of his shoulders, then rolled over hers. Her breath became white puffs as the man bumped him again. Baring his teeth, Westvane turned, palmed the guy's face, and shoved him backward.

The offender went flying.

The crowd scattered, opening a hole as the man hit the pavement with a thud.

She stared at the guy on the ground, then refocused on the Assenta warrior standing at her back. "Calm down, Westvane."

"I hate people."

Truly dug down deep and buried her smile. He wouldn't appreciate her sense of humor. Not right now. Teasing him wouldn't her get anywhere, other than tossed like a caber.

"Westvane, where's Eastbrook? Maybe —"

Latching onto her wrist, he yanked her behind him. Gaze moving over the crowd, he sliced between a light pole and a throng of idiots throwing beer bottles at a store front. Glass shattered. A shout went up. Westvane veered right, then left, knocking people out of his way.

She heard complaints rise around her. Each complaint died an easy death. Understandable. One look at Westvane and, drunk or not, everyone scurried out of the way. A hole opened in front of him, only to close in his wake. Open, then close. Ebb and flow. The human wave felt like a living organism, the reaction of molecules being pushed aside, only to reassemble into proper formation when the disturbance left.

"Tuck in," Westvane growled, rounding a burning SUV in the middle of the street. "Head down."

Truly pressed closer, trying to do as ordered, but couldn't look away. Walnut Street looked like a war zone. Battle credos rose from everywhere. People stood on top of cars, yelling.

Others hung from the sides of lamp posts, shouting. More than one group chanted, waving signs — some masterful, others homemade — creating visual scramble, mesmerizing with color. The sound of breaking glass and the smell of smoke joined the chaos, rippling through the normally peaceful neighborhood.

"Oh my God," she muttered, grabbing the back of Westvane's jacket. She tugged, fighting the hold he had on her wrist. His grip tightened. Pressure compressed over her bones. Ignoring the sting, she yanked again. "Let go, Westvane. You need both of your hands free."

"Stay close." Shoving a group aside one-handed, he released his hold on her. "Don't let go."

In answer, she fisted both hands in his coat.

He didn't slow, towing her through the crowd, moving obstacles when needed, heading for the flash of greenery at the end of the clogged avenue. She saw treetops through the smoke and angry mob, standing tall on the edge of Rittenhouse Square.

Clinging to him with her dominant hand, Truly let go with the other. She pointed at the trees and yelled over the noise, "The square!"

He nodded, and weaving between cars, headed for the corner of Walnut and Rittenhouse Square. Jammed with protestors facing off with police in riot gear, the intersection seemed like a bad place to go. Westvane plowed straight through, shoving people aside, walking around the police barricades, over the sidewalk, right into the park.

The officers didn't blink an eye... or break formation.

A few greeted Westvane with chin lifts as he walked past.

"You know them?" Truly knew it was a stupid question. Of course, Westvane didn't know the police. How could he? He'd spent limited time in Earth Realm, and none of it hanging out with Philadelphia PD.

"No," he said, humoring her momentary lack of mental

acuity. "But they don't need to know me to know they don't want any part of me."

Drawing her in front of him, shielding her from the bump of streaming bodies, he stopped at the edge of the park. His nostrils flared as he scented the air. A growl rumbled from deep inside his chest. Citrine shimmer sparked in his dark eyes as he tipped his chin down and stared at something. A strange stillness overtook him. His cheekbones sharpened, taking on predatory edges.

Watching the change, Truly swallowed, but otherwise stayed perfectly still. Distracting him didn't seem like a good idea. Neither did making herself the subject of such rapt focus.

"Remember what I said," he said, his voice a low rumble as he grew more focused on the center of Rittenhouse Square.

His hands flexed around her upper arms. Something dragged at her jacket, pricking her biceps. She glanced down and caught her breath. His fingernails, normally round and buff, had grown into sharp, short claws. Staring at the proof of his Assenta heritage, she struggled to draw full breaths.

Westvane shook her gently, then released her. "Remember it to the letter, princess."

"Wait," she said, grasping at his lapel. "I..."

"What?" he snapped, his gaze on the crowd... and his target.

"I won't be able to keep up." Feeling like an asthmatic, she drew one shallow breath after another. "You're too fast. I'm assuming the Wendigo is too, so once you take off, I'll never be able —"

Black eyes glinting yellow cut to her.

Truly flinched, but held steady, determined to stand tall in the face of an Assenta warrior on the hunt.

With a nod, he scanned the crowd. His gaze flickered. Lightning quick, he reached out, snagged a cyclist zipping by, and yanked. The speed bike came to an abrupt halt. The rider flew over the handle bars. Westvane didn't wait for him to land.

Manhandling the bicycle, he spun it toward her. She grabbed the seat to hold the Cervélo upright, cringing as the man hit solid concrete.

Sounded awful. Absolutely brutal given the groan the guy expelled.

The pain he caused didn't faze Westvane. Dark eyes focused on her, he growled, "Now, do as you're told. Stay down range, keep up."

Under normal circumstances, Truly would've bristled at his tone. She didn't enjoy being ordered around — or snarled at for that matter. But as she watched him run into the park, footspeed freakishly fast, she didn't waste her energy on anger. She threw her leg over, set her foot on the pedal and, saying a silent apology to guy spread like a broken starfish on the sidewalk, tore after him. She'd rip a strip off Westvane later. Right now, she had a bicycle to ride and an Assenta warrior to catch.

AN UNDENIABLE SIGN

Staying low, Westvane sprinted into the Rittenhouse Square. Pretty place, even in the semi-dark. Lampposts rose at even intervals, throwing light across wide pathways crammed full of people. Thick tree branches cast long shadows, dappling statues in dormant flowerbeds. Humans thronged the square, carrying signs, standing on benches, climbing the many trees, all facing a man with a megaphone chanting "The whole world is watching."

The crowd yelled the slogan back. Over and over. Again and again.

The sound of voices rose and fell, throbbing like a heartbeat, pumping life blood into the protest. A quick sweep made Westvane clenched his teeth. The protest was about to get ugly. Police stood outside the perimeter, surrounding the square, waiting for trouble to start.

And it would.

Frustration and rage were about to boil over. He sensed it. Smelled it. Picking the invisible threads that signaled violence out of thin air. Two potent scents combined, intricately entwined, the frenzy an undeniable sign the beast was close.

Which made perfect sense. Where the Wendigo went, chaos, death, and destruction always followed.

Though the beast never got its own hands dirty. The Wendigo left that to those it twisted into fury, whispering incendiary thoughts into their ears, corrupting the good, elevating the bad... reveling in the fallout.

Infiltrating the crowd, Westvane kept his eyes on the male with the megaphone. The Wendigo must be nearby, egging the crowd on, whipping humans into a frenzy. Soon, the savagery would begin. Small circles were already forming, fists flashing as men fought at the center.

He needed to move faster. To find a way in now, before —

Glass shattered against the path. Clear liquid splashed up and out of the broken container. Fire raced across concrete as a second incendiary device exploded in front of him.

People screamed and scrambled away, onto the grass, back toward the street.

Ramping into a run, Westvane jumped through the flames, skirted a statue of a lion, then leapt over a small pond. His feet touched down without making a sound. The scent he tracked grew stronger, then became sight and sound.

There. Off to one side, standing behind the man on stage leading the crowd. The Wendigo in all his beastly glory. Not that the humans around him could see it. The creature had taken human form, horns tucked away, feet in place of hooves, normal hands instead of paws and claws.

Westvane bared his teeth. His canines lengthened, becoming fangs as he located his prey and allowed the killer inside him out of its cage.

In full stride, he cut across a flowerbed.

He watched the Wendigo's nostrils flare. Its head whipped in his direction. The beast's eyes widened as it saw him. It took a step back, then another. Perception narrowed. Time slowed. Focus and aggression aligned.

His shoulder blades began to itch.

Relief burned through him. Satisfaction arrived hard on its heels. *His wings.* His wings were back, trying to punch through his back to reach open air. Westvane killed the urge to let the pair free, keeping them caged inside his skin. He didn't need the distraction right now. And the drag of feathers in open air would only slow him down.

Eyes locked on his prey, Westvane launched himself over —

The Wendigo grabbed the male with the megaphone and, with a violent spin, threw him like a caber. The human careened off stage, hurtling toward Westvane. Tail tucked between his legs, the Wendigo ran in the opposite direction.

Dodging the human projectile, Westvane growled at Eastbrook. The raven shifted course above the heaving crowd, providing a more accurate view. The screen inside his mind changed its angle. Images of the protest flashed. Westvane zeroed in. Locked on, he tracked the Wendigo's retreat, and shoving people aside, sprinted after it.

Rage swelled, rippling through him as he pursued the Wendigo out of the park. Talk about disappointing. He wanted to fight, not a prolonged chase.

He'd been dreaming about a knuckle-bruising brawl for days. Sinking his claws deep — ripping and tearing, watching blood flow — would soothe him. Settle him. Reset his internal compass so he could do what needed to be done. Now, all he had was a bird's-eye view and the hope the Wendigo wasn't as fast as it seemed. If it escaped him now, who knew where it would go, how much damage it would do... or how many humans would be killed.

PEDALING the bike like a mad fool, Truly chased Westvane down Locust Street and up 23rd. She swerved around lamp posts, careened between cars, jumping curbs to avoid people on sidewalks. Her leg and arm muscles burned. Battling the discomfort, she fought to catch her breath, lamenting all the time she'd spent sitting on her ass inside her car taking pictures.

She needed get to the gym more. Pump some iron. Do more cardio. Join a kickboxing class or something. If she didn't, and this kept up, Westvane would end up being the death of her. Though he might kill her first if she didn't start covering more ground.

Pumping her knees, she tried to steady her breathing. Really. Her sedentary lifestyle needed to be thrown out the nearest window. Chasing an Assenta warrior around classified as an extreme sport. One requiring mastery in multiple disciplines.

A death grip on the handlebars, Truly soldiered on, lungs screaming, muscles burning, scrambling to keep up. Knowing where she was heading would've helped. She could have taken a couple of shortcuts, but as things stood now, she felt direction-less. She sensed Westvane nearby. Could actually feel him somewhere — up there, ahead of her — but couldn't quite get a lock on his location.

Sinking into the stream, she tapped into her magic. Her senses began to sizzle, but... no joy. The signal stayed muffled. Her mind's eye remained blank, forcing her to track Westvane the old-fashioned way — with her eyes and ears. An impossible task. She needed more practice with her newfound abilities.

Keeping up with an Assenta on the hunt required a lot more skill than she currently possessed.

Wheeling around a pile of debris, she stood on the pedals and looked around. Large intersection ahead, steel pole and signal lights scorched black and listing to one side. A car on fire, steel frame gutted sitting in the center lane, fewer people around.

She squeezed the brakes. Rubber squealed. Her boot sole touched down, bumping along cracked asphalt as she rolled to a stop. Alert and focused, senses firing like pistons, she scanned the buildings, both sides of the avenue, the thinning crowd, trying to decide.

Go left.

Turn right.

She studied the clusters of people. In groups of three or four. Walking instead of running, talking at normal levels instead of shouting, most headed away from Rittenhouse Square instead of toward it.

No one screaming in terror.

Nothing exploding in the immediate vicinity.

Or pools of blood on broken concrete left by an Assenta who didn't care whom he hurt. Nary a sign of Westvane.

"Great." Frustration about to boil over, she looked skyward.

Shadowed, barely visible above the city glow, she saw a black blur.

She set her other foot on the ground and, straddling the crossbar, angled backward, her gaze fixed between two buildings. A black bird crested the top of a high rise, banked left, and circled back.

Eastbrook in a holding pattern.

She huffed in satisfaction. Got him. Westvane wasn't far. Her guess? Somewhere near Schuylkill River and one of the bridges crossing it.

Flipping the back tire around, Truly took off in that direction. She stood on the pedals and jumped the curb. Air held her suspended a moment. Her tires slammed down. Pedestrians leapt out of her way, yelling at her to slow down. She didn't listen. Darting down an alley, she sped past dumpsters and piles of trash to reach Market Street.

Hands clenched around twin grips, she checked the sky.

Eastbrook swung into another rotation.

Truly turned right onto the JFK Boulevard and zipped across the bridge. Lit up in the dark, 30th Street Station shone like a beacon in the dark. Massive Corinthian columns stood sentry, protecting the entrance, welcoming good-intentioned travelers through its doors. Running a red light, she zipped across the avenue and rode into the portico.

Eastbrook landed on the huge clock standing between the columns behind her. Cocking his head, he hopped from talon to talon, head bobbing.

"In there?" she asked, attention moving between Eastbrook and entrance. "Did he go in —"

Screaming rushed from behind glass doors.

A roar shook the tall panes in their steel frames. Running for their lives, a stampede of people followed. Doors banged open and travelers streamed out, pushing, shoving, tripping over one another. The human wave swarmed around, then past her.

Truly dropped the bike, and leaping over the front tire, elbowed a straggler aside to reach one of the doors. Another roar. More snarling. The sound of shattering glass. The building shook on its foundation. Chunks of rock and wooden debris exploded out the front doors. The concussive wave picked her up, throwing her backward. She slammed spine-first into one of the columns. Dazed by the blow, she sat unmoving, ears ringing, blood trickling down her cheek.

Blinking, Truly swiped at it as a band of pressure squeezed

her ribcage. Her chest hitched, hiccupping like an old car engine, then caught. She sucked in dusty air and coughed, but managed to drag in a shuddered breath.

Eastbrook landed on her thigh.

He chuffed, nudging her with his beak. She drew in another lungful and nodded. Right. Okay. She needed to get up. Find her feet. Move forward. She couldn't sit beneath the portico while Westvane battled the Wendigo.

Truly didn't care what he said. She refused to let him face the carnage alone.

Pressing her hand into the ground, she levered herself upright. Chucks of concrete and glass bit into her palm. She ignored the sting. A couple more scrapes wouldn't kill her. Eastbrook agreed, hopping to her shoulder as she wiped blood off her cheek and rushed to one of the doors, ignoring Westvane's instruction by running toward the fight instead of away.

WHAT ARE YOU?

For a large structure, the train station seemed too small. Despite the high ceilings and wide main hall, Westvane needed more room to maneuver... and fewer things for the Wendigo to throw. Particularly since the beast had shed its human skin.

Now, it stood twelve feet tall. Thick, hooked horns spiraled from the sides of the beast's head. All six eyes trained on him, its flat nose flared. Jagged teeth flashed as it snarled, causing the venomous snake tipping its tail to rise into strike formation above the Wendigo's shoulder.

Westvane sidestepped, using long benches as cover.

The viper's head shifted sideways. Armored brown scales clicked as its forked tongue flicked out, scenting the air. Westvane's shoulder blades began to itch again, sensation ramping into an insistent throb beneath his skin.

Yellow eyes with slitted pupils narrowed as the Wendigo grinned. "Not so cocky now, are you, Slayer?"

The giant snake tipping its tail hissed.

The itch along Westvane's spine grew into a sting. His wings, still tucked away, drew half circles around the inside of his shoulder blades. His nostril flared. His gaze began to glow, throwing citrine shimmer across the floor.

The Wendigo growled.

Westvane stopped fighting it. With a murmur, he let his wings go, allowing bone to cut through his muscles. Bladed edges punched through his leather trench coat. Rolling his shoulders, he flexed the pair. The lethal claws tipping each wing flashed beneath the overhead lights. Black feathers fell like dominos, cascading into place.

He hummed in relief.

Better.

Much, much better.

When his wings had come to him inside the Parkland, Westvane hadn't wanted them. He was an Assenta, born to be a hunter, taught by his mother, and back then, any sign of his Electi father hadn't been welcoming. In the intervening months, he'd come to appreciate his father's gift. He may not have met the male who sired him, but Westvane no longer wished to deny his birthright.

The powerful magic given to him by his sire was an asset. An advantage most never saw coming. Which left him with a clear path and one option...

Embrace his heritage. Learn how to wield his magic in order to defeat Lyonesse, oust the Electi elite who sat at the High Table, and give freedom back to the Azlandian people. A lofty goal, but a problem for another time. Right now, he needed to focus.

Predatory instinct sharpened as he flexed his wings. The sight caused the Wendigo to pause and reassess. He could almost see the beast's mind turning, the questions not difficult to guess. What kind of opponent did it face? How had an Assenta warrior come to own a set of wings? What did it mean... did it make Westvane less lethal or more dangerous?

Focused on his wings, the Wendigo cocked its head. "What are you?"

Westvane widened his stance. "You're about to find out."

The viper's forked tongue curled, scenting the air before it hissed, "Electi. Assenta. Hybrid."

Huge hooves clicked across the marble floor as the Wendigo flexed its paws. Light from the overhead lights winked off razor-sharp claws. "You are unnatural."

"An abomination, some say." His mouth curved. "But then, so are you."

"I am what the world made me, Slayer."

True, but then...

Weren't they all?

Gaze riveted to the beast and its viper, Westvane entered the center aisle. Still analyzing, the Wendigo stepped back, toward the wall of glass doors behind it. Keeping his feet moving, Westvane circled left and took stock, inventorying what he needed to bring the creature down.

Shield and sword were always good options, but the immediate environment mattered. The benches, the ticket counter, the ornate wall fixtures provided a multitude of interesting options. Westvane could throw any number of them, taking the Wendigo off guard, tripping it up long enough for him to neutralize the threat.

Shifting into a better position, Westvane scanned the interior again. Long wooden benches used for sitting. Slim light fixtures on long cables hung from the ceiling. Steel railing rimming the second-floor balcony.

His attention slid to the doors behind the Wendigo. A statue of an angel — wings spread, benevolent expression, holding a human who looked dead. Cast in bronze. Heavy. Solid. Perfect for smashing skulls. Weaponizable. In truth, everything he saw held potential. Even the board heralding times and places could be ripped from its moorings and —

"You begin to bore me," the Wendigo said, flashing pointed teeth. "What are you waiting for?"

"Just being polite."

The Wendigo's brow creased. "Polite?"

"Giving you time."

"For what?"

"To understand the futility."

The beast huffed. "Think you can take me?"

"Forgone conclusion." Flexing his hands, he relished the feel of his claws. Razor-thin, so sharp the talons sliced through muscle and bone, no sawing necessary. He stared at the Wendigo from beneath his brows. The look was aggressive. Westvane intended it to be. He wanted the Wendigo enraged. Anger would lead to an error in judgement. And a mistake would give him the opening he needed. "So certain, in fact, why fight at all? Give up. Go home. Keep all your limbs attached."

"I'm not going back." Seven-fingered hands curled into fists, it slammed a hooved foot into the floor. Stone cracked. The viper's iridescent scales rose like spikes, then clattered back into position. "I'll never go back to that witch."

"Well, you can't stay here," he said, understanding more than a little. He almost felt sorry for the Wendigo. Lyonesse wasn't anyone's idea of a prize. Neither was the prison cell she wanted to stuff the beast back into.

Claws dragging along the floor, the Wendigo snarled at him.

He growled back. The guttural rumble vibrated from his chest. Subtle, but nasty. Quiet, yet wholly disrespectful. A challenge issued in the old way, an insult intended to infuriate.

The Wendigo's slitted nostrils flared.

Westvane waited for the eruption. When the beast hesitated, he raised a brow and gave it a push. "What's the matter — you scared?"

That did it.

Fury sparked in its eyes.

Westvane almost grinned as, with a roar, the beast ripped a bench from the floor. Bolts exploded toward the ceiling. Steel rivets rained down. Wood creaked as the Wendigo swung the solid length like a club.

Wings flat against his back, Westvane ducked and dodged left.

The bench smashed into the wall behind him. Sharp shards flew across the train station. Pieces of heavy beam slammed into the petroglyph carved into the stone, ripping the figures off the wall. Chunks of rock rained down. Ignoring the spray of shrapnel, Westvane leapt over a staircase and tilted into a somersault. He conjured his twin swords in mid-air. Black flame rose from his hands. The blades solidified, settling familiar grips into his palms.

His feet touched down.

A door at the side entrance slammed open.

Truly ran into main hall.

Westvane cursed under his breath.

Her eyes widened as she caught sight of the Wendigo. Arms pinwheeling, she reversed course. Feet sliding over polished marble, she fought to stop her forward progress.

The Wendigo's head snapped in her direction. Its focus narrowed a second before a gruesome grin flashed across its face.

Westvane clenched his teeth. Not good. The beast didn't hide its intentions. He read the shift of strategy in its expression. Saw the nasty gleam enter its eyes. Knew the precise moment it changed strategy.

Kill the Door Master.

Close all avenues back to Azlandia.

Westvane raised his blades. "Truly — get down!"

Scrambling like an uncoordinated crab, she backpedaled. The clatter of her boots echoed in the huge space. Westvane heard her breath catch, felt her panic, then...

Truly stilled mid-scramble. In a move so idiotic it shocked him, she squared her shoulders and stood to face the beast. The snake hissed. The Wendigo laughed. Westvane mobilized. He didn't know what she thought she was doing, but whatever her plan, it was a bad one.

No one who planned to live stood in the kill zone when faced with a monster. Somewhere along the way, Truly failed to learn that invaluable lesson. So...

It came down to him.

He must be the one to shield her — to save her, and along with her, his world. The future of his home rested on her shoulders. The second the *Ecotone* closed for good, all hope in Azlandia died.

With a curse, Westvane unfurled his wings. Hell of a time to learn how to fly, but... so be it. The timing couldn't be helped. Truly stood in the pipe. The Wendigo had her in its sights. Which made him the Door Master's only hope of survival.

47

HELLO AGAIN

Glass rattled as the steel-framed door banged closed behind her. The slam echoed, rippling across the main terminal of the train station. The noise barely registered. The monster standing on the other side of the aisle glaring at her, however, did.

She'd made a huge mistake. One that grew bigger by the moment as horror pushed disbelief out of the way. The Wendigo. It looked different. Yet another version of the same beast, this variant nothing like the one that had escaped from the confines of her house — or the human it had pretended to be.

Ass-planted on polished tiles, she sat frozen, in open-mouthed astonishment, staring up at it while it grinned at her. Needle-sharp teeth with blackened tips flashed beneath huge pendant lights. Westvane yelled something. His words didn't register. She was too busy scrambling, crab-crawling backward, rubber boot soles squeaking across the floor as she looked for cover. The frantic search was futile. 30th Street Station's grand concourse provided little to no cover. Instinct urged her to turn around and exit as fast as she entered.

With a quick glance, Truly gauged the distance to the doors.

Seven, maybe eight feet behind her. Not an insurmountable distance, but the question was — could she make it before the Wendigo got ahold of her? Inching backwards, she ran all the scenarios down inside her mind and —

"Truly," Westvane growled.

Her attention flicked in his direction and... *shit.* She couldn't do it. Couldn't turn tail and run even as every instinct she owned screamed for her to leave Westvane to it. He was a warrior, an Assenta hunter with more skills in his fingertips than she possessed in her entire body. The expression he wore told her he wanted her to go, but running would be weak. An act akin to waving a white flag without ever having stepped onto the field.

The drumbeat increased inside her head. *Run. Run. RUN!*

Refusing to listen, Truly stopped backpedaling. Stupidity run amuck? Probably, but the reason she'd entered the station hadn't changed. Whether he knew it or not, Westvane needed her help. Two magic-wielders working together were better than one fighting on his own. Their battle with the Earth Octopus was proof enough of that, so...

She couldn't do what Westvane wanted.

Somewhere along the way, Westvane had become important to her, the yin to her yang in an unbalanced game. Which meant she couldn't turn away — or retreat from the truth. She and Westvane were partners. If she let him fend for himself now, she was not only a terrible friend, but the worse kind of coward.

Not that she'd inform him of her decision, never mind the conviction anchoring it. Westvane didn't care what she thought, and right now seemed an especially bad time to point out the obvious. Or start an argument. One look at his face, and she knew he wanted to rip her head off and punt it out into the street.

She leveled her chin.

Westvane muttered something obscene.

Heart pounding, Truly pushed to her feet and sidestepped. A slow, careful shuffle as Westvane cursed and the Wendigo tensed. She did too, but for different reasons. The beast was huge. Much larger than the first time she'd come face to snout with it. Its horns hadn't been as tall, its frame as broad, its clawed fingers as long or —

The Wendigo's tail swung around.

Hard scales clicked. Bright green eyes with vertical pupils locked on her. Her stomach clenched. Suppressing a shudder, she swallowed as the giant snake shifted sideways, preparing to strike. A forked tongue slithered out of its mouth. Curled at the tip, the serpent scented the air, tracking her from over the Wendigo's shoulder.

Working moisture into her mouth, she met the beast's gaze. "Hello again."

"Door Master." Six eyes locked on her, the Wendigo executed a half-bow.

The formal greeting threw her.

It sounded... she frowned... respectful. As though the Wendigo believe it faced a worthy adversary. One it intended to kill, but couldn't execute without first observing the rules of engagement. Odd, but then everything about the beast was out of the ordinary, monstrous but beautiful despite its brutality.

She almost hated to see it hurt... and re-imprisoned.

Almost. But not quite.

Despite their (relatively) cordial interactions, she knew the Wendigo couldn't be trusted. It wasn't her friend. It wasn't a pet. It was a thought-stealing, riot-inducing demon with one goal — to wreak havoc and ruin whatever world it inhabited. Her personal history with it made no difference. The beast might enjoy rules, or the appearance of them, but politesse played a minor part. Protocol, honor, the correct way to annihilate were more important. How she understood the Wendigo's aim was anyone's guess as its straightened from its bow, precepts met, and focused on her.

She saw the violence in its eyes. Recognized the maneuvering of an apex predator — the desperate claw of a cornered animal formulating a new plan.

Raising her hands, she held both out, palms up and to the sides, and retreated. Her feet whispered over gleaming marble tile. Each rasp grated against her frayed nerves. She inhaled calm and exhaled tension, moving with precision, a new plan developing on the fly.

The Wendigo wasn't the only one capable of changing tact mid-sail. It might be bigger. It might be stronger. It might be an accomplished killer, and yet... she held the advantage. She stood in center focus. On stage, lit with a spotlight so bright she commanded the Wendigo's attention to the exclusion of all else.

Maybe she could use it.

Maybe she could become *the* distraction. The bait and bull's-eye that would allow Westvane more room to maneuver.

Done observing the formalities, the Wendigo bared its fangs. Hooved feet planted, long arms flexing, it swung the bench up and back, brandishing it like a club.

"Westvane," she said, voice low in warning.

She needn't have bothered.

He was already on the move.

Twin swords in hand, wings spread wide, he launched himself toward the ceiling. She flinched as he took flight. Gloss-black feathers flashed. The temperature dropped. Ice crystals rolled out in waves as he flew between hanging pendant lights. Heavy ceiling cables swung, sending art deco chandeliers whipping in his wake.

The deep freeze thickened.

Frost crackled across the floor.

The Wendigo's attention drifted.

"Hey!" Her shout echoed, bouncing around the cavernous interior. Flexing her fingers, she felt her blood heat. Power rippled down her spine. Her lips curved. *Magic.* Excellent. Right on time. "You gonna do something with that or —"

The beast roared. Shattered at one end, the bench sliced toward her.

Westvane angled into a dive. "Shields, princess!"

An image formed in her mind. Magic gathered, twisting in front of her as she conjured a sphere. Heat lightning whirled into an impenetrable shell. Surrounded, protected, wrapped up tight, she raised her hands, planted her feet inside the ball and —

Wood struck the shield broadside, making contact like a batter in a baseball game.

A loud *crack!* screamed across the station.

The bench exploded.

Shrapnel rained down. But she was already gone, flying toward the wall above the balcony. As she tumbled inside the sphere, an idiotic thought entered her mind. The Wendigo could play ball. The thing had hit a grand slam, one that would make fans cheer in any major league baseball stadium in America. Her admiration hooked foul, however, when she slammed into the stone wall, then ricocheted straight back into the danger zone.

48

THE PARKLAND

Fighting his wings, Westvane struggled to stay airborne. The flight wasn't smooth. He jerked from one movement to the next, battling to control the angle and his velocity. Too fast, and he'd crash. Not fast enough, and he'd *crash*.

Neither option worked for him.

Not with the Wendigo taking aim at Truly down below. He swung left, then flew right, avoiding thick cables, trying to figure out how to move in the direction he wanted to go.

His feathers rustled in the updraft. Tendons in his shoulders ached as he banked into another shaky turn. Magic detonated at floor level. His focus snapped toward Truly and —

Hell. He hadn't seen *that* coming.

Of all the choices Truly could've made — retreat the smartest option — conjuring a sphere wasn't one he anticipated. The sight of her inside the ball, shimmering liquid spinning off the shell, made him want to skin her alive. What the devil was she thinking? *Not much* was his first thought. His second wasn't nearly as charitable.

If she lived to see dawn, he just might have to kill her. Or...

his brows snapped together... at the very least give her a harsh talking-to.

The downgrade from *annihilate* (his favorite) to *lecture* wasn't a pleasant one. She really needed to learn some restraint. Forethought and strategic planning wouldn't be bad things to instill in her, either. As it was, hearing the crack of wood against the sphere, watching her soar through the air, forced him to switch tracks. He wasn't flying solo anymore. Now he must protect himself from the Wendigo while ensuring the Door Master didn't die in the process.

Beyond annoying. Also... circling overhead, Westvane tightened the grip on his swords... the tiniest bit endearing.

She cared about him. Didn't want to see him injured. Problem was, she'd miscalculated. He was an Assenta warrior, practically indestructible. Truly was nowhere near indestructible. She was human, which made dying a serious concern for her. If her magic faltered and the sphere around her disintegrated, she'd be killed... instantly.

Slicing over the Wendigo, he plotted evasive maneuvers. Everything slowed. He heard the crack of wood. He saw the sphere fly through the air. Blue slime spun off the outside. The Wendigo laughed and corrected its stance, ratcheting the club back into position, readying for the next swing.

Westvane calculated the odds and angles. Attacking from above would be more effective. Faster. Cleaner. A greater challenge for the Wendigo to defend. If his wings cooperated. A big *if* that involved a lot of guesswork. Not the best assumption to hang his hat on, given his current struggle to stay airborne.

Which meant he needed to be on the ground. In a familiar tactical setting, using his usual techniques. Otherwise, he'd lose Truly and never make it back to Azlandia, never mind complete the rest of his mission.

Tucking his wings, Westvane dropped from ninety feet up.

His feet slammed into the floor. He moved right, dragging his swords across marble. Black flame-tipped blades bit into tile. Smoke drew a line, curling up from the cut. The scent of acrid air burned through the train station. Under normal circumstance, he wouldn't have done it. Making noise never made for a good strategy when on the hunt, but...

Stealth wasn't part of the plan.

Turning the beast's attention, forcing it to focus on him instead of Truly, was all that mattered now.

With a snarl, he raked one of his swords along the top of a bench. Varnished wood caught fire. More smoke rose.

The Wendigo swung in his direction, but didn't take the bait. Half of its six eyes on him, the other three on Truly, the Wendigo adjusted its grip on the bench. The shattered end circled over its horns. The viper reared to avoid being impaled on nasty-looking spikes, shifting to its other shoulder.

Truly slammed into the solid wall opposite him.

He heard her muffled yelp. Watched her bang around inside the sphere, then cursed as the revolving ball of slime rebounded, rocketing straight toward him.

The Wendigo laughed again.

Clenching his teeth, Westvane dodged. Blue liquid splashed into his face. The sphere clipped his wing-tip. Pain clawed over his shoulder. Momentum spun him around. He collided with a column, smashing through stone. The pillar crumbled. Part of the coffered ceiling gave way. Light fixtures and cables smashed into the floor.

A death grip on his weapons, Westvane leapt away from falling debris, fighting to recover as the beast swung at Truly again. The make-shift bat clipped the ball. She sailed wide, slamming into a statue.

Ripped from its pedestal, the angel fell. As the bronze idol hit the floor, the ball skipped sideways. Spun three-hundred-

and-sixty degrees, she cursed as huge fangs bared, the snake attacked. One strike, then another, followed by more. The clang of striking teeth echoed. His gut clenched as wings bent at odd angles, Westvane struggled to get up.

Blood dripped into his eye.

With a vicious swipe, he wiped it away and reacquired the target. Hooves planted, standing ten feet to his left, the Wendigo turned on him. The club arched toward his head.

Punching his feet into the floor, he vaulted into a somersault. Spiked wood whiffed over his head. Halfway through the rotation, he angled one of his wings. The underside caught air, setting him on his feet as he unleashed his swords.

Pivot. Sight the target. Strike without mercy.

The three-pronged attack drove Wendigo backward across the station. Gaining speed and strength, Westvane avoided horns, hooves, and claws, dipping beneath the club again and again. Dodge. Parry. Stab. Footwork in perfect balance, he advanced, eluded, and perused, slicing at vulnerable areas. His blades bit, hacking at armored skin, cutting into flesh.

Orange blood ran down the Wendigo's arm. With a hiss, the beast heaved the club. The bench slammed into the floor beside him. Westvane spun into another assault, and using every tactic he knew, battered the Wendigo, forcing it to retreat.

Between one strike and the next, his gaze tracked to Truly.

She was holding her own.

Not elegantly, or even very well, given the snake was trying to swallow her — and the ball — whole. Jaw clamped down on the sphere, its fangs clanked against the hard exterior. Her own mouth working, Truly yelled at it.

Ducking beneath the Wendigo's guard, Westvane carved into its side. The beast hissed. The viper released the sphere and wheeled around. Green eyes with vertical pupils narrowed on Westvane. Spinning right, he struck the Wendigo again. His blades sliced deep. Clutching its side, it fell to one knee.

He stabbed it again.

The Wendigo listed to one side, then collapsed into a heap on the floor. Leaving the Door Master, the massive snake moved to protect its master, scaled body rising, venom dripping from its fangs.

Truly shouted his name.

Westvane ignored the warning. He had one chance. With a single sword stroke, he must behead the viper. Before it got too close. Before it managed to strike. Before it sank its fangs in and sent its venom deep. Westvane didn't know if the poison would kill him. Nor did he wish to find out. Not tonight. Not when he stood so close to achieving his goal. His strategy wasn't complicated — return the Wendigo, use the beast as bait to draw Lyonesse into his kill box.

Swords raised, Westvane unfurled his wings.

The snake lunged, but —

Blue shimmer slashed in to surround it before its fangs reached him. Surprise struck. Feet rooted to the floor, Westvane watched the magic-driven ribbons tighten around the viper's neck. The snake writhed against the bonds. The ribbons turned to razor blades. Sharp edges sliced through hard scales. Blood splattered, arcing up, spilling over as the snake's head landed at Westvane's feet.

The Wendigo's headless tail twitched.

Razor-sharp blades smoothed back into ribbons. Following a crooked path, the slithering cords wound around the Wendigo, tying it up, securing the beast for transport.

Westvane stared at the dead viper a second before redirecting his focus to the trussed-up Wendigo. His brows rose. Impressive bit of magic. The ribbons were flawless — silky and thin, but strong. Coiled tight, hold secure, the triple-tied knots unbreakable.

A splash sounded.

Westvane glanced at Truly. He watched the sphere dissolve and her step out of the remaining goo. A look of horror on her face, she stared at the decapitated snake. "I had no idea I could do that."

His lips twitched. "Handy skill to have in your arsenal."

"Messy, though." Her nose wrinkled. "Really messy."

"Mess is good," he said, taking in the destruction around him. "I enjoy mess."

"Of course, you do. But then, we've already established you're crazy."

"The good kind."

"I'm not sure there's a good kind." Palms up, fingers spread, she looked at her hands. "But if there is, I hope I'm that kind too."

He grinned.

Maybe he'd been wrong. Maybe, at long last, she was coming around to his way of thinking. He'd known it would take time. The adjustment from human to magic-wielder wasn't an easy one... and he should know.

Locked away in the Parkland, he'd had time to come to terms with his magic. He understood it better now. Had spent years testing it, learning what no one had wanted to teach him. Truly hadn't been afforded the same advantages. She'd been thrown straight into the fire, but then, she had something he'd never possessed — a house designed to protect her, a friend like Earl to guide her, and now *him*. A world-class killer, able to shield her until she acclimatized to her magic and sharpened her skills.

"Truly —"

"You used your wings," she said, smiling at him.

The pride in her tone prickled through him.

A curious tightness gripped his chest. A lump formed in his throat. Uncomfortable with the praise, not knowing what else to do, he tipped his chin in acknowledgement.

"Very cool!" Still grinning, she slapped him on the side of his arm. "I wish I had wings."

The idea made him cringe — on the inside. The last thing the Door Master needed was wings. He could barely keep track of her as it was. "You grow wings, I'm cutting them off."

She rolled her eyes.

He glared at her, then looked past the rubble toward the side entrance. His senses webbed, dropping a net over the building and surrounding area. Gathering the web, he pulled on invisible strings. Westvane titled his head and listened harder.

"What?" she asked, gaze sharp on his face. "What is it?"

"Sirens."

"Police. We need to get out of here."

"Agreed." Moving to the Wendigo, Westvane studied it a moment. Six eyes closed. Unconscious from blood loss, but fit to travel. Hitting his haunches beside it, he checked Truly's knots. Warm to the touch, the ribbons stuck to his fingertips. With a nod of approval, he shook his hand free and stood. "Eastbrook — to me."

Black eyes blinking, the raven leapt from the balcony railing. Smooth descent. A few drops of shimmering blue liquid stuck to his plumage. None the worse for wear after witnessing the battle. With a loud caw, the bird landed on his shoulder. One moment, Eastbrook claimed solid form, the next he dematerialized, sliding onto the surface of his skin.

"I need one of those too."

"What — a raven?"

She shook her head. "A cool tattoo."

"Maybe later. Right now —"

"Back to Azlandia?"

"Yeah."

"Where do you want to land?" she asked, stepping over the Wendigo's mangled tail. "Azlandia's a big place. I need to be able to picture a location to get us there. Otherwise, I'll open the wrong door, and we'll end up somewhere we don't want to be."

Startled, Westvane threw her a sideways glance. "You can direct the path? You're sure?"

"No. I mean... not exactly. It's more of a feeling, the strong sense that..." Pursing her lips, she trailed off, then picked up the thought again. "If I hold a location front and center in my mind while opening a door, I'll land in the place I'm picturing."

Interesting. An excellent trick if she could pull it off.

Staring at her, Westvane sifted through the possibilities. Eckizbad Island was out. Returning to the prison would be the kiss of death. One designed and delivered by Lyonesse. She would expect him to play by the rules and return the Wendigo to the place it had escaped. The instant he stepped onto the island, the queen would renege on her word, and the trap would snap closed around him. So...

He must choose a location she couldn't use against him. Somewhere he held the upper hand. His eyes narrowed as an idea came to mind.

Watching him, Truly tipped her chin. "Where?"

"The Parkland."

"Why the Parkland?"

"I was caged there by Lyonesse. I know it well. Taking the Wendigo there will —"

"Give us the advantage," Truly said. "How many years were you imprisoned there?"

"Almost two decades."

A muscle flexed in her jaw. "She's a real piece of work, isn't she?"

"You have no idea, princess."

"I will soon," she muttered, a murderous glint in her eyes. "So... the Parkland."

"Yeah."

"How do we get there? Can you show me —"

"Come here."

As she walked toward him, his attention jumped to the cut on her forehead. No longer seeping, blood crusted the wound. "I'm going to need you to trust me, Truly."

"It's already a done-deal, Westvane."

He shook his head. Incredible. He'd never thought it possible. Other than Eastbrook, no one wanted to be his friend, but as the Door Master stopped in front of him, Westvane acknowledged that having her trust felt good. Felt right. Felt like a missing piece in the puzzle of life as he gazed down at her and she looked up at him. He should probably warn her but...

Westvane didn't bother.

Doing it quick and clean, he sliced open his palm with one of his claws. Truly flinched, opening her mouth to protest. He was faster. Holding her steady, he wiped congealed blood from the cut on her forehead and pressed his open wound to hers. Magic swirled. A tingling rush swept over his skin as his life force reached for hers.

A cosmic connection opened.

His mind aligned with hers, running on a parallel track.

Staring into her bewildered eyes, he pictured the Parkland. Heavy forest laden with thick brush and green moss. Rolling rivers and meandering streams. Valley trails and mountain peaks to the North and South. The clearing and cabin he'd called home for years.

"Can you see it?" he asked softly, respecting the immensity of the moment.

Her eyes lashes fluttered. "Got it."

Sirens grew louder. Cars screeched to a stop outside the train station. The sound of doors opening. The pounding of human feet.

Truly drew a deep breath. "Ready?"

"Go."

Blue shimmer hit her eyes.

A magical doorway opened behind her.

With a smile, Westvane kicked the snake head out of the way and grabbed the Wendigo. Truly stepped through the portal and vanished into the *Ecotone*. Dragging the beast behind him, Westvane crossed the threshold, disappearing from view as damaged steel doors rattled and human authorities poured into the train station.

49

APPEARANCES MUST BE MAINTAINED

Interrupted by the knock on her door, Lyonesse twisted the lid back onto her favorite lip stain. Settling her wings, she shifted on the stool, then twisted to set the small pot on her make-up table, making the guard who stood outside wait. No need to rush. Zero inclination to soothe his nerves or make him comfortable.

Not after the debacle on the cliff.

The servant attending her picked up a container of blush, tilting the blend into the light for her consideration. With a flick of her fingers, she waved the girl away. New servants always annoyed her. The tips of her fake eyelashes fluttered, impeding her peripheral vision, as Lyonesse glanced at her from the corner of her eye. What was her name again? The girl had told her already but...

Her eyes narrowed.

The girl flinched.

Ah, yes — Korah. A dull name for an uninteresting girl.

Why Priestly believed she needed a new slave, Lyonesse had yet to determine. Everything about the Cropper bothered her — the lush sheen in her dark hair, her youth, her height and luscious stature. Each and every one of Korah's clumsy attempts to please her.

Inspecting the girl, Lyonesse wondered at her Priestly's generosity, then let the thought go. He'd fallen out of favor. Stood to reason, the warrior wanted back into her good graces. The Cropper he'd given her simply needed more training, and yet...

Her dislike of the girl grew by the moment.

Unsure of herself, Korah bowed her head, stepped back, and waited. For more instructions. For her queen to decide. Lyonesse rubbed her fingertips across the pads of her thumbs. Magic moved in the mist beneath her skin. She stared at the Cropper beneath the fan of her lashes.

Awkward.

Inept.

Unfit to serve in the palace.

The servant wasn't worth the fine clothes Lyonesse dressed her in. A singular regret, but sometimes, incompetence must be suffered. Appearances must be maintained. She couldn't refuse a gift from a royal member of the Electi elite. Tradition dictated she give the girl a chance. Allot an acceptable amount of time. Find better reasons to dismiss her. Otherwise, Priestly would pout, and right now, she didn't need the criticism... or to hear any rumbling from the High Table.

"Majesty?" Gaze aimed at the floor, a slight tremble in her hands, Korah raised a pot of rouge. "More blush?"

She glanced at the girl. A delightful chill crept down her spine as the urge to eviscerate almost overcame her. She contemplated it a moment. Croppers were thick on the ground. One fewer wouldn't make a bit of difference. Heat gathered in her palms. She smoothed the magic, remembering she didn't need the trouble, or the inconvenience of training another servant.

She had enough on her mind.

"Majesty?" Korah whispered, becoming more nervous by the moment.

Lyonesse looked at herself in the oval. Turning her head one way, then the other, she inspected herself in a mirror taken from Earth Realm. A rare commodity in Azlandia. A birthday present from her father, and not a kind one.

"It will do," she said, motioning for the rouge to be put away, thoughts drifting to her sire.

Leonidas had called her vain, lacking, less than an ideal daughter. His gift of the oval reinforced her suspicions about him — and what he thought of her. Pragmatism forced her to accept the truth long ago. But much as she tried, the accusation still bothered her, worming beneath her skin, straight into her heart. She shouldn't care what he'd thought of her. Her father could go to the devil.

Her painted mouth curved.

In fact, she'd sent him there. For being a terrible mentor, certainly. For risking Azlandia and those under her rule, without question. But more for the lifetime of insults he'd delivered — the barbed corrections disguised as kindness, the criticism couched in concern, the neglect concealed by endless hours spent in his presence, under his tutelage.

Death by a thousand tiny cuts.

Her father had specialized in slicing her to ribbons. Almost to the quick, but... no matter. She'd won in the end. He rotted in his grave while she sat on the Azlandian throne, ruling the realm much better than he had.

Lyonesse smiled at herself in the mirror. Despite his scathing opinion of her character, she knew he was wrong. She was regal. She was cunning. She was born to be a *Queen*... and a queen deserved her comforts — exquisitely crafted make-up vanities included.

Another rap on the door, this one less polite.

With a flick of her lashes, she dismissed her servant. "See to the door."

Bare feet pattering across hand-painted wooden floors and mosaic inlay, Korah scurried beneath the archway and crossed the antechamber. Stopping at the double doors, she reached for one of the ornate handles. A moment before she grasped it, Lyonesse snapped her fingers. Pink sparks flared against her skin. Magic spun across the chamber. The door swung open, making Korah stumble back in surprise.

Lyonesse laughed under her breath.

Standing in the hall, Anckar scowled at the girl.

Korah genuflected and backed away, face pale, head bowed.

Enjoying the results of her game, Lyonesse's lips curved. Killing the Cropper might bring momentary satisfaction, but putting the slave in her place felt so much better. Lines must be drawn. A strong message must be sent. Boundaries must be respected. The lowest among her subjects must never be allowed to forget Electis ruled the land. Their superiority to other races and species should never be questioned.

"Anckar," she murmured, disappointment ringing hollow in her chest. The captain of her guard was not who she'd been expecting. Lyonesse waved him into her bed chamber anyway. "Where is Priestly?"

"He was delayed, Majesty."

An awful suspicion prickled through her. Her silk gown pooled, sliding across the floor as she swiveled on the stool and raised a brow. "Delayed?"

"Unexpectedly."

"You lie," she said, scenting the deception.

"Majes —"

"Where is he?"

Standing at the foot of her four-poster bed, he shuffled from foot to foot.

"You do not know?"

"Well…"

Shoving the stool back, she popped to her feet. Her wings bounced, tangling her feathers. With a jerk, she resettled the dark pink plumes and frowned at her guard. "I was to receive an update from him."

"As to that…" he paused to deliberate, choosing his words with care. "If you'll permit me to —"

"You have news?"

Anckar opened his mouth.

"Get on with it." She flung a hand out, temper seething, impatience snapping at its tail. "Tell me."

"The gargoyle has not been found," he said, taking a step back when she flexed her fingers.

Hot pink flames rippled over her shoulders, then flared off the hooked claws on her wings. Heat blasted into the room. Still in the antechamber, hiding behind heavy damask curtains tied to the sides of the archway, Korah cringed and —

"*Yet*, Majesty," Anckar said, swallowing before resetting his courage. "He's not been found *yet*, but… the hunt is still young, barely begun. There are many more places to search."

"It isn't complicated, Anckar."

"I'm aware, your majesty, but —"

"Then what is taking so long?" Given Priestly's skill, the traitor should've been found by now. The task wasn't a difficult one. Or shouldn't be for Electi warriors. Find the gargoyle. Bring him to her. Ipsalar might be a large city, but it was hers. No one who lived in the shadow of her palace, in the place her magic was the most powerful, would deny her guard the information they needed to —

Anckar cleared his throat. "The House of Scholars."

"What about it?"

"The Scholars have been..."

"What?"

"Uncooperative."

Her eyes narrowed. "They dare?"

"The gargoyles are merely protecting one of their own," he said, watching her, preparing to retreat. "We would do the same."

"I am their queen." Magic ghosted beneath the undersides of her nails, threatening to claw free. "No one defies me."

"My queen, I would advise that we tread carefully with the Scholars. They are well respected by the people. Perhaps, if we change our approach. Might we try —"

"I will not change my approach." The lethal edge in her tone made Anckar flinch. Unease flared in his scent. Drinking in the delightful smell of fear, she walked toward him. The train of her silk gown hissed over the floor in her wake. His throat bobbed as she stopped within striking distance. "Electi bow to no one, least of all Scholars. Tighten the screws, Anckar. Make them comply, or I will burn the House of Scholars to the ground."

Head bowed, Anckar nodded.

Raising her hand, she placed her index finger under his chin and tipped his face up. Wary blue eyes met hers as she traced his bottom lip with her fingertip. Her touch made his pupils dilate. Her mouth curved as satisfaction took hold. He wanted her. Was ravenous for her touch, desperate to be invited to her bed, to service her the way Priestly sometimes did. Not that it happened much anymore.

Shifty and evasive, Priestly found ways to avoid her... and his duties. At least of late. A problem, given the lack of contact made him much more difficult to control.

With a hum, she pressed the sharpened point of her fingernail to the corner of his mouth. "And what of the other matter?"

He cleared his throat. "The machine is en route."

"They didn't touch it?"

"No, Majesty," he said, his voice hoarse, his body aroused. "Royal valets packed it up with care, table and all, and put it on a secure transport. The machine will arrive here within the week."

"Good. Very good, Anckar," she said, leaning in, giving him hope as her breath whispered against his jaw.

His lips parted.

She nicked the corner of his mouth with her nail. Blood beaded from the small wound. He moaned. She smeared the droplet across his cheek, then dropped her hand and turned away, her mind no longer on her guard, but the Yeomanry. The second the machine was installed in its new chamber, she'd reengage with Isaac. She had a new mission for the human commander—locate the place the Door Master slept. Destroying the witch's sanctuary would uproot her power, making it more difficult for her to open doors and cross into Azlandia.

"Let me know when the machine arrives and —"

A pricking chill needled across her senses, interrupting her train of thought.

Lyonesse turned her attention inward, searching for the source. Gathering the magical threads, she drew each one to her. She inhaled deep, filling her lungs, then exhaled a continuous, long breath. Mental focus shifted, moving her into a trance-like state. The heat in her veins grew hotter. Her focus narrowed.

A door.

Another door stood open in Azlandia.

With a snarl, Lyonesse strode toward the floor-to-ceiling windows. Moonlight glinted through the glass, showcasing what lay below. Nestled in the valley, far below her royal perch on the mountainside, the towers of Ipsalar stood in the distance.

Thick walls rose between massive turrets, protecting the city's white stucco homes with squared-off roofs.

She clenched her teeth.

Another door.

Damn the demon's hide. The Door Master was at it again, using the *Ecotone* to infiltrate her realm, defying her authority. Anckar called to her, trying to recapture her attention. Ignoring his prattling, Lyonesse went hunting without leaving her room. Following the magical trail, she scoured her domain for a location.

There.

To the north.

Deep in the Parkland, beneath the invisible dome, inside Westvane's cage.

"Anckar!"

Yanked from his diatribe, her guard jerked to attention.

"Gather the others," she said, spinning away from the windows. Swiping her mantle off a hook, she rushed past him. "Meet me in the Crystal Den."

"The Crystal Den?"

"Now!"

Racing across the antechamber, Lyonesse wrenched the door open with her mind. The ancient, hand-carved panels whipped open. Korah gasped and jumped back. Ignoring the idiotic Cropper, she sprinted into the hall, uncaring she left Anckar looking confused inside her chamber.

Time was of the essence.

She couldn't delay.

The most skilled of her fighting Electi needed to leave at once. The Parkland wasn't close to Ipsalar. Flying the distance would take too long, at least half the night. She'd never reach the Door Master before she slithered back to safety if she didn't move to intercept the witch now.

Using the last of her crystals to teleport into the Parkland was a risk. The remaining stones lacked the strength they'd once possessed. The depletion of power couldn't be explained, but Lyonesse knew what it meant. Transporting so many guards at once would drain the last of her crystals' power. So...

Teleporting would be a one-way trip. In order to get back, she and the others would be forced to fly. A risk, certainly. But one worth taking if it ended the Door Master's life.

Wings tucked tight to her back, Lyonesse turned a corner and ran down a set of steps. Releasing a burst of magic, she unlocked the door and pushed into the armory. She paused at the railing rimming the labyrinthine space, getting her bearings, mind flipping through the possibilities.

What did the Door Master's sudden appearance mean?

Westvane wasn't stupid. Returning to Azlandia with the witch was dangerous, unless...

Her senses rippled. Unless...

He intended to keep faith with her and deliver the human into her hands.

The possibility seemed like an unlikely scenario. But then, much like Priestly, the Slayer had never been predictable. He wanted his freedom. Longed for the ability to come and go — do as he pleased in Azlandia. But was he ruthless enough to sacrifice the Door Master to achieve his goals?

Yes.

He was... without question.

Even so, she must proceed with extreme caution. Westvane, for all his faults, was cunning. A skilled predator, the most accomplished Assenta warrior in Azlandia. She needed to be ready for anything. Use every resource at her disposable to rid her realm of the threat. Otherwise, the Door Master would escape her net before she'd gotten a chance to spring the trap.

50

RIBBONS OF MAGIC

Exiting the *Ecotone*, Truly stepped into a clearing. Lush floral scents. A thick carpet of green grass. Huge trees hugging the perimeter, and nestled at one end, a log cabin. A cool breeze ruffled her hair as she moved out of the doorway and walked toward it, giving Westvane enough room to drag the Wendigo over the threshold.

Westvane's home.

Small, but serviceable. The place he'd spent more than half his life.

Her gaze ran the gauntlet, picking up more details.

Small windows in a timber-frame structure. Narrow, tall wooden door with a rope handle. In front of the cottage, a chopping block, knives embedded in the wooden top, well-worn hilts issuing a silent warning. Large oaks did the same, branches curving over the thatched roof like a protective angel, on guard and at the ready. Her focus tracked right. A lopsided shed, sharp, homemade tools hanging inside, some propped against barnboard sidewalls.

A brook babbled somewhere nearby.

Birds sang in the arms of not-too-distant trees.

Truly took a deep breath, enjoying the fresh air. Beautiful place. Calming. Peaceful. Full of the kind of quiet anyone would embrace.

Footfalls sounded behind her.

She turned to watch Westvane drag the Wendigo into the clearing. Leaving the monster in a heap, he strode toward his home. Curious, she trailed in his wake, walking past raised garden beds, full of growing vegetables. Leather hinges creaked as Westvane pushed the front door open, and dipping his head beneath the lintel, disappeared inside.

Truly bit the inside of her lip. She should no doubt wait for an invitation to enter, but with curiosity running rampant, didn't bother. She invaded his space instead, following him into the small cottage.

The smell of fresh herbs and wood smoke greeted her. The plain interior struck her next. Everything had a place inside the one-room cabin constructed with squared-off logs. Even the white mortar between heavy wood lengths fell into line, the joints straight and even. Her gaze drifted over the scant array of cooking tools hanging above a short stretch of butcher block countertop. Neat. Tidy. Utilitarian. Walls without pictures. Walls without personality. Walls designed to shelter, but not nurture.

Feet planted on the dirt floor, she stood silent, watching Westvane move around the cabin, picking up more details. Every single one of them stark.

A sturdy table anchored the center of the space. Fat candles sat in a pool of once-melted, now-hardened wax on the wood planked top. Suspended from metal hooks screwed into the timber-beam ceiling, a huge hammock hung motionless in the back corner. And an ancient armchair, stuffing sticking up through holes where the upholstery had split, made its home in front of a fireplace that took up most of the wall to her right.

Truly stared at the chair.

No matched set for Westvane. Just a single place to sit, alone in the candlelight with no one to talk to and nothing but hunting and killing to occupy his time.

The idea sent a pang through her. In her mind, the chair — *that stupid solitary chair* — represented all the crimes committed against him. Forced into isolation, when it was clear he was a social guy who enjoyed interacting with others out in the greater world. Knowing Westvane the way she did now, she knew the starkness of his existence until now (until her) must've nearly driven him mad.

Her chest tightened. She cleared her throat. "I like your place."

He shrugged, but she could tell her comment amused him. She'd gotten better at reading him. Attention on his face, Truly studied him from across the room. Maybe, *better at reading him* wasn't quite right. Maybe, he'd simply become less skilled at hiding his reactions from her.

Toolkit in hand, he stopped beside the table opposite her. Dropping the leather-bound bundle on the wooden surface, he began to unroll it, revealing a wicked set of sharp knives.

"You're a good liar, princess."

"You deserve better than this, Westvane."

"It's a roof over my head," Strapping on arm sheaths, he slipped twin blades into the leather casings. "That's all it's ever been."

"I can see that, and given the circumstances, it's done its job."

"What's that?"

"It kept you alive," she said. "But now, you've got a new home. One where people care about you."

His black eyes sliced to her.

"I know what you're thinking... and what you're preparing

to do... but I need you to pull your head out of your ass. You're not staying here."

"You think you can stop me?

"Where I go, you go now, remember?"

A muscle ticked in his jaw.

Without answering, he skirted the end of the table and headed for the door. As he exited the cabin, she turned and followed him into the clearing. Hovering above the ground, the door from Earth Realm into Azlandia opened wider, the fire around its frame banked but still burning.

He gestured to it. "Close the door, Truly."

"We're not staying, Westvane. The Parkland is perfect for the Wendigo. There's no way it'll be able to escape. We've brought it back, now we need to go before —"

"I'm not going back."

"Westvane —"

"Lyonesse cannot be permitted to continue." His dark eyes sparked, beginning to glow with familiar citrine light. "The cruelty needs to stop. Her rule must end, and I'm going to be the one to end it."

"You —"

"No one else is strong enough."

Staring at him, Truly grappled with his argument. She needed to find a way to counteract it. Neutralize it. Make him see staying in Azlandia wasn't the most effective strategy. As an Assenta, a Slayer, Westvane liked planning, but...

What should she say to change his mind? How should she say it? Words mattered, sure, but the delivery of them mattered more.

Be honest.

Hitting him with the truth was the only way to win with him.

"I see your point, Westvane. I do. What you have suffered —

horrific. The injustices others have endured — brutal and unfair. My mother was one of those people, remember? I never got to meet her because of Lyonesse and her hatred of... well..." Truly tossed her hands into the air. "Everyone and everything. But sacrificing yourself is not the answer."

His eyes narrowed on her.

"It isn't," she said, digging in, desperate to make him see standing alone against a queen who commanded an army wasn't a plan, but martyr-driven suicide. "You're strong. Skilled. Deadly. I'm not denying that, but you can't defeat her alone. God knows, she won't show up alone. Her guards will stand firm against you, me, and anyone else who tries to dethrone her. She'd got a stranglehold on Azlandia. Her tentacles are wrapped around everything."

"Truly —"

"We need a game plan."

"I have one."

"A *good* one. One that doesn't involve you getting dead," she said. "I understand your mission — she needs to be stopped. The thing is, if we do it smart, it'll be surgical. A clean cut that'll benefit everyone here. Think about it, Westvane. No more caste system. No more discrimination. Equality and justice under the law for all." She paused, letting silence hammer the point home before continuing, "Isn't that what your parents wanted? Isn't that what they died trying to do?"

"Low blow, princess."

"I'm not above kicking you in the balls to make a point." Striding toward him, she thought out loud, voicing the beginnings of her plan. "We put a team together. A small, dedicated group with lethal, but varied skillsets. Do some intelligence gathering. Get an information chain going. Enlist Assenta and Croppers from all over the realm. They'll be our eyes and ears, help us infiltrate Electi infrastructure... at every level."

"Grassroots."

"Exactly," she said, warming to the idea. "We strike with intent, attack with precision. Run Lyonesse ragged while we build our network from the ground up. I'll even let you be in charge."

He scoffed, but didn't attack her plan. He stayed silent instead, gaze drilling into hers, the gimmer in his eyes growing more and more intense. His expression gave nothing away, but she swore she heard his mind turning. He wanted to believe her. Wanted to believe achieving his parents' goal — freeing all Azlandians from the yoke of a zealot queen — was possible.

"How soon will they get here?" she asked.

"Lyonesse and her lackeys?"

Truly nodded.

"Fast," he said, glancing skyward. "Probably before —"

Light exploded like fireworks overhead. The wire structure undulated in the shockwave. Armed to the teeth, a contingent of winged Electi dropped out of the sky.

Conjuring flaming twin swords, Westvane shoved her behind him. "Go, princess."

"I'm not leaving you here."

He snarled at her. "Don't argue. Just go. I'll buy you enough time to get out."

Heart raging, Truly scanned the clearing. What to do? What to do? Listen to Westvane and retreat, or stay and help him? Staying would divide Westvane's attention between her and a fight he needed full-focus to win. Going would mean leaving him to fight alone. Neither option worked for her.

Surrounded by her guards, Lyonesse landed on the other side of the dell. Pink feathers fluttered as she folded her wings and smiled at Westvane.

A chill rolled down her spine. Magic sparked through her in response.

With a hum, Truly welcomed the burn, and fingers flexing, strengthened her hold on the threads. Shifting into a fighting stance behind Westvane, she surveyed the shitshow about to unravel, searching for a solution, trying to figure out how to make Westvane leave Azlandia with her.

Something moved in her periphery.

Without turning her head, she glanced that way. The Wendigo. Still trussed up by her magic, the monster lay face down on the grass, horned head turned toward her. She watched two of its eyes crack open. Black as night, its pupils contracted, reacting to the light. Her mouth curved. The beast's lip curled in reaction, displaying rows of razor-sharp teeth.

A new plan formed.

The Wendigo's tail twitched.

Watching new scales form, Truly gathered the ribbons keeping the monster contained, and without warning Westvane, prepared to unleash hell.

51

A DANGEROUS VICE

Black swords blazing in his hands, Westvane watched the contingent of Electi warriors land in his clearing. He heard Truly murmur a warning. She wanted him to be smart and leave Azlandia with her. *Live to fight another day* — one of her favorite sayings — while he plotted the end of an empire using less direct means.

He hated to admit it, but knew the Door Master had a point.

So much of one, he wondered why he hadn't thought of it first. Or moved to put a plan like the one she proposed in motion sooner.

Frowning, he glanced at her from the corner of his eye. Maybe she wasn't just a pain in the ass. Maybe she was on to something. Maybe now wasn't the time to make his final stand against the faithless witch who called herself a queen.

Up until now, he'd been so focused on killing Lyonesse that changing tactics to deploy an alternate strategy seemed an impossible task. He decided to try anyway, given Truly's stubborn insistence, and the fact she might be right. Beheading the queen today wouldn't solve the issues plaguing Azlandian society. Truly's plan would take more time, sure, but at least it struck at the heart of the problem. The systematic dismantling of discrimination opened new avenues, creating the possibility for lasting solutions.

Ones that would benefit all Azlandians, not just him. Though, assuaging his need for vengeance ranked high — he was his mother's son. She'd been selfless, putting him and the health of the realm before herself. His mother would want what Truly wanted — to right the wrongs done to the people and heal old wounds. To put the past behind them in order to forge a brighter future — and eliminating the queen wouldn't stop the cruelty.

Power was a dangerous vice. Seductive, addictive — in the wrong hands, a sadistic tool used to bludgeon the living.

The Electi elite who replaced Lyonesse wouldn't relinquish authority. The balance of power would simply change hands. Everything else would stay the same. The deeply ingrained attitudes and institutions — the very ideas and systems perpetuating the injustice — would continue to flourish. The queen's death would be treated as a form of martyrdom. The highest in the land would build altars in her honor. Songs would be written. Assenta and Croppers would be forced to sing her praises for generations to come.

The thought sickened him.

Widening his stance, Westvane spun his swords. Well-worn hilts whirled against his palms. Black-flamed blades blurred, cutting through verdant scent of forest musk as Lyonesse and her guard settled into battle formation.

His gaze narrowed on the witch responsible for his parents' murders. For his unfair treatment and jailing. For perpetuating hatred in the place he'd made a home, the only one he'd ever been allowed to claim.

Yes. Without a doubt. The Door Master was definitely onto something.

Her insistence, the strident belief new ways must be tried for a different outcome to be achieved, tempted him with the possibilities. Undermining Lyonesse, digging beneath the rot of Azlandia — installing intelligence networks, striking when least expected, ensuring the foundation Lyonesse stood on crumbled — would work better than challenging her dynasty head-on.

Different ways of thinking. New hope for a generation of subjugated people. And eventually — new laws that ensured Azlandia never went back to the old ways.

His nostrils flared. Westvane stilled the whirl of his swords. "Truly."

"Already ahead of you," she said, her voice soft, yet infused with iron.

Without looking, he located her. To his right, standing five feet behind him. Watching his back even though he'd told her to go. He resisted the urge to shake his head. So very stubborn, defiant to the core. Normally, he found that annoying about her. Right now, he appreciated the dedication. The loyalty she showed humbled him.

"Slayer." The purr in Lyonesse's tone raised the fine hairs on the back of his neck.

"Lyonesse," Westvane said, shrugging away his adverse reaction.

Surrounded by an Electi platoon, the queen shifted her stance, moving from one foot to the other. Westvane smelled her unease... and understood her restlessness. She never knew what to make of him. Unlike Truly, Lyonesse had never learned to read him, so the fact he continued to break protocol threw her. No one in Azlandia called Lyonesse by her given name. Not without permission.

The queen's expression tightened. "Are you here to make peace?"

He raised a brow. "Peace?"

"To collect your reward."

"What reward would that be?"

"You already know."

"Remind me," he said, relishing the idea of forcing her to admit it in front her guards.

"Your freedom in exchange for the Door Master."

Anckar cleared his throat. "Majesty, I don't think that's a good —"

"Quiet," she snapped, slashing her hand through the air.

He adjusted his grip on his swords. "You intend to honor your word?"

"I am an Electi of the royal line," she said, bristling at the question. "I never lie."

Westvane swallowed a growl. *Never lied.* Right. Lyonesse rarely, if ever, told the truth. She spoon-fed those around her falsehood after falsehood, heaping one on top of the next. She didn't know how to be honorable. And loyalty? He huffed. Lyonesse wouldn't know — or understand — loyalty even if it walked up and stabbed her with a knife.

The urge to paint the forest floor with her blood rioted through him. He clung to control, knowing all that stood between Lyonesse and the Door Master was him.

"Prove it."

"How?"

"Deactivate the cage." Stalling for time, giving Truly what she needed to set the play, he unfolded his wings. "Let me fly free."

Lyonesse glanced toward the structure she designed. She stared at the powerful web curving over the Parkland, her hesitation palpable.

One side of his mouth curved up.

And there it was — the lie in living color.

He knew she had no intention of letting him go. The deal

she'd struck to ensure his compliance was nothing more than a ploy. Not a surprise. He'd known it the second she proposed it inside the Wendigo's cell. And although chatting with her was the last thing he wanted to do, he needed to be smart.

He recognized her caution. The fact she engaged him in conversation instead of ordering an attack, gave her strategy away. She didn't want to risk any of the Electi standing between him and her. Lyonesse, more than anyone, understood his abilities, knew he could cut through half her personal guard in seconds, taking the Door Master out of reach forever.

"Step aside, Westvane," Lyonesse said, refusing his demand to deactivate the cage. Dark pink feathers glimmering in the fading light, she stepped up behind her guards. "Hand her over and go."

"The cage first," he said, hedging his bets.

Lyonesse pushed through the frontline. Her guard objected, trying to step in front of her. She waved them to silence.

"Get ready," Truly murmured behind him.

"About time," he muttered back, listening as she retreated toward his cabin.

Eyes glowing with unholy light, Lyonesse raised her hands. Magic whipped into a windstorm around her, battering the trees. Branches swayed. Leaves bristled and —

"Now!" Truly yelled, gathering the ribbons of her magic.

Pivoting toward her, Westvane tucked his wings and got low.

A roar ripped through the clearing.

Unleashed, the Wendigo rose, growing taller, broader, hooves hammering the ground, claws lengthening into thin blades. Fangs bared, six eyes glowing orange, a regenerating snake head growing from its tail, the beast charged Lyonesse. With a curse, the queen retreated. Anckar rallied the front line, and swords drawn, shields at the ready, defended as the monster attacked.

The Wendigo clawed through the middle guards.

Electi warriors screamed in pain. Severed limbs flew into the air. Blood splattered across green grass. A severed head rolled across the ground toward his foot. Sidestepping the bloody skull, Westvane spun his swords. Maybe he should join the fight. Help the Wendigo. Witness the carnage up close. Watch the beast run free in the Parkland, just for a minute or —

A thud sounded behind him.

"Westvane!"

His attention snapped toward his cabin.

Grappling with Lyonesse's watch dog, Truly elbowed Priestly in the ribs. The male grunted, but hung on. Twisting his hand in her hair, he dragged her backward.

Westvane bared his teeth and, without thought, unfurled his wings. An updraft lifted him. Feathers carried him. He landed with a thump behind Priestly.

The childhood friend swung around.

Golden eyes met his black ones.

Westvane reabsorbed his blades. Black flames scorched over his palms. He ignored the discomfort and focused on the threat. He didn't need his swords. Killing Priestly with bare hands would be much more satisfying.

Using Truly as a human shield, Priestly dragged her behind the butcher block. "Don't. Stay back, Westvane. Listen to me. I'm on your —"

Truly jerked her head. The back of her skull slammed into Priestly's nose.

He grunted. His grip went slack.

She slipped loose and, hitting one knee, spun. The white points of her knuckles flashed. Without hesitation, she punched Priestly in the groin. His former friend made a high-pitched noise and doubled over.

Vaulting over the table, Westvane unleashed an uppercut

beneath his chin. Priestly's head snapped back. Blood splashed across his face. Folding like a tent, the Electi hit the ground, wings bent at odd angles, arms flung wide.

A bright light flashed his periphery as Truly opened a door.

The Wendigo roared again.

More screams of agony from the queen's guard.

He hit Priestly again — and again — putting power into each punch.

"Leave him." Fisting her hand in his coat, Truly yanked him sideways. "Let's go."

"I'm not done killing him."

"Some other time," she yelled over her shoulder, running toward the open door.

Westvane wanted to argue, but resisted the urge. He considered himself a fast learner. Arguing with Truly never ended well for him. So, instead of ripping Priestly's face off, Westvane dropped his opponent, leaving him where he lay.

He must live to fight another day.

Truly kept reminding him of that, so even though it went against the grain, Westvane abandoned the fight, listening to the Wendigo roar and warriors scream, and followed the Door Master out of Azlandia, back to Earth Realm.

WRAPPED IN HEALING ENERGY, Truly traversed the *Ecotone*. Her flight wasn't wild like the first time. She walked across instead, gliding through warm mist. Gentle breaths brushed her skin, curling over her shoulders, touching her with a purity so fresh, she became wonderstruck. Allowing the awe to carry her away, she paused a beat.

Water lapped against faraway shores. Purple mountains rose beyond miles of pristine forest, vibrant grasslands and...

Something traced the wound on her forehead. The cut closed, knitting in the wake of the gossamer touch.

With a whispered "thank you," she became one with the *Ecotone*. Centered, at ease, she started walking again. Strides even and pace steady, she navigated a path she shouldn't know with ease. The innate *knowing* seemed odd, but felt right. She was plugged in here, at one with nature, at peace with herself. A slice of beauty sitting between worlds in turmoil. A balancing place. A nurturing place. A connecting place ruled by magic — the origin point where all things began.

The idea should've shocked her. It didn't anymore.

The things she'd seen and experienced had settled deep, finding a home inside her. Truly accepted her role now. Didn't feel like a novice. Didn't feel out of her depth, even though she still had a lot to learn. Each trip to and from Azlandia taught her something new — strengthened her magic, sharpened her skills while revealing new ones. Making her want to hone her abilities and develop greater facility with her magic, but...

Baby steps. One thing at time.

She'd accomplished enough for now.

The most notable achievement involved getting Westvane to leave the Parkland. Convincing him to chart a new course — to play the long game instead of a short one — had been touch-and-go. He was stubborn. He also had ambition and drive. One fueled by the need to avenge his parents and his own experiences.

She understood better than most his need to make things right. He was an Assenta warrior who lived to obliterate an enemy. The path he traveled would always be the most direct. Objective driven. Attack heavy. More bloody than necessary. His approach blinded him to other ways of operating. Without his kind of training, she viewed things in a different light. Believed in looking in all directions, down every avenue and alleyway... no matter how dark.

Tackling the old ways using the same tactics wouldn't work. Lyonesse was too entrenched, her followers too loyal, the guard she commanded still too strong, which meant...

New strategies must be developed, tested and deployed. Building a network of spies and strong alliances was just the beginning. Excavating the filth underpinning Azlandia would take time, but with a concentrated effort on multiple fronts, she believed Westvane would eventually get what he needed — a revolution, and an army of like-minded individuals to lead.

Walking along the shoreline, Truly paused on the edge of the *Ecotone*. She glanced over her shoulder. Wreathed in white, she located Westvane's blurry silhouette through the mist. Heavy strides said *unhappy*. Coiled body language screamed *murderous*.

Truly pressed her lips together to keep from laughing. He was in a *mood*, which meant she was in for a lecture when he caught up. She already knew the subject matter — the rules of engagement and principles of non-interference.

Truly didn't regret sticking her nose into his business. She'd saved his life. He'd saved hers. Teammates to the bitter, messy end.

Dragging her gaze from the angry Assenta stomping in her wake, Truly murmured her wishes. The *Ecotone* bloomed like a rose around her as she searched the back of her mind. Light sparked in the darkness. A door frame appeared. With a nudge, she pushed it open and crossed the threshold, stepping into the vestibule of the house on Isadore Street.

"*Turnbolt,*" her home murmured.

"*Hello,*" she said, returning the greeting inside her mind.

The Victorian mansion exhaled, humming in contentment.

Leaving the door open for Westvane, she started down the hall. "Earl!"

"Yeah!"

"Home safe!"

"Well, finally," he said, voice drifting from the kitchen. "I almost —"

A thud echoed across the entryway.

The magical door crashed open behind her.

The crack of fists against flesh ricocheted. Cursing ensued. Grunts of exertion came next. The slam-bang of boots hammered the wooden floor, rampaged inside her foyer.

Halfway down the corridor, Truly whirled around. Her mouth dropped open as wings with golden feathers entered her house.

Not understanding what she was seeing, she stood stock-still, like a dummy on the hall runner, and watched Westvane grapple with...

She blinked.

Priestly. Westvane's nemesis was in her home, on the wrong side of the *Ecotone.*

Feet planted in billowing mist, standing on the wrong side of the door, Westvane kicked Priestly in the chest. The gold-feathered Electi reeled backward. Wings tangled, he landed spine-first on her oriental rug. The hall table jumped to the left. The carpet crinkled. Feathers flew. Priestly didn't care. Moving like a pissed-off ninja, he surged to his feet and attacked Westvane.

Black eyes aglow, Westvane punched him. Knuckles cracked against cheekbone. Priestly's head snapped to the side. With a snarl, Westvane stepped over the threshold. The instant he cleared the frame, Truly shut the door, trapping Priestly inside her house.

Shifting right, Westvane met the on-coming assault. Black

wings slammed into tawny ones. Fists pummeled. The smell of blood rolled up the hallway.

Avoiding the fray, Truly backtracked as the guys fought, searching for an opening. Priestly's back was to her. His wings acted as a barrier, protecting him from a rear assault, but...

Maybe if she tripped him, Westvane would get the upper hand.

The brawl couldn't go on, although... Truly frowned at Westvane... he certainly looked like he was enjoying beating the crap of out Priestly. Though, even backpedaling, the Electi continued to hold his own, getting his own licks in against an opponent who out-matched him in size and strength.

Westvane drove his rival across the entryway.

Blood running from a cut over his eye, Priestly slammed into side of the staircase.

The chandelier rocked, swinging overhead.

Truly searched the side table for a weapon.

She grabbed the base of a heavy lamp. Ripping the shade off, she raised it like a club, waiting for her chance, timing her attack and —

A streak of white blew past her. A clang rose above the cacophony of fighting. Priestly's head lolled on his shoulders. An instant later, he hit the floor.

Shocked, Truly stared at Earl.

"What the hell, girl?"

"Ah..."

Chef hat askew, he pointed the cast iron skillet he'd slammed into the back of Priestly's skull at her. "Bringing a strange Electi home! Are you insane?"

"Excellent question," Westvane said, wiping blood from the corner of his mouth.

Her brows popped up. "How is this my fault? I told you to leave him there."

"You told me not to kill him," Westvane said, correcting her.

"Leaving him there was implied."

He scoffed.

"Great, just great. One of the queen's guard in Earth Realm — total disaster," she snapped, tempted to toss Priestly out of her house, back into the *Ecotone*, knowing she couldn't. The Electi would wreak havoc in there. Ruin the peace. Obliterate the quiet. Though, maybe the sea serpents would cooperate and eat the idiot. Jamming her hands onto her hips, she scowled at Westvane. "What are we supposed to do with him now?"

He opened his mouth, no doubt to suggest torture.

"I swear," Earl said, cutting him off, glaring at her. "Trouble. Nothing but trouble... that's what the two of you are."

Shades of Montrose.

Truly stifled the urge to laugh. The gargoyle would've scolded her, too. Although with a few more foul words inserted into the lecture. And as ever, she would've ignored the gargoyle's reprimand, just as she intended to disregard Earl's.

Staring down at an unconscious Priestly, she nudged him with her foot. "Seriously, though — what we going to do with him?"

Finding a secure place to keep him came to mind. Locking him down seemed the best strategy. The Wendigo had taught her a few things. Westvane had added to her lessons. Allowing a lethal warrior with magical abilities free rein inside her house — and Philadelphia — would end in disaster.

"Well?" she asked, picking a broken plume off the floor. "Any bright ideas?"

"Other than killing him?"

"Next," Truly said, tone sharp. "Think of something else."

Amusement in his eyes, Westvane shrugged. "It's your house, princess. Your plan."

Irritated by his unhelpfulness, Truly threw him a dirty look.

"For the love of all that is holy," Earl huffed, tossing the skillet at Westvane. As he caught the cast iron handle, her new chef grabbed Priestly by the wings. Creepy-crawling, hind-end swiveling, he hauled the Electi beneath the swaying chandelier. "I'll see to it."

"Where are you taking him?" she asked, turning the tawny feather over in her hand.

"The dungeon," Earl said, pushing against the wood paneling. Hinges creaked. A secret door swung opened. With a grunt, he disappeared over the threshold with Priestly in tow.

"I have a dungeon?"

"So it would seem, princess."

"All right... well," she said, gaze on the secret door, unsure what to think. "That's handy, I guess."

Westvane chuckled.

The lovely sound rippled through her. Her annoyance with him faded. She took heart as it did, understanding for the first time what real progress looked like. For a lethal warrior who wanted to kill everyone he met, Westvane was coming along. And honestly...

The thought gave her hope.

"The house left you a Grimoire. It's on the table!" Earl yelled, disembodied voice rising above loud thumps as he dragged Priestly into the basement.

"A what?" she yelled back.

"Huge book! Thick. Old. Picture of a bridge on the front, and oh..." A grunt echoed up from down below, then, "Almost forgot — blueberry muffins 're on the cooling rack on the kitchen counter!"

Glancing at Westvane, she raised a brow. "A bridge?"

"Homework," he said, sounding amused. "No rest for the wicked, princess."

Truly sighed. "I need a drink."

"I'll pour." Jet-black feathers brushed her cheek as he walked past her.

Straightening the crumpled floor runner with the toe of her boot, she set the lamp back on the hall table and watched him stride toward the back of the house. Wings tucked tight to his back, he sent the kitchen door swinging, dipped his head beneath the lintel and entered Earl's domain.

Slower to follow, Truly trailed behind, listening to the house breathe around her, feeling the hum of magic in her veins, aware the future stretched like an open field in front of her. She hoped the Grimoire filled in some holes. She didn't like the gaps in her knowledge, or flying blind, but with Westvane on her side and change on the horizon, the future looked brighter than it had in while.

Her mind flipped through the possibilities as she made her way to the kitchen. Plans needed to be made. The details must be hammered out, allies identified and approached. So many angles to consider, but...

Later.

Neutralizing Lyonesse and the Yeomanry, along with the other problems plaguing the Mirror Kingdoms, would have to wait. So would reading the Grimoire, at least for a little while. Right now, she had fine whiskey to drink, Earl's blueberry muffins to eat, and Westvane to get settled into his new home.

ACKNOWLEDGMENTS

This book nearly didn't happen. I started writing it when I was suffering from burnout, though I didn't know it at the time. And yet, when I needed her most, Truly Turnbolt walked into my head and began talking to me. At first, in whispers. Later on, much louder, compelling me to return to my keyboard and immerse myself in my love of storytelling. Truly and Westvane kept me entertained, but also helped me heal. I hope my telling of their story does the same for you.

I'd like to say an enormous thank you to Christine Witthohn, literary agent extraordinaire. You believed in me when I couldn't do it for myself. I'll love you forever. We make a great team.

To Katherine Ward – thank you for digging in to help me not only fill in the gaps, but deepen the story overall. It was incredible working with you.

Thanks as well to Tanya and the wonderful team at Oliver Heber Books. I love working with you all. I'm so grateful to be part of your crew.

To my family — you're the best. Words cannot convey how much you mean to me. Love you to the moon and back again.

A NOTE FROM THE AUTHOR

Thank you for reading **The House of Starlight and Shadow**. If you enjoyed it, please help others find my books so they can enjoy them too.

Recommend it: Please help other readers find this book by recommending it to friends, in readers' groups, and on discussion boards.

Review it: Reviews really help authors find the right audience. If you have a minute, please let others know what you liked about **The House of Starlight and Shadow** on Amazon, Goodreads, or wherever you buy your books.

Follow me on Facebook, <u>Instagram</u>, and Bookbub to get all the latest news.

Sign up for my Newsletter and get exclusive VIP giveaways, freebies, and sales throughout the year.

Book updates can be found at www.CoreeneCallahan.com

Thanks again for taking the time to read my books! You make it all possible.

The Mirror Kingdom Chronicles

The House of Starlight and Shadow

Rise of the Slayer

The Clash of Two Queens

Dragonfury Series

Fury of Fire

Fury of Ice

Fury of Seduction

Fury of Desire

Fury of Obsession

Fury of Surrender

Fury of Destruction

Fury of Aggression

Dragonfury Scotland

Fury of a Highland Dragon

Fury of Shadows

Fury of Denial

Fury of Persuasion

Fury of Isolation

Fury of Frustration

Fury of Misfortune

Dragonfury Bad Boy Shifter Series

Fury of Fate

Fury of Conviction

Circle of Seven Series

Knight Awakened

Knight Avenged

Warriors of the Realm Series

Warrior's Revenge

ABOUT THE AUTHOR

Coreene Callahan is the bestselling author of the Dragonfury novels and Circle of Seven series, in which she combines her love of romance and adventure with her passion for history. After graduating with honors in psychology and taking a detour to work in interior design, Coreene returned to her first love: writing. Her debut novel, *Fury of Fire*, was a finalist in the New Jersey Romance Writers Golden Leaf Contest in two categories: Best First Book and Best Paranormal. She lives in Canada with her family, a spirited Anatolian Shepherd, and her wild imaginary world.